LIES AND FLAMES

Also by Jenny Jones

Fly By Night
The Edge of Vengeance

LIES AND FLAMES

Volume Three of *Flight Over Fire*

Jenny Jones

HEADLINE

First published in 1992
by HEADLINE BOOK PUBLISHING PLC

10 9 8 7 6 5 4 3 2 1

British Library Cataloguing in Publication Data

Jones, Jenny
    Lies and Flames
    I. Title
    823.914 [F]

Hardback ISBN 0-7472-0456-X

Royal Paperback ISBN 0-7472-7943-8

Typeset by
Letterpart Limited, Reigate, Surrey

Printed and bound in Great Britain by
Richard Clay Ltd, Bungay, Suffolk

HEADLINE BOOK PUBLISHING PLC
Headline House
79 Great Titchfield Street
London W1P 7FN

For Edward
he knows why

Acknowledgements

Thanks to Tim Crawley and all at Guppy's. To Richard Evans and Caroline Oakley, and everyone at Headline. To my family and friends, for everything . . .

Extract from W.B. Yeats *The Collected Poems of W. B. Yeats* published by Macmillan, London, 1967 edition.

Contents

PART TWO

Glossary and Main Characters

Eleanor Knight
Chorolon – a world governed by the flight of the Benu Bird.
The Benu Bird – the original phoenix. A blind hawk, whose cycle of birth, death and rebirth provides the framework for time to pass. It was captured by Lucien Lefevre (q.v.) for a period known as the Stasis.
Lycias – The Sun God, whose great love for a mortal woman called Mariana dictated the existence of the Stasis.
Astret – The Moon Goddess, to whom the unchanging sterility of the Stasis was anathema.

Stromsall – the Northern Continent.

Felicia Westray – Countess of Shelt, daughter to the Duke Javon of Eldin (q.v.). She defeated the dragon Ladon, which was in league with the Sea Lords of Shelt. She is married to Jolin Rosco, the newly elected Earl of Shelt.
Lukas Marling – a Caver, who assumed the name Jolin Rosco on arrival in Shelt. He befriended Eleanor after she came to Chorolon. They grew to love each other. His apparent death was the price of the breaking of the Stasis.
Javon Westray – Duke of Eldin. Felicia's father, and brother to Torold, previous Earl of Shelt.
Merield – Javon's wife, Felicia's stepmother.
Olwyn Mitttelson – Mage, who engineered the marriage between Rosco and Felicia.
Ferant and Alex Aldrich – apprentice Mages.
Dederic – deposed Sea Lord and Mage.
Yerrent – Merield's (q.v.) court Mage.
Annis – Felicia's maid.
Kester Robart – Annis's lover and a captain in the Shelt Castle Guard.
Philp Cammish – retired fisherman.
Vere Holtby – flautist.
Gawne of Aquile – First Sea Lord. A Mage trained in Peraldon, lost in the ocean after a fight with Jolin Rosco.

Garulf – hermit and mystic.

Esmond – Garulf's son, and lover of Torold, the last Earl of Shelt.

The Eloish

Serethrun Maryn – instrumental in rescuing Felicia from the Sea Lords of Shelt.

Irian Maryn – shaman, sister to Serethrun.

Jerr Morrelow – traveller.

Lara Valde – Archon of Gerune clan.

Brianne Querille

Haddon Derray – ex-Caver, cursed by Lycias for daring to love Coronis, a lover abandoned by the Sun God long ago.

Coron – the son of Lycias and Coronis.

mereth – an eloish term to describe non-nomadic people, city-dwellers (derisive).

Peraldonia – the Southern Continent.

The Emperor Xanthon

Emile Blanchard – the Warden. Secular power in the city of Peraldon.

Phinian Blythe – ex-member of the Warden's Watch. He left Peraldon to join Eleanor Knight and Lukas Marling on a quest to break the Stasis. As a result of his actions, he was afflicted by the Shadows, Children of the Night (q.v.). Coron (q.v.) lifted the Shadows from him.

Neque – Mage.

Dion Gillet – Priest and mystic.

Katriana – Gillet's ward.

Cassun – Gillet's disciple and apprentice.

Weard – the Fosca King's pupil.

Lucien Lefevre – In his incarnation as Great Mage and High Priest he set up the Stasis to satisfy the Sun God's love for his own sister, Mariana. Since then, he has undergone a number of transformations, including Fosca King and Desert Rose.

The Fosca – creatures engineered as fighting machines by Lefevre. They ride on dark angels, reptilian flying creatures.

Edine Malreaux – her lover, the Mage Imbert, lost his life in their attempt to reinstate the Stasis by burning the Desert Rose.

Harren – poet, acquaintance of Phinian Blythe during his time as Captain of the Warden's Watch in Peraldon.

The Cavers – followers of Astret.

Matthias Marling – Mage, brother to Lukas, responsible for bringing Eleanor Knight to Chorolon. He was blinded by Lycias in revenge.
Thibaud Lye and Aylmer Alard – Caver Mages.
Letia – foster-mother to the Marling brothers, who first made Eleanor welcome on Chorolon.

The Arrarat – sapient hawks.

Astrella – aligned to Lukas Marling.
Amery – aligned to Matthias Marling.
Adila – aligned to Coron.
Zaeus

The Children of the Night, Shadows – afflictions of the guilty.

Prologue

He was a man of purity. He had left Peraldon long ago to pursue a life of solitary contemplation. Meditation, prayer. . . . He studied sacred texts long into the night. At the new Moon, he fasted and mortified his flesh with barbed whips.

In extreme states of great intensity, he found the pathway to magic opening up before him. The sacred texts, the Cabbalah and Scriptures can lead to such a perspective in a soul so isolated, so unbalanced.

Sometimes he dreamed. As his life was given over to excess, so were his dreams. His visions showed him that the Lord Lycias was the Lord of Love. He recognised the passionate sensuality of the Sun, and found himself torn. He was himself dismayed by women, and acknowledged their power to divert men. He knew it was dangerous.

And yet his God desired to be united with the feminine.

He watched the Moon, too, hoping for an answer. He became fascinated by the brilliance of it, by its cold clarity. He wondered if the two could ever be reconciled, leaving the world free for men.

One night, he walked along the rocky seashore close to his hermit's cave. Although it was midnight, the Moon was full, and he could see the outline of rocks and waves quite clearly.

He saw something disturb the smooth swell of waves. Something delicate and frail, something emerging from the pull of the tide.

A hand, reaching towards him.

Dion Gillet was a man of God, and it was with prayers on his lips that he brought her from the waves.

A young girl-child, dressed in rags, only half conscious. He took her to his cave and watched as she revived. He saw that her form was perfect, that her features were without flaw, but it was not her beauty that moved him to keep the child with him.

Her black eyes were flecked with silver. She had no memory of the past, no knowledge of her parents or home. She had no name.

He did not try to find out more. He made no attempt to return her to her parents. He gave her a name, 'Katriana'. And then he began to teach her, to instruct her in the ways of the God. And, although he was a priest of the Sun and it went much against his instinct, he told her about the Lady.

He said that the Lady, beautiful though She was, brought death in Her train, that She was untrustworthy and vicious. She must be tamed, he said, as should all women. Listen to me and learn, for you shall be an example to the world.

And as he spoke, he saw the silver flecks in her eyes intensify. She turned her head, and he gasped at the clarity of her gaze. He thought, I have here a means to satisfy the Lord.

A woman, taken from the waves. It had happened before; he knew the legends, none better. Dion Gillet knew how to interpret this strange gift of the sea. Katriana was dedicated to the Lady Herself. He saw in her the means to unite the unhappy Gods.

So that the danger would pass.

PART ONE

Chapter One
Meeting

The door opened. Lukas was there.

From the time that the Sun God Lycias had told her that Lukas Marling still lived, she had longed for this meeting. She had rehearsed it a thousand times in her dreams, every hour of her waking life, too. It had been a thread through all her thoughts: Lukas's arms open for her, his head against her hair, the warmth of his hands.

She took half a step towards him, reaching out for him.

Why were his arms not open?

He was not alone.

'Are you. . .you're looking better, Eleanor.' His voice was light and even, and his eyes, searching her face, were intense and brilliant as ever. Why did he not move towards her? There was a tall man at his side, watching. Against her will, her attention was caught by the stranger. What was he doing there?

'Lukas, who is this person?' The old imperiousness, an arrogance she thought she had lost, surfacing under the pressure.

There were still yards of floor between them, a wall of polished wooden planks. 'Do we need him here?'

'His name is Olwyn Mittelson. A Mage.' His voice was still neutral, his hands loose at his side, his eyes still scanning her face.

'Do we need a chaperon, then? Lukas—' The words began to fall in a torrent, she could not think, not imagine what was happening. Another step, but the distance was still too far, and the Mage was there. . . . 'Lukas, I thought you were dead! Why are you standing so still, have you changed? I needed you so, but I thought you were dead! Lukas. I was told. . .Lycias *showed* me that you were dead! I didn't understand. . .'

'However, he survived.' The stranger's cool words broke into the flow. 'And now rules the city of Shelt, married to the Lady Felicia—'

In the intensity of the moment the fact of his marriage had eluded her. Now it struck with the force of a mortal wound. She halted, frozen, crippled.

'Get out, Mittelson!' Lukas had turned away from her, the whole blazing force of his eyes directed at the ugly, frail Mage with the pointed chin. 'Get out of here,' Lukas repeated softly.

'Olwyn, please come here. I wish to talk to you. . .' Another voice from the open door behind them. A slight, pale girl stood there, the girl from the wedding procession. Lukas's wife.

Eleanor found herself saying, again, 'I thought you were dead. . .'

And the look he gave her, turning away from Felicia his wife, was shot through with a fury she knew was directed anywhere but at her.

'Well, we all make mistakes, don't we?'

She could not believe it, could not believe that this was happening. In that cold drawing-room, looking at Lukas across those miles of floor, it became clear at once how it was to go. No passionate reunions, no reaffirmations of a love that would never die.

It's over. He might as well have broadcast it from the city walls. It's over and we can be nothing to each other, now.

She saw him standing by the door, still looking at her. His wife, that pale drab of a woman, lurked at his shoulder. The tall ugly Mage was unmoving at his right hand.

She saw him fenced round by them all. All his wild energy and force contained by bonds and loyalties she did not understand. Alien, in every way.

In blackest depression she saw him begin to turn away from her. 'Lukas!'

She couldn't help it.

It made no difference. He barely hesitated as he left the room and did not look back.

'Lukas?' Only a whisper now. The door was already shut.

Later, she thought that she might have remained calmer, might have managed to talk about it all without shouting, if only the thunder had relented. Those first days in Shelt became blurred in her memory, losing definition under the weight of the storm outside.

Arguments, scenes, cold silences, uneaten meals. Restlessly, she prowled the damp and draughty Castle, sometimes accompanied by Serethrun, more usually alone. She could not bear to talk to anyone who was not Lukas. And he was always busy, caught up in meeting after meeting, attending councils of Mages, fishermen, townspeople, bureaucrats.

She watched him whenever she could, standing where she could see the door to his offices, waiting for a glimpse, a glance, a shared moment of understanding. . . .

It never happened. Did he do it deliberately? she wondered. Was he trying to avoid her? But he was preoccupied all the time, and there was no end to the business of serious, importunate men who needed the new Earl of Shelt to decide economies, strategies, plans, lives. They ate up his attention and energy day after day, holding him far away, on the other side of closed doors.

Eleanor tried to be patient. It could not last for ever, she told

herself. This was a time of crisis and sooner or later the government of
Shelt would begin to run smoothly, and he would have time to talk to
her, to be with her.

Rain distorted every window and the Castle was a web of cold winds
and darkened rooms. She saw lightning illuminate pale and anxious
faces, interrupting vivid and secret glances. She saw his hands
suddenly clench at their few, unexpected encounters, his step
hesitate.

The scenes in her memory were fragments shot through with pain.

'Divorce? There is no such thing under the laws of Stromsall.' Felicia,
a cold, white, insubstantial figure weighted by heavy robes, dwarfed
by ponderous furniture. 'Marriage endures for ever, as the Lady
decrees.' Her voice was very quiet. 'But I would end this if I could.'

Eleanor had no difficulty believing her. Never had she seen
anyone look so miserable, so ill. Eleanor could not afford to regard
it. She had forced this meeting, refusing to leave the drawing room
after breakfast one morning. She was not going to let it rest there.
She pressed on. 'Annulment, then. Call it off. There must be some
loophole.'

'There are no grounds for annulment.'

Lukas was by the window, watching the sea crashing against the
Castle walls. 'No grounds. . . .'

'Oh, Christ, were you tricked, too?' She looked at him helplessly.
More lies, more tricks, more treachery.

'No. Not tricked. . . .' And a glance, an understanding, passed
between him and Felicia, and Eleanor ran from the room, slamming
the door.

She was ashamed of herself, her lack of control.

No one was unkind, no one ignored her. They brought her soft,
warm clothes, delicious food. She was given an apartment in the
guest-wing, a suite of richly carpeted rooms, a maidservant to tend her
every wish.

She was made welcome in the Castle of Shelt, an old and trusted
friend of the new Earl. The Earl who was too busy to meet her,
still tied up in committees, meetings, councils. Petitioners queued
outside his door, lined the corridors of the Castle. At every meal,
there was a sheaf of papers at his elbow, awaiting signature and
authorisation.

He had little free time. She saw his eyes glitter with suppressed
impatience as yet another dignitary interrupted him, as Mittelson
approached with arm-loads of files and document cases.

How could she add to it? She drifted from room to room,
purposeless as a fallen leaf.

Eleanor told Lukas what had happened to his brother Matthias. One long, cold afternoon, while the wind whistled in the hangings, disturbing the lie of tapestries on the walls.

They were not alone, of course. They were never alone. Usually it was Mittelson who accompanied the Earl of Shelt, sometimes Ferant Aldrich, Mittelson's assistant, or a taciturn fisherman called Philp Cammish. Sometimes one of the officers of the Guard. Never Felicia herself.

This time, Mittelson was there to stop them touching each other. He was sitting at a table close to the window, surrounded by files and papers. He was thoughtful, scribbling pencil notes.

They were in the long gallery on the second floor, with its wide views of the heaving grey sea. Fires burnt in the fireplaces at intervals along the wall, but it was always cold.

It seemed strange to remember the pattern of Lycias's revenge on Peraldon. She described the drought, the burning sun and what it had meant to everyone there. She did her best to explain why Matthias had brought her back.

Her voice halting, she told him of the blinding and the treachery, and the attempt to recapture the Benu Bird.

He listened in silence, his long fingers still on the table between them.

'Come back to Peraldon,' she said desperately in the end. 'You're needed there. Your family will need you, now.'

'They need me here, too. There's a long way to go before there's any real peace in Stromsall.'

'It's not your responsibility!'

'But I think it is.' He frowned. 'No one's indispensable, of course, I do know that. But there is a vacuum here in Shelt, and at the moment, only I can fill it.'

'Surely not! Can't you leave them to it? Come away with me, back southwards, perhaps we could find that island again. . . .'

Mittelson was not quite out of earshot. She had been aware of his interest in her story, but she didn't care. Recklessly, she kept on trying. All her attention was focused on Lukas.

His face was drawn as he looked at her. For the first time, she thought she saw the weight of the immeasurable Stasis shadowing the blue of his eyes.

'Eleanor. . .*no*. I can't leave Shelt now. Things are going to be hard here for a long time yet. The city is deeply impoverished, the government in chaos. The rebellion took place at my instigation and the fisherpeople followed me. I can't desert them now, I don't even want to. Things have changed, life has moved on for you and me, and there's no way of recapturing the past. We have to adjust to a new world, new responsibilities. . . .'

'You never used to settle for less than the best! I never thought you would change so much!'

'But haven't you changed too, Eleanor? You've been through so much. . . .' She heard that rage again, flickering beneath the surface of his words. 'So much has happened to us both that I sometimes feel we don't know each other at all—'

'Do you? Do you really?' She was beginning to shout again, her back to Mittelson. Anything to break through this control. 'Lukas, is that really what you think?'

She did not see that Mittelson was on his feet, as if drawn by the intimacy of their exchange. Lukas did not speak again, there was no need. She saw complicated things in those eloquent eyes, but still he said nothing.

There was only a long pause as he looked at her, and she felt her breath stifle in her throat. And then Mittelson coughed politely and started to talk, about Castle affairs, the Guard, the *eloish*. . . .

Lukas turned away from her, almost as if glad of the distraction, and she walked from the room alone, out on to the battlements, to the windy towers and rainswept evergreens.

On the whole, Felicia kept well away, but was unfailingly courteous whenever they met. Eleanor found it hard to dislike her: this thin shadow of a woman, too pale, too weak to be a serious rival. She was always quiet, unobtrusive, avoiding Eleanor's inevitable curiosity with gentle self-deprecation.

I would end this if I could, she had said. Eleanor sat in her lonely apartment wondering if Felicia meant it. And because Lukas was so unapproachable, so out of bounds, she knew she would have to get to know his new wife. She needed to find out whether Felicia had been telling the truth.

It was surprisingly difficult. For a start, Felicia was rarely to be found in the public rooms, and anyway formal occasions offered no kind of privacy.

Twice, Eleanor had been invited to Felicia's own suite to take tea, but there had always been other people there. They were women from the aristocracy of Shelt, who looked at Eleanor with some curiosity but were too well bred to ask direct questions. The conversation revolved round children, and gardening, and the eternal, dreadful weather. Eleanor took little part in it, preferring to observe. Felicia introduced her as a traveller from Peraldon, in the far south. It was nothing less than the truth.

Grudgingly, she had to admit that Felicia knew very well how to handle these situations. She drew out her guests with subtlety, leading them to talk about their most pressing concerns. Occasionally these touched on politics and government, and Felicia listened carefully.

Eleanor saw her give these women exactly what they wanted, sympathy and more than that. There was the tacit implication that Felicia might do something for them.

She made an excellent Countess. Eleanor could not deny it. She was

the Duke of Eldin's daughter and accustomed to privilege and
responsibility, or so it seemed to Eleanor.

More than that, Eleanor recognised that there was something undeniable between Felicia and Lukas. It kept her awake at night. Not lovers,
no, she could see they were not – no longer – lovers. But friendship, that
was what existed between Lukas and Felicia, a deep, committed trust.
Eleanor's voice became acid and sarcastic, talking to Felicia, cold and
grudging to Lukas. She hated herself for it.

The Mage Olwyn Mittelson was wary, ignoring Eleanor's ill temper
and flaring rages. He was always distant, always preoccupied, always
close to Lukas. It was he who placed the papers on Lukas's desk, who
reminded him of the next meeting, each essential and urgent responsibility. He was always there, keeper, minder. Chaperon. She loathed
him.

They called Lukas 'Rosco', even Felicia called him Rosco, and
Eleanor wondered why he let the masquerade continue. At least his
hair was losing that deadly, deceitful fairness. His eyes always
watched her whenever they were in the same room, but there
was no contact, no touch, no warmth between them. How could there
be?

Rosco had been invested as Earl the day before the wedding, the
day before Eleanor had arrived in Shelt. Nominated by Torold,
elected by the fisherpeople, attended by an Arrarat hawk. He had
defeated the Sea Lords, and they languished now in lonely exile,
scattered among the offshore islands. They were accompanied only by
servants and a garrison of the Guard. Their staffs had been burnt in a
ceremony of great celebration. The people of Shelt looked to Rosco as
their saviour from the unreliable force of magic. They could deal
with him, they thought, soldier and leader that he was. . .and his
marriage to Javon's own daughter broke down any last resistance.
There was no one else possible to rule Shelt. He was welcomed with
open arms.

Shelt was his to command now. The fisherpeople were ready to
return to their trade, the townspeople to their shops and businesses.
For a while, it seemed that peace might be possible. Once the storm
was over.

But this storm had gripped Shelt on the morning of Rosco's
wedding to Felicia and not an hour had passed, not even a moment
since then, when the wind did not howl through the city. It seemed to
search out every small area of comfort, every scrap of warmth. It
screamed through the city with a near-human voice, crushing and
punishing a world already exhausted by the stresses of civil conflict,
the depredations of tide and dragon.

There was no rest in Shelt, no peace, no calm. The fishing boats
rocked on their moorings and the waves crashed against the Castle
walls.

★ ★ ★

Once, Eleanor met Lukas accidentally on the balcony overlooking the gardens.

She was watching the gardeners attempt to reinforce the smaller trees against the stressful winds. The three men were drenched with rain, their hair whipped into dark strands over their faces, getting into their eyes. She watched them struggle with stakes and props, and listened to the anguish in the wind.

She did not hear him approach. And his voice, when he finally spoke, was carefully neutral.

'Aren't you cold? Wouldn't you prefer to be indoors?'

She spun round, and then halted. Oh my dear, my love, what can we do?

For once he was alone. For once unattended. And immediately her words let her down. She was betrayed by emotion into ungraciousness.

'Good heavens, they've let you out. Isn't Mittelson scared you might run off?'

'No. Don't, Eleanor. He's a good man. Don't take against him. He has done his best to help the people of Shelt—'

'Really? What about you, has he done his best to help you?'

Lukas did not answer her. He leant forward, resting his forearms on the parapet. 'He says this wind is unnatural. That there's something wrong with the storm.'

'And he doesn't know what? There you are, Lukas, he's not infallible. He might not even always be right.'

'You're making a mistake, blaming everything on Olwyn Mittelson, Eleanor.' He turned towards her, and reached out his hand to her face. She thought she might cry.

His fingers brushed aside the hair from her brow, and she saw that he was looking at the moon-shaped scar on her temple.

'The Lady runs our lives, Eleanor. Remember that. Our choices are strictly limited.'

But even as he spoke, the door to the ballroom opened. Felicia stood there, looking at them both. She came no closer.

'Lukas, can we talk soon? I must. . .I need to know—' Eleanor could not go on. His face was whiter than death.

'There's nothing we can do.'

'*Nothing?*'

But already he had turned away, was walking back to where his wife waited.

Her fingers traced the scar on her skin. She heard the wind howl, and remembered something. She had heard the human voice of that storm before, screaming down the deserted avenues of a deserted city far away. Searching for health, for healing.

As were they all.

★ ★ ★

Eleanor did not cry that night. She sat by the window of her comfortable room on the north wing of the Castle, and watched the storm-torn water seethe. She heard the howling in the wind, but it was nothing to the torment in her heart.

This was intolerable. Of all the terrors she had survived, this was the worst. Sitting quietly in a warm and pretty room, surrounded by people who would do anything to put her at ease (except what she most wanted), who would provide for her in luxury until she died, she felt finally alone.

This was not her world, these were not her friends. Lukas was not her lover. Perhaps he still loved her; she thought that probably he did. But he would not touch her now. That all seemed to have been put aside, completely and irrevocably, with no reference to her.

Obsessively, her mind traced and retraced every word he had spoken to her. You're looking better, he had said, across those miles of wooden floor. *Better*. Had he watched by her bed when she was unconscious? What had he felt, seeing her carried into the Castle? Or had they hidden her away so as not to spoil the party? A familiar prick of anger here, quickly subsiding. What was the use of it?

What did Lukas feel now, looking at the pale girl who accompanied him through every official function? She sat next to him at meals, tasting almost nothing, pushing away still-full plates. She was like a ghost, drifting through the Castle, fading almost as they watched.

Perhaps Felicia would leave Shelt. On the surface, she seemed to have no will, no desire even to defend her own interests. Today had been the only time that Felicia had chaperoned Lukas. Perhaps she would conveniently disappear from their lives, drop out, or return home.

Die. Eleanor acknowledged the thought at last. She looked frail enough. And then Lukas would be free. . . .

It wouldn't work like that. She recognised a streak of obstinacy in Felicia, a steady flame or courage which would not easily be extinguished. Felicia was here to stay.

Chapter Two
Felicia

At first Felicia tried to exorcise the demons by drawing them, by trapping them in paper and pencil.

Every afternoon after lunch she retired to her rooms, in search of a little peace. The tension of watching Rosco and Eleanor together was difficult to handle, the situation ultimately depressing. She thought that sketching their faces might defuse some of their power in her mind. Coldly, like a surgeon, she would dissect them in pure white paper and black pencil. They would lose their power over her. . . . It had always worked before, when she had caricatured the powerful men who had ruled her life.

She began a new pad. It was an uncomfortable exercise. Eleanor's pencilled face was sour with unhappiness. Carefully, Felicia copied the moon-scar at the temple and then suddenly realised what she was doing. She put the pad down, the pencil back in its pot, and leant back in her chair.

This was a marked woman. Felicia knew, mainly from Serethrun, who Eleanor was and what had happened in the past. She wondered, looking at that fine scar, just what the implications were.

There was no way she could discount the significance of Eleanor's presence in Shelt. This was no mere accident, an unlucky mischance. Eleanor Knight might once have been a victim, a pawn in some unknown strategy, but she had crossed a continent to find Rosco. Against all odds, she had escaped great danger to come *here*, and no one could now ignore her presence, scowling and ungracious though she might be. She was an undeniable force.

Of course Felicia wanted Eleanor to leave. Felicia was in love with the man she knew as Jolin Rosco, the man whose real name was Lukas Marling. She loved him, and she was married to him, and that was the end to it.

But there was a situation to be resolved. She thought, watching Rosco and Eleanor together, that their love was still potent, still locked in the 'for ever' phase. . . .

How did they know? she wondered. How do you recognise that once-in-a-lifetime change of perspective, the passion that endures? How do you tell it from lust or infatuation or even the love that burns itself out, over-balancing into jealousy and possessiveness? How can you trust so much in something which might fade?

In Eleanor's face, caught unawares on the pad on Felicia's lap, love was vivid and potent.

No comfort in that. She picked up the pad and turned the page. What truth could she see in Rosco's likeness? There were no scars there, she knew, to point to arcane meanings.

Rosco's face blazed with fury. Her accurate hands traced only the truth. She sighed. He was unfailingly kind to her, courteous in every way and yet she wished that he would shout, wished he would yell and scream against this strange strategy that bound them together.

She still did not understand it, she did not know why it had been so designed. She had tried to talk to him about it, but it had been so difficult. . . .

About a week after the wedding, she had caught him waiting, most unusually alone, in one of the anterooms for a deputation of farmers from the western plains. She had intercepted a message from Mittelson.

'Your meeting will be delayed,' she said, closing the door behind her. 'The bridge is down. The farmers are going to get their feet wet. . . .'

He smiled, quickly, charmingly. 'And I suppose Mittelson intends to amuse me with a pile of paperwork?'

'How did you know? But, if you don't mind. I'd rather talk.'

'Of course, Lady. At your service.' He moved towards the fire and adjusted a chair for her, but Felicia heard the wariness in his voice.

'Tell me, Rosco. What is going on here?'

'Do you mean Eleanor's presence here?' As always, his thoughts went straight to his old lover.

'No. That is understandable, given the past you shared. But why should you and I have to endure this awkwardness?'

He looked at her, candid blue eyes thoughtful. 'Is it so very bad? Don't answer that. . .I wish I knew, Felicia. Mittelson said that our marriage was the only way to bring peace to Shelt, but I'm not so sure. . . .'

'Do you think that Mittelson is behind it all?'

'No. Not at all. It's true that he wanted us married, that he ensured Eleanor did not interrupt, and that has been hard for all of us. But there's more at stake than Mittelson's ambitions for Shelt. . . .'

She felt the tug of other ideas, difficult to express. She hesitated, and saw that he was looking out of the window again, away from her.

Her voice was clear, although the words were impossible. 'Did you offend the Lady?'

'The Lady Astret relinquished Her claim long ago.' He spoke dryly. 'She is nothing to do with me now.'

Felicia waited in a silence that extended like a dead hand between them, an unbridgeable chasm.

At last he spoke again. 'Do you think that that's it?' His voice had dropped abruptly and she heard nothing but cynicism. 'Just one denial, a single rejection of the Gods' will, and vengeance takes over?'

'How can I answer you?' Sharply, anything to break this mood. 'Do you think I'm privy to special knowledge?'

'You are the Lady's chosen, are you not? Think about it, Felicia, what freedom do you have?'

She said nothing, knowing that he would not want to hear the only reply she could give. And then Mittelson knocked on the door and came in with six men, damp, cold air still hanging round their sodden cloaks, their boots soaked and caked with mud.

She saw Rosco turn to face the farmers with a warm and easy welcome. She stepped forward, exclaiming in sympathy, calling for mulled ale and fresh clothes for them, the fire to be built up. . .Felicia settled their ruffled spirits, and reassured them that the delay had inconvenienced no one. . . .

At last she escaped to her rooms. And turned over in her mind the reply she would have given, if he had forced it. She thought, I have had every freedom. I made my choice long ago, to marry Jolin Rosco. And whatever the pain of it now, I regret nothing. Because he trusts me, and talks to me with honesty.

Looking at the drawings on her pad, she thought that they too were honest. They showed the truth: the undeniable and awkward reality of it all.

She tore the pages in half and threw them away.

Truth. Uncomfortable and difficult. It was her only refuge.

Chapter Three
Night-time

The door opened. Eleanor swung round in her chair.

Lukas. Alone. The door shut behind him.

In that same instant, she was in his arms, her lips raised to his, her arms reaching to press him closer.

In desperation, at an ultimate edge of passion, for one moment his arms tightened, his lips locked on hers, his body welded to hers. . .

And then she was pushed away, with violent force.

'No! Eleanor, no. Not like this.' His voice was uneven, his mouth grim.

She would not be ruled by this. Not this time. She thought, this is my last chance. . .

He had moved away from her, crossing the room to the table by the window, and she had released a stream of words. Don't you love me, have you forgotten, how can you let this happen. . .?

'Eleanor, where is Matthias now?'

The question, so unexpected and sudden, stopped her in mid-flow. 'Matthias. . .? In Smintha, I suppose. Or Peraldon, somewhere. Why? What has he to do with what happens here?'

'Was he going to come here? Will he follow you?'

'I don't know.' She stared at him, mistrusting the preoccupied, masked expression on the mobile face, the pretended coolness of the light, pleasant voice. She knew him better than that.

He was brother to Matthias. Acquainted with Mages, with danger, with betrayal.

'If he comes. . .' Lukas continued evenly and then she knew what he was going to say.

'You want him to send me home.' She could see it in his eyes. It was why he was here.

'Do you want to stay? You can, of course. I owe you that much, at least. Or your own house, in Shelt or anywhere else. But—'

'But actually you want me to leave. For ever, this time.' Her voice was brittle as glass.

He was looking at his hands, lying empty on the table between them. He would not meet her eyes. Why would he not be direct with her?

'Felicia – is pregnant.'

For once she could think of nothing whatever to say. She stared at him, but still he would not look at her.

'Congratulations,' she said at last, her voice thin and distant. 'When is the happy event to take place?' Words from other places, other lives.

'In midwinter. Eleanor, I'm *not* throwing you out. I don't think I could—' A small betrayal of something there, but not enough. 'But – does it make you happy to be here?'

'What makes you think I want to stay? As soon as Matthias gets it together, you won't see me for dust—' But her voice cracked shamefully on the last word, and she felt rather than saw his face change.

She backed away. 'I know,' she said brightly. 'I'll go and stay with Phin. I needn't trouble you further. You can get on with running Shelt, and looking after the family. It was all a mistake, I see now, coming north. But, as you said yourself, we all make mistakes, don't we?' And then she turned her back on him, so that he wouldn't see the tears which ran and ran.

He did not touch her. He said, 'If you ever need me. . .really need me. . .I'll come. Anywhere, anytime. I'll find a way. You know that, don't you?'

'Sure. I'll drop you a line. Keep in touch. . .' She stopped.

A long silence. Then the door opened and closed quietly over the deep carpet. He was gone.

She needed him. Really needed him, *now*. And there was nothing either of them could do about it.

Chapter Four
Serethrun

Serethrun Maryn haunted the corridors, paced the galleries, shadowed the hallways. He watched Rosco and Eleanor with sharp interest, and although there was nothing he could do about the situation, he did not return to his sister and the rest of the *eloish*. Because of Felicia.

There was also unfinished business between him and Mittelson.

A few days after Eleanor regained consciousness, Serethrun had searched out Mittelson, had found him in the Castle library. It filled one of the towers of the Castle, on several floors, all connected by a spiral staircase. There were tables and chairs on each floor, and books lined the walls.

The wing where the Sea Lords had lived ran from this tower. It was far away from the Earl's apartments, and from the public rooms. And although the Sea Lords were no longer present, it was not dusty or neglected. The wooden floors were swept, the narrow windows cleaned regularly. But there was a smell of disuse, as if some creeping worm were infecting each volume with disease.

Or so it seemed to Serethrun. He started to mount the staircase, running his hands along the leathered spines, his eyes catching the occasional title. *Governaunce*: *The System of Fief and Fealty, The Way of the* Eloish. He paused, drawing the volume from the shelves.

'Curious, Serethrun?' Mittelson's voice was friendly. He was sitting in one of the chairs on the ground floor, just below the younger man.

Serethrun flicked through the pages and then let the book drop to the floor, where it lay awkwardly, pages bent, spine cracked. 'Why do the *mereth* always seek categories? Does it make them feel safer? There is no past, no history to be analysed, no lessons to be learned. . .and yet. . .' He paused deliberately. 'I think I would like an explanation from you, Mittelson. Some reason for what you did.' He moved downstairs so that they were both on the same level.

'I have been waiting for you to ask just that.' The Mage stood up, his yellow eyes unblinking.

'You drugged me. The marriage could have been prevented. Do you know what you've done?'

'Yes, I know.' Mittelson shrugged. 'It doesn't matter. Nothing on earth would have halted that marriage. You heard the girl's story, the fisherwoman and those few, fatally lost hours.'

'It was no damn fisherwoman, as you well know—'

'No, that is the point. The fisherwoman was an emanation of Astret, of course. As I said, nothing could have stopped it. That marriage was planned right from the start.'

'How do you know?'

'Dreams, Serethrun, dreams and visions. Surely, as one of the *eloish* you can understand that?'

'There are lies, too, as you know.'

'This dream came true—'

'Because you went along with it. What of your own responsibility? Do you seriously think that we have no choice? No freedom at all?'

'No, none whatsoever.' The new Earl of Shelt had now joined them. He stood in the doorway to the library. His breeches and jacket were of a green so dark as to appear almost black. A plain white shirt, a severely practical sword-belt and scabbard. No other ornament, and yet there was no impression of austerity about the man. His eyes were glittering, his voice was very hard.

'But it's no good complaining. Mulling over the mysteries of the rule of Astret, were you, friends? Surely we can find subjects more rewarding to discuss. Javon, for example. Serethrun, we need to talk. About the *eloish*—'

'Reinforcements for the Castle Guard. You want them to fight your battles, right? In case Felicia's dear papa and all his merry men take it into their heads to depose you?'

There was no way Serethrun could keep the acid out of his voice.

'Will the *eloish* fight for Shelt, do you think?' Rosco came forward into the room, considering Serethrun.

'Not if I have anything to do with it.' He tried to push past. To leave the room and these treacherous, difficult men, leave Shelt and Felicia for ever. But Rosco stepped sideways, blocking his way.

'If Javon decides to attack, he will almost certainly win. We'll have him in charge here, and your precious *eloish* will be pushed back into the wilderness again. Too wild, too subversive to live in peace under Javon's rule, don't you agree?'

'Is that what the books say?'

'It's what I have observed. Do you want a return to the conditions of the Stasis?'

'It would be better than fighting for you.' Serethrun raised his chin, meeting the taller man's gaze directly.

A long pause. 'Very well. If that's what you really feel, you'd better leave right away. The *eloish* will be needing you to tell them what's

happening. You'll have to get them out of the line of fire, too. I
wouldn't bank on Shelt being safe or comfortable for some considerable time yet. North, or north-west would be wisest.'

'What of the Sea Lords?' Mittelson asked. 'They are powerful.
They may cause trouble, too.' All at once Serethrun knew that this
was something that mattered to Mittelson. After all, Olwyn Mittelson had been a Sea Lord himself, long ago. It was true that he had
fought against them, had worked with Rosco to overthrow them
. . .and his anger against their despotism had been genuine. But, but,
but. . .

Serethrun looked round at the serried rows of books and thought
about the *mereth* who cling to their histories, cling to old allegiances.
They may fight against it, they may revolt and rail against these ghosts
from the past, but they cannot deny where they belong. They can only
act on, or react against, what they have been. They have no real
freedom.

Mittelson had been a Sea Lord, was still a Mage. He was a man who
used magic as power in the lives of others. He had used magic to
ensure that Felicia married the man Rosco—

'You should not have let the Sea Lords live,' Serethrun spoke
abruptly. 'Mages will always mean trouble to you.'

There was a curious smile on Rosco's face, a caustic self-awareness
that Serethrun mistrusted.

'To execute the Sea Lords would have meant alienating every
powerful family in Shelt. Without Gawne, they pose very little threat.
They have no staffs, they are kept separate from each other.' His
mouth twisted. 'It's not ideal, and perhaps one day this stability will
change. But in the meantime, they're out of the equation.'

'But still, Rosco, the *eloish* must stay. We'll need all the help we can
get.' Mittelson was leaning against the bookcases, speaking softly.
Faintly, from afar, Serethrun could hear rain drumming against the
windows.

'I don't want unwilling troops. There have been too many betrayals,
Olwyn. Let them look out for themselves.'

'Javon's army is numbered in tens of thousands, we'll need every
man!'

'On the contrary. We'd do better to surrender immediately,
because we have no chance whatever against an army of that size.
Anyone with a grain of sense would refuse to fight for Shelt against
Jovan.'

'You?' asked Mittelson.

'I'll do as I promised. Remember, the investiture oath? To defend
Shelt from all her enemies, at the cost of my life?'

'What are you planning, Rosco?' There was a strange gleam in his
eyes that neither Mittelson nor Serethrun trusted.

'To defend Shelt, of course. . . .'

★   ★   ★

Felicia was drawing when Serethrun found her.

She still drew all the time, a ceaseless flood of caricatures and cartoons, in thick black charcoal on fine paper. Ravens with human heads, hybrid cat creatures, winter-stripped trees, the hidden expressions on lying faces. . .Ladon, over and over again.

Never Rosco. Never Eleanor. Never again that particular truth.

Once Serethrun had found a sketch pad lying discarded on a windowsill. He had taken it back to his room, had stared with concentration at every line, every face. He saw such loneliness in her drawings. The pad was full of portraits, people caught unawares at windows, in the distance, walking alone. Not one of the faces laughed, no one smiled.

She is trying to come to terms with a life of loneliness, he thought. With the prospect of solitude. For although she is married to the man she loves, he has nothing to give her. Through the machinations of Mages and their gods, she will have to become reconciled to something less than the best. He could not bear to stand by watching, and know that there was nothing he could do.

As Serethrun entered her room, she was crumpling up yet another sheet of paper. The floor by her chair was littered with discarded drawings. He wanted to speak, but there were no words. She was so alone.

'Lady Felicia. . .' he began and then stopped, struck afresh by her beauty.

She forestalled him. 'You're leaving, Serethrun? With the *eloish*?' It was this same quick intelligence, this sensitive awareness that made him love her. It was difficult to tell what she thought about him leaving, for her voice was as calm as ever.

He nodded. 'There may be war. It's nothing to do with the *eloish*. We're getting out of the way.'

'Very wise, if there *is* going to be a war. But it's not inevitable, you know.'

'The Earl and his Mage seem to think it is.'

'They don't know everything. My father. . . .' She stopped. Then, quietly, almost a whisper. 'Serethrun, will you do something for me? Before you return to your people? Take a message to my father?'

He was watching her face, tracing the patterns of her words expressed in delicate bones and pale skin. She was beautiful without compare, glowing softly with the energy of the new life within her. No one had told him that she was with child. He had seen it on his return from the South, had found it in the faint bloom on her skin, in the added grace in the way she walked. To everyone else she looked pale and thin, her eyes dark-shadowed. To Serethrun she was fine-drawn and fragile, infinitely precious, infinitely powerful, carrying new life within her.

It was this that had finally decided him to leave Shelt.

'What about diplomatic means? Surely there will be ambassadors, envoys and so on going backwards and forwards before too long?'

'I want to prevent it getting to that stage. Once they start talking it will all be caught up in politics and pride. Who will back down first, who will give ground, lose face and so on. Negotiation won't work. My father is not noted for compromise.'

'Neither is Rosco.'

'No. I'll have to try something else. *Will* you go to Javon for me?'

'Of course. If you think it will help.'

He would do anything for her. For although she was so beautiful now, although her skin shone with her miraculous secret, he recognised and shared the still centre of misery within her.

He was reluctant, though. Another long journey. A useless errand, he thought, like that mad dash to bring Eleanor to Shelt.

Would Javon even receive him at the end of it? Still, Felicia was his daughter. He could hardly refuse a message from his only child, even if it had been brought by one of the untrustworthy *eloish*.

In the end he took more than a simple message to Javon. Felicia gave him a long letter, and something else, a small wax plaque upon which she had etched two faces.

Her own, coldly drawn, the thin lines and unhappy mouth without disguise or softening. It was in profile, looking with concentration at the full face of a man between middle and old age, fierce brows over implacable eyes, heavy lines between nose and mouth, between the brows, beneath the eyes. Long hair was swept back from the lined forehead to tumble arrogantly over his shoulders.

'My father,' she had said to Serethrun, wrapping the plaque in a small piece of silk. 'You may use this as proof of the genuineness of your message. The letter should explain everything else. And, Serethrun, you will answer with honesty whatever he asks, won't you?' For a moment, her wide green eyes looked at him, and then quickly she went on, as if she had to get the words out before her courage failed.

'I want no more lies, no more deceits. No more manoeuvres on my behalf, with or without my knowledge and consent. He will try something of this nature, Serethrun, be warned. Threats, subtle promises, appeals to your honour, violence, bribery. . .my father will try to draw you into all sorts of plans. Do not be diverted, you are free of bonds, one of the *eloish*. You have your people and another life to live. That is what matters. Hang on to it, Serethrun. It will keep you safe.

'My father will try to construct a different set of rules, and he'll want to overturn your true priorities. And then he'll make his own vision real with the strength of his armies. He may even succeed. . .he has done so in the past. Do you understand what I'm saying? Be honest with him about yourself and honest about what has happened here in Shelt, and stick with it. It may just keep him steady.

'There is no need for him to attack Shelt, no need for war. There never is.'

He remembered those words a week later, looking down over the Central Plains. He and and his horse Oriel were standing amidst a rough terrain of piled rocks on the bluff ridge of Jarr's Walk. The Walk formed a natural barrier between the Central and Western Plains. Far in the distance he thought he could make out the high towers of the city of Eldin, but the glare of sun against metal was too dazzling to be sure.

Between the Walk and Eldin lay the army of Javon. It filled the open grasslands as they stretched away into the blue haze on the southern horizon.

Tents, banners, drifts of cooking smoke, pens for goats and sheep, the sudden glint as the sun caught a drawn sword, a sharpened knife. The smell of leather and smoke, of canvas and food and middens and tobacco. . . .

From his high point, Serethrun could see that the army was well ordered, well provisioned, and competent. No unruly rabble, this. No untidy stragglers and camp-followers. The only bright colours were white and orange, Javon's own, vividly impractical. Uniforms everywhere. It was a professional, disciplined body of men numbering more than a hundred thousand.

Serethrun sighed. If Javon decided to mobilise, Rosco would indeed have no chance of defending Shelt. It would be a sledgehammer to swat a flea. He had never seen anything like it before.

A sudden unease. The knowledge that he was being watched. Quickly, he pulled on the reins, bringing Oriel round, but as he did so there was the sound of scattering rocks above him. A flaring pain burst at the back of Serethrun's head.

A deadening blackness dropped across the vision of sky and rocks and grass. He began to fall.

Chapter Five
Javon

Serethrun awoke to a feeling of grinding misery. Overwhelming depression blocked his every thought. A sickness, something deadly. . . . He struggled feebly against it, and an image formed. Felicia? His mind reached out in anxiety.

He opened his eyes. He was lying on a couch in a large, light and airy room. There was a vicious throbbing in his head, and the taste of nausea in his mouth.

Through all the misery and the pain, he saw the silhouette of a man against the streaming white light of the window. He was standing perfectly still, looking down on him. Serethrun lifted his hands to shield his eyes from the sun. He craned his neck to look at the man.

About fifty years of age, dark and swarthy, he was wearing full military uniform, all brilliant white and glowing orange. The brass buttons were polished, his tall leather riding-boots shone. Even his neatly cut hair gleamed with oil.

Serethrun's headache intensified. He sat up abruptly, looking round for his saddle-bag with the all-important letter. It had gone. He stood up, swaying, clasping the back of the couch. 'Where am I?'

'Where you want to be, I imagine. This is Castle Celair. Northern residence of Javon Westray, Protector of Stromsall and Duke of Eldin. . .' The voice ran on, listing Javon's many titles but Serethrun paid little attention.

'I have a message for the Duke—'

'It's on its way there right now, don't worry.'

Serethrun believed him. The man's voice was calm and unstressed, free from artifice. Serethrun trusted his own instincts in these things. But his sense of unease continued. It wasn't only the fate of Felicia's letter. The room they were in disturbed him. He looked around. He had never seen anything like it before. The *eloish* lived in tents or the open air, the people of Shelt in a heavy city of grey stone and high walls. There, windows had been small, to keep out the biting sea winds, to provide protection from enemies and rebels.

Javon's Castle could not be more different. Pale parquet flooring, pale panelled walls set with tall windows. He was in a large room: a hall perhaps, for there was a series of doorways in the wall to his right, set in ornately carved arches. A free-standing open-spiral staircase led to a balcony which spanned the length of the room. The ceiling, high above, was divided into a series of domes, each subtly ornamented with carved wood, set with glowing glass panels. Sunlight filtered across the pale floor in rainbow patterns of gold, green, indigo and scarlet. There was no speck of dust anywhere, no heavy dark, deep colours. No hidden corners, no room for subterfuge.

The only other colours came from the landscape outside. The hallway was not at ground level; the windows framed an overview of the plain and the army.

Serethrun saw men moving back and forth in orderly fashion, tending horses, polishing weapons, preparing food. In the mid-distance some kind of tournament was in progress, a series of men tilting at a dummy, trying to impale it on their long lances. Generally, they succeeded. But the glass of the windows must have been specially constructed, for Serethrun could hear nothing of all the activity outside.

'It's quite a view, isn't it?' the man at his side said companionably.

'Who are you?' Serethrun turned to look at him.

'Bladon is my name. Master of the Duke's own horses. I was out exercising a string when we saw you on the ridge. Rather careless, we thought. A trained soldier would have been aware of the vulnerability of such a position—'

But Serethrun had no chance to answer. One of the doors at the side of the room opened. A man stood there.

Serethrun recognised him immediately. The face on the waxed plaque, the source of his unreasoning misery on waking: Javon Westray, Eldin's Duke, Felicia's father.

'Serethrun Maryn. *Eloish*. Why did my daughter send you?' There was nothing overtly aggressive in his tone.

Trust. Be honest, be cool. Don't let him draw you in. . .Serethrun tried to remember Felicia's words, but the green eyes regarding him were distracting. Javon was still handsome, undeniably intimidating with his straight back and forbidding eyes. The greying hair and web of lines which covered his skin only added to his authority. But there was sickness there, and unhealthy pallor, Serethrun decided. For a moment he allowed his mind to wander, his senses to register impressions and instincts without the constraints of logic. He noted the taint of decay, slight and insignificant, that soured Javon's breath. Probably the Duke was not yet aware of his own malaise. . . .

Serethrun had turned round when Javon entered. Bladon was standing beside him, stiffly to attention. 'Has she no one more – prestigious? What of the servants and attendants I sent with her?' Javon was frowning.

'There was a shipwreck. . . .'

'So I understand.' A long pause. 'We'll come back to that later. My brother's dead, she tells me. What did you have to do with it?'

'I was not in Shelt during the week immediately preceding the Earl's death. I arrived there only in time to see his dying act.'

'Naming Jolin Rosco as his successor!' A short, unexpected crack of laughter. 'Does she really expect me to believe that rigmarole? What *did* happen the day my brother died, Maryn?'

'I only saw the end of it. The Lady Felicia's account would be entirely accurate. Torold spoke to his Captain, and the Sea Lords all capitulated. The fighting stopped immediately. Rosco was the popular choice.' He could not keep the bitterness from his voice.

'How convenient.' Javon's tone was expressionless. He was still staring at Serethrun, as if trying to weigh the honesty in his eyes. 'Let's start at the beginning, then. In your own words, Maryn. Let's have it all. When did you first meet my daughter?'

The shipwreck. Bleakly he recounted it, reliving somewhere in his mind the inquiry which had cost him his job.

'An odd circumstance, wasn't it? They were all experienced sailors, chosen for their familiarity with that coastline.'

'The ship was deliberately wrecked in a Mage-created storm. By Lammon, a member of one of the old families of Shelt. An acolyte Mage who resented the influence of Torold and yourself on Shelt. He is now dead. . .did not the Lady Felicia explain this in her letter?'

The green eyes stared back at him impassively. The Duke did not answer Serethrun's question directly. 'Torold was ever incompetent. . . .' The words were spoken half under his breath, and Serethrun only just caught them. 'The letter mainly concerns the man Jolin Rosco.' He was pacing the room now, up and down the length of the wide window over the plain. He wore a white surcoat of arctic-fox fur, over a full-sleeved shirt and breeches in tawny orange. He was not much taller than Serethrun, of slight build. When he moved there was an impression of energy, a sick, febrile energy that had its source in some distortion.

A cancer, thought Serethrun. Felicia's father is mortally ill.

He was still talking about Rosco. 'Tell me about him. Who is he, where does he come from? What is he like?'

Some of it was easy; a skilled warrior, a stranger from the far south. Riding an Arrarat hawk—

'*Does* he, indeed? Well, well. Perhaps she's not so silly, after all.' Unwillingly, Javon was impressed. 'And a warrior, you say. That means nothing. What's he like as a leader? A good judge of character, would you say?'

'He chose his lieutenants well.' Cammish, Lindel, Mittelson . . .himself. 'People follow him. He has charisma and the cause was just. The Sea Lords, under Gawne, were acting with evil intent. Disenfranchising the fisherpeople, mortgaging the city to a dragon. . . . And Rosco, he has – vision. He saw that it was all going wrong, and knew what to do to change it.'

'Why don't you like him?' The question was unexpected.

'I don't – dislike him.' Serethrun was caught off guard. 'The Lady Felicia would not be alive now if it were not for him.'

'And you, she says. First the gallant rescuer from the shipwreck, and then again from the clutch of the evil Mage Gawne. I shall need to know more about the Sea Lords and this dragon, but not now. Perhaps we are in *your* debt—'

Serethrun swept on. He could not allow this line of thought to be pursued. 'Rosco is honourable. Used to command. He demands loyalty, and receives it. He will do his best by Shelt.'

'And by my daughter? No, don't answer that.' For a moment, the Duke turned away, facing out across the plain. When he turned back the green eyes were withdrawn, his voice dry and expressionless.

'I have only one answer for my daughter. She is to leave Shelt, leave Rosco. If she returns to me, here, I will dissolve her marriage.'

'But the law—'

'Is safe in my hands.' There was no questioning the statement. Javon had made and enforced his own law throughout the southern and central lands of Stromsall.

'But the Lady Felicia—'

'Yes?'

'She – Felicia loves him!' The words were infinitely bitter on Serethrun's tongue.

'You are very simple. My daughter is not free to chose where she will.' He glanced once more at the letter, and folded it carefully. 'Love is irrelevant. Her hand has been sought in marriage. A marriage of far greater significance than that to an upstart adventurer, even if he does ride an Arrarat hawk, commands loyalty from his followers, and inspires love in my daughter. . .' And here, with deliberate slowness, he tore Felicia's letter in half – once, twice. He scattered the remains on the fire. 'She is destined for something more than that. A marriage promising peace and security for all the people of Stromsall and Peraldon.

'Felicia is to be the next Moon Empress on Peraldon. She will unite the two continents. Her marriage to Rosco must end. *Will* be ended.'

Serethrun stared blankly at the thin face already turning away from him. His message was being disregarded. Felicia herself was to be disregarded. He had not presented it well, he had allowed his dislike for Rosco, if that was what it was, to colour his words. He was aware of undercurrents he did not understand in everything Javon said, too. Plans and strategies, just as she had foreseen.

And the threat of death.

'But you can't just pass over a marriage, just like that! There's going to be a child!' What had she put in the letter? Was this general knowledge or not?

A sudden, dangerous pause. 'A child, indeed?' For a moment, Javon's face, always masked, became completely devoid of expression. Serethrun waited for the explosion.

But there was no anger, no violent assertion of power. Javon smiled at him gently. It was far worse than any explosion of fury. 'Perhaps – it has gone too far, then. Perhaps I will reconsider.' Another pause, and Serethrun realised that Javon's attention was elsewhere as the Duke stepped back and lifted his head to stare at the balcony above them.

Serethrun followed his host's gaze. Standing there, dressed in the subtlest of golden yellows, was the small figure of a woman. Laughing, darting eyes smiled at him. Curly black hair was threaded through with gold silk. Her skin was a warm olive, dusted by golden powders, so that she seemed to shimmer in the cool sunlight.

Still the silence went on. Then Javon sighed, and turned back to Serethrun. 'This is Merield, Lady of Berrice. She will accompany you back to Shelt. I have long thought that my daughter would benefit from the guidance of her own sex. And in her present condition she will welcome support from her family. Merield is my daughter's new stepmother. My honoured and esteemed wife.'

Chapter Six
Phinian

'The wedding will have taken place,' Matthias said. 'Eleanor will have been too late to stop it. A child. . . .'

The words dropped into the quiet, spoken neutrally, without stress or pressure. Matthias Marling and Phinian Blythe were sitting on the verandah of a sun-drenched villa, the louvred doors opening on to a cool, mosaiced hall. The house was deserted and in a state of some disrepair. It was one of three farms on the island of Massiq, south-west of Peraldon.

Blythe had stayed there often in his childhood, long before the Stasis. Even then, it had been shabby and run-down. The tattiness had been part of its charm. He and his sisters had run wild down crumbling brick paths along the sides of slow-moving watercourses. Willows still overhung the dark canals, but the drought had dried up every drop of water:they were now silted up with leaf mould and other debris.

There was no need for Blythe to pursue Matthias's bald statements. But he was sensitive to many nuances now, and knew that Matthias was concealing something. 'Why didn't you take her there straight-away? After leaving the Palace of Blood? Why did you come back to Smintha?'

'There was the Rite to stop, remember? And Weard, running loose. . .'

He halted, and Blythe looked away from the thin Mage, along the narrow canal-bed leading from the villa grounds to the open sea. Bleached grasses struggled for survival along its length. The sun-baked stone was warm and dusty. He found words.

'And me, of course. The Shadows. . .she came back with the baby to find me, didn't she?'

Matthias said nothing. There was a long silence. They watched the light breeze disturb the willows, the shifting shapes of narrow oval leaves.

'She'll need me,' Matthias said at last. 'She'll want to go back to her own world. I shall have to find a way to do it.'

'Alone? Could you do it by yourself?' Blythe remembered other rites, the rites that had always required the powers of more than one Mage.

'What do you suggest, Phin? Another pact with Edine? She would of course be delighted to work with me. . .'

'Thibaud and Aylmer. What about them?'

'They'll have other things on their minds. Negotiating with Peraldon, for a start. No, I shall have to find a way on my own. . .'

It seemed important not to leave Matthias alone again. The reworking of the Hidden Rite had left scars, unseen, but no less real than the ones on his face.

'There may be other Mages in Stromsall—'

'Almost certainly there will be. But I've had enough of collaborations.'

He had left later the same day, and Phinian Blythe was not sorry to stay behind. He stood on the landing stage and watched the hawk and rider disappear into the clear, blue air. The trees behind him rustled faintly in the warm on-shore breeze. He could have been there too, skimming the thermals on the back of Amery, Matthias's golden Arrarat.

He was glad to be alone. He was tired. It was almost as simple as that. The Shadows had drained his last reserves of energy, and the reworking of the Hidden Rite had been an exhausting and violent ordeal for him also. Then there had been the hurried journey northwards until they reached Massiq, the last island of the Octal archipelago, owned by Blythe's family for as long as anyone could remember.

Eleanor would not want to see him. It would be hard for her to forget why she had delayed. Why she had been too late to stop the wedding. Blythe could not imagine how she would handle any kind of rejection from Lukas Marling, after so much waiting, so much anticipation. And he felt, somehow, that rejection was all too likely. He did not want to dwell on something he could not change, but he

found his thoughts returning again and again to her, wondering what
she would do, hoping that she would at least find herself among
friends. . .

Perhaps he should have gone with Matthias. . .He turned away
from the landing stage and walked slowly through the burnt-umber
grasses back to the house, the home of his childhood.

He was back in Peraldonia. A countryside he knew intimately, a
climate he liked and trusted. His mother, sisters and friends lived
across only a narrow stretch of water. He hoped the heatwave of
Lycias's revenge had not caused them too much suffering.

What would be happening in Peraldon now? How was the new
Emperor faring with post-drought conditions? What advisers whispered in his ears, how had the factions fallen out, who was High Priest
now? And did a Moon Empress sit at his side, chosen from the
northern dwellers of Stromsall, as tradition required? Had life slipped
back at last to the ancient patterns? For the first time since the Stasis
had broken, Blythe found himself wondering about the political
situation.

It had nothing to do with him. His life as a Captain in the Warden's
Watch was over. It had ended when Karis died. His family thought
him dead, and perhaps it was best that any resurrection be indefinitely
postponed. The citizens of Peraldon might not thank him for leaving
them to endure the doubtful pleasures of old age and death.

He was sitting on the verandah again, watching the sun sink over
the calm lagoon. The other farms were deserted. The drought had
killed some of the smaller trees on Massiq, but most of them had
survived. The grass was already beginning to show streaks of fresh
green, and he knew there would be rain again that night, as there had
been every night of the journey northwards.

And as the shadows beneath the trees grew longer, the first light
spattering of rain refreshing the dank canals, he found himself
speculating. Where had those other Shadows gone, the Children of the
night, the Shadows which had hung round his shoulders for so long?
Now that Imbert was dead and thus released from their grip, were
they still flying free as black ravens, waiting to alight somewhere,
somehow? Or were they already weaving living nightmares round
some other suffering, sin-freighted soul?

That night Blythe dreamt of them, as the rain outside drummed
against the wooden shutters of his room. They were laughing and
chattering at the end of his bed, their faces hidden in the dark of the
room. But they came no nearer, playing a game of dice, back and forth
across the covers, the ivory cubes tumbling and lightly clashing
together.

He slept on, undisturbed.

Chapter Seven
Weard

Weard sat alone beside the ruins of the Temple to Lycias. Not far away a wide chasm yawned. Ash and dust clung round the skeletal remains of a great flower, stretching skywards out of the ruins of an endless stairwell.

The framework of the Desert Rose still reached up to the sun. Blackened stems and ashy flowers looked as if they might crumble to dust at the least breath of air. It appeared as fragile as charcoal, frozen in a moment of precarious stillness.

A cloud of dust billowed beneath it. Weard caught the suggestion of a flower, a fold of leaves, a showering of petals within the smoky clouds. But then it was gone, and he decided that it was a trick of the light. The ruins of the Desert Rose lay there: perhaps the clouds had picked up some reflection.

Weard wondered at the smoke. There were no flames, no heat. The fire had cooled long ago. And yet the smoke shifted, wisping through sunlight, and petals were wreathed in its midst.

He was unsure how to probe it further. He had a spiral staff, but he needed more than mere power. He needed instruction and knowledge. Matthias had promised. . . . But he was gone. Weard did not need the staff to tell him that Matthias and Phinian Blythe and Eleanor Knight had all gone. He had searched Smintha thoroughly, using the few remaining scurries. Even Edine seemed to have left.

As he watched over the smoky cloud, with its disconcerting suggestion of florescence, he heard the sound of wings beating in the air above him. He looked up and a heavy, spiky black shadow flew across the bright disc of the sun. Then another, and another.

The sky became full of wings, leathery flying creatures with their predatory riders, scudding over the Temple of Lycias. They came to settle around the ruins of the Temple arena. The Fosca and their dark angels.

Weard was on his feet now, his large heavy hands clasped firmly round the spiral staff.

He didn't trust them. They were avid, greedy and savage, and only Lefevre had ever been able to control them. But Weard was not seriously frightened, for he held a staff of power made from the body of the Great Mage himself, and he had faith in its strength and its untried powers. He was not defenceless.

They made no move to attack him. The riders slid from their mounts, and the movement sent a wash of putrid smells through the still air towards him. He felt the nausea rise in his throat, his stomach heaving at the stench.

He considered moving back, but even as the thought crossed his mind, there was another disturbance in the air and a further company of Fosca alighted just behind him. With an uneven gait, the riders closed in. Their faces were grinning, but that was not unusual.

'What do you want?'

Silence. They no longer laughed and chattered. Their faces still smiled, but there was determination in their uneven gait as they came nearer. The chasm was completely surrounded by them now. The Fosca behind him were pushing Weard towards its edge.

He shot a barb of power from the staff at them, and two of them were blasted silently to the ground, double-jointed limbs splayed wide by the force. Others took their place. Weard used the staff again, and yet more of them fell. But still the sky was filled with swinging, stinking shapes and their numbers were constantly replenished.

Only a few feet from the edge, he stared wildly round at the ranged petal faces, the grey skin fraying and rotting even as he watched. Each face was divided by a wide-grinning mouth, small, dagger-sharp teeth forming fringes round the non-existent lips.

He could use the staff again and again, and stave them off for some considerable time.

But Weard was beginning to realise that brute force might not always be enough. He would do better to conserve the staff's power for some more worthy task. He looked round for escape.

He could only consider the chasm below. There was nowhere else, ringed as he was by clawed, puppet-like figures. He knew that passages ran off the stairwell, doors and gates through to the City of Stairs. But as he looked into the depths of the chasm, his concentration was suddenly interrupted by a jagged outline swinging down from the sky just in front of him, and by the sickening smell that accompanied it. Rustling wings swooped down to settle on the broken steps of the ruined staircase. Only then did Weard realise that the sky was full of them, skimming down into the chasm, ranging themselves like dead leaves around the fractured spiral staircases. All the exits and doorways were blocked.

The Rose. Smoke still wound through the black stems. For a moment he thought he caught a glimpse of flowery tendrils again, of white falling petals, but then it was gone and he decided that the smoke merely reflected its surroundings, mirroring now the flower-faces of the Fosca.

In its charred, weakened state, was the Rose strong enough to bear his weight? He thrust the spiral staff into a loop hanging from his belt, and leaned over to touch one black stem. Part of it crumbled under his fingers – but beneath the fine dust green flesh grew.

Incredulous, Weard leaned further, towards a wide branch with several offshoots. Again: the showering of black ash from strong and living stems.

He glanced over his shoulder. The Fosca were still there, still nudging forward, the nearest of them less than an arm's reach away. Its clawed tentacle ripped through the air and as he dodged sideways to avoid it, Weard's foot slipped on the edge of the chasm. There was a half-choked cry at the sudden heart-stopping loss of stability and balance as he fell. His hands grabbed wildly for the blackened, fleshy stems.

His right hand caught.

The branch trembled and juddered, but held solid. He moved his other hand and hung there for a moment, looking at the edge of the stairwell. The Fosca riders were ranged along the wall, littering every half-ruined step, every landing. In that brief glance he saw in the grey, fraying faces – what? Amusement, malice. . .satisfaction.

No answers there. Swiftly, moving with agility, he hoisted himself, hand over hand, along the charred branch towards the centre of the Desert Rose, where the stems were thicker and stronger.

A thorn ripped at his side, almost dislodging the staff. His hands were black and slippery with greasy ash. He cursed and tried to wedge the staff more securely, but a tendril from the Rose had wound itself around the carved spiral.

It wanted his staff! Furious with rage, forgetting quite what the Rose was or had been, Weard slashed at the stem with his knife.

In response, a thorned stem wrapped itself around his body. He struggled, but was constrained by having to hang on to the branch above.

It wrapped itself around him with love and care, and the thorn found its home in brown-skinned flash.

He hung, screaming, as the thorn pierced his heart, lodging there.

The flower-face bloomed once more.

Chapter Eight
Edine

The woman crouched in the dust of the desert outside the city of Smintha was drawing patterns in the sand.

Under her fingers, shapes grew from the hot white grains. She was muttering under her breath, a stream of words in a language known to few. Every now and then, hissing with fury, she would spread her fingers wide, smoothing over the surface, cancelling out a careless line, an uneven trough.

Her knuckles shone white. Short dark hair, damp with perspiration, clung to her forehead. Her hands moved with a kind of desperate haste, as if this were some race against the glaring sun. The back of her neck, already burning under the midday sun, was scorched red, and the seam of her cloth-of-gold cloak grated on her skin.

Two small heaps of powder lay on the sand at her side. The muttering went on, a monotonous drone of ugly words. The woman's eyes were fastened on the sand-carried patterns, unblinking in the dry desert wind that subverted her attempts at order. And although it was hot and dry, and her throat was parching with thirst, her skin burning under the sun, a ceaseless flow of moisture ran down the pale planes of her face, tears, salty and bitter, falling from her eyes to spoil the patterns in the sand.

At night, her task completed, the woman returned to the city. She moved slowly, reluctantly, shivering slightly in the cold desert darkness. This was a gamble, the ultimate risk.

The gates of Smintha stood open, lopsided against their hinges. Drifts of sand clogged their base. The rain that was bringing life to the North had not yet reached this far outpost of the Peraldonian Empire.

Smintha was deserted. The path of the Stormbearer still betrayed ruinous destruction, buildings torn apart, roads ripped up, bridges broken and crumbling. The fountains and ornamental lakes were still dry and dusty, the avenues abandoned, the great halls and temples empty.

Two beings moved towards each other through Smintha that night. Edine, still soundlessly weeping, carefully carrying in roughened hands curious glass shapes: a crescent moon, a strange oval, a blazing sun. An offering, perhaps. A placatory gift of power.

And someone else, released from an embrace of thorns. He still wore a patterned leather jerkin, and the other trappings of that crude, forceful body; he held a spiral staff in brutal hands, striding through the streets of Smintha.

At his shoulders dark angels flew. Like a mantle of black they spread out through the night air, eyes glowing. The rotting rags of skin that fell constantly from their riders showered in grey flakes behind him, as petals had once fallen through the Forest of Flowers in the Palace of Blood.

A smile curved the full lips. There was a certain pleasure in the strength of a gross human body. His hands were wide and powerful, and could caress or crush with equal efficacy. He felt the brush of the cold air through his long curling hair; he was walking quickly and the dark angels were cutting swathes through the night all around him.

'Edine.'

'My Lord.' For a moment, she wondered whether her nerve would fail and lead her to run screaming down the deserted avenues, although there was nothing in Weard's voice to inspire this terror.

Nothing about his appearance to explain why she trembled so, why her hands were sweaty in the cold night air.

It was not the Fosca either, hovering in the air over the figure of the man before her. She was used to Fosca; although she had never controlled them, she had learned enough from Imbert to defend herself. But her weeping eyes were wide with fear and her breast moved quickly under the pressure of faint, gasping breaths.

'My Lord—' she said again, falling to her knees, bending her head low over the fragile glass shapes.

'Well, Edine, so we meet again. A long time since we last spoke. . .' A slight pause. She looked up at him, meeting his eyes at last. 'Tell me Edine, what fate do you deserve? Death by burning, perhaps? It would not be inappropriate.' A faint smile flickered over the lips of the man standing over her. 'Or shall I instruct my sweet flowers to run their thorns through your flesh, to strip from you in ribbons of crimson the burden of your sin?'

A faint, inarticulate sound from her lips as she crouched there in the dust. A longer silence this time. He seemed to enjoy the length of it, still smiling, the thick fingers stroking the wooden spiral of the staff.

'You have doubly offended, Edine. The weight of heresy lies heavy across your shoulders. . . . Have you nothing to say in your own defence, little one? No words of regret and remorse, no professions of loyalty to expiate your past sin, no oaths or prayers, or blandishments, subtle and enticing? No words at all? Nothing?'

She found speech then. 'There are no words adequate to the task. What could I possibly say? I can only prove my loyalty through my actions. Lord, I have used my tears to conjure shapes of glass.' Although her voice was steady her hands still trembled, holding out the three shining forms. 'These are for you.'

'And still your tears flow, Edine, washing your pale, pretty skin. . .' Carefully, he laid the staff on the ground. He looked at her again, examining the anguished planes of her face, and the smile flickered once more. 'How touching. You grieve for your lover and colleague, the clever Mage Imbert. . .'

He did not even glance at the glass shapes. His hands, wide and powerful, reached forward and smoothed the tears from her face. Others flowed in their place. His hands cupped her face momentarily, and then moved down over her throat, over the thin slope of her shoulders, over the soft skin of her arms to her wrists.

She shuddered under his touch, a quiver of unmistakable revulsion, but she said nothing.

'I will accept an offering from you, Edine, but not these fragile toys.' Inexorably, his fingers round her wrists tightened until, with a gasp, she allowed the frail shapes to fall to the stone pavement. A showering of glass, a shattering of hope. 'I will accept. . .the gift of your body, Edine. Vowed in eternal loyalty to your lover, I am sure. Moved in love with him less than a sennight since. . . .'

The eyes and hands still held her captive, but at last she found courage.

'I would rather die.'

'I know.' He laughed softly. 'Death by burning, or by flensing would come easier to you, proud Edine, than this. I remember, you see. You rejected Weard many times in the past. Your abhorrence was plain then, as it is now. Weard was in no position to argue.

'But I am not Weard. And you are not going to die.'

In the morning, Edine and her master left Smintha. They rode on dark angels, skimming high over the desert. Only one other Fosca accompanied them, a petal-faced baron with unusually intelligent eyes.

Another incarnation, another chance. Lucian Lefevre was returning to his Empire. To his palace at Solkest, where he would resume his old rôle as trusted and esteemed advisor to the Emperor: in his hands the spiral staff, sharing and augmenting his powers to an unprecedented degree. The spiral carving was no longer merely wood. It moved all the time now, twining round and round, wreathing away into nothing, like the smoke that billowed beneath the spiral stairs.

The broad, crude face was unsmiling, concentrating, planning. There would be a long way to go before his power was recognised and accepted by the Peraldonians. Much depended on the character of the Emperor, of course. And whether there existed still any Mages or priests powerful enough to challenge him. He had every confidence in his abilities. Whatever the challenge, whatever the strength of character in priest, Mage or Emperor, he would prevail. It was only a matter of time.

He had been forgiven by his God. He had survived an abyss of fire, cleansed, purified. He would start again, and the world would echo to the praises of the Sun God. . .

A little to his right flew the third dark angel, ridden by Edine. Her hands were slim, resting lightly on the scales of the reptile's neck. Her mouth was drawn wide in a soundless smile, and short dark hair flew behind her in the wind.

Her eyes were gleaming in the reflection of her master's power. Beautiful, calm and aware, she looked out into the blue skies, over the pattern on dunes and mountains beneath them. Every now and then, she raised her hand to the corner of her mouth where a small trickle of blood fell from the torn lip.

Her eyes gleamed and her mouth smiled. But tears still fell, ceaselessly washing down over her face, and mingled with the blood.

Chapter Nine
Decisions

One afternoon Eleanor walked on the northern brigg below the Castle of Shelt. She was longing for home.

Spring. The sky was a vivid cloudless blue, the tide far out, just on the turn. There was a light wind. Listlessly, she wandered over the slimy rocks. She was wearing smooth-soled boots, and slipped on the green-stained rock. She did not gaze into rockpools, or gather shells. Instead, she looked out over the bright sea, out towards a distant horizon.

She was watching the birds wheeling there, high above the waves. Gulls and cormorants, petrels, shags, blown about a sparkling sky. She had dreamed of Ash, the night before. She had been standing in the cave on Arrarat Isle, waiting for him. She had held out her arms, waiting for the wide sweeps of midnight-power to centre in towards her.

He had come, laying his great head against hers, and her arms had folded round his neck. She remembered the quality of his welcome. She had never really mourned Ash. Her grief for Lukas had overwhelmed every other emotion.

She did not want to think about Lukas now. A bitter wash of pain distorted every image of him in her mind. There was nothing she could do, except get out of the way. If only a great hawk would come for her, now, and take her away from Shelt. She hated this cold northern shore. It reminded her of dull, rainy childhood holidays on windswept coasts. Lonely holidays, lonely times. The past is a foreign country, she remembered reading somewhere. They do things differently there.

There seemed little enough difference to Eleanor. She had always been lonely, although she had never realised it before. Some people she knew saw their childhoods through a glow of affection and laughter. Hers had been gilded with gifts; parcelled out between nannies and au pairs.

Still, it had been home, as this was not.

She turned back towards Shelt. The Castle was in deep shade now, the sky behind it tinged with red. There were already lights in the ballrooms and in the large galleries on the second floor. There was to be yet another reception that night, she remembered. An exercise in binding together all the wealth of Shelt, to ensure that loyalties would remain true in the difficult days to come.

She faced the prospect with resignation. And then saw a shadow shift against the base of the cliff. She stood still, hesitating. With incredulous, delighted shock she saw the shadow solidify into a familiar, graceful shape; a great hawk. Amery. Eleanor recognised her immediately. The hawk was standing in the shadows of the cliff below the Castle, and there was someone with her.

'Matthias!' She began to run across the rocks, slipping and splashing in the pools. His blind face was turned peacefully towards her, his hands held out.

'Eleanor? Is that you?' He clasped both her hands briefly and then drew her closer, brushing the hair from her eyes, touching the tears on her cheeks. 'Are you all right?'

She could hardly speak. 'I'd rather. . .Tell me what happened, Matthias. You got away, you managed to get out of Smintha? All of you? What about Phin?'

'He's all right, back in Peraldon, getting used to ordinary life again. . .There's so much to say, I hardly know where to begin. The Rite failed, of course, as you must have realised.'

'And Thurstan?'

He didn't answer, and she found tears in her eyes once more. 'The others?' she asked, her voice like a thread. 'Imbert? Edine? What happened to Weard?'

'Imbert died. The Shadows, Children of the Night, had taken him, and there was a struggle on the edge of the stairwell. That was when Thurstan fell, too. I don't know about Edine, or Weard. We didn't stay around for long. It's all very far away, now, Eleanor. I came here to find you, to see how you are.'

'I can't stay here. I need. . .I want – Matthias, can you send me home?' She looked at him in painful anxiety.

'I don't know that I can.' He sounded guarded.

'You've done it before. You've sent people to my world.' People in a taxi: two ambitious, driven Mages.

'I had help then. It will be difficult alone.'

'Can't I do it? Teach me what to do!'

'How long are you prepared to wait, Eleanor? Five or six years? It's a long road, learning magic.'

She was aghast. 'That long? I can't stay here for six years!'

'Is it so very bad?'

'It's impossible! Lukas is. . . .' She stopped. She still found it difficult to say.

'Married. Yes, I know.'

'Is that what you saw, all the way through the desert surrounding Smintha? Did you know what would happen?'

'I saw him married, yes. But I didn't know if it was unavoidable, more than just a possibility. I didn't know how accurate the vision was. I was wrong about the Rite. I really thought that it would work, and that the Stasis would start again—'

He was trying to change the subject. She let it pass.

'Can you see the future still?'

'Some of it. Not all, I'm glad to say. I only ever see pictures, and they are always open to misinterpretation.'

'What do you see for me, Matthias?' She stared at him, trying to read honesty in the thin, blind face, caught in the gathering twilight. As usual, he revealed nothing.

'You, back in your own world. I cannot follow you further there. But yes, you will return.'

'Right then. Let's get started.'

He almost laughed. 'You haven't changed at all, have you? Remember that beach outside the cliff? A light to follow, and to hell with the consequences?'

'So long ago. . .I was young, then.' She paused. 'Lukas thinks I've changed. That he doesn't know me any more.' Her voice was only a whisper.

A long silence. 'Perhaps he has other things to worry about. . . .'

'Armies, politics, laws, government. Yes, lots of things.'

'Eleanor.' His hands were on her shoulders. 'Tell me about his wife. Before we go to the Castle. I must know who she is.'

'Why?' A tight, bitter little voice.

'She must be – of significance. A part of the pattern for some reason. This marriage was planned without reference to any human consideration. Who is she?'

'The Lady Felicia, daughter of Javon Westray of Eldin. She's thin and pale and pregnant. She looks as if a puff of wind would blow her over. Honestly, Matthias, as a figure of significance she doesn't even begin to rate! You wouldn't notice her even if she wore full ceremonial regalia at breakfast. Which she doesn't, never eating breakfast anyway.' Eleanor stared at her boots. 'I don't dislike her. I was all set to loathe her. Lukas's wife, but really it would be irrelevant. She's quite unhappy enough as it is.'

'So it's not much fun in Shelt?'

'It's dreadful! Anywhere else has got to be better. Take me away, Matthias. Send me home, there's nothing here for me, no one needs or wants me!'

'And Lukas?'

'It's over. He's not even – interested. And I can't stand it any more.'

Matthias said nothing, taking her arm as they walked together back over the rocks to the Castle. His heart ached for her, but there was nothing he could say. The future he saw contained Eleanor, whisked back through the dimensions to her own world.

There would be someone with her. And although it wasn't clear, he didn't think it would be Lukas.

Four days before Matthias arrived, Felicia had watched Serethrun Maryn cross the Castle courtyard towards the gates. He was returning to the *eloish*, and would ride with them far away, to the northern pastures.

She was deeply puzzled by the message he had brought from Eldin.

She knew her father well enough to understand that he would do anything to procure her marriage to the new Emperor. Javon had already succeeded in uniting the whole of the Northern Continent under his rule. He would not be content to let it rest there.

She could not quite believe that the existence of her unborn child would change his mind.

But perhaps she misjudged him. Perhaps, now that she was no longer chaste, he would accept with a good grace her marriage to Rosco. She hardly dared think it could be true, but there was no way she could be presented as a suitable bride for the Emperor now. Her hand went to her abdomen, still flat. As yet, the only evidence of her pregnancy lay in the ceaseless vomiting and the tenderness of her breasts. She hardly noticed it. She was used to feeling ill.

'Should you not be sitting down, Felicia? I am persuaded that you should rest more. The early months of pregnancy can be very draining.'

Her stepmother, Merield, spoke languidly. Within the space of two days she had established herself as a person of exquisite and frail sensibility. She drifted around the Castle, pale silks wafting in the cold draughts. Gradually, layers of fringed shawls were added to the ensemble.

Rosco's eyes had sparkled dangerously when she arrived. 'A visit from the mother-in-law already? We are of course delighted to receive your congratulations, Lady Merield. Tell us, how fares the noble Duke of Eldin?'

She had looked at him, consideringly. A faint smile flickered over her serene face. 'Quite well, I thank you. He looks forward to meeting you.'

'It is good of my esteemed father-in-law to spare you to us, so early in his marriage. Will you be staying long?'

She shrugged. 'I do not know. . .as long as necessary.' She raised her chin slightly, looking him in the eye, and Felicia was amused to see him, for once, hesitate.

'And your entourage. You're all settling in, I see.' He was not even polite to her. Felicia began to feel annoyed. Her father was at least making a gesture of reconciliation. Could Rosco not reciprocate?

Merield introduced her personal staff. A thin, elderly wisp of a woman, Louisa, her companion and lady-in-waiting. Cherry, her neat, silent maid. Yerrent, a Mage in Javon's employ, a small, self-satisfied man with thin lips. And Bladon, the Duke's own horseman.

Brilliant eyes swept over them all, lingering not at all.

They had been assigned apartments on the west wing, away from the sea, away from Rosco and Felicia's private quarters.

'There will be a reception for the nobility of Shelt, the day after tomorrow. I shall be glad to see you there.'

The dismissal could not have been clearer. Merield's cheeks were flushed, her lips slightly compressed.

However, her farewell to Rosco was a model of elegance, a gracious inclination of the head. Felicia she ignored. She swept from the room, followed by her servants.

Felicia turned to Rosco. 'No good can come of offending her, you know.'

'No good can come of her being here at all. Why on earth did he send her? It's a bit late for a chaperon.' He was already glancing at the pile of papers on his desk. 'Rather sudden, this marriage of your father's, isn't it? Did you know Merield before you left Eldin?'

'Only by repute. She was widowed rather suddenly soon after her marriage to the Count, three years ago. Some mysterious illness. At the time, there were rumours. . .'

Rosco looked at her thoughtfully. 'How are you feeling these days? Off your food, as usual?'

She stared at him. 'Surely you'd be the one at risk. If that's what you mean?'

He laughed. 'Don't look so worried, Felicia. Just an idea. Have a word with Olwyn, if the sickness gets too much. I expect he'll have something to help.'

'No doubt.'

But she avoided Olwyn Mittelson, and kept to her rooms.

She was not alone, however. Her new stepmother visited her regularly, bearing with her pills and potions. Felicia meekly accepted every one, hiding them away in a handkerchief, a reticule, a posy of flowers.

But one night, she opened the window of her lonely room, and threw every powder, every pill and drop of medicine down into the quiet waves below. Then, for the first time she noticed that the wind had dropped, that the skies were clear.

The storm was over.

Chapter Ten
Irian

Irian rolled over, disturbed not by noise but by silence. Something had happened, something had been cleared from their lives. She knew at once what it was. The storm had passed. She felt it in the unstressed air, she knew it from the calm whisper of the new leaves. The howling had finished, the battering wind had died. The grief was ended.

Iran pushed back her blanket and stood up. She looked round at the other shapes nestling in their bracken shelters, listening with concentration to the steady sound of their breathing. They were all asleep, the *eloish* that survived. They would sleep the night through, she thought, dreaming of the open plans.

Why should they not? It had been hard enough. First the storms of the Stasis, matched by the violence in the City. The *eloish* had endured persecution from Torold and the Sea Lords, the enclosure of their hunting grounds, the theft of their horses. They had been driven into the deep forest, and there a creeping, feral quality had overtaken them all. They had begun to forget the open plains, the open spaces. It had been a time of subtle danger, but her brother Serethrun had brought them horses, had rescued them from the forest's grip. He brought horses on the condition that they joined the fisherpeople's fight against the Sea Lords of Shelt.

So the *eloish* had followed Serethrun into battle. They had been caught up in the city's struggle, and many had lost their lives. It was the price of forgetting the open spaces, the calling wind.

Iran had watched them die in silence, knowing that the price had to be paid. She had thought that would be enough.

But then they had delayed. She would not forgive them that. It was so stupid as to be beyond belief. They had horses, and the plains were calling. But the *eloish* decided to wait for Serethrun, although she knew no good would come of it. And while they waited, this other storm had shattered the air over Shelt, driving every last reserve of energy from them all. She had worried that the forest would reclaim them.

That final storm was over now. As suddenly as it arrived it had died. With relief, the *eloish* had fallen into a deep and exhausted sleep.

But Irian had woken, had moved out of the shelter of the camp. Something was calling her, and she could not rest.

She left the clan peacefully entwined about each other in their bracken shelters, and walked swiftly away from the camp. The fires were dying, the sky bright and clear. A thousand stars, the quiet Moon.

She turned away from Shelt, black-shadowed in the East, and looked out across the plains to the North-west. They would ride the next day, whether they wanted to or not. She would make it happen. There was no reason to remain, nothing to keep them here now. Even her brother Serethrun was back, grim with an inexplicable fury. She had warned him that no good would come of this involvement with the city. . .with the *mereth*.

She stood watching the open plains which were scattered with the horses Serethrun had brought. She saw a breeze ripple through the grasses and a kind of triumph filled her. Tomorrow they would leave, and then the riding would be everything, would contain their whole world. They would leave behind the complications and mess of Shelt, nothing would matter but the horses and the wind and the grass. . . .

She crouched down on her heels and closed her eyes. In her mind a shape formed, a sharply defined image of fleet strength. She hummed quietly beneath her breath, and sent the shape of her desire out into the calm, horse-strewn plains.

At her side, suddenly appearing from nowhere, the image of her wishing was given flesh. She stared into his velvet-dark eyes and smiled. She lifted her hand to salute the long, smooth forehead. A ride, tonight. It was lunacy of course, when they had so far to go the next day. . .

She was getting soft. City-sick, forest-feral. A short, disdainful laugh at herself, and then she swung herself up on to the horse's back.

As the night deepened before dawn, they danced over the plain, wheeling and carolling, following the light breezes in patterns of a grace that was not quite the other side of savagery. A salutation of the night, a celebration of intense power.

As dawn broke, they found themselves south-west of the city, on the outskirts of the forest. The horse slowed to a walk, and Irian pushed back the hair from her face, as if emerging from deep waters.

He was called Kerol. She knew it now, just as he knew who she was. They would be companions on the ride and perhaps for longer than that.

There was dew on the fresh grass, sparkling in the early sun. Kerol's hooves left a delicate pattern behind them. Tired now, Irian was content to let her horse choose their route.

She could tell that the storm had passed that way not long ago. Trees had collapsed against each other in haphazard devastation, their branches interlocking, slanted at unsteady angles. Others had flared up in a shock of lightning, and only charred skeletons remained, bleak in the dappled light. The undergrowth was crushed and battered all around. A pathway of destruction cut deep into the forest and Kerol was having to tread carefully to avoid the worst of it.

The jagged scars of the storm's path would soon fade, she thought.

In the course of one ordinary summer the bracken and brambles would cover those stumps and uneven gashes. The *eloish* wouldn't be here to see it, running through the northern forests to the tundra. It would be cool there, and the hunting wolves would howl in the night and the terns and plovers call overhead in the massive silences. . .

And although it was a quiet, sunny morning south of Shelt, Irian shivered. She pulled her cloak more tightly round her throat, and glanced back the way they had come. Calmly, the forest stood around her.

The sun was beginning to warm the air, and there was a faint scent of newly disturbed leaf mould, of green growing things. A pungent taint of wild garlic. Birds were singing, too, an uneven chorus. She lifted her face to the growing sunlight, concentrating on the patchy warmth.

Kerol stopped. They were standing in a small clearing, brightly lit, shining in the dewy light.

A man lay there, sleeping peacefully.

In the crook of his arm, wide awake, and watching her approach with interest, was a baby.

Irian did not move, watching the man and child. This was why Kerol had brought her here, this was why she had been unable to sleep that night. And yet she did not at first understand what she should do. The camp would be waking soon, would wonder where she was. She looked up, assessing the path of the sun. It was still very early. There was time. . . .

She dismounted and crossed the grass, watched all the time in silence by the baby.

She frowned. She was not a maternal woman, far from it, but there was something about that wide, black gaze. The *eloish* were short of new blood. There had been too many lives lost recently. A half-formed idea. . .

The man puzzled her. He didn't at all look like the kind of person to be in charge of so small a child. He was more likely a vagrant from Shelt, a criminal or a drunkard. He was thin to the point of emaciation, his eyes were circled in red, deep-sunk in a white, lined skin. He was locked in a deep sleep of exhaustion, his hands flung wide and abandoned, his mouth slightly open, the breath gasping faintly in the quiet morning. But for all the frailty of the ragged figure, she thought that he was young, that his broad back was wide enough to bear much.

She shook his shoulder, but he did not stir. The baby was still watching her, dark eyes serious. It held out its arms to her and without thinking, she tried to take the baby from the man's embrace. But although the man was still unconscious, his grip tightened on the child. The baby looked up and smiled, as if it were sharing a joke with her.

She sat back on her heels, wondering what to do.

Kerol was cropping grass a little way off, unconcerned. As she watched, the man shifted slightly and sighed. She found herself yawning in sympathy. She had not slept last night, after all, and there was a long day ahead.

She would just sit down for a while, and rest until the man woke up. They were probably lost. She'd point them the way back to Shelt, and then return to the camp. The baby was bound to need something soon, anyway. Babies *always* did, in her limited experience.

She wouldn't sleep, of course, not in the middle of the forest close to a strange and dissolute-looking man, although she had to admit that he didn't appear dangerous. He was not even carrying a weapon.

She laid her cloak out on the grass not far away, and settled herself. In moments she was asleep. And not long after, she stirred, turning over on the soft springy turf. Her outflung hand touched the baby.

It reached out to her, bending all its small fingers round her thumb. And in that way, not touching, but linked by the baby, Irian and the ragged man slept through the early spring morning.

He was still unconscious when she awoke some hours later. The sun was high now, directly overhead. She sat up stiffly, irritated with herself for having slept so long. The *eloish* would be wanting to set off, wondering what had happened to her. She should be getting back.

The baby was asleep now, but she knew it wouldn't last long. She should come to some decision about it. Irian sighed, and leant over, shaking the man's shoulder once more.

This time he mumbled, half raising his hand to brush her off, but she persisted. It was nothing to do with what the baby was like, of course, a pretty enough child, but of a different racial mix, like the man. No slant eyes there, no touch of wildness in the curving mouth. But new blood could not just be passed over. The clan numbers were down. It would do them no harm. . . .

The baby would need feeding and changing soon. She didn't want to leave it here with this wreck of a man. Was he drugged, perhaps?

She was about to lift his eyelid – she was a healer, after all – when the eyes flicked open, meeting her look.

She sprang to her feet with a gasp, her hand flying to the knife at her side. His eyes, his eyes—

—Were open and staring, and the memory of madness lurked there.

Her only instinct was to get the child to safety, and quickly. She bent down swiftly, reaching out.

He snatched the child away, clasping it close, his whole body hunched over the small downy head.

Irian did not hesitate. Breathing hard, she pulled a knife from her belt.

'Put the child down,' she said forcefully.

There was no reply. Perhaps he did not speak the same language. She took a step closer, and then stopped.

There were tears falling on to the child's head, a running stream of salt. She saw the man's shoulders shudder, but there was no sound.

Impatiently she said, 'Give the child to me. You are in no condition to look after it. You are weak and ill. I am a healer, I will not hurt you or the baby.'

'Nothing can hurt me now.' His voice was very low, his words halting and uncertain. As if he had not spoken for a very long time. His head was still bent.

'Who are you?' she asked. 'What are you doing here?'

He was not one of the *eloish* clans. He was true *mereth*, large and clumsy. Dark, round eyes; light brown wavy hair, streaked with grey. He looked as if he had been seriously ill. She doubted whether he'd even be able to stay on a horse.

He glanced up at her again, and again there was that shock. She took an involuntary step backwards, repulsed by the echoing blackness at the back of his eyes. 'I. . .don't know. I have been mad, I think. . . .' His voice trailed off uncertainly. 'I. . .this is my son. His name—' He stopped again, as if unsure. Then his voice became stronger. 'His name is Coron. And I am Haddon, Haddon Derray.'

'Where are you from?' His boots were barely holding together, his clothes only filthy rags. But he spoke with courtesy, and his arms, cradling the baby were infinitely gentle.

'I – can't remember. . .I've come a very long way. Someone stole Coron, you see. I had to find him.'

'And now you have your son again, what will you do?'

He seemed incapable of understanding her. 'What will I do? I. . .don't know. I haven't thought.' Unsteadily, he lurched to his feet, still holding the child carefully to his breast.

He was unstable, she thought, in every way. As if he had neither rested nor eaten for a long time. On the run, no doubt. He swayed. As she watched, he dropped to his knees.

Automatically, she moved towards him, wanting to take the baby from him. He was going to drop it.

He turned away from her, brusquely. And then seemed to feel that it was awkward, impolite. 'I'm sorry,' he said, 'but I've spent so long looking for him. . .I can't let him go.'

'All right.' She spoke on impulse. 'You'd better come with me. You need food, I think. And so does the child.'

Let the clan decide, she thought. They had spare horses now, and a baby would be valued. Derray had been strong once, she could see that. He would recover, given a little food and rest. She was a healer, and did not grudge him that, *mereth* or not.

'You can ride my horse, if you want. It's quite a way from here.'

He staggered to his feet once more, and turned towards Kerol. He was too exhausted by the effort even to reply.

'At least let me take the baby while you mount. You're in no shape for walking.'

She thought he was going to argue, for there was a mulish look to those exhausted brown eyes. But then he shrugged, and slowly, reluctantly, handed the baby over.

It was as if his strength had suddenly drained away. His knees began to buckle once more, but his hand was on Kerol's mane and somehow, with a groan, he managed to haul himself on to the horse's back. And then he would not move, would not start, until she had given him back his son, so that the child was resting on his lap.

Probably the clan would find it ridiculous. This was an act quite out of character for Irian. She was not prepared, for the moment, to question her motives. Kerol was going along with it, too. Irian walked at his side through the forest, while the stranger's weary head drooped towards the baby, his hands helplessly cradled round the small body.

She did not notice, in the bright midday light, the two glowing eyes watching them from behind the thicket of trees. Did not see the great golden hawk spring up into the air, following the path they had taken.

Chapter Eleven
The Riders

Back at the edges of the plain, the *eloish* were waiting.

They moved quietly through the tall grasses and she could see from the eager groupings of the horses that each rider had already made a choice. They were waiting only for her, and she was aware of the impatience in their glances.

The pile of leavings rose high in their midst.

As she approached, the *eloish* mounted their horses. They stood stamping in the late afternoon sun and watched her.

One of them rode forward.

'No passengers, Irian. Remember?' Serethrun, of course, unsmiling and bleak.

'He will recover,' she said shortly. 'He only needs rest.'

'No one's going to wait around while he puts his feet up. We're leaving now. He's *mereth*. We don't need him.'

No, perhaps they didn't need him. She stared doubtfully at the wrecked man, his chin sunk deep in his chest, the baby still calm on his lap. He would be a liability, there was no doubt of that. It would be a long time before he would be ready to contribute to the life of the *eloish*. If, indeed, that was what he would want to do. It was all too risky.

She didn't want to leave the baby behind. The man didn't matter, but she wanted the baby, an unreasoning and passionate desire. It would never do to admit such weakness, especially not to Serethrun in his present mood.

'Is everyone else ready?' she said, looking round. She had noticed that someone had packed up her own possessions. There was a small pile of belongings on the ground near the leavings. Perhaps Ferna had helped, for once. Or Rusarrian, more likely.

Serethrun's voice was still unfriendly. 'We're all here. You'd better get rid of these two. We're leaving now. There's a long way to go.'

'Lara should decide.'

There was a pause while he considered it. She raised her chin, staring him in the eye, daring him to challenge her.

'Very well. Five minutes.' Serethrun turned away from her and rode back to the *eloish*.

Five minutes. Time at least to ask Lara, although she knew what the decision would be. Leaving Kerol with the man and child, she pushed through the mass of horses and riders to the familiar figure she knew she would find at their centre.

Lara Valde, Archon of Gerune *eloish*. She was old for a rider, over fifty, and her yellow skin was creased and leathery. And yet she was still potent in all their lives, the lines on her face the marks of laughter and compassion. She had braided her hair with even more ribbons than usual, Irian noticed sourly. To celebrate the ride?

Well, it was not inappropriate. Irian put aside her irritation and bent her head, formally.

'Ah, Irian. We were wondering where you were. How could the *eloish* ride without the Lady's own sayer?' And although the words were sharp, the Archon's tone was not unfriendly.

Irian said, 'You have never had to wait for me before.'

'True. The first to leave each camp, the first to respond to the calling wind. . .yes, Irian, we know you well. I'm glad you are not letting us down after all this time.' The wise eyes were smiling. And then she looked beyond Irian to the slumped figure on Kerol's back.

'Who is that?' The teasing quality had vanished.

'His name is Derray. He appears to be homeless. The baby is his son, a fine child.'

'Irian! What is this? Are you asking that we take them with us? You, the most severe practitioner of the One Rule?' Lara leaned forward over her horse's neck. 'This is most unusual.'

'Where does he come from?' Jerr Morrelow, the maverick traveller who sometimes joined them, had approached. He had been watching Derray and the child. His hat was frivolously tilted, his slant eyes mischievous. 'I must admit to some curiosity. . .'

'There can be no question. We don't take *mereth* passengers.' Serethrun was there too, now, frowning from the back of his black mare.

'Our numbers are down. We need new blood—'

'He is not one of us. And ill, besides.'

'But the baby is self-evidently healthy.' Jerr Morrelow again, interrupting. Irian stared at him. She was not accustomed to support from his quarter. She was uneasily aware that she had never understood him.

'Years will pass before he is of any use to us,' said Lara.

'We *need* new blood!' Only five children had been born during the last year, and one of them had sickened and died in the wild forest. Twenty men had lost their lives during the battle at Shelt. There were fewer than two hundred now to ride the plains.

'Not the man. He will only drain our resources. You may offer to take the baby, Irian, but it will be up to you to look after it. And you have other duties to perform.' Lara Valde spoke decisively. There was no arguing with her. Her decision was more generous than Irian had expected.

Jerr Morrelow was already fading back among the other riders. But not before Irian had seen something in his face. Satisfaction, she thought. He's got what he wanted.

She nodded to Lara and turned back to Kerol.

Heavy brown eyes watched her approach. Through the exhaustion, incredibly, Haddon Derray was smiling.

'You want your horse back, right? Never mind, we'll walk.'

'You can't come with us. Do you understand? We leave very soon. The child can come, he is healthy and would be of use to the clan.'

There was a genuine sparkle of amusement in the shadowed eyes. 'Don't *you* understand, wild lady of the plains? This is my son, my only salvation. We stay together.'

Salvation? For the moment, Irian put the word aside. 'If you truly love this child, you will let us take him. You are in no shape to look after him, and this is not a region where people will live in peace for years to come.'

'*Love?* Love has nothing to do with it. We stay together, that is all. It's not open to discussion.' He looked down at the child on his lap and, as Irian watched, the little boy reached out one hand, touching him lightly.

It was as if the touch had given strength and purpose. The man gathered him up into his arms, swung his leg over Kerol's shoulder and slid to the ground.

Irian started forward immediately, expecting him to fall, but somehow he managed to stay upright.

'Which way is the city?'

'You won't make it.'

'I only need to sleep now. Tomorrow I shall be all right.'

'But what about the baby? It will need feeding before then!' She was exasperated by his easy acceptance of the situation.

'Leave us some milk then. . .bread. If you can spare it.' His voice implied that he couldn't have cared less what she left. As if it didn't matter at all.

Frowning, she turned to her small pile of belongings on the muddy ground. Someone had taken care to tie it securely. It did not take her long to release the knot. She needed to find a leaving, anyway. So she unrolled the bundle, and drew out the waterproof container that held her food. Dry, dark bread, a little mare's milk, an onion and some withered apples. An unappetising collection. She put it aside.

Then, the leaving. She looked at her possessions. Which object had given her most pleasure during their life in the forest, when the *eloish* had run in silence through the trees, tracking the deer. . .?

She considered. Her clothes were all functional, there was no one garment that meant more to her than any other. She owned no jewels, no weapons beyond her bow and knife. She had never decorated her resting places with wildflowers stuck in pretty jugs. She possessed nothing that was not useful, nothing extra to the most basic requirements.

But something must be left, something of value in her life. Her eyes fell upon the rough bone comb she used to straighten her hair. Inessential, surely. She could always cut the hair off if it became troublesome. Without a further thought, she dropped it on the pile of leavings in the centre of the camp. Derray could set up as a pedlar, she thought with a flicker of amusement. There was enough rubbish there to tempt the citizens of Shelt.

She gave him all her food as a gesture of goodwill towards the baby, but didn't linger. The wind was blowing, the afternoon sun warm and bright, the horses stamping with impatience. She was distracted by the longing to leave.

No one spoke as she mounted Kerol. The silent moment of distilled concentration: of prayer or longing, of passion or regret. . .who knew how each of them faced a ride? It was never taken casually, the instant before the race.

And then the wind changed. A sudden veering round to the West and, as one, the *eloish* looked towards that direction. An alteration in the wind, now, was unforeseen – something contrary to the pacing of the ride.

For a moment they thought that the storm had returned. As they watched, the clouds began to race, the wind to gather. Would they be delayed again? A ripple of disquiet, of dissent and distress.

They looked across the plains and saw man and child framed by dark clouds. In the hectic light, the last rays of the Sun caught on the child's upraised hands.

'They must come with us.' Jerr Morrelow spoke quietly, but they all heard him.

And no one said anything at all. Silence held them all still and acquiescent. Irian urged Kerol forward and as they moved towards the two figures standing alone in the sunlight, one of the horses, a large chestnut, joined her.

Wordlessly, she helped Haddon and his son on to their mount. Then, as the wind swirled round to push at their backs, they began to ride.

In the twilight, the *eloish* followed Irian and Haddon Derray. Together, they began the long trek to the North.

Chapter Twelve
Gawne

The ocean rejected him.

The passing of the dragon had left the deep waters free. They moved under the luxurious energy of the tide, and recognised something neither living nor dead souring the rocky caverns of the off-shore kingdoms.

Moon-driven, the green depths had turned against the intruder. The ocean plucked carelessly around the grey rags and hunched shoulders, and moved Gawne, gently and relentlessly, away from the land of the Moon Empress.

The power he desired, the power he coveted, had betrayed him. He had courted the Lady, had bargained with a dragon for eternal life and he had failed.

Failure is its own reward. He felt everything slipping away from him as the tides took him northwards.

He tried to resist because it was not in his nature to accept defeat. He had tasted immortality, after all. Gawne knew where his centre of power lay, where all dreams and visions led: in a gleam of silver light, in a twisting spiral. In the Rites of Astret, which belonged only to the men of Shelt.

To the Mages of Shelt, the Sea Lords. Gawne had been a Mage once; he had used the tide to dictate the paths of life and death. . . . He had failed, and his reward now was to languish beneath uncaring waves.

He tossed and turned in the cold currents that drew him through the forests of weed and shells. In dark, uneven light, he reached out to the passing fish, trying to catch at a fin, a tail. In a flicker of bubbles and a flash of colour they whisked aside, contemptuous of the Sea Lord's desire.

The waters grew ever colder about him, caught in a north-wards drift, but he was unaware of mere temperature. His eyes burned with frustrated energy, pitched this way and that beneath the waves.

In the end, that unconquered medium of moving currents and shifting outlines, the origin of life, began to freeze around him. He found himself rising through the viscous water, trailing slivers of ice from the ends of his long fingers, from the soft tattered silk that still clung to his unfairly mended body.

At last, he found his home within a drapery of diamond ice, at the far north of the world. During the long days of summer light, when night never fell, the Sun caught at the glassy shroud and made it shine, as sparkling as the snow all around. Then, he could watch the bright, white land and the soaring of the terns, pigeons and fulmars through the cold blue sky.

In the winter night, when the Sun was forgotten for endless months, he waited in darkness, colder than the blizzards that tore the air beyond his home of ice. Gawne watched the Moon, and thought of a mystery he had once manipulated.

The ocean had rejected him, but he need not depend on his lordship of the sea now. As the summer day turned to winter night, he considered what had happened.

The winter storms lent him power.

Chapter Thirteen
Party

Prawns, crabs, mussels, oysters, cockles, lobsters, squid. Strange shapes curling and curving on silver dishes, dressed in delicate sauces, light mayonnaises. A salmon as the centrepiece, silvery rainbows over pink flesh set on a castle of ice. Glistening towers of black caviar, sprinkled with paprika. Trays of tiny sardines glinting with oil and garlic; herrings, their tails in their mouths. . .

Eleanor had never liked fish. Listlessly, she pushed the food around her plate, attending with only half an ear to the conversation of the man on her right.

He was a musician, he said. Vere Holtby, a flautist. He was slightly plump, earnest but eager to please, and did his best to amuse her with stories from the history of Shelt. It was very dull. She smiled politely.

They were in the draughty great hall. The soaring ceiling was supported on rows of ornamented pillars. Hundreds of candles flickered constantly in the unsettling currents of cold air shivering all around them.

The tables were covered in white linen, the cutlery and glasses shone. People were dressed in silk and velvet, satin and fine wool. It was all rather splendid, almost decadent.

A strange context in which to find Lukas Marling. She found it hard to reconcile the cool, arrogant and elegant figure presiding over the central table with the man who had camped out through the length of Peraldon. He seemed a stranger to her now. It was almost as if he had undergone a transformation, a sea-change, and someone reborn from the waves stood there, washed clean of any connection with the past. Any connection with herself. . .

The luxury in the Castle surprised her. The wealth of Shelt itself was a shock. The city sprawled untidily over the cliff and headland, stretching out beyond the walls, encroaching on the open plains. At first sight, much of it had seemed to Eleanor to consist of slums, shanty towns. In one region, bleak tenement blocks lined dark-shadowed streets. The crowds that pushed through the narrow roads seemed shabby, grey-faced, aimless.

But nearer the Castle, the great houses set in generous gardens indicated a considerable degree of wealth. The old families of Shelt, Eleanor supposed, the families who had given their most talented sons to learn magic.

The Sea Lords now languished on lonely, windswept islands, deprived of their staffs, of their leader and of ambition.

She remembered a reluctant conversation with Olwyn Mittelson. The new Earl had decided not to alienate all the powerful families, he had said. He had decreed that the Sea Lords should be merely exiled, neither executed nor imprisoned, and their staffs confiscated and destroyed. He wanted the city at peace. He recognised that to execute the eleven remaining Lords would cause resentment. He was prepared to allow members of their families, those who swore allegiance, to retain their homes and positions.

The rest of the aristocracy had gone about their usual businesses, banking and speculation. They had abandoned the revenue from the healing industry with a shrug, and had turned their skills to exploiting the flat grasslands beyond Shelt. Farms and market-gardens now clung to the windswept fells, and their produce would be traded with the cities of the inner and southern plains.

But another breed of men was emerging, the ruthless opportunists who find their feet after every revolution. They were a different matter. The best of them the new Earl kept by his side, men he had tested in the course of the revolt.

Most of the fishermen had returned to their trade. Such was the aim of the revolt, after all. The boats were renovated and repainted, their original names restored, the nets repaired. Their women gathered bait, and watched the rhythms of the waves.

It was a relief once more to find their lives ruled by the weather and the tides. They owed nothing to the machinations of men that way, nothing to the politics of the city. The fishermen were glad to escape the confines of dreary interiors, the aimless days of unemployment. Wind and waves were challenges more exhilarating than the struggles for power within the city.

Only a few stayed behind to help the new Earl in his difficult position. Philp Cammish, too old to be comfortable for the long stretches at sea. Joss Ferral, who had drafted so much of the propaganda used by the fishermen before the rebellion, and who'd been crippled in the final battle which brought Jolin Rosco to power.

Eleanor knew why they were there, watching the new Earl, watching the way he was handling these disparate elements. They laughed and ate and drank and enjoyed themselves, but essentially they were there to see how Rosco would manage.

The dining hall remained chilly, for all the candles and the fires burning in great fireplaces along the length of the wall. Tall, uncurtained windows looked out to the black sea beyond Shelt, a restless prospect.

Eleanor turned away from the windows and watched instead the group of figures at the centre of the table. They were not within earshot, although Eleanor had been seated way above the salt, on one of the arms of the long, raised table at one end of the dining hall.

Matthias was not with them. He had disappeared with Lukas on reaching the Castle, and on reappearing hours later had gone straight to bed. And if it was difficult to come to terms with Lukas's presence in this gathering, it was near impossible to imagine Matthias making polite conversation over the soup. A blind Mage who could see the future would hardly cheer up the party, she thought. But *something* was necessary.

The pretty woman called Merield, Felicia's stepmother, seemed to feel it too. Half-way through the interminable sequence of courses, she stood up, leaned across the table to Lukas and spoke a few words. Eleanor saw him lean back in his chair as he considered. Merield spoke again, and he nodded briefly. She made a signal to her companion, Louisa, who was seated further down the room. Louisa left the table and went to the double doors, opening them a little. Then she stood to one side as they were flung fully open.

A small man stood there, dressed in a silvery cloak with ragged edges. He gazed unwinkingly back at them all, and then disentangled from the folds of his cloak a spiral staff.

Beside Mittelson, there were two other men with training in magic in the room: Alex and Ferant Aldrich, Mittelson's assistants. They were men who had sworn allegiance to Rosco, and had studied long and hard to acquire a few necessary powers. They were not accustomed to seeing their hard-won skills demonstrated as an entertainment.

'May I introduce to you all Yerrent, the court Mage of Javon of Eldin,' said Merield in the sudden silence. She paid no attention to the evident disapproval of the assembly. 'With the permission of the Earl of Shelt, we would be happy to display a little of the art of the Mages in the Lord Javon's employ.'

She gently smiled at the disconcerted guests, and sat back in her chair. There was more than a touch of cynicism in her attitude.

Eleanor looked up with interest. A cabaret! She had always suspected that Mages leant more than a little towards pantomime.

Not Matthias, of course. But Matthias was resting somewhere in the guests' wing.

She leaned towards Vere Holtby and whispered to him. 'Does this kind of thing happen often in Shelt?'

'No, never,' he said sombrely. 'Mage-craft is not to be taken lightly.'

'Are you sure about that?' She was watching the small, grey-clad man weaving shapes with his right hand around the spiral carving at the top of his staff.

Smoke began to weave in and out of the curling wood. The scent of it filled the room, large though it was. With almonds, cardamom. . . oranges. It made Eleanor feel light-headed, as if she'd had too much to drink, too quickly.

The smoke gathered together into shapes of butterflies, birds and flowers, fluttering, wreathing, taking on colour as they watched. Rose-pink, turquoise and amber, doves and swallows soared over their heads, weaving in and out of the tall pillars around the room, leaving trailing clouds of mist to drift slowly through the air.

Rainbow colours of light began to shoot out of the mist in fizzy, unpredictable patterns and there was a light smattering of applause from the guests.

A superior and tasteful firework display, decided Eleanor. She drank more wine, and was irritated to find herself glancing towards Lukas. It was an action she was trying to give up. He looked up, and met her eye. He was totally unsmiling, cold and withdrawn. Almost immediately he began talking to Merield again.

Eleanor shivered. It was a relief to turn away.

Her attention was caught by Felicia. Normally pale, now she was almost grey, her fingers clutching the edge of the tablecloth. Her head had dropped forward against her breast and, for a moment, Eleanor thought that she was going to collapse face-forward into the fish bones. She felt rather than saw that the tall, ugly Mage Mittelson was on his feet, staring at Yerrent with those disconcerting, yellow eyes.

Lukas was leaning towards Felicia, his arm round her shoulders, talking to her with every evidence of affection and concern.

Cold tension gripped in Eleanor's stomach. She did not pause to examine its cause, but dragged her eyes away, fastening them on the display of hacked-around fish still on the table.

There was something nauseous about those pale, sinuous sea-bodies, rainbow skin glinting in the candlelight, oily sauces congealing, eyes wide and staring, mouths open and redundant. . . . There was ice everywhere, preserving the dead in a semblance of life. The display was brilliant, glittering with cold white light.

She did not see Felicia push her chair back, and surg to her feet, the white linen cloth rucked up and stained by the tumbled wine glass.

The stink of vomit suddenly filled Eleanor's senses. She was aware of Felicia crouched heaving over the stone floor behind the table, Lukas supporting her, Mittelson pushing him aside.

She looked across the table to the small grey man by the door and saw him smile thinly, saw him wrap his flexible hands round the spiral staff once more, this time to quieten the activity of the scented smoke and fluttering lights.

He looked up from the spiral staff and Eleanor saw, inexplicably, that his eyes were flickering towards Alex Aldrich at the side table halfway down the hall. A message seemed to pass between them.

Then Yerrent's gaze moved on, and caught the gaze of the cool, elegant woman still sitting at the top table. Merield, Javon's wife, Felicia's stepmother. Eleanor saw the thin mouth curve slightly, and an almost imperceptible nod, before Merield turned to the collapsed figure of her stepdaughter.

Lukas had lifted her, was carrying her out of the side door, away from the feast. Olwyn Mittelson and the Duchess Merield followed.

Alex Aldrich advanced across the floor to Yerrent, his brother Ferant close behind. Eleanor pushed her neglected plate aside and muttered an excuse to Vere Holtby. She stood up, frankly curious, and moved down the room until she was standing behind a pillar, well within earshot of the group of Mages.

She had no qualms about eavesdropping. She didn't belong here, she was going to be leaving soon anyway. And she owed them nothing.

She pretended to fiddle with the strap of her shoe in case anyone should notice her. She heard an argument, a clash of wills, just as she expected. But the point at issue was a surprise.

'Foolish, very foolish and ill-considered, Yerrent! This is not what we planned!' Alex Aldrich, his eyes glaring with fury.

'Irresistible.' The small Mage looked not in the least abashed. 'It will work, you'll see. And the sooner it takes place, the more quickly we will be consulted.'

They were talking of Felicia, of course.

'Mistress Eleanor – can I assist?' One of the uniformed guard, a man who had once been introduced to her as Kester Robart, was stepping forward to lend an arm.

'Oh – yes, thank you.' Briefly, she leaned against him, replacing the shoe.

'They are about to clear the tables for dancing. The Earl has returned and wishes the evening's pleasures to continue undisturbed.' His deep, pleasant voice was entirely neutral.

'No doubt.' Her mind racing, she barely noticed Lukas drifting among his guests, reassuring, smiling. . .

The perfect host. The perfect Earl and governor of Shelt. He would not allow himself to be diverted by his wife's indisposition. Eleanor didn't know whether to laugh or cry.

She had something more urgent to consider. She nodded to Robart, and pushed her way through the people beginning to assemble on the dance floor.

Chapter Fourteen
Dialogues

The wide hall with its double staircase was deserted. She ran up the stairs, turning to the right at the top, towards the Earl's private apartments.

She had never been there before. She paused at the line of heavy wooden doors leading off the plain stone corridor. Richly woven rugs lined the floor, and there were stands holding candelabra at intervals. Hesitantly, she tapped on the first door. No reply. She tried the handle, but it was locked. She moved on, down the corridor, trying each door in turn.

One opened; she slid inside warily, wondering if she would find what she sought.

The room was apparently empty, although a fire burnt in the grate and the curtains were drawn. A keyboard instrument stood by the window, smaller than a piano but more solid than a harpsichord. Fresh flowers bloomed in profusion on the table and mantelpiece.

She was about to turn and leave when she noticed another door in the panelling beside the instrument. It was slightly ajar. Cautiously, she looked round the edge.

'He's not here.' Although the voice behind her was very quiet, it made Eleanor jump. She swung round. There was someone sitting by the fire, curled up, so as to be almost hidden by the wings of the chair. Felicia, white as alabaster, sweat still shining on her upper lip. 'The Earl has returned to his guests' she added coldly.

'I know. It's not Lukas I want.' Eleanor moved towards her. 'Look, shouldn't you have someone with you? A doctor, a maid or someone?'

'I sent them away, but they'll be back soon. There's nothing they can do anyway.' Her head was leaning back against the cushions, her eyes half-closed. 'I just wanted some – peace and quiet.'

It would be unkind to disturb her further, but Eleanor was determined to tell Felicia what had happened. For although she had longed for Lukas's wife to vanish from the face of the earth, Eleanor felt impelled to warn her of the dangers she faced. She had discovered a conspiracy of Mages, and she knew evil when she saw it. 'I think there's something you should know.'

Felicia opened her eyes and looked directly at her uninvited guest. 'No.' She seemed to feel that this was too bare a denial. 'If you don't mind, I don't think there's anything you can usefully say—'

'It's not about Lukas or me. It was that Mage. . .Felicia, you must listen to me.'

'You'd better sit down.' Her voice betrayed nothing but weariness.

Eleanor moved the other chair away from the oppressive heat of the fire and sat facing Felicia. 'What do you know about that new Mage? Did you meet him at your father's court?'

'Yerrent? No, I know very little about him. Merield brought him from her own country. I've never met him before.'

'He's in league with the Aldrich brothers.'

Felicia shifted slightly. The movement could almost be interpreted as a shrug.

'I *heard* them say "the sooner it's over, the quicker she'll recover." They were talking about you.'

'Just how did you manage to "hear" this?' There was a speculative gleam in Felicia's eyes.

'I stood behind a pillar.' There was no reason to elaborate. 'Anyway, I think I know what they meant.'

'The pregnancy?'

'How's it going? How do you feel, Felicia?'

'Awful. But then, I usually do, pregnant or no.'

'And I'm no expert. Women are often sick in the early stages. . .'

There was a pause. Felicia was looking into the fire. The glow of flames tinged her face with colour. Then she sighed, and looked up at Eleanor. It was as if she had come to a decision. She spoke slowly. 'I was not just sick. If it had been only that I would have managed to leave the hall in time. But the nausea was accompanied by cramping pains.'

'Something in the smoke?' Eleanor asked. 'I felt a little of it too. I'd get rid of them, if I were you.'

'Who? The Mages? I'd have as much chance of getting my father to change his mind.' For the first time, her voice was edged with bitterness.

'You can't trust Mages. They deal with distortions, with trickery and treachery.'

'Even Matthias? Rosco's – Lukas's brother? I thought you were friends.'

Eleanor frowned. 'Matthias is different. Of all the Mages I've ever met, he's the only one who accepts responsibility. He pays the price. He knows what he's doing.'

'An interesting theory.' A cool voice from the doorway. The two women looked up. Olwyn Mittelson stood there, watching them. He was smiling faintly.

Eleanor was immediately on her feet, feeling as guilty as a naughty child. She did not like Lukas's self-appointed chaperon.

He was a Mage. More than that, Serethrun had told her that Mittelson was directly responsible for Lukas's marriage to Felicia. And as if that were not enough, she found him everywhere she went. He was present at every major event in the Castle, and he was always, always there, wherever Lukas was.

She did not want to stay in the room with him.

Felicia reached out a hand to her. 'Don't go,' she said calmly. 'I'm quite all right, Olwyn. I shan't be needing you again tonight.'

'I'm glad to hear it, my lady.' But instead of leaving, he moved further into the room. 'Forgive me,' he said politely, 'but I couldn't avoid overhearing a little of your conversation.'

Well, we're all at it tonight, thought Eleanor to herself.

'You were discusssing the trustworthiness of Mages.'

'Are you going to offer us a defence of your profession, Olwyn? Inspired with missionary zeal?' Felicia smiled at him, but her eyes were guarded.

'What can I say?' He came further into the room, joining them at the fire. His hands were upturned, his shoulders hunched. 'Ours is a double-edged power, certainly, and can be used for good and evil. Much depends on the morality and motives of the Mage.'

'Do you not think that the possession of power – any power – is a corrupting influence?'

'A cliché, where I come from. *Power corrupts*. . .' Eleanor found herself commenting.

'Of course. And with such wisdom, do the people of your world shun the uses of power, Mistress Eleanor? Do you come from a place of anarchy, free from hierarchies?'

'No, far from it. Power is exerted all the time: in all relationships, at all levels. It's not all that different. But we don't have Mages. I dread to think what would happen if things were complicated by people who made use of magic.'

'Are you sure there are no Mages in your world? It is most properly a hidden skill, employed in secrecy for covert ends,' said Mittelson.

'No, there's no real magic there. I can't wait to get back.'

'Really?' Felicia was looking at her with concentration.

'Really. You can all relax then. Get on with running Shelt undisturbed. Matthias said he'd find a way.'

'Ah, the Mage who takes responsibility. The exception to your rule, the Mage you trust.' Mittelson was equivocal.

'Well, you have to trust someone, don't you?' Moodily, she stared into the fire. 'It gets very lonely otherwise.'

'Yes.' Felicia echoed her words. 'Very lonely. . .'

'And has this trustworthy Mage, the Earl's brother, always proved himself so worthy of regard?'

Before Eleanor could answer, Felicia spoke. 'What is this, Olwyn? Jealousy?'

'I think not. My Lady Felicia, you know the force of Mage-lore. None better.'

'True.' A guarded expression again, her face turned away.

Eleanor said, 'Matthias has made mistakes. All the way, he made mistakes. But he did try to do the right thing!' It seemed important to defend him. 'And in the end, it worked.' The Stasis had broken, because Matthias had brought Eleanor to Chorolon. He had been behind it all. He had even brought her back a second time, although that had been dreadful. But in the end, the attempt to recapture the Benu Bird had failed, through his vision.

'Bringing you here? Did that work?' said Felicia, accurately divining the centre of Eleanor's thoughts.

It was an impossible question. Even with this new trust between them, she could not answer it. 'He's promised to send me back.' Eleanor met her eyes. 'And he's not in it for the glory. You wouldn't catch Matthias giving a cabaret.'

'Nor Olwyn, here, I'm sure.' Felicia glanced at him.

'Which brings us back to your original point, Mistress Eleanor. Which Mages do you suggest the Lady Felicia should dismiss?'

'You *did* overhear a lot, didn't you? You must give me lessons one day.' Eleanor considered him thoughtfully before turning to Felicia. 'All of them. Alex and Ferant Aldrich. That man Yerrent. Anyone else with half a training in distortions. . .and I'm sure our friend Olwyn Mittelson here could find alternative employment. He's clearly talented in all sorts of odd directions.'

A sudden crack of laughter from the ugly figure standing by the fire. 'It's almost a shame you feel obliged to return to your nicely uncomplicated world, Eleanor! You have much to offer us.'

'Possibly. But there's no point in regrets. I can't stay here.' She stood up, suddenly nervous that Lukas might return. 'But I still think, Felicia, that you should be wary of all these Mages in Shelt. There's an imbalance. Far too many running loose in the Castle.'

'Perhaps. . . .' Felicia looked at her. 'I'll be careful.'

Eleanor left the room, and walked quickly down the corridor to the stairs. But instead of returning to the party, she paused and took the other passageway, the one leading to the west wing where Matthias was resting.

She needed his advice. Also, she was lonely, and trusted Matthias even though he was a Mage. Mages, she thought disdainfully. She couldn't wait to leave the rest of them behind.

Chapter Fifteen
Matthias

Matthias thought at one stage to join the party. He thought, Eleanor will be so lonely, it's so difficult for her. Finding a rack of clothes in the wardrobe, he touched velvet and satin.

With no regret he shut the door. They could take him as they found him. He splashed water on his face, dragged a comb through his hair. He wondered whether to ring for a servant to show him the way to the banquet.

No. He would explore on his own. He opened the door on an empty corridor. Felicia's Castle. Odd that he should think of it like that. It didn't feel as if it had anything to do with his brother Lukas. He was constantly aware of Felicia's presence, quiet and retiring though she might be. For a moment he stretched the limits of his imagination, wondering what the future would show for his brother and his wife.

A child. Yes, he saw that, a child and a difficult birth. Felicia? Would she survive? It was unclear. And what about Lukas, where was he during all this? Impossible to tell.

With some relief, he found that everything else was lost in the mists. This was an unpredictable curse, and the way through to the future increasingly vague, since coming to Stromsall. This land owed allegiance to Astret, in name at least. His precognition had been the curse of Lycias, and perhaps therefore belonged to Peraldon.

Matthias shut the door of his bedroom behind him and paused there, listening to the sounds of the Castle. Far away he heard the murmur of conversation, the clash of cutlery. He smelled food and sweat, wine and candles: other indistinct things from the kitchens and living quarters. The sound of sea and wind underlay it all. A door banged far away, someone raised their voice in the kitchens. . . . Nothing unusual, nothing out of the way. Except the left-over scent of sour magic, a diminishing drift of weakening significance.

Party tricks, he thought. Nothing more. Or was it? Again he thought of Felicia, of some threat to her. He frowned, and stepped out into the corridor.

He stopped dead. Something was moving, something happening. Footsteps, very light and delicate. Close to him. A rustle of silk, a faint perfume, someone coming along the corridor towards him. Some lady.

Lady. Here, now, at this moment, present in his life.

He was on his knees, welded to the stone floor, his hands trembling uncontrollably, thoughts spinning off into chaos. What did She want? Why was She here? What could he offer Her?

Coldly, cruelly, She gave him sight.

Herself, wrapped round in icy silks, swathed in satin smooth as steel. Her eyes were wells which drowned all his defences. His own eyes were blind, and so there was no way of looking anywhere else. There was nowhere else, only the Lady, demanding his attention.

'*Listen.*' Fingers like claws drew his face towards Her. '*Forgiveness is not enough, and compromise is only distortion. The truth lies elsewhere. Remember that. We are not the same, and never shall be. He understands nothing, He is the eternal fool, the dupe of all time.*

'*Tell Him that, little man. This city is mine, this land, these people, and shall always be so.*'

'Lady—' He struggled for words. 'Is there only division, then? What hope for us?'

'*Hope?*' Derision, hard as iron. '*No hope, none at all.*'

He said, despairing, 'It was not always so.'

The whiteness of Her skull was barren as a desert. It filled his mind, an empty and deadly expanse of pure white.

'Ah, Lady, is there nothing more than that?'

'*Only this.*' And he saw the white begin to break with blood. It welled over the surface, its complicated promise of death and life filling his mind. '*Only this. . .*' And She abandoned him, and all men, letting him fall.

'*Tell Him,*' She said, the words slicing through his brain. '*Tell Him. No compromise, no hope, no forgiveness.*'

Betrayal. That was Her message. Somehow Matthias found his way back to his room and sat on the bed, shivering. Astret was betrayed in humanity. People had lost faith, and used power to change the shape of the world. Magic, science, politics, religion. Religion, even here in the Lady's own country. All the male-dominated icons to will and ambition.

Hard and desperate, She used such methods, too. She lied, too.

He knew what this meant. A fight to the death.

Matthias Marling sat alone in the room in Shelt and wondered if he could bear to do it. Whether he had the courage to face Lycias once more.

He thought, I am a Mage, and have spoken with Gods. What happens now is at least partly my fault. I will have to try it.

He knew none of the Rites of the Sun. He knew no way into the realm of the Lord. He was celibate, and the most rapid summonings were beyond him. He fumbled round the room until he managed to light a candle. He could see nothing, but he held the image of flame in his mind.

He widened the limits of thought, while all the time his body shivered with tension. He used everything he knew to call the Lord. Wild promises, words of power, prayers and pledges.

It should be possible, he thought. I am a man, and have allegiances dictated by the patterns of the body. We are relevant to each other, and the Lord is active in my life, too.

But nothing answered, nothing came.

In the end, he blew out the candle and lay back on the bed. It seemed to take hours, but in the end he slept.

'*Matthias.*' The voice seared through his dreams in a lancing fire-light.

'*Matthias, you must give Her to me and not fail.*' A voice, smaller than ions, than atoms or protons, screamed down the paths of his nerves and thrilled them with flame. He lay there, immobile, unable even to think, while the God answered his call.

Lycias revealed His nature. He lived in Matthias's own body, revealed in the inner pathways of the blood. Desire scorched through Matthias's limbs. His celibacy was no defence from this. He was strung high on burning wires, a home for incandescence, a place of agony.

'*She must be Mine. There is nothing else.*'

An overload, a howl-back of blazing fire. His skin was charring, unable to hold together this excruciation of flame.

His inner vision was blind, his other senses were all consumed in this same fire. He was probably sweating, probably moaning, but he was so locked inside torment that he had no knowledge of it.

The blaze was intensifying: consuming itself, red, white, black-hot, drawing everything inwards, gathering everything to itself. And in the blackness of that final consummation, in that last, incestuous loneliness, Matthias saw the gift of the God.

He brought death, as surely as the Lady. The price of this blazing love was death. For man, woman, Mage and priestess, for every creature in the world. And there was no way out of it because the death He brought was also His own.

Matthias awoke, shivering, sweat running through the scars on his face. He could not move. And as he lay there, trying to assemble thought, his mind skidded into triviality. He could no longer tell dream from waking, now he lived only in darkness.

Chapter Sixteen
Late Night

At three in the morning, Felicia heard the carriages draw up, the
guests leave. A respectable time for a party to end. It had probably
been a success.

She waited, hesitating, until all sounds of activity from the Castle
ceased. She heard Rosco's steps pass by her door without pausing. His
own room was at the end of the corridor.

She slid out of bed and pulled on her wrap. The passage was in
darkness. She returned to her room and took the small candelabra
from the mantelpiece. Her hand shook slightly. She stood still for a
moment, willing it to steadiness. Then she walked to Rosco's room,
and knocked on the door.

There was a pause before he opened it, but she did not consider
turning back. He was still dressed. The curtains were drawn back, the
window open. The night was blowing cold through the room.

His eyes flickered in surprise as he looked at her. 'Felicia. Is
anything wrong?'

'Should there be?' Crossly, she walked past him and sat at the foot
of the bed. 'Can't a wife visit her husband at night without arousing
suspicion?'

He shut the window, pulling the heavy velvet carelessly over the
leaded glass. He never managed to draw curtains competently, she
thought critically. There was always a gap to let in the light or dark.

'Don't be difficult Felicia, you're not usually given to social calls at
four in the morning. Couldn't you sleep?'

'I had a visitor tonight, while you entertained the aristocracy of
Shelt. Eleanor Knight. She made some interesting suggestions.'

He was very still watching her, completely unmoving.

'How was the party tonight, Rosco? A success, was it?'

'I would say so, yes. Go on.'

'Tell me about Mages. Olwyn Mittelson and the Aldrich brothers.'
She looked up at him. 'How's it going? Do you believe these
professions of loyalty? Are they being helpful?'

'What are you getting at, Felicia?'

'Sometimes an outsider can observe things more clearly. . .than the
protagonists. Your friend Eleanor doesn't like Mages – except for your
brother Matthias, who appears to be exempt from all suspicion.'

'She has reason.' Abruptly, he turned away from her, beginning to
pace the room. He spoke evenly, distantly.

'Very well. Mages. Without the support of the Mittelson *and* the
Aldrich brothers, I doubt very much whether I would be able to retain
control of Shelt. In many ways they are the stabilising power behind

the city, uniting fisherpeople and the aristocracy. Your father recognised that any Earl of Shelt would have to win the support of men trained in magic.'

'And you have that support?'

'Yes. Mittelson – is my friend, I think. His first priority, his only priority, is that Shelt should prosper. The Aldrich brothers are loyal for different reasons, not because they particularly admire me, my skills or talents. . .'

'But because they think to manipulate you,' she finished for him.

'Yes. You know all about that, don't you?'

'Is it a situation you're happy with?'

'Were you ever?' He smiled at her, quickly. 'Of course being someone else's puppet is unsatisfactory, but it is open to misrepresentation.'

'The manipulators manipulated, in fact.'

'Perhaps. What have you in mind, Felicia? A unilateral declaration of autonomy?'

'I don't like Mages.' She spoke very quietly, looking down at her feet. 'They use unfair advantages, unfair skills. It's open to abuse, to every corruption. I'd like to get rid of them all, dispossessed or not. The Sea Lords on those lonely islands, the Aldrich brothers, Yerrent, Mittelson—'

'Matthias?'

'He'll be leaving here soon, anyway. Eleanor Knight will go with him.'

'Yes.' A long pause. 'Felicia, think of this. A banished Mage, bereft of the obvious pathways to power, would be infinitely dangerous. Resentful, ambitious. . .treacherous. I would really rather keep them under my eye. And I trust Olwyn.'

'Do something for me, Rosco.'

He looked at her with curiosity. She had never asked anything of him before.

'Get rid of Yerrent. He's the worst of them. Find him some useful, prestigious task far away from here.'

'And how do you think your esteemed stepmother would like that?'

'I can handle her.' An unusual degree of confidence here.

'And your father? Can you handle him, too?'

'Well, one has to start somewhere. You said so yourself.' She smiled at him, quizzically.

'And you are a match for dragons, after all. . .It's a risk, Felicia.'

'Trust me.'

'Very well.' He leant towards her and lightly kissed her forehead. 'You look tired, Lady. You should rest now.'

She allowed him to escort her back to her room, and paused at the door, the Castle quiet and calm about them.

She could not say it. Her body would not move. She had no means of expression.

'Goodnight, Felicia.'

She saw him turn away, back down the long corridor. She entered the room and closed the door behind her.

Far to the North, a shroud of ice cracked. In the sudden noise, a fleet of arctic pigeons sprang into the bright air, wheeling in wide arcs until they settled further away on the sodden grass.

Diamond shards fell into icy water, glinting in the sun. Slowly, grey and indistinct, a darker shape moved under the ice. All at once, the shroud fragmented completely, a swift falling away of rectitude.

Water, chill and clear, washed over his ankles. Unaccustomed fingers flexed, stiff and uncomfortable. He lifted his left hand, nerveless and pulseless, and wiped the last splinters from his eyes.

A step forward. Snarling, a white-coated fox backed away. He halted, watching.

The fleet of pigeons wheeled in the air, circling high, way beyond the grey figure standing on the edge of the fast-thawing ice floe. Impassively, grey eyes followed the spiralling drift of birds, and memory stirred.

Another step, and he stood on land. He was tall, and the shadow fell long and narrow from his feet across the new grass and sky-reflecting pools.

He stood in sunlight and scented the released land.

Chapter Seventeen
Leaving

'Eleanor—' She was carrying a candle but otherwise the room was in darkness. Matthias was standing by the window, with his back to the door.

'How did you know it was me?' She shut the door behind her. 'Couldn't you sleep?' The bed was rumpled. She saw that he had removed the scarf with which he usually covered the scars on his face.

'No. No. No way of sleeping now, not for me. No rest, no peace, no love, horror on horror, grief on grief—'

She stood still, rooted with shock. 'Matthias! What's wrong?' Frantically her eyes scanned the darkened room, perhaps expecting to see strange smoke in the fireplace, glass shards on the carpet. . .or ashes, powders traced with spirals, patterns and scents, signatories to a life drawn from dreams and magic and intuition.

He was drifting across the floor towards her, carried on the wave of something she could not sense or articulate. He was frail and white, blindly seeking expression in words she did not understand.

'Matthias!' She was shouting, holding out her arms to ward off the fear. She found herself clutching his thin forearms in a strong grip. 'Matthias! Are you dreaming?'

The noise would wake the Castle.

'No, I don't think so, not dreaming now. . .I will never sleep again, never dream again—'

'You must explain! Matthias, what *is* it?' He was shuddering with tension, every fibre attenuated and taut.

She couldn't bear it. She wanted the cool voice of sanity from him, not this torrent of passion.

'Eleanor, you must leave Chorolon. Leave it as soon as you can, because I see the Gods—'

'What Gods? Lycias, Astret?' What other gods were there?

'It's the end. They will destroy Themselves and us. . .I see it clear and deadly, death for us all, forever. . . .' The wild surges in his voice were fading now, dropping to an appalled whisper. 'Eleanor, you must get out of here, you don't have to suffer this.'

'What? What are you talking about?'

'This world will die. Torn apart by warring gods or by our own indifference, wherein lies the solution?' Light and fluent, his voice gathered volition once more, plunging and soaring with the cadences of bird-flight. 'I thought I could understand death, that I knew what it meant. But not for everyone, not for everything!'

'This can't be so, Matthias, stop it!'

But the Mage's words tumbled on, 'This is why hell is full of flames, because our God lives there – and we will fall, fall into his black blaze of destruction, each and every one of us, because God exists only in passion and conflagration—'

'Astret! What of the Lady?'

'Nothing. Nowhere, only cruelty. I don't know—'

She could not see a way to contain or control this outpouring. She drew back her hand, far flung away from him, and released it in a slap to his unknowing face. He fell away from her, wrecked to the floor.

A moment's silence. Then, as if she had not touched him 'Eleanor, it's final annihilation. It will be insupportable, beyond bearing, beyond understanding. I never knew.' Flat and dull, the bird-song was grounded.

She was on her knees beside him, tears of terror on her own face.

'What do you mean, oh, Matthias, what is this?'

'The danger. The danger of what we have done, of what will happen.' He was in the grip of some vision of the future, some dreadful dream of inexorable changes.

'Nothing is inevitable! There is still chance, and hope and change! The Benu is free! Listen to me, Matthias, I know it for sure!' She was saying anything, a perfect flood of words, trying to blot out the unsteadiness of the room. the Castle, the voice.

'Liar.'

Now drained, now empty, he looked towards her in blindness and called her by the Gods' name. 'Liar. The Gods lie, and so do you.'

She took his face between her hands, her tears falling between them. She said nothing, her lips pressed to the scars.

'I've seen it, Eleanor, I know what will happen, and there is no way out. . .I have to get you out of here. Let me send you home. Let me find a way.' He drew back from her, crouched now, head buried in his arms. And then the awful, unforgivable thing. *'Don't tempt me to use you again.'*

She sat back on her heels, no longer needing to touch the power in him. 'What do you see, Matthias? The end of the world. The Day of Judgement?'

He did not understand the term, but its meaning was clear. He shuddered. 'What hope is there for us, when the gods leave us?'

'Gods cannot die!'

'They are given shape through our imagination. And in horror, the mind fails, the spirit falls away, and the Gods live only in hell. . .'

She had no idea what he was talking about. Did the burden of the future lead only to madness?

'When I go home, Matthias, come with me.' Anything, anything to give him relief.

'That's no answer.' A long pause. And then, very quietly, 'You won't be alone.'

'There will be someone with me?' Lukas? Leaving Shelt, leaving Felicia, a second chance? Wild hopes.

'Not Lukas. I don't know who it will be. But not Lukas.' He had no kindness left to give her, no comfort or relief.

There's no way round the decision I made, she thought bleakly. For ever and always, he is dead to me. A small voice within herself, finally acknowledging the inevitable.

'We need to go now, Eleanor. There is no time left. Come with me now, somewhere quiet where I can find the way.'

'The way home?'

'Yes. I need to concentrate somewhere, in peace. I'd like you there, because it's easier with two. I'll have to teach you certain procedures.'

'Where shall we go?'

'Amery will find somewhere for us.'

The Arrarat hawk was standing on the battlements outside the window. She could see golden eyes glowing in the deep dark before dawn.

'Are you ready to leave, Eleanor? Now?'

He had stood up, was blindly feeling his way around the room, searching for a few items which would be of use. Fruit from the bowl. Blankets from the bed.

She watched, aghast. 'Not now, Matthias! Let's leave it until tomorrow, I can't go now.'

'We should leave now. We must.'

'But I haven't said goodbye. Lukas—'

'Will understand. It's over, you say. What can be gained by your presence here? A formal farewell would be only useless pain for you both.'

'I can't just leave! Not like this!'

'Eleanor.' He had crossed the room towards her, had found her shoulders with his own hands. He was no longer shuddering, he felt steady as a rock. 'There is a pattern to the events here in Shelt, a pattern I have foreseen. Felicia's child, Felicia and Lukas's child, will unite north and south. The future lies with that child, and you and I are not part of it. Our only path lies elsewhere.'

'Would we make things worse for Lukas?'

'Your presence here does not make anything easier for him. You know that.'

'Then he does care!'

'You are not, surely, in any serious doubt of that? It makes no difference. You know him well. He would no more abandon Shelt or Felicia than – deny his hawk Astrella. You should leave with me.'

'I must. . .must just see him. Once more!' A catch in her voice, desperate and determined.

His hands, resting on the back of a chair, were held still and calm. Deliberately.

'Very well.' He did not move. 'I'll wait here. Don't be long.'

The door to Lukas's room was unlocked. On the brief walk through the dark corridors, her thoughts ran wild. She could not bear the tricks her mind was playing, inventing impossible conversations. You shall not go, he would say. Or, I will come with you, Shelt/Felicia/the baby mean nothing to me. Let's make love, stay here. . .

The unlocked door swung open into an empty room. The bed had not been disturbed. For one appalled moment she imagined him lying with his wife in companionable comfort, and then she saw that the window was wide open.

She moved across the cold room towards it. The heavy curtains were lifting in the breeze. She stood still there for a while, waiting for him to return.

But there was no graceful grey shape pushing through the clouds. She heard no steady beat of wings. Eyes like lanterns did not glow through the night towards her.

There was writing-paper on the desk, pen and ink. She would leave him a letter, a statement of love eternal. She even started one such creed.

Lukas, I will love you for ever.

Words would not do. She crossed them through, heavily, and tore it into small pieces. Then, scrap by scrap, she fed them to the dying ashes in the grate, watching the paper distort and curl until it, too, became only ash.

She had no more tears. She stared at ash, and then stood up and left the room.

As dawn touched the eastern horizon, tinting with rose the calm, glassy surface of water, she clung to Matthias's waist on his great hawk Amery, and left Shelt.

For ever.

Chapter Eighteen
Summer

The days lengthened into summer. The warm glow in the air was quite unlike the punishing heat of the drought. Phinian Blythe slowly rediscovered his deserted island and watched the canals begin to fill.

Rain fell every night. The grass lost its pinched, dried-out look, and the leaves on the poplars and willows showed grey and green, rustling softly in the on-shore breezes.

It was quiet. A wide calm washed over memories and nightmares. He slept deeply each night, and if the flickering shapes of Shadows drifted through his dreams, still oddly throwing dice across his bed, they were unthreatening and irrelevant.

The island was divided by brick paths set in herringbone patterns. Washed by the nightly rain, they glowed with a rich terracotta, running between the three farms that shared the island's sun-strewn orchards. Cherry trees, peach, damson, apricot. . .some still survived. White blossom fell like snow across the paths.

Small birds chattered, and crickets hummed in the long grasses. He watched emerald lizards basking with unblinking eyes in the sunlight, and butterflies sunning themselves on the bright early summer flowers.

He found food easily enough. Chickens still ran wild in the gardens round the house and, as the canals filled, ducks and geese returned to their old haunts.

Inside, the larders were still stocked with grains and rice. There were jars and bottles of preserves and dried fruits. Rough local wine in the cellars. He wandered through the old house, replacing fallen chairs, straightening the pictures in a desultory fashion. Sometimes he pulled back shutters and let the sun shine through clouds of dust.

He preferred to spend his time outside. Most days he fished the undisturbed waters of the lagoon, from one of the small boats he had found still tied to the jetty. He kept to the north side, furthest away from Peraldon, and trusted that his family and friends would have better things to occupy them than visiting the island. But he knew at the back of his mind that sooner or later someone would come. That someone would walk down the terracotta paths and that he would have to start responding to people again.

And although he was not looking forward to that day, he was not lacking in confidence. He was beginning to feel stronger in every way. Even the wasted muscles of his left arm and hand seemed to be regenerating. He could hold a cup now without dropping it. He practised each day, lifting objects, clenching and unclenching the stiff fingers, and gradually strength and feeling returned.

He walked, and fished, and sat in the shade watching the crickets jump. Tension and doubt drifted away.

They arrived at night. On a sighing wind, as the owls called and the guinea frogs sang their lovesongs. The early evening rain had long finished. It was the very depths of night and the moon shadows were long everywhere.

Suddenly the gentle sounds of the night ceased. Half locked in sleep, Blythe rolled over and sat up. His eyes were open, looking round the dark room. Nothing, no sound, no movement.

Why had the frogs stopped calling? Noiselessly he swung himself out of bed and reached for the knife he had been using to repair the window catch.

The wooden floor was rough and warm to his bare feet. Quickly he pulled on the dark clothes he wore most days. Quiet still, he slipped out of the room into the hall. There was no sound, no whisper of movement or breath of life.

Something stopped him. He did not know why he paused there, on the threshold of the hall, looking at the dark, dusty shapes of furniture.

A mirror hung on the wall by the side door. There was a glint of moonlight through the unshuttered windows, palely reflected.

He saw someone move out of the shadows, and pause by the mirror. A slight figure, a woman, silhouetted against the silvery surface. She lifted her hand to her face, and seemed to wipe something away. Blythe moved slightly, so that he could see the surface of the mirror, but remain concealed himself.

He saw Edine, hair immaculate, face grey in the moonlight. She was smiling, but tears still fell. A small trickle of blood blurred the outline of her mouth.

Their eyes met in the mirror. With deep shock he saw her recognise who he was. He waited for the quick movement, the muttered spell, the dangerous swirls of Mage-powered spirals, but she was motionless.

The distorted mouth still smiled.

For a moment they stared at each other. Then she turned away from
the mirror and walked steadily across the hall to the door. A thin hand
pulled it open.

He followed her, even though he knew it was unwise. He was
unwilling to question his motives. He should of course hide. Run back
out into the orchards, dodge among the trees. . . .

He had had enough of fear, of running. He followed Edine along
the silent brick paths, the night-grey leaves turning in the moonlight
as they passed. They were walking beside the narrow canal leading to
the jetty. He was some twenty yards behind her, keeping to the deep
shadows beneath the willows as far as possible.

He slowed when the distinctive Fosca stink began to filter through
the quiet air. Edine, Fosca. . .what else? Spiky outlines, triangular
points of wings. He hung back, straining every sense towards the
strange meeting at the end of the jetty.

It was not yet dawn and the moon still gave a dull luminosity to the
world. Drained of colour, the silence hung heavy. One shape changed
in the greying light. A man stood up, moving away from the red-eyed
angel, coming towards Edine.

He was tall and heavily built. Light brown curling hair fell over his
shoulders, and the patterned leather jerkin hung open over a broad,
muscular chest. But the voice that disturbed the air held not the
coarse, brutal tones Blythe had learned to expect:

An unexpected fluency, an uncaring arrogance.

'Who have you found here, Edine? Who lives on this lonely island?
For there are signs that someone has sailed this boat, that someone
has fished from this jetty, and that recently. Who lives here, Edine?'
An unwarranted sharpness in the voice. Contempt, and something
else.

'A peasant,' she said. 'A farm labourer, left to scratch a living on
one of the farms. . .he will not disturb us.'

'The island is large enough for us all, you think?' The voice was
now courteous, simply inquiring.

'There are other farms further round the island. They are probably
deserted. They may suit us better.'

'And we will not be here for long, after all. . .'

The man who looked like Weard, walked up to Edine and lifted his
hand to her face.

She did not flinch as he cupped her delicate chin.

A long, slow kiss, and he looked deep into her eyes. Holding her
gaze, he wiped the blood from his lips. 'No, we won't be here for long.
Just until we have found out who you have met here. And why you
still think it worthwhile lying to me.'

Weard? No, Weard never spoke with such control, such measured
fluency. Weard had never held the upper hand over Edine, either.

Someone else, riding Fosca. . .Blythe faded into the shadowy willows, moving swiftly and carefully back towards the house.

He would have to be quick. The man who looked like Weard would investigate. There were bows in the house, and a few arrows, left over from the archery competitions of his youth. He still held the knife.

He stopped, just outside the gate to the garden. Violence. What could he hope to achieve with children's toys, kitchen knives? What did violence ever achieve, even the professional weapons of the Warden's Watch, against the shifting spirals of a Mage? Blythe did not know what had become of Weard, but he knew enough to recognise the occult power of the man who had kissed Edine.

As he hesitated, he heard a light footfall on the path by the canal. There was no other course: he stepped out of the shadows, to stand in the centre of the path.

'Phinian Blythe. . .again. Phinian Blythe. We meet like lovers, fated to destruction, time and time again. Do you know me, Phinian Blythe?'

He stood there, the spiral staff at his side wreathing like smoke into the overhanging trees. He came no closer, and Blythe caught a taint of something unexpected in his voice. Was it fear?

'You are not Weard.' The fantastic knowledge that was beginning to colour his mind was beyond articulation.

'No, not Weard. Look again Blythe, we have met before.' He moved three paces forward and then paused.

The eyes looked directly at Blythe and their expression was familiar. So had the Desert Rose looked towards the Sun. So had the High Priest to Lycias watched his enemy burn in a cauldron.

'Lefevre. . .' Half a breath, half a prayer.

The man smiled faintly. 'You hold a knife, Blythe. Are you going to use it?'

The knife hung from his fingers. With no regret at all he let it drop.

'Giving up? At this late stage?' Brown eyes that had shone with greed and ambition were now coldly mocking.

Blythe said, 'What weapon could prevail against the Great Mage? What would you advise?'

'That is for you to decide. You swore an oath, once.'

'Yes. . .irrelevant, now.'

'You have lived with shadows, after all.'

'Yes.'

A half-laugh from the tall man standing so close. 'We will not be here for long. We will not disturb you. You may live out your retirement in peace.'

'Where are you going?'

He was already turning away, walking back towards the jetty. The word flung over his shoulder was alight with laughter, open and full-throated.

'Home!'

Chapter Nineteen
The Ride

For four weeks they had pressed northwards along ancient trails, following landmarks familiar to the *eloish*, but entirely new and strange to Haddon Derray. The twin fords over the Quenild river and its tributary, the Bren, needed only minor repair; the rushing rivers had brought rocks and fallen trees, storm-debris from the Western Mountains to shore it up. It had taken them only half a day to cross.

'They work well together, don't they?' said Jerr Morrelow.

Haddon Derray was sitting against a tree, high up on the south bank of the Quenild, watching the *eloish* clear a log-jam downstream from the ford. There was a fresh wind, a light spattering of rain and the baby on his lap was warmly wrapped in wool and oilskins. Haddon was aching with weariness and yet obscurely content, watching the *eloish* at work. The baby was gurgling, clapping his hands together as Morrelow approached.

Haddon stirred himself to respond. 'They certainly don't seem to need us.'

'I could hold the baby, if you're feeling left out.' There was more than an element of malice in Morrelow's teasing.

'Thanks, but I'm quite happy here.' Haddon did not really have any alternative. He was still shaky with exhaustion after the morning's ride.

Jerr Morrelow squatted down beside him, holding his finger out. With concentration Coron reached out to grasp it, intent and serious. Haddon watched Jerr's face, the slant eyes and the untrustworthy mouth softened, gentled. Jerr looked up, and caught his eye. A pause, and then a sudden grin of self-mockery as he straightened up, and mounted his horse.

Haddon watched him ride down the bank towards the river. He did not entirely trust Morrelow, although he had no reason for any kind of suspicion. Morrelow was a birth-right member of the clan, even if he had chosen to spend much of his life apart from the *eloish*. He had always been fascinated by other ways, Irian had told Haddon, somewhat sourly. And indeed, the man had appeared at Haddon's side more often than any other of the *eloish*, apart from Irian. He was friendly, offering to share food, offering to help with the baby, and Haddon, still so infuriatingly feeble, could only be glad. The *eloish* made no concessions to the latest additions to the clan.

In those early days of the ride, Haddon contented himself with observing his adopted clan. They were impressive. They worked together in silence, and it seemed that the flow of the river had calmed as they approached, that the wind was always behind them.

Haddon thought it a good omen, to cross the wide double-ford with so little trouble.

Two days' plainsriding, fast and unimpeded, and then a forest. The wide circle of beech trees known as Calter Wood was largely intact, although several of the younger trees had fallen in the storms, their intricate tracery of roots exposed to the sun. There was nothing there to delay the riders. Haddon braced himself for another sprint.

At first they galloped until their horses stumbled with exhaustion. It was all he could do to stay in the saddle. The last year had been an unimaginable devastation, one his mind could not begin to apprehend. He remembered nothing but howling. . .

A black wind had devastated his life. He knew nothing else.

This was a hard existence. He was too tired to think, to remember, to regret. Everything was lost in the pounding of hooves, the cold air rasping in the throat. And all the time, the baby smiled, or slept, or held his finger.

They travelled fast. There was an unspoken agreement that they must put Shelt behind them as quickly as possible. There were only the briefest of breaks, snatched meals, short nights. Haddon Derray and his son were largely ignored. He understood why, he knew what the parameters were: they kept up with the ride, or they did not. No one was going to make any allowances.

They kept up. The baby rarely cried, quietly accepting the wind, the sun, the pounding hooves, the meagre food. By the end of each day, Haddon moved like a man in a dream, in a daze of exhaustion, while Irian unrolled the bedding and prepared food.

She seemed to have adopted them. She was not precisely friendly, certainly not accommodating or easy to be with, issuing orders, coldly dismissive of Haddon's efforts at cooking and childcare. But somehow her presence helped smooth over those first difficult days with the riders. This was an enormous concession and Haddon did not then appreciate its significance.

'What's the rush?' he asked one evening, watching Irian prepare a rabbit-stew.

'Shelt,' she said briefly. 'The sooner we leave it behind, the better. A city. . . .' She shrugged, contemptuous. 'People living on top of each other – filthy, crowded. Corruption and compromise at every level, laws and habits and customs trying to prop up a consensus that doesn't exist. There's no trust there. A place of lies and distortions, cursed.'

'How *cursed*?' he asked, curious.

'They've forgotten the things that matter.' She stared, unseeing, into the small fire. 'It will be like death for the *eloish* ever to return there.'

After ten days' riding, they came to Ristmere, the tufted, treacherous plain of shifting bog, with its wide causeway of white-stone blocks. A haze of moisture hung over the mire, clouded with mosquitoes and gnats. The riders were prepared; each wore a light veil which protected nose and mouth, and carried a burning torch which gave off repellent, bitter-smelling smoke.

Each night they surrounded the camp with burning torches, and choked down food which seemed tainted by the acrid smell. It was better than trying to avoid the clouds of insects which hovered, waiting, just beyond the smoke.

It took them three days to cross Ristmere, three uncomfortable, malodorous, nerve-racking, gnat-haunted days and nights. Although the causeway was over thirty feet wide, some of the blocks had crumbled under the pressure of the weather, others had submerged. But none of it was impassable: with patience and caution they managed to trace a route over the ancient road, the horses carefully picking their way over the damp, slippery stone.

Then another wild week of galloping, across flat grasslands, through calm plains. They rested for longer each night, now, and sometimes paused in the day to hunt. Herds of wild deer roamed these wide spaces, and Haddon watched the riders use their small, double-curved bows to great effect.

They invited him to share in the hunting, and although he was still weak and long out of practice, he acquitted himself well enough to earn a little respect. There were communal feasts each night, singing and story-telling round the fire. For the first time, Haddon Derray felt strong enough to begin learning their customs.

He knew nothing of the reputation of the *eloish*. Nothing of their wild magic and black witches. He did not expect them to fade into the wilderness, to laugh in the wind, to slide through the night, and indeed they did nothing of the kind. The riding, the horses, the changing scenery bound them firmly to the earth. They were plains-riders, that was all. Ruthless, inspired by savagery, strangers to ease and content. Their life suited Haddon Derray, who had forgotten what it was like to rest.

He did not always know himself how he managed to keep up with them. His horse was strong and graceful, although Haddon hardly had even the will to stay upright. But whenever he held the baby, energy flooded his limbs, and the past receded even further from him.

There were huge gaps in his mind, areas of trauma he was unwilling to examine. So often, dreams drove him in screaming into wakefulness, but the baby was always there, and the nightmare phantasms lost potency and drifted away.

He did remember his past with the Cavers, but it seemed distant and irrelevant. More vivid to him was Coronis and their brief, miraculous marriage. He knew she was dead, and that the baby was not his. Mercifully, the knowledge of the baby's real father was hidden from him. He felt that it was unnecessary to know. Coron's father had relinquished any claim, for he had made no effort to find the child.

Haddon remembered searching for the baby, the howling pain of it all but not what it meant to be the Stormbearer. He was unaware of the divine nature of the child. There was just the unreasoning conviction that the baby was infinitely precious and as far as Haddon knew, this was a conviction shared by most parents.

He was content to ride and hunt with the plainspeople, sharing their austere and passionate life.

Gradually the plains became more hilly, the air a little cooler. The land was rising, and they saw in the distance a line of deep, dark green edging the horizon.

Falby Forest: mile upon mile of pines and larches, birches and spruce. There was no temptation to linger. They found and took what they needed: rabbits and deer; berries and nuts. No one went hungry. And at last they came to the barrier that divided the plains from the northern wastes. They came to Pallon Cliff.

The crag was a wall of white stone, traversed by a single, narrow zigzag path. The path had been hacked out of the cliff long ages ago. Great blocks of limestone had been carted through the forest, and over the plains to Ristmere, to build the causeway. An incredible undertaking by a race long forgotten.

The path led from the evergreen forest to the high moors, some three hundred feet above. Nothing grew on the cliff, no mosses or lichen. Its white surface was gleaming bright, uninterrupted. During the Stasis, the path had been virtually impassable, partly through the rockfalls brought about by the violence of the storms, but mainly because it offered a favourite trap for thieves.

Lara Valde, the Archon of the tribe, looked up, craning her neck, shading her eyes against the morning sun. Irian followed her gaze. The path certainly seemed to be reasonably clear. There was no sound in the calm morning beyond the slight rustle of horses' hooves against the bed of pine-needles underfoot.

As always, there were falls of stone here and there. Any problem would arise around those areas. Either the path would be blocked, or thieves would be in hiding. . . . The usual thing was to send two or three riders ahead, to check the route.

'I'll go,' said Irian to Lara, the Archon.

'Don't be ridiculous, Irian, you're the last person I'd choose. You'll be needed. . .' Thoughtfully, Lara's eyes ran over the assembled group of riders. One of them moved forward.

'I, however, am dispensable.' Jerr Morrelow, the traveller who rejoined the clan only as it suited him. He was still wearing his absurd, deep-brimmed hat. He turned to Irian. 'Leave me to bear the standard of *eloish* honour, black lady.'

'Don't call me that,' Irian said sharply. Although technically she was indeed the black-painted seer of the clan, it was rarely mentioned. There was no need. Jerr Morrelow, the erratic outsider, was always outrageous, always difficult. She didn't like him. He smiled too much.

But Lara had other ideas. Irian sighed. The Archon had always been intrigued by Jerr Morrelow.

'Very well, Jerr,' said Lara Valde, as Irian knew she would. 'Who else?'

'What about Brianne?'

Irian glanced from Jerr to the tall woman who was often to be seen in his company. Brianne Berruffon was strong and wiry, unusually athletic. She had embraced austerity with enthusiasm and had been one of the first of them to discard her comb. Her dark brown hair had been cut very short and clustered round her head in soft curls. The younger girls looked to her with admiration, the men with desire. She was not austere in the matter of her favours.

Her other advantage was an extraordinary degree of skill with the thrown knife. She could hit a running rabbit at thirty paces. She was a central figure in the life of the clan, trustworthy in every respect. She would be a wise choice, a steadying influence to the wild Morrelow.

'Who else? It has been so long.'

'I agree. It should be at least three, this time.' Lara looked about her as she spoke. Irian knew that some riders were already out of sight. They were spread out through the forest, the dark shapes of their horses in shadow under the dense trees. Her brother Serethrun was nowhere to be seen, evidently at the farthest fringes of the group.

He had not yet settled back into the clan. Irian had seen him stand apart from the others on almost every occasion. Too long in the city, she thought. He was finding it hard to recall the old ways.

But it was Lara's duty, as Archon, to ensure the cohesion of the *eloish*. Irian wondered how. She knew what *she* would do. If Irian were Archon she would choose to send Serethrun, not because he was her brother, sad and unhappy, but because he needed to belong again. To feel useful, necessary to the clan. In Lara's place, she would be willing to overlook Serethrun's recent silences, his black ill-humour. He was theirs, she knew. *Eloish* through and through, notwithstanding all that time in Shelt. This was a chance for him to break through his loneliness.

'Serethrun, perhaps,' she said, feeling her way.

Lara sighed. 'Asking for trouble.'

'No, I don't think so. He needs to feel that he still has a rôle here.'

'Jerr and Brianne don't need looking after.' Lara paused, thinking. 'And yet, perhaps you are right. Jerr and Brianne won't need him, but someone else might. That is why I shall ask Haddon Derray to go, too.'

'Devious, Lara, devious and risky.'

'Nervous of a little risk, Irian? This *is* out of character.' Small, bright eyes crinkled with amusement.

Irian twisted, peering through the trees. As usual, one figure was a little way off from the others, bent over the child on his lap. 'Physically, Derray is sufficiently recovered, I would say.'

'Yes, I think so.'

But still he is vulnerable, Irian thought. Much more alien to the clan than Serethrun or Jerr Morrelow would ever be. He needs to prove his worth. Perhaps this was the way to do it. 'Will he leave the baby, though?' Irian was doubtful.

'His first allegiance must be to the ride, of course.' Lara was undisturbed. This was the quality of ruthlessness that had entitled Lara Valde to the rank of Archon. 'I think that we should find out.' She motioned to Morrelow. 'Jerr – what about Haddon Derray?'

Morrelow's eyes were hidden by the brim of his hat. He smiled, lazily. 'He was useful during the hunting. He is certainly capable of shifting rocks. He can come,' he turned to Irian, '. . .if you say so, black lady.'

'Will you ask him, Irian?' said Lara. 'He trusts you with the child.'

It was not that difficult: a brief discussion and then Haddon reluctantly leant over and gave the baby to Irian. He went to join Lara Valde.

Jerr had gathered up Brianne and Serethrun. The four riders stood before her, their horses eager and frisky. Jerr and Brianne appeared pleasantly excited, Serethrun bored and Haddon neutral. For a moment, Irian was doubtful. This was an unstable mix, a difficult bonding. But Lara rarely acted unwisely. Let them work it out together, she thought. Brianne would hold them together, and Irian knew that Serethrun would not fail. Haddon Derray would do his best, such as it was. . . . Of them all, Jerr Morrelow was the only one to worry her seriously.

Lara gave her hunting horn to Morrelow. 'Blow it three times from the top if the way is clear, twice if you need help. We will wait here until tomorrow, before sending anyone else.'

Jerr Morrelow rode off, his head held high, Brianne laughing at his side. Serethrun was just behind. Haddon Derray was a little separated from them, sitting straight and tall on his horse. He looked solid there, steady and in control. A more mature figure perhaps than the others. Irian shrugged. It was a chance, Lara was quite right. But the day was clear, the air quiet; it was worth the risk.

Chapter Twenty
Rockfall

'A fine day for a ride, don't you think?'

'Delightful.' Haddon Derray squinted against the sun, looking over Morrelow's hat to the high edge of the cliff. An Arrarat would be of use, here. The rock all about them was dazzling bright, almost painful to the eyes. Great spars jutted out, concealing myriad cracks and holes in the surface. Shadows of deep black lay behind each brilliant white slab. He could see why it was a favourite place for ambush. A thieves' paradise, he thought. He used to be good with a sword and knife himself. . .

The riders' swords were short and broad, quite unlike the slim, serrated blades of the Cavers. Irian had lent him her own sword, but it felt unfamiliar and heavy. He would have to get used to it. These were his people now, and the past nothing but a void behind him.

'The view from the top must be worth waiting for.'

'I suppose so.' Jerr Morrelow was uninterested.

'Forests, grasslands. . .' Brianne shrugged. 'Just what you'd expect.'

'You see strange patterns sometimes, looking down. I used to. . .' Haddon stopped.

'What? What did you "used to"?' Morrelow looked at him.

'Ride an Arrarat hawk.'

'Oh, yes. And pigs do fly, of course!' Jerr Morrelow took it lightly as a joke, but Haddon heard other resonances in his voice. Morrelow knows about the Arrarat, he thought. And he is more than interested in my child. . .

Jerr spurred his horse on, galloping ahead up the steep incline, Brianne just after him.

Haddon followed, leaving Serethrun Maryn to bring up the rear. He did not look back at Serethrun, not suspecting that he had heard every word.

He did not see the way Serethrun was staring at him.

It was early afternoon. The air was still, clear and calm about them. The sun, bright and unclouded. Somewhere in the distance a lark sang a filigree of elaborate trills.

They had moved slowly up the cliff face, examining each crack and cave on the way. In one, they found the remnants of a cooking fire, and some dried bracken that had recently been used as bedding. But the fire was cold, the bracken dusty. There was no other sign of life.

Further still they came to the rockfall.

A massive tumble of boulders and rocks blocked the entire width of the path. Sighing, handing his hat to Brianne with theatrical courtesy, Morrelow dismounted and began to scramble to the top of the pile. Small stones skipped and jumped beneath his feet. A cloud of white dust billowed.

The other three waited below, exposed in the sunlight. Brianne was wearing Jerr's hat, shading her eyes against the sun as she watched his progress. Serethrun was staring out over the forested plain beneath them, his brow faintly creased. His mind was clearly elsewhere.

Haddon Derray had drawn his unfamiliar sword. There was something strange in the air. A half-remembered smell, something that made his heart beat unevenly, his breath quicken.

Mages. He recognised the scent of magic, the sweat of concentration. He glanced at Serethrun and Brianne; they seemed oblivious. Would it be left to him to instruct them in the presages of man-made enchantment?

Jerr Morrelow had disappeared over the top of the rockfall. For a moment, everything was quiet.

Then, the rumbling sound of rocks crashing, and a muffled cry. An unpleasant slithering, dragging sound. Silence, again.

'Jerr! Are you all right?' Immediately, Brianne had slid from her horse and was scrambling over the rocks.

'Wait, Brianne.' Haddon was also on the ground, reaching out, grasping the girl's shoulder. 'Let's take a look from higher up.' He nodded up to the cliff face above the rockfall.

Serethrun had moved to the edge of the cliff, looking down at the rock face. 'It will be easier this way,' he said. 'There's a crevice just beneath the overhang.'

'I'd rather look down.' Already, Haddon had slung a rope over his shoulder and was clinging to the rock face. He moved swiftly over the surface, without hesitation or error.

'You've done that before,' Serethrun murmured.

'Yes.' He was above the rockfall now, and paused, looking back. 'There's no sign of Morrelow.' Then they heard him raise his voice, yelling at something on the other side of the fall.

'Morrelow!' They heard Haddon's furious shout, and then he abruptly dropped from the rock face, out of sight on the other side. There was a crash, a breath released on a curse. The sound of fighting, of scuffling, of bodies rolling and kicking in the dust.

'Keep together.' Brianne was climbing over the heap of stones, her knife jutting from her belt, Serethrun only two feet from her.

The rockfall was some fifteen feet high, composed of rugged and uneven stones. It was not hard to climb. Dust lay over every surface, rising into the air as they moved. They were climbing quickly, drawn by the sounds of violence.

With caution, Brianne lifted her head over the top, and at the same moment there was an explosion of sound from beyond them.

The two watchers at the top of the rockfall looked down on an extraordinary scene.

They saw Morrelow, falling back against the cliff face, pushed there through the force of the blow from Haddon Derray's fist. Haddon, standing some distance from Morrelow, his face suffused with anger and disgust.

And, on the ground between them, face down in the dust, the body of an old man.

There was no one else there. For a moment, no one moved.

Serethrun stood up, sheathing his knife. He half ran, half jumped down the other side of the rockfall until he was standing on level ground once more. In moments Brianne was at his side, alert and watchful.

'What's going on here? Jerr, what is this?'

'Ask our strange friend here.' Morrelow pushed himself away from the cliff, and drew his knife. He was breathing hard, his face running with sweat. He was very angry.

'Why did you kill him?' Haddon Derray was shouting at Morrelow, disregarding the other two. 'What harm could he have done to you?'

'Listen, Derray!' Morrelow was staring at him. 'Old men lurking in shadows only mean trouble! Why else hide in caves on cliffsides?'

For one impossible moment Haddon stood still, as if rooted in incredulous shock. His mouth twisted with a bitter amusement.

The crumpled, discarded body at his feet was undeniable.

'He was an old man, for Lady's sake! A Ma—' Haddon suddenly stopped. 'There was no need for murder!' He was kneeling at the man's side, feeling for a pulse.

'No need?' Morrelow pushed him aside, and roughly rolled the old man over on to his back. 'Look at that!'

The jaw fell slackly open, the eyes blankly reflecting the blue sky. No one was looking at the man's face, or at the hilt of Morrelow's knife, jutting from his breast. Underneath the frail, elderly body, half-covered by ragged and torn folds of grey cloth, lay a wooden staff, still clutched in bony and bloodless hands.

At one end, the wood was tortured into a twisted spiral, disappearing into a vanishing point.

'A sodding Mage! What does it matter if he's old? There's more harm in one of those spiral staffs than in any weapon!'

Brianne was standing beside Jerr, her hand on his arm. Her eyes were sparking, flashing with anger.

'You did right,' she said, her voice low and passionate.

Haddon could not believe this. 'Rubbish! A staff is only as dangerous as the person who uses it. There was no way of knowing that he wanted to harm us. He could have just been travelling, like us!'

They were all staring at him now, as if they had never seen him before.

'Hiding in a cave beside a rockfall! Oh, sure. He was probably just resting up!' Jerr was still furious.

Serethrun Maryn looked up from the man's body. 'Shut up, the pair of you. Whatever he was doing, it doesn't matter now. It's probably just as well. Nothing but trouble comes from mixing with Mages.'

'Not in my experience.' Haddon spoke forcefully. 'There are good Mages too.'

'Not where I come from!'

'What does that matter? It's done now.' Brianne shrugged. 'There's no point in regret.'

'Morrelow murdered him!'

'He was using the staff to build a blockade.' Morrelow's voice was patient, as if he were talking to a child. He was still watching Haddon, his eyes glinting. 'I saw it happen. He moved one stone, and then said something, and that damn spiral began to fizz, and all of a sudden there was a heap of rubble where the stone had been. There was no doubt about it, he was deliberately blocking the path!'

'Did you ask him why?'

'For Lady's sake! What good would that have done? He'd probably have turned me into a lizard or something!'

'And anyway, as you yourself said, he was old.' Brianne looked bored. 'A waste of space.'

Haddon could not quite believe what he was hearing. Slowly, he looked from one to the other. Morrelow was already turning away, dismissively. Brianne cold and contemptuous.

Only Serethrun looked uncomfortable, but he said nothing, he turned back to the pile of rock, and began to shift stones out of the way.

Chapter Twenty-one
Forests

Haddon Derray had not moved. He stared at the other three in amazement. They were already at work, methodically shifting rocks and stones from the blocked path. Didn't the death of an old man, Mage or not, matter?

'What are we going to do with the body?'

'Carry him to the top, I suppose. There's soft ground up there.' Jerr Morrelow straightened up for a moment. 'Unless you feel we should build a mausoleum here to commemorate the place where he fell?' There was an edge to his voice.

'The staff should be destroyed.' Haddon knelt down at the side of the crumpled figure again. Carefully, he moved the spiral staff to one side. 'And any other belongings. It wouldn't do to let them fall into the wrong hands. What *was* he doing here, do you think?'

'He was travelling,' said Serethrun shortly. 'Northwards, I think. There are berry stains on his cloak. He was on the way up, blocking the path behind him. He didn't want to be followed.'

'But we do. They're waiting for us below.' Morrelow looked with severity at Haddon. 'This is going to take a while. We could do with a hand, Derray. You can bury your Mage later.'

Haddon joined them at the rock pile, and began to shift stones.

By late afternoon they had cleared a way through the rockfall. With no further comment at all, the Mage's body was loaded on to Haddon's horse. They reached the top of the cliff an hour later without incident, although the path became increasingly narrow and precipitous.

The forest below them was cast into twilight cloud. Smoke arose from a number of small fires where the rest of the *eloish* waited. Morrelow blew the horn three times, and it was answered from below.

'They'll wait till morning. That path's no fun in the dark.' He turned to the others. 'Supper?'

They were all hungry from the physical exertion of the day. Morrelow had brought with him two rabbits.

'Always prepared, that's Jerr,' Brianne smiled at him. She found wild thyme, and Serethrun built a fire.

Haddon took no part in the preparations. He stood some way from them at the edge of the cliff top. The countryside around them was flat and treeless, marked only by bracken and heather, vanishing into a rapidly darkening distance. Cold winds blew across the heath.

The body of a Mage lay at his feet.

Jerr Morrelow was a murderer, and the others thought it trivial. What kind of people were these? For the first two weeks of the ride he had been too exhausted to notice. And as he had recovered, he had found most of his attention taken up by the baby.

A half-smile flickered across his face at the thought of the child. Suddenly, he longed for the soft downy head and warm embrace of Coronis's son.

Coron made him laugh. A thousand years had passed since he remembered laughing, but there was something irresistably comic about the way the child regarded everything around him. It was as if the world were a source of exquisite humour. He had a trick of carrying his head to one side, dark eyes not quite serious, considering his surroundings. . .

He stopped. He hadn't liked leaving Coron behind. But Irian would be good to him, and Haddon did owe the riders something.

Irian was all right. He trusted her. And most of the others had been reasonably friendly. He had thought that he recognised in them an integrity that reminded him of his own past with the Cavers. And yet there was a wildness, something unaccountable about Jerr Morrelow that was not just violent, but also obsessive.

He had killed without compunction or remorse.

Haddon Derray knelt down on the ground and began to cut away the surface layer of peat. He had no proper tools, and it took longer than he expected to dig out the shallow grave. Darkness had fallen by the time it was deep enough to take the body.

Carefully, he laid the old man in the soft earth. At the back of his mind there was a memory of a rite to attend the death of a Mage. He worked quickly and silently, trusting that the memory was accurate.

At last he stood up, brushing the dirt from his hands and looked back at the others. A figure was approaching him, silhouetted against the fire. Serethrun Maryn, carrying food. A truce?

'Here. We saved some for you.'

'Thanks.' He took the knife-skewered roast meat. 'There's more wood there for the fire.' He gestured towards the small pile of belongings on the other side of the grave.

'Where?'

Haddon walked round the disturbed earth and picked up the staff. He brought it back to Serethrun, who he held it for a moment, tracing the spiral with his hands. Then he looked up. 'So,' he said slowly. 'You can see in the dark, too. You claim to have ridden an Arrarat hawk and have a liking for Mages. You wouldn't happen to know a man called Jolin Rosco? Or, what was his other name. . .Marling? Lukas Marling?'

Haddon Derray stood very still, holding the cooling food in his hands. 'Lukas? How did a plainsrider get to know Lukas Marling?'

'He calls himself Jolin Rosco now. He lives in the city of Shelt. He's the new Earl.'

And because an old man who was also a Mage lay dead at his feet, Haddon Derray turned away from Serethrun and tried to order his responses. He failed. He lifted his head and looked at Serethrun through streaming eyes.

Haddon was laughing.

He did not think he would sleep that night. There were a number of reasons. Jerr Morrelow was not a comfortable companion, whispering to Brianne on the other side of the still-burning fire. They had made no attempt at friendliness towards him.

Serethrun Maryn was different again, moody and difficult. Haddon was not particularly worried by this, seeing it as a natural response to a stranger. Serethrun was somehow suspicious of Haddon's friendship with Lukas Marling, but refused to expand on this. And when Haddon tried to explain something of his own past, what it had been like living at the Cliff with Lukas Marling, Serethrun had merely shrugged.

Knowledge of Lukas's presence in Shelt opened up all sorts of possibilities for Haddon. Perhaps he should return south, and rejoin his old friend. From what he had gathered of the stories told every evening on the ride northwards, Lukas would probably welcome support in Shelt. Serethrun Maryn had said that there would be trouble. That it was unlikely the Earl would retain his power. Haddon lay on a rough blanket beneath the stars and wondered whether to join the struggle.

It would be like trying to recapture the past. The old camaraderie, beleaguered together on the Caver's Cliff, no longer existed. The Stasis had ended, and everyone had moved on. Even the Cliff was only a pile of rubble.

Coronis was dead.

You can't go home again. The year lost from his memory was like a barrier in his mind, insurmountable and immovable. He did not want to lift it.

He judged a year had passed, because Coron was now sturdy and strong, on the verge of walking. He had no other way of knowing what time had passed.

He lived differently now, riding the plains with a remarkable people. He was not going to leave them, yet. The life suited him: the hard riding, the pared-down exigencies of their existence. He did not have to pause to think or remember. Apart from Serethrun and Irian, no one had asked him anything. No one seemed in the least interested. It was a relief.

And if he was disliked by Jerr Morrelow and mistrusted by Serethrun, he thought such problems would pass. Left to themselves, Serethrun and Brianne would not have killed that old man so casually, he was sure. They would at least have given him a hearing. He did not consider the *eloish* naturally cruel: they had allowed him to ride with them; Irian had helped, in so many ways. There were bound to be difficulties in fitting into such a tight, cohesive group of people.

He would stay with the *eloish* and learn their life. His son would grow up part of an extraordinary race.

It was not these thoughts which prevented him sleeping. He tossed and turned, and eventually got up, wrapping the blanket around him like a cloak, and walked along the cliff top away from his three companions.

It was the thought of the child that was keeping him awake.

Would Coron be missing him, would Irian be loving enough? He rarely cried, and Haddon could imagine that others might find it possible to forget he was there.

Deep down, he knew Coron would be all right. After all, Haddon had chosen the life of the riders for his sake. And he had done so because he trusted them. They valued young, new life. No one would neglect a baby.

There was something else that made him ache for Coron. He did not want to sleep that night in case he dreamed. He could not bear the thought of a night unprotected by the baby. How could he drive away nightmares alone?

There was a barrier in his memory, and only during dreams did he begin to realise what lay behind it. He could not face that knowledge.

Chapter Twenty-two
Morning

Felicia took breakfast privately in her quarters, as usual. The east-facing room was bathed in warm sunlight. For once there was no sickness and she ate rolls and marmalade, coffee and fruit, with enjoyment.

She knew nothing of the rumours running through the Castle.

She dressed slowly, while Annis replaced the flowers and straightened the room. That day there were no constraints, no formal events or ceremonies to attend. She experienced a slight lift to her spirits, remembering that Rosco had promised to get rid of Yerrent.

And Eleanor Knight would soon be gone. They could settle down, and perhaps things might become easier between them.

There was a knock on the door. Annis went to open it, and Felicia saw over her friend's shoulders the tall thin figure of Olwyn Mittelson.

'Come in, Olwyn,' she said pleasantly. 'A fine morning, is it not?'

There was something clouding his face.

'The Earl—' She had never seen him so discomfited before. 'The Earl is not here?' He came towards her over the deep carpet, his triangular, ugly face serious.

'No.'

'Nor has been this night? Forgive me, Lady, this is urgent.' He was embarrassed, she noticed, as well he might be, and more than that.

'No. What is it, Olwyn? He's probably flying with Astrella. On such a day as this, who could blame him?' But even as she suggested it, a cold cramp seized her stomach.

'He was due to meet Philip Cammish over breakfast. There was some talk of commissioning new fishing craft. He would not forget such an appointment.'

There was a pause. She felt the cramp knot and twist within her. Then it came.

'Eleanor Knight has gone. And the Mage Matthias.

'And Jolin Rosco is no longer in the Castle.'

She turned her back on him, the sickness rising and crippling thought. For a moment the room seemed unstable, the triangular face of the Mage, the pretty eyes of Annis mere drifting smoke in a reality which was fast fading.

Deliberately and painfully, she dug her fingernails hard into her palm. A deep breath, battening down the nausea. Another breath, to give her strength to speak.

'You're sure?'

'I would not be here, else. Felicia.' He was looking directly at her. There was kindness in his face, and pity.

She spoke again, distantly. 'Is Cammish still here?'

'In the library, I'll send him away.' Mittelson was beginning to move back towards the door, the pale eyes unblinking and opaque.

'Tell him to wait. I will be down to talk to him – in ten minutes. Give me ten minutes. Now go, both of you.'

Quick glances were exchanged between Annis and Mittelson, and then they left her.

Alone.

She decided to get Cammish to talk. She was good at listening, good at observing, and knew he would not want to deal with a woman. A follower of Astret, he would certainly grant her respect, but that was about as far as it would go. He had little contact with women apart from home and temple.

The elderly, thick-set man was pacing the room, his step heavy on the polished boards. He stopped dead when she opened the door, staring at her beneath heavy brows. She saw surprise and wariness in his eyes.

She spoke quickly, before he could say anything. 'The Earl sends

his apologies. He will not be away for long. His brother brought
urgent news from the South. . .his family need him.'

'I would have thought there was plenty for him to do here.'
Cammish was uncompromising.

'He has left me explicit instructions. You may talk to me as you
would to him.' She waited. Still the older man stared. There was a
pause. She took a deep breath. 'Do sit down, Philp Cammish. It's
about new fishing craft, I understand. Tell me about the present fleet.
How many are in good repair?'

'There's not one in good condition. About half of them, some forty,
need completely refitting. All the others need repair of some sort.'

'But that's not what's bothering you?' She could hear aggression in
his voice.

'No.' There was another silence.

She said gently, 'I need to know what the problem is. You must tell
me. I cannot act wisely in ignorance.'

'Tradition. This is not women's work. You cannot understand
what's involved.'

'You will have to tell me then.' She was patient, undemanding.

There was a pause. She could see him weighing up the issues,
weighing up the authority of the woman before him. Two mutually
contradictory things were in her favour: her father was Javon of Eldin,
overlord of most of Stromsall and extraordinarily powerful. Felicia
had more than words to offer him.

The second issue worked in his soul, not his mind. It depended
on the fact that, here, Felicia was dealing with a man who had
attended ceremonies at the Fisher Temple in honour of the Lady
Astret.

Goddess of life and death. Of the tides of the sea, and the tides in
humanity's life.

He sighed, a breath of wind over the sea. 'Very well, then. The Sea
Lords. Traditionally, the Sea Lords financed the building of new
boats for each generation. In return they received a proportion of the
catch.'

'And there's a new generation coming up who are in need of their
own boats?'

He nodded.

'You have sons yourself?'

'Yes. I can provide for them, there's no worry there. But there are
others.'

'How many? How many boats do you need?' She did not want to
prolong the discussion.

'A dozen would not be enough. Two, to be realistic, twenty-four
boats, commissioned from the builders and you'll have gone some way
to helping the unemployment problem in Shelt.'

She thought. 'I'll talk to the Council. Remind them of the Castle's
obligations.' She stood up, reaching across the table to shake his hand.

'I'm grateful to you, Philp Cammish, for trusting me with this. I will try not to let you down.'

He glanced at her, beneath heavy brows. 'When do you expect him back then, Lady? No discourtesy intended, of course.'

'Of course.' She paused. 'I hope, soon. But I will be honest with you. I do not know for sure when the Earl will return. You may have to deal with me for some time yet.'

She looked at him with steady green eyes and for a long cool minute he met her gaze. Then he nodded, sketched a brief bow, and left the room.

She stared blankly at the rows of books.

Rosco. You should be here. I do not question your decision to leave me, and your child. It would not be the first time such a thing has happened. I always knew it to be a risk, loving you. I know, all too well, how imperative love can be.

I hoped, somehow, to offer you enough to divert you from the past, but I failed. I was not the right person to do this. I could never be the right one. This adds to the long tally of my failures.

But you should not have left these people.

This was a moment of strange and subtle knowledge. She thought, the people of Shelt need you even more than I do.

It's running out. Desertion.

They deserve better than this. The huge weight of sadness was enlivened by anger, then. It was a pricking, a call to action. She thought, you have left me here to hold things together against your return. There can be no other course for me.

Shelt was an inescapable responsibility. She remembered Rosco's fury in the face of it, and wondered if she would be able to accept the burden any more gracefully.

She would have to try. She would abandon no one.

She rang the bell-pull by the fire. 'Send for the Lord Chandos please, and Olwyn Mittelson. I would speak with them. Now.' The servant bowed and left the room, a look of slight surprise on his well-trained face. Although her words had been courteous as ever, there was something the matter. Walking down the long corridors of the Castle, he found himself shivering.

She didn't want to tackle all the Council at once, and so she arranged many meetings over the next few days, catching them in twos and threes to enlist their support.

She was not averse to using underhand methods. Every now and then she would mention her father. Remind them of the strength of Duke Javon of Eldin. She invented messages left to her by Rosco. Played, disdainfully, on their self-interest. It was not difficult.

'There will be a good rate of return. Twenty per cent of the catch, for ever, as a reward for an initial investment of a few hundred guilden.'

How could it fail? Within a few days she had good news for Cammish.

More difficult was the encounter with Merield and Yerrent, later that week. For this, after much inner debate, she enlisted the help of Olwyn Mittelson. She reasoned that he had always put Shelt first. Even more than she, Mittelson was interested in maintaining the equilibrium in Shelt, in keeping things going in case Rosco ever returned. They worked out a strategy in advance together.

'We would be grateful for a little advice, Lady Merield.' Felicia met her with the triple kiss of family greeting in the formal antechamber off the Hall. It was a cold room, cramped with heavy furniture and gilded portraits.

Since Rosco's disappearance, Felicia had avoided her stepmother. It was not hard, there was so much to do. But there was no way of concealing what had happened, and the last thing Felicia wanted was hypocritical sympathy. She wondered whether Merield was planning something.

A small nod to the Mage at the Duchess's side. Yerrent was Merield's constant companion, and it was his presence, more than anything else, that led Felicia to mistrust her stepmother.

It had been Yerrent who had conjured that foul smoke, who had tried to induce a miscarriage. What Felicia did not know was how far Merield had been involved.

Looking, now, at the way Merield's eyes flickered uneasily towards Yerrent, Felicia had her answer. These two were in league, but only Yerrent had power. They would both have to go.

Felicia seated herself on the grand, uncomfortable chair at one end of the room. Meriald she invited to sit beside her. Mittelson and Yerrent were left standing.

'I think it is time that Shelt sent an embassy to my father's court, don't you agree?' She looked at her stepmother. 'He should be informed of the position here.'

'The position? To what are you referring, my dear?'

She was unconcerned. Her days had been filled with meetings with the aristocracy, with hunting parties and balls and parties. Rosco was busy, Felicia had said, and Merield had questioned her no further.

'Jolin Rosco has left Shelt. I don't know when he will return.'

'My dear!' Merield had hoisted herself closer, her eyes sparkling. 'What are you saying!'

'The ties of the past. . .' Felicia spoke vaguely. 'His brother and the woman Eleanor Knight left at the same time. I don't know when he'll be back, if ever.'

Merield reached across and took Felicia's hand. She let it lie there, passive and unresponsive. Felicia spoke coldly.

'I need to send a messenger to my father's court. He must be told.'

'Indeed he should!' Merield's voice was shocked. She removed her hand, and instead reached her arm round Felicia's unyielding shoulders. 'You poor dear! And at such a time! You should not have to bear this terrible situation alone, I agree. Your father's support would be invaluable.'

'Yes.' This was more than distasteful to Felicia. She pressed on. 'Yes, Olwyn and I have been discussing it. We have decided that the Lord Chandos of the Council, Gereth Hallan, would be a suitable envoy. He has the trust of the rest of the Council, and comes from a well-respected Shelt family.'

'Felicia. Consider.' Merield looked at her seriously. 'This is a matter of delicacy. You must not think of involving a stranger.'

'But who else is there? Oh, Merield, can it be that you are offering to go yourself? This is so kind of you—' Felicia rushed on, ignoring Merield's sudden pallor. 'There are messages that can only be conveyed with a woman's sensitivity. . .' She leaned forward, and took Merield's hand.

Her stepmother looked hunted. 'My dear! I could not for a moment think of leaving you at this difficult time!'

'Bladon,' said Yerrent, stepping forward. He was outwardly cool, a small neat figure, his slashed grey cloak embroidered with silver. 'Bladon must go. Your father's own Master of Horses, Lady Felicia. He could be trusted with any message.'

'Unfortunately, the captain left yesterday on a week's exercise with members of the Castle Guard.' Mittelson spoke with smooth regret. 'They have gone northwards in pursuit of the wild horses . . .the stables are in need of restocking.' Unblinking, he looked at Yerrent.

'Send someone after him!' Yerrent spoke sharply.

'There is no need to waste time in chasing after the Guard. They could be anywhere on the northern plains.' Mittelson bowed to Felicia. 'Chandos is ready to accompany the Lady Merield as soon as she is ready, my lady.'

'No! I mean, I cannot possibly think of leaving you to bear this alone!' Merield was clasping her hands together, not bothering to conceal her dismay.

'But Merield, there is no one I would rather trust.' Felicia was beginning to enjoy this.

Merield looked at her with dislike. 'Dear Felicia, I am deeply honoured by your confidence. But to leave you here, amongst strangers. . .you are too trusting!'

'But I know how you must feel, Merield. To be separated from my father so soon in your marriage.' Felicia smiled at her sweetly. 'You must feel the separation.'

'Naturally. However, my duty is clear.' Merield's voice was no longer quite smooth. 'Yerrent will accompany your Lord Chandos. That is the best compromise!' Her lips were drained of colour.

Felicia disregarded it. 'But really, I would much prefer such messages as I have for my father to be presented by you, Merield. You will know just what to say.'

'I could not consider leaving at this time!'

'I am determined that you should neglect your marriage no longer. . . .'

'I cannot possibly leave Shelt now!'

'But it is urgent that my father receives this message.'

Merield pursed her lips. 'Yerrent can carry a letter as well as anyone.'

'I want *you* to take it.'

There was nothing more Merield could say. It was settled.

That afternoon, Felicia and Olwyn watched the Duchess Merield leave Shelt in the company of her Mage, Yerrent. Several mounted guardsmen attended them and their preposterous piles of luggage.

Felicia looked up at Mittelson.

'Will it work, do you think?'

'Who knows?' He hunched thin shoulders. 'Merield is not a fool, and must know that she has failed. Quite what she will tell your father I cannot judge. But it is a long journey to Eldin, and the coach in which their luggage is stored has not been renovated, of late. . .' He paused, and his voice dropped. 'And Yerrent is a storm-cloud looking for somewhere to break. I don't think we've seen the last of him.

'But at least you have won yourself a breathing-space, Lady Felicia.'

She said nothing. But that night, alone in her bedroom, she found unwelcome thoughts resounding in her mind.

Small victories, petty triumphs. What was the use of it? Why bother: manipulating, planning, organising, deceiving, teasing? What was the point of it?

She ran her hands over her unfamiliar body, the breasts heavy, tender, the slight swelling of her abdomen. She was not strong, there was a baby coming and no one to help her. Why didn't she just abdicate, return to her father's court, let them all get on with it? And then another thought struck her, one she found impossibly distressing.

What if her father had been in league with Merield? What if she and Yerrent had been acting on Javon's instruction?

She could not go home, even if she wanted to. She looked out of the window to the empty skies.

She had turned the tide once, defeated a dragon. She would not go back, whatever the circumstances. She would not run out. Her coming child had changed everything. There was a wider future to consider, something beyond the span of her own life. Her child would not reproach her for cowardice. She would try to rule Shelt fairly, and if her nights were made desperate by loneliness, that was nothing new.

Rosco was gone with his bright-haired lover. She could not find it in herself to wish them happiness, but the anger was no longer arrow-sharp.

It's not fair, she thought, the truest cliché of all. All those manipulations, all those missed opportunities. . .The world, as run by warring gods, was a place of sub-standard values, of unequal chances. What hope was there for humanity, marked for unwilling rôles in a bitter feud? And then another, subversive thought, undercutting all that wild resentment.

We get the gods we deserve. We have only ourselves to blame.

So where did I go wrong, Rosco? What have I done to deserve this?

Nothing. Nothing at all, was the only answer she could find, and for a while she could not prevent the tears falling.

Exhausted at last, she fell into an uneasy sleep, attended by a strangely comforting, unusual idea. The idea of a pattern, a sequence of events that reached beyond her, through her child, to shape all the world.

Chapter Twenty-three
Southwards

As he moved through the rapidly thawing northern wastes, Gawne found that the world still bent beneath his breath. With ancient hands, he took the northern winds to his heart and promised them joy. Winds from the East he tempted with the bribe of power.

In return, his wind thralls pledged snow for him, snow and spreading ice.

Always the pull came from the South. From Shelt, the city he had made his own. At the joining of the winds, where north and south met, he absorbed the auguries of change.

In Shelt, a power shifted. As yet unconscious, but inevitable, the force which had defeated him stirred again. He had underrated the Lady and Her servants, but he would not do so again.

Revenge inspired him. To take, to grasp what was his. With steps slow and quiet, he lived in patience. He moved again, always southwards.

Animals still ran screaming from his path. Wolves, bears, deer and foxes disappeared into the deep forests, spreading their news or invasion. Birds, in wheeling drifts, soared high into the cold skies, fluttering in wild, heady panic away from their traditional feeding grounds.

Men were not so wise.

This clan lived with reindeer. Herding them, tending them, harnessing them to pull sledges, using their pelts for clothing and tents, their flesh for food. It was a hard existence, pared of all luxury and ease.

They were suspicious of strangers. In the manner of their kind, they abandoned their old and sick according to ritual and tradition. They surrounded the ragged man who had wandered into the camp and watched him warily. How could an old man, with ice on his breath and sparse, wind-blown grey hair command their compassion?

His hunched shoulders raised high around his ears, he held out his upturned hands to them.

'What harm can I do you? I am old, but not without knowledge. Have you need of healing, of someone skilled in medicine and herbs? I know many secrets. I know the meaning of portents and omens. I can read the stars.'

'Prove it,' came a rough, mocking voice. Gawne fastened deep-sunk eyes on a face in the gathering crowd.

'You will lose your dearest possession before the night is over.' You are marked for grief, he nearly said, but he didn't want them panicking.

A roar of laughter from the crowd. The man Gawne had identified was tall and strong, with quick eyes. He tossed fine black curls and laughed with his friends, but there was a flash of doubt behind the bluster. He slept that night with his hand on his sword, with the ring that his wife had given him glowing on his finger.

Before dawn, his daughter died.

Gawne was waiting, two miles beyond the camp, crouched unsleeping through the cold night. The wind thralls were quiet at his shoulders. He was too far away to hear the keening voices, but he knew what would be happening.

He heard the thunder of hooves first, the soft swish of the sledges over uneven snow and grass. He was waiting in the shelter of slender birches. He was tall and thin like the trees, but where they shone vernal-white and beautiful in the early morning sun, he was dull and attenuated.

Their swords were drawn at his throat. He caused the sharp metal to become heavy, weighted with the crawling ice of his making.

He laughed. 'Who else would care to test my skill? Have I any takers? You are in need of guidance, my friends, in need of direction and leadership. How else will you learn the ways of power? How else will you learn the will of the Lady?'

All the time, as the flow of lies ran on, light and emotionless, the weight of ice spread along the metal to trembling flesh and crept along veins and nerves. Their fingers cramped round the swords, welded to iron, and a long, low moan was wrenched from rigid throats.

He waited until the threnody had ceased, until he saw the cold gleam of ice in their eyes. Briefly, he allowed the northern winds to rustle around them as it fed from the dying remnants of warmth. He waited quietly until they turned towards him once more. Wordlessly, he crossed the sodden ground to one of the sledges.

Attended by wind, the ice warriors carried him back to the camp. One by one, they sought out their wives and children and kissed their puzzled faces. The ice spread. The women took up their weapons, finding in them a natural extension to the biting cold now at their centre.

The children died. The ice ran through their living tissue with barely a pause, and in seconds small hands fell slack. Rosy cheeks turned to grey and bright eyes dulled.

The reindeer snickered and whinnied, rolling their eyes and stamping in the pens. Calmly, the adults entered the pens and ran their hands over the coarse, tough coats. The animal distress quietened. No one bothered to close the pens again; the deer waited patiently, their keepers at their sides.

The wind still lifted the warriors' clothes, ran through their hair, disturbed their breath. But now they had no essence that was not composed of crystalline ice, no atom of flesh that pulsed to the heart's beat.

They were ready. Mastery of humans and animals, mastery of ice and wind. Gawne glanced over his people and a thin smile flickered on his face.

Ready. Gawne set his face to the South, the winds gathering force behind him, and continued his journey.

Chapter Twenty-four
Astrella

The rider of an Arrarat hawk in no way controls his or her mount. The bond between rider and bird is described as a partnership, a marriage of equals, and neither party can exert ultimate control.

Lukas Marling, that morning, did not believe it.

Never before had he found himself so at odds with his beloved companion. He was used to communicating with her in silent pictures and unspoken thoughts; and although she would often respond to an idea, to the suggestion of an idea, he would always find himself taken where he wanted to be.

Not that day. As she flew steadily northwards, away from Shelt, he found himself reduced to tugging at her feathers, a huge and furious question in his mind.

Why?

She took no notice, gave no reply.

He looked back at the rapidly diminishing outline of the north brigg. They had passed over the massive rock formations that lined the Bay of Marqun, where the dragon had arisen at Gawne's bidding.

He felt a thrill of anticipation from Astrella. *Gawne?* Was she taking him to Gawne? Had the First Sea Lord survived his watery grave to threaten the kingdoms of the North?

Jolin Rosco was needed in *Shelt*. Felicia would think he had run out. Eleanor—

But no. He would not allow himself to think about Eleanor, even now. She was no longer part of his life, no longer anything to do with him.

Thinking of Eleanor, Lukas did not notice the miles of open plains pass beneath them. Part of him registered the River Quenild, a slim ribbon of silver across the flat grey grasslands, and the oddly regular outline of Calter Wood.

But other shapes filled his mind: other words, other feelings. All centred on someone he was resolved to drive from his thoughts. He gazed unseeing at the fleeting landscape below, carried moment by moment further from the Castle of Shelt and its various and complicated responsibilities.

At last Astrella swooped down on to an empty plain to settle for the night. Cold with fury and hunger, Lukas slid from her back and began to walk southwards.

She would not let him pass. The sudden rushing sound of violated air, a long low swoop over grass and she was before him, wings outstretched and quivering, a wall of feathers.

Compressing his lips, Lukas turned to one side and ran swiftly, diagonally, past her. A swirl of wings, a sudden lashing of claws, and she had caught his cloak, tearing through the cloth to graze the flesh beneath.

He saw dark eyes flashing, experienced distress, anger, regret and determination in equal degrees from her. He shook the cloth free from the curving talons.

'Astrella, what *is* the matter? Why are you doing this?'

Never before had he found himself compelled to use mere words to her. She had never before opposed her will to his in this way. Always, she had perfectly understood his least desire, and they had moved together in harmony and peace. He glared into her dark, liquid eyes, willing her to explain.

And yet again, there was the picture of Gawne, the First Sea Lord, somehow shining. . .glinting, as if covered in a shroud of running water. . . . No. Ice. An image of ice and snow.

Astrella had moved again, to stand with her back to him, looking northwards once more. The message was unmistakable.

Gawne was alive, living somewhere in the North. And Astrella had unilaterally decided that it was up to him, Lukas Marling, erstwhile Earl of Shelt, to do something about it.

How did she know what was happening in the North? Was there another Arrarat hawk in Stromsall, sending telepathic warnings to Astrella?

A warm surge of assent from Astrella. Another Arrarat, then, here. But who was riding it? Would it be someone he knew, living in exile in an alien country?

Reassured that he would not try walking again, Astrella brought him a rabbit for supper. She laid it at his feet, as if in apology, and waited for him to gather some dry brushwood for a fire. Fortunately, he was still carrying a knife.

He settled for the night by the dying embers of the fire, leaning against his Arrarat hawk. There were probably wolves, he thought, at the very least, but Astrella would warn him.

Matthias had promised to send Eleanor home. It would take time, preparing the Rite, but it could be done. He might never see her again.

In Shelt, crucially involved in the daily business of running the place, he had been almost unwilling to consider the implications of her presence. But now, alone on a moonlit, windy plain far north of anyone or anything he knew, he found his mind returning again and again to the woman he loved.

He acknowledged it. He had sworn once to love her for ever and although time and events had driven them far apart, he had not, essentially, changed. Neither had she. Still courageous, still passionate. He saw it written in her every expression, in every movement she made.

She had broken the Stasis, thinking him dead. She had survived the appalling toll of the God's vengeance. She had endured every hardship, had crossed Peraldon and Stromsall virtually alone, just to find him. . . .

To find him married, withdrawn, ungiving, distant and preoccupied.

He had not behaved well, and now it was too late. He had married Felicia out of a desire to bring peace to Shelt. He had thought himself indispensable to that process, although Shelt would have to manage without him now. Somehow, Mittelson, Felicia and the Council would have to work it out together.

And they would manage. Shelt would somehow, of course, survive without him. He should never have married Felicia. A thought of overwhelming clarity and force. He should have refused the crown, and then he would have been free to be with Eleanor now.

The marriage was unworthy of Felicia, too. He could offer her only friendliness, respect, companionship. She deserved more than such debased currency. She was miserable and ill, plainly deeply unhappy.

The child. He looked, unseeing, into the red embers of the fire. A branch cracked in the heat, and a shower of ash fell on to the glowing cinders.

There was no point in these regrets. There was a child on the way, his child with Felicia. The chains had been welded fast long before either investiture or wedding.

He was even tired of cursing the gods. Mittelson had spoken no less than the truth. And he had seen it for himself echoed in Matthias's blind face. There was no way out, nothing to be done.

He shifted his position, leaning back against the soft grey wings, his knees drawn up. Somewhere, in the deep dark, he heard the wild call of an owl, the scream of a mouse or rat.

He turned his face to the grey feathers, and tried to sleep.

The wide sweep of Astrella's wings carried him northwards. He lost track of the days and nights, the changing levels of plain and forest beneath them. He observed the white causeway across Ristmere as a glinting brilliance through the shifting mists of vapour and insects that overhung the mire.

In Falby Forest, he found an old acquaintance.

Astrella had swerved aside from the northwards flight, and they were passing west over the dark evergreen forest. Lukas was resigned, now, to letting her have her own way. No doubt there was some reason for this diversion. . . .

He saw no streams, no paths, no clearings apart from the one wide dirt-track which led north to the white cliff at the edge of the forest. The trees grew densely together, a mixture of pine, fir and spruce.

Astrella put him down in the middle of unmarked trees. It was very quiet. He was not given to superstition but the forest seemed unfriendly in its silence. He saw no sign of wildlife, no rabbit burrows or deer tracks.

He looked around him. Astrella was standing still, calmly waiting. There was nothing she wanted to tell him, no message beyond the usual affection. He shrugged, and began to walk through the trees towards the cliff. The forest was silent. The spring sun fell in slanting rays through the trees to create dappled patterns on the forest floor. Fresh green shoots were beginning to thrust their way through the carpet of pine-needles. In distant, warm air, he heard a bird leap untidily into the sky, a partridge or pheasant, alarmed by a breeze, a movement, a dream.

Brambles, dried and desiccated brown by the previous winter, gripped at his cloak. Why had Astrella brought him here?

And yet, he felt somehow that he was not alone. He smelt the fresh evergreens all around, the scent of earth disturbed by new spring life, and recognised something else. The scent of woodsmoke, was it? Together with a faint sourness, a damp dirtiness. . .blood? He stood still for a moment, allowing his senses to run over the combination of sound, scent, light and warmth.

He looked around warily. There was someone here, there had to be. He knew eyes were watching him. He started walking at an even pace, although every sense was finely tuned. Occasionally he paused, looking round and behind him.

The forest waited, blank and empty. The trees were tall and straight like the bars on a cage. He could still see Astrella through them, waiting patiently like some poor imprisoned creature.

He realised then, with irony, that the prisoner could equally well be himself, held behind bars formed by trees.

A sudden rush of sound, of branches breaking, and there were hands and claws clutching at his throat. He was pushed off his feet by the force of the attack. Something wild and ragged tore at the skin of his neck.

Forcefully he brought his arms up, and slashed outwards. Quicker than thinking, his right hand grasped the dagger. He rolled over on top of his assailant, and saw the glint that betrayed steel.

Lukas flung himself sideways as the knife whistled past his head to thud into the tree behind. Instantly he rolled over, scrambling to his feet and dodging round behind one of the trees.

There was something familiar in the set of his assailant's head, although the individual features were difficult to make out through the dirt and grime. Heavy cloth hung in rags and tatters, almost obscured by filth.

The creature gave a scream, a howl of frustration, and wildly hurled itself at him. It was not difficult to dodge. Again Lukas stepped to one side, and it almost fell, reaching out one hand to clutch at a branch.

There was a flash of familiar sapphire on the raking hand. Lukas realised who it was.

'Esmond! What's the matter with you?' he shouted as the smaller man launched himself forward in renewed attack.

Lukas sheathed his knife, and swung a fist, knocking the oncoming body backwards to the ground and there was a dull knock as his head struck a branch. The man half shifted, and then fell back unconscious against the pine-needles.

Lukas bent down, gently tilting the filthy face to one side. A small bruise, a slight cut. . .Esmond was only stunned. Quickly, he drew a cord from the seam of his cloak and turned the frail figure over, drawing the wrists together.

For a moment his hands hesitated. Esmond's once-elegant, graceful fingers were now tipped with filthy and broken fingernails – yellowing, discoloured with dirt, mud. . .blood.

He pulled Esmond over on to his back, examining the begrimed face. Lines of dirt mapped a wasteland, downturning at the mouth, creasing the forehead. New lines, Lukas thought, lines of sorrow. The rust of old and new blood stained the chin in uneven streaks, dried mucus clogged round the nose.

The man was wrecked, degraded by something worse than grief. And round his neck there was an iron collar, with the ends of a chain attached to it. He had been held prisoner, chained like some wild animal.

As Lukas looked on, shocked, the figure began to stir. The eyes flickered, the blue lights in them flashing with unholy brilliance. At once every muscle seemed to contract, so that Esmond's body curled up in a tight ball. A bizarre paroxysm almost tore the cord at his wrists as the energy was released. Gripping the thin shoulders, Lukas saw blood splatter over the forest floor beneath him.

Leaning down heavily, Lukas changed his own position so that he was kneeling astride the writhing figure.

'Esmond!' he shouted, urgent to break through the savage mask. He lifted one hand to slap, lightly, the snarling face. Esmond nearly overbalanced him at that point, moving with uneven energy.

'Esmond! Remember me?'

The creature spat in his face.

'Don't you know who I am?'

'Rosco, fucking Earl of Shelt! Usurper, murderer!' The light tenor voice was hoarse and grating, discoloured with violence.

'With your connivance.' Lukas spoke softly, eyes fastened on the other's, willing him to steadiness.

'Torold is dead, and whose fault is that?' There was another violent surge of energy, and then Esmond suddenly relaxed, as if released.

'The Mage Lammon killed Torold. Not I. His death was not what I desired.' Lukas kept his words slow and even, trying to prevent the violence reappearing. 'We wondered where you'd gone,' he said easily.

'You think I should have stayed in Shelt?' Esmond's voice was rising again, the edge of hysteria flexing and expanding. 'There's nothing for me there! Only ashes and treachery and enemies and evil. Shelt is a bloody cauldron of horrors. . .' His voice dropped to a sibilant whisper. 'But not for you, Jolin Rosco. . .or do I speak to Sharrak, or a wraithe or the Children, or some other bloody fraud?'

'I am Rosco.' He would not lie. 'Rather, that is a name I have used.'

A long pause. 'What price integrity now?' The voice was dry and distant, an echo of the old Esmond. A faint smile flickered over the dirt-scarred face. He no longer moved. Breath barely stirred the wrecked body. A ray of sunlight drifted through the trees, animating the filthy hair, somehow picking out the remaining blond strands.

'The man known as Rosco could not afford honesty.' Lukas decided to chance it. He moved away, so that he was sitting with his back to a tree. And although Esmond was now lying motionless, Lukas kept his hand on the hilt of his knife.

There was no reply. Esmond continued to stare blankly ahead, at some vanishing point between trees and sky.

'Are you alone here?' Lukas had last seen Esmond in Shelt, desperate, at Torold's funeral. He assumed, as far as he'd considered it at all, that Esmond had been taken to one of the grand houses of Shelt and there nursed back to health.

'Why does the Earl of Shelt leave his city?' At last Esmond dragged his gaze towards the man sitting at his side. Not only were the words barbed, but there was again a flicker of something wild in his eyes. . .hatred? Fear? Lukas could not decide.

'It was not by my will. My hawk brought me here.'

'Your Arrarat hawk. . .' The voice trailed away into silence.

'What are *you* doing here, Esmond, of all places?'

'This is my home. Where else should I go?'

'Your *home*?'

'I lived here as a child. My father owns this land, and the plain south of here. This was and *is* my home. The land of generous trees, trees which do not mimic death in winter, the land where love lives eternal.' He spoke quietly, dreamily.

'And you met Torold when Javon took over the area, and you returned with him to Shelt. . .?'

The face beside Lukas was totally blank. Devoid of emotion or expression.

Then the voice started again, drifting into the shadowy wood as if from a great distance. 'And now comes another Earl of Shelt to disturb my peace.'

Lukas stood up. 'Who looks after you, Esmond? Surely you're not alone here?'

For the first time Esmond moved, turning on to his side, so that he faced away from Lukas, his hands still roughly imprisoned behind his back. Blood ran from the wounds in his wrists.

There was a moment of complete silence, and then a whisper of breath seemed to ripple through the air.

'No, I'm not alone.' And then the whisper became a giggle; the giggle, a laugh. The sound of it made Lukas feel sick.

'My father. . .' Between one second and the next the laugh turned to tears.

Lukas stood up and moved round so that he faced the man on the ground. He saw rivulets of salt staining tracks through the grime. Red-circled eyes were clenched shut, great shuddering sobs shook Esmond's body. Lukas knelt down, pulling the stinking figure on to his lap, cutting the bonds around his wrists.

As a child clings to its mother, Esmond clutched at Lukas's cloak, nuzzling his head into the soft folds of cloth. For a long time he was held there, until the wracking sobs had quietened into sleep. Gently, he was then lowered to the ground once more.

Lukas looked up into the dark lines of the trees, and saw the prison-straight bars hiding the sky.

Chapter Twenty-five
Garulf

Astrella? His mind received an answering reassurance of love and loyalty, but nothing resembling an explanation.

Lukas needed water, to clean the cuts on Esmond's wrists. He glanced down at the man asleep at his feet, who was lost in deep oblivion. Perhaps the fury of madness would soon regain him. . .?

There was running water not far away, he knew that. He could even hear it now, a faint rushing sound. He did not like leaving Esmond. For a moment he considered tying him up again, but Lukas disliked the idea of imposing restraints on such a wounded creature. There were chains enough around him as it was. He decided to chance it. He began to walk quickly through the forest, following the slight downward slope towards the sound of water.

The stream was a narrow foaming torrent, overhung by bracken and the low branches of larches. No wonder he had not been able to see it from above.

He had no vessel or cup. Only the hood of his cloak. He had used it before to transport liquid: it was waterproof against rain and could perfectly well be used to carry water the short distance back to Esmond.

He took off the cloak and knelt down at the side of the stream. It was the last thing he remembered for a long time.

There were bars around him, and a repeating refrain in his mind. No way out now. No choice, no diversion, no freedom, no way out.

The bars were tall and straight, like trees, not quite obscuring the midday sun as it poured down on him. He was lying on bare stone, his cloak folded neatly as a pillow under his head.

He felt perfectly well, instantly alert. There was not even the suggestion of a headache. *Had* he been hit? How else did he get here, unknowingly?

'A drug,' confirmed a dry voice behind him. Lukas sat up.

A small, delicate figure sat cross-legged on a narrow mattress close to the wall. The man was old, straggly grey hair fringing a bald head, and yet he sat there erect, quite calm and self-contained.

Lukas moved round the room, so that the light from the barred window was no longer in his eyes, and then stopped.

The man was blind. Blank white eyes with no pupils stared at nothing. The man continued, turning his head towards Lukas's new position. 'I hope you will forgive the use of such unsubtle methods. It was necessary.'

His voice was dry as ashes, but Lukas heard something else there. The ruins of passion howled beneath the bare words.

'Why?'

'My home, here, has remained hidden for a very long time. I have no desire to have its whereabouts revealed.' He smiled graciously in Lukas's direction. It made it worse, somehow. 'My thanks are due to you for your kindness to my son, Esmond.'

'Your *son*?' It was not inconceivable. The old man was of a slight build, with fine hands and a pleasant, cultured voice. But still, here, dressed in coarse linen, in a barred, stone cell in the middle of a forest? With such terrible echoes under the breath of his voice? 'What is your name?'

'My servant calls me "Master", my son calls me "Father". You may call me "Garulf", if you wish, or anything else. . .it doesn't matter.'

'Where are we?' Lukas asked. There was a door opposite the window. It was shut, but he could not tell whether it was locked.

'In the centre of Falby Forest. That is all you need know.'

'Esmond said that his father – you – owned this area. That all this territory is under your control.'

The old man smiled slightly and the sunlight seemed to sour. 'It could certainly be viewed like that. But such concepts are always open to debate.'

Lukas decided to pass over this. 'Where is Esmond? He needs care.'

'He has been found. My people will look after him.' Garulf was unconcerned. 'I did not bring you here merely to offer thanks. I would ask a favour of you.'

'I am not a free agent. My hawk brought me here—'

'At my behest. I have a little knowledge of the Great Hawk. My other skills include. . .an inkling as to the future. It is for that reason that I requested your hawk to bring you here.'

'My brother has that gift. He also is blind.' Lukas stood quite still, watching the terrible figure sitting so upright on the floor. Garulf was very thin. There was a suggestion of ill-health about the texture of his grey skin. As if years of abuse had deprived it of colour of resilience. It lay stretched over skull and gaunt ribs. His muscles were slack.

And then that voice, the gentle passivity concealing so much. 'Does your brother view his prescience as a gift?' Garulf's face was faintly enlivened with curiosity.

'More – as a curse. I think.'

Esmond's father nodded. 'That is why I live here, withdrawn from the world. It is impossible to act, when the future is known. . .' This was the gaping horror behind the words, the extraordinary degree of suffering. The calm, sun-filled cell was a battleground.

'You want me to do something for you?'

'Sometimes. . .it is necessary to descend from the ivory tower.' He smiled. 'There is danger, coming from the North. And worse still in the South, but that peril is not my responsibility nor yours. I would not have asked you to help, but the advent of an Arrarat hawk was too significant an opportunity to miss. Without it, I would have to risk the lives of others to find out what has happened to Lassan.' He paused. 'Lassan is my Mage. I sent him to the cliff, to block the road. I hoped it would delay the evil a little, but he has not returned. And for some reason, I cannot see what has happened to him.'

He was no longer smiling, the surface of the calm face now cracking to reveal what lay within. The lined skin rearranged itself into patterns of torment. 'There is some power blocking the path of my sight, something in the way.' Another lengthy pause while he struggled to regain serenity. The lines on his face smoothed out once more, and the calm voice continued. 'The rider of an Arrarat hawk would be able to tell me what is happening, at no risk to himself. I am asking you simply to act as a look-out for me.

'Tell me what is happening, so that I may make sense of the future. . .'

Lukas moved across the room to the door. It swung open easily at his touch, leading to an empty stone-lined corridor.

'You may leave whenever you wish,' said Garulf. 'Although I would be grateful if you would give me your word not to betray the position of this place.'

Lukas turned back to the old man. He watched the calm plains of his face carefully. How disabling was Garulf's fear? He would have to find out. 'What you have foreseen in the North bears some relation to a message I have received from Astrella, my hawk. She has shown me that a Mage called Gawne still exists, to the North of here. For a time he lived as a Sea Lord at Shelt, but before that he came from Peraldon. He was an adept at the use of Parid.'

Garulf sighed. 'There's no need for hallucinatory monsters now. His breath chills flesh and blood instead. He rides on the back of the North wind, crossing the empty tundra to regain his territories, his world of power. He challenges more than you think.'

'I have more than a personal stake in keeping him out of Shelt.' Lukas spoke softly.

'You have been crowned Earl of Shelt, I know. And you will return to enjoy that rôle, to protect and care for the City of the Sea. . .' It was impossible to ignore the shadows beneath his words.

'What else do you see, Garulf?' Lukas's hands were painfully clenched. 'Death?'

'Death, certainly. For each and every one of us. Everyone owes a death.'

'That's not what I'm asking.'

'I know. But I have no other answer for you.' Garulf smiled again, turning his hands palm upwards to the ceiling. The gesture was a disconcerting, sick echo of Olwyn Mittelson.

'Very well.' He knew there was never any profit in pressing a madman too far. 'When shall I leave?'

'It is urgent. My servants will have prepared food for you.' He waved a graceful hand towards the open door. Standing there was a another man robed in the same coarse linen. He bowed to Lukas and held out a hand, inviting him to follow.

Lukas turned back to Garulf. 'I would like to see Esmond again before I go.'

Esmond's father shook his head. 'No. Eat, and then take your hawk and go. Esmond will be all right. It is necessary that you make haste. There is no time for delay.'

He was taken to sit outside, on a bench against the stone wall. A bowl of lentils and some bread was brought for him. The servant, an elderly man with hunched shoulders and colourless eyes, did not speak. He smiled pleasantly, but shook his head in answer to Lukas's questions, retreating quickly back into the stone fastness.

The hexagonal building stood in a small clearing, a strange angular shape. The late afternoon sun was beating down on the bench where he sat. Lukas ate quickly, curious to find out more. But just as he was about to call Astrella, he heard from the forest ahead a thin wailing noise.

It sounded like Esmond. He was in no state to be left running loose. Lukas left the shelter of the stone wall and moved out into the forest.

He found him without difficulty. Esmond was sitting hunched on the ground under the dark trees, his back to Lukas.

'Esmond? Are you all right?' Lukas spoke quietly and at first he thought that the other had not heard him at all.

But then Esmond turned round, shuffling against the dry pine-needles and Lukas saw, with shock, that there was now a chain running from the crude iron collar. He was tethered to a stake jutting from the ground. It was not quite long enough to allow him to stand.

'You've been talking to him. He's mad, you know.' Esmond's eyes were brilliant with hate. 'You know what he does, my sainted father?' The voice was beginning to soar again, uneven as flame. 'All day he sits there, knowing the future, trying to persuade himself that there's still chance. He puts bars on the windows to show that he has no freedom, and he pays his servants to throw dice!' He began to giggle again, an insane bubbling laughter, his eyes gleaming, throat thrown back.

'They throw dice and if it's an odd number they feed him, and if it's even, they don't. Simple, isn't it? Sometimes he goes weeks without food, sometimes it's okay and there's bloody lentils twice a day. One day, he'll die of starvation and he'll be glad then, because he'll have proved his submission: total obedience to the Laws of Chance, total disdain for what the gods ordain. He'll have proved that he doesn't know everything that's going to happen.'

'When I leave here, do you want to come with me?' Lukas had been listening with only half an ear, running long fingers over the length of chain. 'I'm going north, and there's going to be trouble there. But I can get you out of this.'

The chain was padlocked. Lukas sat back on his heels, regarding the pale and beautiful wreck before him. Esmond began to giggle again, the brilliant eyes flickering shiftily. 'Propositioned by the Earl of Shelt! Yet again! Are there no new lines anywhere?'

'No. . .but I'm not propositioning you. Just offering a way out; a lift, if you like, to somewhere else. Do you want to come?'

'My father has bars at his windows because he knows humanity is not free. I wear chains round my neck because I know that my love is imprisoned in cold earth. I am chained to the earth where he lies and no longer want to fly. . .'

In his hands he held a small key, the key that fitted the padlock. There was no sense to be had from him. Lukas touched his hand to Esmond's cold cheek. 'I'll be back soon,' he said. 'Think about what

I've said. I'll take you away from here.'

'But chains are chains, wherever you go.'

A hollowing of madness lived within Falby Forest. Centred around a stone cell, madness reached out to entrap the grieving and the guilty.

Flying on Astrella, springing into the cooling air, Lukas felt as if he had escaped death itself. He did not know if he would return with the answer Garulf sought. He might, however, return for Esmond.

The forest was dark and dreary beneath them. The clearing round the stone house was soon lost in the shadows of trees. Ahead, he could see only the blank wall of the Crag. Low cloud hung round its upper reaches. The white wall showed grey in the twilight, grey like the cloud above.

He saw the path: a narrow, precipitous track running through many zigzags. There were caves, and the occasional rockfall. One major fall had been cleared only very recently. There was no sign of life.

At one point Astrella alighted on the path, and he looked at the tracks in the chalky dust. Horses, he thought, riders travelling lightly and swiftly.

Serethrun's plainsriders? It could well be. They had left Shelt rather than help him fight Javon. Were they instead going to form the advance guard, inadvertent or not, against whatever horrors Gawne had in store?

Together, they flew along the course of the path to the top of the cliff, through the barrier of cloud. It was a relief to leave the dark forest behind, out of sight beneath the clinging grey mist. The moors stretched out far into the distance, cast now into deep shadow by the setting sun.

Astrella put him down again, near the edge. There was something she wanted to show him. He saw the disturbed turf almost immediately. A grave.

Garulf's Mage, perhaps? He would have to make sure. Distastefully, he knelt down and began to dig away the loose earth with his knife.

The grave had been only recently dug and was not deep. The body, soon revealed, was almost untouched by worm or damp, but not quite. The smell of rotting flesh hit him like a blow. Breathing through his mouth, he pulled back the cloth which protected the face from soil. An old man: of slight build and sunken eyes, his arms folded peacefully across his chest. This could indeed be Garulf's Mage, although there was no sign of a spiral staff.

Lukas was about to replace the earth when a movement caught his strange night-vision. A spray of heather, released from the pressure of cloth and earth, stirred beneath the folded hands.

Gently, he moved the hands aside, and then sat back on his heels for a long moment.

A plaited pattern of heather, bent round and round into the

eternally vanishing form of a spiral. Worked with care and skill.

So, the gravedigger had recognised the old man as a Mage. Had he also stolen his staff? Was it now held in irresponsible, unknowing hands?

But even as his mind raced along these worrying paths, Lukas found himself wondering that such an unusual rite should take place this far north. He recognised the heather spiral as an ancient tribute to the Mage, given when the staff was lost, or passed on to a successor. An obscure practice, even amongst his own people. It was more than surprising to find it here.

Unless there was a Caver here, too. Someone else riding an Arrarat hawk, as Astrella had implied. Someone who might understand a little of all that was happening.

The Mage had been stabbed. It was not a natural death. Had the rider of an Arrarat hawk, the putative Caver, wise in the more esoteric by-ways of Mage-lore, committed murder?

No. He would not have left the plaited spiral of heather, if he had spilt the blood of a Mage.

A plaited spiral of greenery, laid on the body of a dead Mage, gives to that resting place power. Thoughtfully, Lukas replaced the cold hands over the springing heather, and drew the cloth over the body. Without haste he pushed earth back over the slight figure and then stood up, brushing the dirt from his hands.

Astrella was waiting for him, waiting for him to decide which way to go. Back to Garulf, to tell him of the death of his Mage and to rescue Esmond from that black forest? Or northwards, following the tracks of the riders, in a heedless, wild run into the waiting arms of some other dispossessed Mage?

Gawne and his actions were a matter of urgency. He could not afford to wait. In the morning, they would set off northwards.

Lukas settled for the night, close to Astrella, some distance from the disturbed grave. He fell asleep quickly, untroubled by dreams. But somewhere behind the quiet rhythm of his breathing, he heard the wailing of a bird.

Chains are chains, wherever you go.

Chapter Twenty-six
Blizzard

Astrella was flying high, so high that the empty moorland beneath could only be seen in washes of colour: grey-green, purple, russet, deep brown. . .

Ahead and to the East, the sky was full of heavy cloud, great banks of cold, grey moisture blotting out the sun every morning. Lukas felt a chill in the air, and high tension and wariness in Astrella.

They travelled for four days towards the cloud banks, passing over a bleak landscape of heather and bracken. Very occasionally the moorland was split apart by the fast-rushing courses of streams and rivers, running through deep, narrow ravines, nameless and turbulent.

The only man-made features were ancient stone bridges and the path of a rough track that linked the bridges, heading due north. Astrella followed this line and Lukas noted the small signs of camps that had been built along its length recently: the remains of cooking fires, the heather and bracken crushed and broken. The camps were often more than sixty miles apart. The riders were moving fast. He wondered if they always kept up such speed. Ahead, the banks of softly rolling cloud seemed to be tumbling to meet them. The chill in the air became more intense, the wind rushing past them, biting and acid-sharp.

Gawne rides on the back of the North wind, the madman had said. And at last they were racing through the wall of cloud, into the teeth of a blizzarding gale where the air was full of flying ice splinters that tore painful scratches through every inch of exposed flesh.

Astrella wheeled about and, in that moment's respite, out of the direct lash of the wind, Lukas pulled the hood of his cloak forward so that his face was almost totally concealed.

Astrella was flying with eyes nearly shut. The wide perspective he was used to sharing with her had narrowed down to a shaft of vision through a tunnel of white. She was being drawn down, through the cloud, to the drifts of tawny colour below. Colours that were rapidly being veiled. Snow was falling thickly, in gusting drifts, and Lukas could see nothing more than three feet ahead.

The ground beneath them suddenly rushed up to hit them. Astrella, pulling back and outwards with wide wings, so that they touched down lightly as feathers.

The cold clamped itself round them like a vice. It battered its way deep into the body, and in seconds his teeth were chattering, his hands shivering uncontrollably as he held the cloak fast.

Lukas slid to the ground, thinking hard. Why should it be colder on the ground than in the air? It felt as if the cold were emanating from the earth itself. There was something fierce in the waves of stress he was receiving from Astrella, something wild and aggressive. Her feathers were standing out, and it was not just an effort to trap warm air. She looked twice her normal size, savage with fury. Her eyes flashed with suspicion, gleaming through the snow, in a predatory stare that twisted the neck far around.

For a moment he stood beside her, his hand resting on the warmth of her shoulder, trying to make out shapes in the swirling snow-dance. The flakes seemed to congregate in whirls and eddies, to cling and then leap. There were people there. Surely those shapes were human? He heard shouting, and took half a step towards the sound, but in an instant it was cut off.

Something rushed at them, suddenly appearing from the blizzard.

'Don't touch me!' A ragged figure, grey with exhaustion, ice hanging from hair and beard, stumbled away from Lukas. The man's eyes were wide and stricken. 'Get out of here!'

'Wait!' But the man had disappeared back into the cloud of white beyond them, and the silence spread outwards like congealing blood.

But there was no scarlet, no gleam of colour, no leaping flash of violence. Another long moment of thick deadly silence, and although the snow continued to fall in those strange eddies he could no longer make out any suggestion of human shapes. His fingers were slow and clumsy with cold. Soon they would be numb. He sheathed his knife, and dug his hands into pockets. Fragments of snow and ice clung to his eyelashes. The exposed skin of his face was aching in the plummeting temperature.

Three horses emerged from the cloud to his left, galloping past him at a reckless rate, their riders crouched low. The racing hooves sent sprays of wet snow and slush flying.

Astrella lifted away into the air. She would try to get some kind of overview of the situation. He needed to know what was happening. Where were the riders going? Did they sense safety, somewhere? And from what were they running? Gawne?

Lukas stood still, conserving energy, trying to concentrate on the drifting snow around him. It was like no other snow-storm he had ever experienced. The snow was being driven into strange spirals by the wind, whirlwind shapes that danced in random sequences. As the flakes were drawn into each vortex they began to spin, twisting round until an opaque funnel formed.

Pulling his hood down low over his face, Lukas started to move towards one of the snow-spirals.

It was spinning with enormous speed over a hunched shape on the ground. The shape was already covered in white, but Lukas knew that it was – had been – human.

Warily, he circled the figure. The spiral was winding upwards from its breast. There was something predatory about it, as if it were feeding from the abandoned figure. Lukas considered running at the maelstrom, trying to push it out of the way, but knew it to be a foolish risk. He didn't know what this thing was, or the extent of its power. He was no Mage: brute force would be irrelevant against such a phenonemon.

He moved smoothly and soundlessly, allowing the snow to gather on his cloak. All at once the spiral detached itself from the hump on the ground, as if sated, and rose upwards into the air above Lukas. He watched it dissolve into the cloud above, and then turned to the shape at his feet.

He bent down and cleared the snow from the figure's face. A young woman, lying on her back. Her eyes were wide open, staring ahead with dreamy vagueness.

She was quite dead. But her hands were still locked in a position of agonised tension, the fingers splayed wide and curving at her breast.

Don't touch me! the fleeing man had said. Lukas wound a length of cloak around his hand, and pulled the clawed hands apart. They had been bent round a hole in the rough wool cloth of her shirt. The flesh beneath the ruined cloth was unbloodied, unbruised. . .but a grey flush of ice was spreading outwards from the point where the spiral had been anchored.

Unhesitating, he ripped the shirt aside exposing the taut body with its narrow waist and small breasts. He watched with revulsion as greyness ate into the skin, robbing it of softness and colour. It was like a cancer made of ice, moving with frightening speed, and in less than a minute even the distorted, rigid fingers were coloured grey.

The eyes blinked and looked at him. They were bright and gleaming. A faint smile curved grey lips. The hand, no longer clawed, reached out to touch his face.

With a muffled exclamation, Lukas sprang back from her, his knife ready. This was monstrous and unnatural. He saw the predatory, avid greed in her eyes and knew he had to get away.

Which way? A frantic, non-verbal message to Astrella circling above the snow-storm. She showed him nothing but swirling snow, winds hurling in from north and east – and a centre of coldness that was the focus for the flying ice and spinning spirals: Gawne.

The creature rising up from the snow ahead was coming towards him, fingers reaching for his flesh. A cloud of snow clung round her shoulders, mixing with her hair, drawing it out into waves behind her. Lukas ran. He followed the direction of the riders and the running man, away from the cold centre of the blizzard.

More riders passed him, thundering through the snow. Some horses were already doubly laden, but one slowed beside him. An arm reached out.

Lukas grabbed for it, swinging up behind the man on the big black mare. Only to find he knew the horse, recognised her rider.

'Serethrun! Where are we going?'

The wind almost drowned his words, but the man in front twisted round in the saddle momentarily. Lukas saw wide surprise in the dark brown eyes. And something else, a deep fury.

'What the bloody hell are *you* doing here?'

'Trying to get warm. You?'

'Oh, fuck it!' Serethrun said nothing more, hunched over the glossy, straining black neck of his mare.

Ahead of them the other riders had halted. Their horses were wheeling about, stamping in panic, blowing hot steam into the freezing air. The riders were shouting at each other, fear and disbelief in their voices.

Lukas saw what had dismayed them. Astrella. Almost unfamiliar in the covering of white, she stood squarely in front of them, blocking their path. The riders were dodging, trying to pass her, but she was swifter than they. In a concerted effort, just as Lukas shouted, 'No! There must be danger ahead! She will not hurt us!' the riders divided, just passing on either side of the snapping, slashing hawk. Alone she could not hold back this dual action.

A rush in the air, the sound of heavy wings, and another Arrarat swooped down to join Astrella. The hawks separated, blocking the way, and at last the riders found themselves forced to listen to the words shouted by the stranger sitting behind Serethrun Maryn.

'We cannot go that way. The hawks are warning us!'

'Where else?' At last one of the riders swung round to face him, eyes narrowed against the blizzard. He was looking past Lukas and Serethrun to something approaching from the storm.

A line of grey figures was moving through the snow towards them, moving with inexorable steadiness. And from the shoulders of these ice warriors spread a mantle of snow, rippling like a wave.

A flood of knowledge reached Lukas from Astrella, a blinding light in his mind, pulling him in one direction only.

'West!' he shouted, pointing obliquely along the line of ice warriors. 'Serethrun, trust me! There's a way through—'

Without a word, Serethrun pulled his horse around and galloped off along the direction Lukas had indicated. Lukas did not look back to see if the others were following; they had no choice. He heard the thunder of their horses' hooves and knew he was right.

Screams from Astrella and the other hawk behind them, made Lukas glance round. There was a wild flutter of wings behind them, stirring up the snow into a cloud of white. The hawks were creating a smokescreen between the riders and the ice warriors.

To their left, Lukas saw the ground suddenly drop away into one of the deep ravines. It was too wide for the horses to jump. Their only hope was to find some kind of a bridge, and that very soon. For although the snow cloud whipped up by the two hawks had slightly deflected the ice warriors, it had been only a temporary diversion.

For half a mile they raced alongside the ravine, hoping to leave the ice warriors far behind. When Lukas snatched another glance over his shoulder, he saw a strangely familiar outline, someone he recognised from another life, Haddon Derray on horseback just behind him. And on his lap, swaddled in blankets was a baby. . . . For a moment, Lukas's blank astonishment overrode his anxiety, but at the same time he had seen that their pursuers were far too close.

Lukas cursed. They were moving smoothly and swiftly over the snow, as if lifted by the wind, propelled by clouding ice. Ice that hung around their shoulders, dribbled from their fingertips.

A bridge, narrow and crumbling, lay across the ravine. And about halfway across it, the grip of the snow ceased. Instead of ice they saw stone, set in regular patterns, discoloured by moss and lichen. Without hesitation, the riders thundered across.

Serethrun's horse, heavily laden, was the last one over. Only then, did everyone halt to look back at the bridge. Although its sides were crumbling, the paving uneven and stained, it was clearly secure enough to hold for some time.

'We shall have to destroy it.' A woman, her clothes threaded through with silver ribbons, spoke with calm authority.

A man at her side, tall, with long dark hair, a wide-brimmed hat. 'But the others! Brianne—'

'Brianne is dead. Something. . .is using her body, it is not she.' Another woman with short-cropped hair, fierce eyes. Her voice was colder than snow. She stared into the freezing cloud. It was moving very swiftly towards them. 'There won't be time. . .'

'Fire.' Lukas looked from Serethrun to the other riders. He could no longer see Haddon in the milling crowd. And no one seemed to recognise him. 'Have you the means of making fire? It might hold them off while we break down the bridge.'

There was bracken beneath the light covering of snow, dried fronds that would burn easily. Quickly the riders dismounted. Some set about gathering up the fuel, ranging out over the moor, while others began to dislodge the heaped stones at the end of the bridge. They all ignored the stranger in their midst. Lukas put Haddon out of his mind and concentrated on finding firewood. Sheafs of rust-coloured ferns were passed along a chain of willing hands towards the bridge.

Several of the riders carried tinder-boxes. All the time, the older woman with the silver ribbons watched the approach of the snow cloud billowing over the other side of the ravine.

She was their leader, Lukas thought. That air of authority, that calmness of purpose. He saw her consider the situation and knew what she must be thinking. Too soon and the fire would exhaust itself before the ice warriors reached it.

The snow cloud drifted towards them, clearing in patches so that they could see the grey faces and glittering eyes on the other side of the chasm. Among them were friends and relatives. . . . A disturbed

murmuring ran through the riders, names muttered: a few stepped
forward.

The Archon held up her hand, and at once everyone was quiet.
Then came a moment of distilled concentration as she watched, and
waited until the first of the warriors was halfway across the bridge.

'Now,' she said. Simultaneously, four riders bent down and ignited
the heap of bracken. It flared up at once, a clear line of flame running
across the bridge. Grey smoke blotted out the gathering snow cloud.

The oncoming faces drifted closer, seemingly unaware of the heat or
the acrid smell. But as they reached the flame, each ice warrior started
to sag, to crumple. The front line had fallen to their knees, men and
women alike. Some were dressed in the same cloaks and breeches as
the riders, others wore the braided jackets and long caps of the
reindeer clans.

A low groan ran through the watching riders. As the warriors sank
to their knees, they looked up through the smoke with cold ice-eyes.
Memories of awareness? Shadows of personality? Then they pitched
forward, face down in the snow.

'They are not dead! They are our friends, our families!' The man
with the long dark hair was pushing past those working at the end of
the bridge, towards the burning barrier of bracken. Those labouring
looked up, dismayed.

'No! Morrelow—' The small woman with the cropped hair dug her
heels viciously into her horse's flanks and followed. She leaned down
to him, clutching his shoulder. 'There's nothing you can do! She's
dead!'

'We can try!' He dragged himself free and, as she tried to reclaim
her grasp, slashed at her arm with his dagger.

A smothered exclamation from her, bright blood springing to stain
the wool of her jacket. He ran free from her, curving his cloak round
to protect his face, and leapt straight over the narrow line of fire.

It had almost died down. Lukas saw him on the other side,
wreathed by whirling eddies of snow. Morrelow was turning from one
ice warrior to the next, searching every face. None of them touched
him. Eventually he halted, bewildered, looking back through the
smoke and snow to the riders. Lukas saw incomprehension in his face.

The cloud of snow that trailed around the fallen warriors parted. A
tall figure stood there, taller than the dark-haired man. A figure with
shoulders high-hunched, hands clasped together.

'Do you search for someone?'

To most of the riders on the other side of the bridge the voice was
audible, yet unfamiliar. But Serethrun Maryn exclaimed, suddenly
and violently, his hand drifting instinctively to his bow.

And Lukas Marling recalled a figure in drifting grey silk, courting a
dragon, spirals, ambition and pride all woven together. He recalled all
these things and one more. He remembered that he was the Earl of
Shelt, pledged to protect the city from attack. And this was Gawne,

First Sea Lord, coming to regain his seat of power. Over the bridge, above the dying crackle of the flames, he saw a farce enacted.

A woman stepped forward out of the ranks of the warriors. She was tall, her hair short and curling. Her eyes shone with ice, but at one strange flicker from the hands of the hunched Mage in the centre of the snow, the crystals seemed to drop away.

She staggered momentarily. And then lifted her hands to her head as if dizzy. Morrelow did not hang back, he caught her in his arms.

Ice did not spread from woman to man. She was warm to the touch. Her skin was flushed with relief, her eyes smiling at him.

The old man watching them almost laughed. He looked across the bridge towards the riders.

'Why do you run from me? I mean you no harm. Come and join your friends and families. There is no need to fear.'

There was a murmur through the riders and some dismounted, beginning to move forwards.

And all at once Lukas saw Haddon Derray again, blocking the way over the bridge, the baby still held in the curve of his left arm, a sword in his right hand.

Other swords were drawn, other weapons raised.

'If we value our lives, we must get away from here!' Serethrun was shouting at the riders.

'This is evil,' said Lukas softly. The woman with the beribboned cloak looked from him to Serethrun.

And the riders stopped their movement towards the bridge: uncertain, cautious. As they hesitated there, with a roar and a crash the bridge suddenly collapsed, tumbling amid an avalanche of snow into the depths below.

It would give them a little time. Lara glanced around her. 'Ride!' she shouted. 'South. Fast!'

They had sworn to follow her. They owed her ultimate loyalty, obedience without question in moments of crisis. And so the plainsriders, and the strangers who had joined them, turned away from the bridge. Away from their friends and families trapped within the snowstorm of Gawne's making, and began the long trek to the South.

Chapter Twenty-seven
Returning

High summer. He knew he would have to return.

Phinian Blythe had drifted through spring watching the orchards revive. He had seen the wildlife of the island flourish, the flowers and shrubs blossom with petals, with leaves and sweet scents. Rain still fell each night. The canals ran once more, and dragonflies hovered over their dark, gently shifting surfaces.

He put aside the knowledge of Lefevre's reincarnation. He did not know what he should do, or if there was anything at all he *could* do. He lived in tranquillity, waiting for the way to become clear.

As the days became hotter, he found himself spending more time indoors. He had kept the shutters closed, and the house had been designed to keep out the sun. Outside, it burned with unabated vigour. He found a battered straw hat and wore it whenever he went out in daylight, although he no longer found the brightness threatening. He remembered a figure of fire, smiling at him over an abyss of ashes. . .

One day, searching upstairs for something to read, he found himself passing yet again the door to his mother's bedroom. He had not entered it since arriving on Massiq. Similarly, he had not opened the door of his sister's room. There was no need, he thought.

He stood in the wide upstairs corridor and gazed unseeingly at the dusty watercolours on the wall. Was he deliberately ignoring the claim of his family? For he could not deny that there was such a claim. They had mourned for him, and he had repaid them with the ambivalent legacy of old age and death. What could he say to them? How could he explain?

He fretted for a couple of days, and then made a decision. Watching the path of the sun, he estimated that it was almost midsummer. Unless matters on Peraldon had changed beyond all recognition, the summer festival would soon be under way, a month of carnival celebrations and religious ceremony.

He could mingle in the crowds and catch up on the gossip. With luck, no one would recognise him. He could find out how his family was.

He packed food and water and a change of clothes. Without regret he chose from the house a few small, valuable ornaments to sell. He would need money to exist in Peraldon, especially at carnival-time. He took a sailing dinghy and set out eastwards for the calm lagoon.

Like Lefevre, he was going home.

He joined a stream of people approaching the city from the South-west. It was a mixed crowd: pilgrims, revellers, the simply curious and those interested in the commercial aspects of the festival. In his dark clothes and sombre demeanour, Blythe thought he would not be obtrusive among the solemn religious figures. In fact, he felt at best uncomfortable and at worst, hypocritical.

He heard their voices joined in song, their fervent prayers. God is good. God is great. With love He rules our days, in justice He weighs our sins. All honour and tribute to the Lord of the Sun, for He maintains the order of life.

Impossible to accept without irony. He shared their belief in the existence of Lycias, unavoidably, but it went against the grain even to pretend allegiance.

With some relief he dropped back into the crowd, and found himself walking alone. He overheard snatches of conversation, watched the kaleidoscopic play of human relationships: the laughs, irritations, smiles. The way people touched and looked, or didn't look, at each other. He took no part.

There were hawkers all along the roadside, shouting out goods and services. Fruit, bread and sticky, honey-coated cakes, barrels of water and wine at exorbitant prices. The spicy smell of roast meat hung over the jostling crowds. Wayside barbecues were strictly illegal, as there was still considerable danger of fire, but the Warden's guardsmen on their elegant horses were few and far between. There were flies everywhere.

Young men and women, wearing very little besides their heavy make-up and masks, lounged outside shrouded tents. Some seemed no more than children, but Blythe knew them to be old. As old as he was, with countless years lost in the limbo that had been the Stasis. He knew that under the make-up and masks their eyes would be cynical.

Trapped in beautiful, unaging bodies, they had seen it all. Now their time would be running short: there was a kind of desperation in the way they moved and the knowledge that if they did not make enough, now, soon, it would all be too late. In the end their bodies would betray them. And then who would buy?

He turned away from them, his thoughts in chaos.

To what had he led them? Death, yes, he had almost come to terms with that. With wisdom, death might be regarded as a friend, a release from the muddle and mess of life. The inevitable and natural conclusion of lives lived to the full. Lives filled with children and music, passion, change and growth.

Under the Stasis, evil had proliferated. Without the constraint of death, people had recklessly pursued selfish desires. They had no children to look after: there was nothing to teach them that someone else could be more important. Cynical eyes showed as much.

Amongst the various religious groups along the trail he had noticed a number of fanatics. The women were shrouded in grey and strictly segregated, the men dressed in sackcloth, or black, as he was. They included flagellants and other extremists. He saw one man bind his thighs with thorns, so that every step would hurt. He saw another group walk with their eyes downcast, denying the appearance of the world around them. At every junction, every place where people paused, these men shouted the scriptures, promising all the fires of Hell for those who sinned, for those who gave way to the pleasures of the flesh.

There seemed to be little tolerance or happiness in any of it. How could it be otherwise? For so long, there had been no children to teach them how to be flexible, no death to show them what their priorities should be.

There would be a hiatus before the effects of the new life were felt. Already he saw women, heavy with pregnancy, others carrying babies. He heard children crying at night, as he lay wrapped in his cloak by the wayside. The oldest of them was not yet walking. There was a long way to go before life returned to any kind of normality.

Snatches of conversation interrupted Blythe's thoughts.

'. . .boat race, build your own, the first prize is a thousand solons!'

'. . .sister's house. She's pregnant. . .'

'. . .a booth against the walls. . .'

'Easy pickings in Peraldon. They're all soft there, the buggers. Peraldon didn't roast, oh no. Not the Lord's own city. A bit of sun-burn, some water rationing. . .*they* were all right.'

'That cake, there—'

'Different orders of love, the God—'

'. . .open day at the College, spiral games.'

'. . .and the Emperor's wedding.' For a moment Blythe almost stopped the elderly couple to ask them, *what* wedding, who will the bride be? He thought better of it. Such a degree of ignorance would not be merely unlikely, it would cause suspicion. He did not want to be noticed.

He walked on.

Towards evening he bought himself some food from one of the stalls and sat down a little way from the main drift of people to eat it.

He had found a slight rise, overlooking the bright, noisy stream of people approaching Peraldon. It was a relief to be away from all the pressure of the crowd. He could hear the clamour of voices raised in prayer a short distance away, and the conflicting scents of food and sweat reached him, but for the moment he was free of the northwards drift.

The road wound across the plain of Peraldon towards the South gate. It ran roughly parallel to the River Perald, at a distance of about quarter of a mile. He could see the dark line of cypresses which bordered the river. He was glad they had survived. Nothing in the countryside seemed to have changed. It was almost as if the drought of Lycias's revenge had passed Peraldon by. Of course, no one in Peraldon had wanted the Stasis to end. There had been no reason to punish them severely.

The carnival would follow its usual course. Every home in Peraldon would open its doors (at a price) and let rooms for revellers and righteous alike. For seven days the gates would be open to all comers. Then they would close, for Peraldon would be full to saturation, and only accredited travellers would be allowed to pass.

It would be chaotic and impossible and full of incident. He was not sure whether he was looking forward to it or not. He was glad to have some time on his own.

Then, he heard voices just behind him.

'I don't *like* leaving you here, of course I don't. I do not do this for amusement.' An elderly man, dressed in a dusty black robe which proclaimed his religious affiliations, was speaking coldly to the woman at his side. For Blythe, the voice brought with it a flood of memories, an echo of the past in no uncertain terms. He looked up, disconcerted beyond reason.

Blythe could not hear the words the woman spoke in reply, but he saw her lay a hand on the man's arm. She was swathed in coarse black linen, her face hidden by a heavy veil. He saw her hand tremble against his sleeve, and thought that she was frightened either of the man, or for him. There would probably be a row.

'Oh no. Not like that. . .' He was much taller than she, towering over her. 'You'll have to wait here. There's no other way.'

The man whose voice he knew was a priest. Blythe remembered him well. Those deep-set eyes and narrow nose. He was a Peraldonian Priest of the Sun, a man of power and influence. Dion Gillet, that was his name.

His dark hair had been shorn, and his black robes were dusty and patched. A sun-medallion hung round his neck, but all the other trappings of authority were absent.

This could not be chance, Blythe thought. Not in all these crowds, within all this space of time. With regret he saw all his dreams of peaceful seclusion fading away. So much for a discreet, unmarked return to his city. . .unless he could get out of the way before he was noticed.

Quietly he stood up, but the man heard the movement and immediately swung round to face him.

A long, disturbing silence as they looked at each other.

'I've seen you before,' Gillet said slowly. 'In the Watch, aren't you?'

He had raised his right hand in a formal salute that Blythe recognised as the mark of the Sun. The middle finger curled down, the others extended. With relief, he realised that this man did not know his name.

It would have been amazing if he had. Blythe had been only one of hundreds of ranking officers in the Watch. Dion Gillet had presided over public ceremonies throughout Peraldon, the centre of all attention, the focus of all eyes. He had often deputised for Lefevre within the Temple.

He was assuming that Blythe was a fellow disciple. Black clothes proclaim allegiance all too clearly, thought Blythe and remembered something else. Gillet had left Peraldon to go into retreat: to pursue the way of contemplation and meditation.

Gillet's eyes under the heavy brow shone curious, greeny-yellow, like a cat's. His skin was pale and waxy, his hair cropped so short that he seemed naked and defenceless under the hot sun. But there was nothing weak about this man: he might have chosen paths away from obvious power since leaving Peraldon, but Blythe recognised a tight, reined-in energy, something held apart, under wraps. . .

Gillet was speaking. 'I welcome your advent, sir, surely a gift of the God! I would ask of you a kindness, trusting in your vows as a brother in God, in the allegiances of the past. My name is Dion Gillet, you may know it. . .I would entrust to you the honour of my ward.'

His words were courteous, but Blythe knew that in revealing his name Gillet was also stating his authority. This was a man accustomed to obedience from others. 'I would be grateful if you would consent to bear Katriana company for a short time. She is to wait here. There is something I have to do.'

And before Blythe could reply, denying any religious affiliation, the man who once held such high position in Peraldon had vanished down the hill into the winding stream of people, just like any other insignificant, unmarked traveller.

Blythe looked at the woman. She was facing down the hill after her guardian, very still, quite hidden beneath the layers of cloth.

He stood up. 'It's hot, isn't it?' he said neutrally. 'Have you come far?'

For a moment he thought she was going to ignore him, but then she turned and looked at him.

At least that was what he assumed she was doing. There was no way of telling. Even her eyes were concealed behind cloth. A dense mesh covered her entire face. He felt a moment's sympathy. It had to be desperately uncomfortable.

He heard her say distantly, 'There is no reason for you to stay. I'm not a child.' Her voice was clear, every syllable carefully enunciated.

'No, indeed. But it might not be wise to leave a woman unattended here.'

'But I don't know who you are. What recommendation is it to be an
ex-member of the Warden's Watch?' She spoke sharply. 'Your
presence is not required.' She turned away from him decisively, and
settled herself a little way off further along the bank.

Blythe remained where he was. He could easily ensure that no one
bothered her without forcing his company on her.

He took the food from his rucksack, and began to unwrap it. The
rustling paper disturbed the woman. He was aware of her attention,
watching his every movement. He looked up.

She began to speak. Her words were crisp, almost clipped, quite
unmuffled by the veil. 'There's no need for you to wait here. My
guardian will be back soon, and I am quite capable of looking after
myself.'

The veil gave the lie to her words. Veiled women, on the whole,
were not renowned for their independence. And there was something in her tone. She didn't want him to go now. Was she frightened of something, or merely inquisitive? Certainly she seemed to
be on edge, uneasy. She had turned back towards the plain
again. Was she searching for the man who called himself her
guardian?

Blythe wanted to see what she looked like. It was more than simple
curiosity. There was a contradiction in her demeanour. Her dress
proclaimed the protected, passive woman, exempt from action or
decision. And yet her voice was cool, almost contemptuous. The
precision of her speech made him wonder if this were her
natural tongue. There was no shyness or reticence in her words, no
meekness or even nervousness. And her voice was all he had to go on:
the veil and shapeless black robes hid everything else. He didn't
know whether she was fat or thin, her hair brown or fair, because all
he had seen of her was one hand laid trembling, on Dion Gillet's
sleeve.

'But I haven't finished eating yet,' he said easily. 'Are you
hungry?'

'No. I don't want your food.' There was an edge of desperation to
her words. He broke a bread roll in two and stood up. He held the
larger part out to her.

'Sorry about the fingers,' he said. 'I can't eat all this.'

There was no further pretence. She took the bread without
speaking and turned away from him, lifting the veil. Again he saw the
white skin, the fine bones of her hand, but nothing more. She was
ravenous. He watched the passing crowds, and when she finished gave
her the other half.

'When did you last eat?'

'What's it to you?' she said. The veil was securely back in place.
'Still, that was generous. My thanks.' It could hardly be more
grudging.

He decided to ignore the hostility in her voice. Who was this woman, how did she come to be connected with Dion Gillet?

'Are you thirsty? I've got some wine here, or water if you'd prefer it.'

In silence she accepted the water, turning away to drink it.

And then she began to talk. Perhaps she felt she owed him something, perhaps she did want company after all. 'The last of our food was finished two days ago. We were robbed.'

'Oh dear. And far from home?'

'Too far.' She paused. 'It was my dowry. All the money I have in the world.'

'Are you not visiting for the festival, then?'

'No. Our purpose lies beyond festivals. For some, Peraldon is the land of opportunity, where all is possible and the streets are paved with gold.' Cynicism in her voice, and some ambivalence. 'Not for us.'

'How did you meet Dion Gillet. . .?'

Her voice was carefully neutral. 'My dear guardian. I owe my life to Dion Gillet. Without him, I would be nothing, I would have nothing.'

'What happened? How did you meet him?' The contradictions were deepening. A degree of detachment, almost contempt underlay her words. He began to wonder if she were involved in some kind of charade.

The veil gave no clues. 'My parents died in the plague. Father Gillet was living in seclusion in the desert just beyond our farm. As soon as the disease struck, he came to help us, and did what he could with no regard for his own safety. My parents made a will, they knew the risks, they trusted the Father.' She shrugged. 'He is a man of God. He saved my life and watched over my recovery. Dion Gillet has looked after me ever since.'

'Why are you coming to the city?'

'He's brought me to find a suitable marriage-partner.'

'Have you no other family?'

'No. Our farm was very remote. You're very curious.'

'I knew Gillet long ago. When he lived here. He was a man of considerable power then.'

'He is a man of considerable holiness now.' Again, her words were entirely neutral. They were playing a polite game. Her hands were elegant, smooth-skinned, not at all those of a simple farm-girl. Her speech was educated and fluent. Blythe did not believe in the existence of a farm, remote or otherwise. This was no country girl coming to the big city to find a husband.

'My name is. . .Tourneour,' he said. Lies proliferate, he thought. 'Phinian Tourneour.'

'Why did you leave Peraldon?' she asked.

'I travelled during the Stasis. I had relatives in the South, and was delayed there.'

'My name is Katriana Lessure,' she said. He thought, if she's ever going to lift that veil, now is the time. She did not move.

He was intrigued against all his better judgement. He thought, there are lies and contradictions here and Dion Gillet is not someone to underestimate in any circumstances. This is all playing with fire, almost certain to lead to trouble.

On the other hand, he did not think that he could in all conscience leave Katriana on her own amongst this carnival crowd. He would have to stay, and find out what he could.

After only a little prompting, Katriana told him more about the farm she had left behind. Her story was consistent, plausible and well-constructed. Blythe could detect no flaw in any of it. Nonetheless it confirmed his suspicions that this was a smokescreen, an elaborate diversion. A *lie*.

She was too confident, her speech too precise. Too sophisticated. She would have been married off long ago in the peasant society she described.

Still, it was pleasant enough to listen to a woman talk. For a while he put aside the disconcerting contradictions, and her involvement with Dion Gillet. As the shadows lengthened and everyone began to settle for the night, he found himself relaxing. She made no attempt to question him further. It was refreshing.

And although she was still aloof, she revealed a certain arrogance. She dismissed the loss of her dowry to thieves as if it didn't matter. Trivial. She would survive, she and Father Gillet. Nothing would harm them now, they'd come so far. . .

As darkness fell, Gillet's absence became something of a problem.

'When do you think your guardian will be back?' Blythe said eventually. 'Will he expect you to wait here all night?'

She tilted her head to look at the rising moon. 'Yes. But you needn't stay. Everyone's settling down now, there won't be any trouble, I'm sure.'

'No, probably there won't be, but that's not the point. Where is he? Does he often disappear like this?'

'Every night.' A pause.

'Well, why? Tell me about Gillet. What does he plan to do in Peraldon anyway? Surely he's not going there purely for your sake?'

'He. . .he has certain connections in Peraldon. He received letters. He's needed there.'

'*What* connections, exactly? Who wrote to him?'

'He is learned in the Scriptures, passionate in the service of God. There is need for someone wise in the ways of the Lord in Peraldon now. There's a feeling that – standards – are slipping. Dion Gillet has acquired many skills, he will be invaluable in the Temple.'

'What skills?'

'Katriana,' A quiet voice out of the dark behind them. Dion stepped forward, holding something in his cupped hands. 'I have retrieved your dowry.' He opened his hands, and a shower of gold coins and glittering jewels tumbled into her lap.

She was looking up at him, unmoving. The expression in her voice was neither relief nor gratitude.

'Oh, dear God, what have you done now?'

Chapter Twenty-eight
Dion Gillet

The priest turned to Blythe, ignoring Katriana's extraordinary words. 'My thanks, sir, for keeping my ward company. It was most kind of you.'

The dismissal could not have been clearer.

Katriana stood up, ignoring the bright clutter on her skirt. It fell into the dust. 'In the Lord's name, where did you get these?'

'From the thieves, of course. They were happy to return them.'

She lifted her hand to her masked face, the fingers wavering and unsure. '*Happy?* And what did you do to *them?*'

'Katriana.' His voice was very quiet, but she immediately stepped away from him, drawing herself up. Was she bracing herself? Gillet looked back to Blythe. His face was colourless in the frail moonlight, the bones of the skull plain beneath his shorn hair and pale skin. 'I believe we need trouble you no longer, sir.'

He bent down and extracted a small green stone from the dust. He held it out to Blythe. 'Please accept our good wishes for the midsummer celebrations.'

'It was a pleasure.' Blythe slightly inclined his head, ignoring the proffered jewel. He turned to Katriana. Her hands were composed now, calmly folded in front of her. The moment's uncertainty had vanished. He knew, without any shadow of a doubt, that she could look after herself.

Besides, he felt a huge disinclination to stay around. This was a nest of vipers. He said neutrally, 'Perhaps we will meet in the city.'

'Perhaps. . .' Katriana did not even look at him. She was still focused on her guardian. And as Blythe watched, Gillet pointed silently to the jewels in the dust. Without a word, she began to gather them up, her white hands precise and delicate.

Blythe bent down for his rucksack. As he walked down the hill back

to the road, he heard nothing further from them. Dion Gillet and
Katriana Lessure were entirely lost in silence.

Later that night he heard wailing, the desperate keening of the
bereaved. Two voices, high and bitter sopranos, cut through the
murmur of the resting crowds. A horse thundered down the road
towards the sound, and he knew that one of the Warden's men would
be investigating.

In such a mixed bag of people, so excitable, so eager, it was not
surprising that there should be accidents and injury.

Death, however, was unusual.

There were flickering torches everywhere, illuminating the tents
and wagons of the wealthy, the reclining forms of those travelling
light.

Blythe could just see the man in silver-grey uniform guiding his
horse through the resting masses. The guard stopped at last, and
dismounted. A crowd was beginning to gather, drawn by the sound.

He saw the guard's horse stamping, whisking its tail, eyes rolling. It
needed reassurance. There had to be something very wrong: a horse of
the Warden's watch was trained not to panic.

The chances of being recognised were remote, but Blythe did not
want to attract attention. At the fringes of the crowd he hung back,
moving round until he found passage through to the tethered horse.

He saw a small, shabby tent, its flap hanging open. The interior was
in darkness. Two hunched female shapes were crouched on the
ground outside the tent. Thin hands tore at hair, rocking. Howling.

He placed his hand on the horse's neck. The creature had been
unsettled by the wailing women, and by something else, something
almost visible in the unsteady torchlight. The crowd felt it, too, a
scent in the air, a vibration of power. He heard a voice shout,
'Mage-power! God protect us, Mage-power!'

It was taken up by others; a ripple of mixed terror and excitement.

The Warden's guard squatted down by the two crouched figures on
the ground. Blythe heard him speak calmly and reasonably, but the
noise went on and the figures rocked back and forth in distress.

The guard straightened up. In the torchlight Blythe saw the face of
a stranger, a hard-faced man with narrow lips and tight-curled hair.
The guard pushed aside the flap to the tent and went inside.

There was a long pause. The murmuring of the crowd died away,
but still the women wailed. No one else tried to comfort them, almost
as if their despair might be contagious.

When the guard came out, his face was ashen. He pushed swiftly
through the crowd to where Blythe stood by the horse. A quick glance
at him, weighing, estimating – a split-second decision.

'Have you a weapon? Can you fight?' He saw the knife in Blythe's
belt. 'Wait here, will you? Don't let anyone in that tent.'

The guard threw himself up on to the horse and dug his heels in. The horse surged through the crowd, and people were pushing each other in their haste to get out of the way.

Blythe moved to stand between the moaning women at the tent's opening. He drew his knife, but the crowd showed no inclination to approach. Others had joined them, drawn by the sound of wailing. The torchlight flared over pale and anxious faces. Blythe glanced over his shoulder into the dark tent.

He saw two faces twisted up towards him, grimacing in the difficult light. They were frozen, locked together in death, the eyes squeezed tight shut in a terrible final spasm.

He faced out into the crowd, no longer caring that he was still on public display, that soon the guard would return with reinforcements, that one of the reinforcements would quite possibly recognise him and reveal to the world that Phinian Blythe was not dead after all.

None of these things mattered, compared with what he had seen in the tent.

Each man's right fist had been buried to the wrist in the gut of the other. He could not imagine what force had compelled such an attack, what might have driven the two men together in such an obscene embrace. Blood had splattered widely over the sides of the tent.

Mage-power. The words continued to flare around the crowd, and Blythe saw some fall to their knees, others crying and moaning.

He looked down to the two terrified women on the ground. Although their mouths were distorted with grief and fear, and tears stained every plane of their faces, he saw that they were both cheaply made-up, dressed in gaudy, skimpy clothes. Glittering jewels hung round their necks and wrists. Without much hesitation, he labelled them as thieves' accomplices.

He was breathing hard. He would give even money that the two men in the tent were the thieves who had robbed Katriana and her guardian.

The priest with the unusual skills, an unusual companion: Dion Gillet, a man capable of standing in for Lefevre himself. Invited back to Peraldon. Going home.

Blythe found lodgings close to the docks. It was not a fashionable area, jammed tight with the more penurious visitors to the festival. He hoped to avoid old friends there. No one had recognised him so far, not even the Warden's men who had come to investigate the murders.

He rented the attic of a crowded tenement, sharing a corridor with two young men who intended to make their fortunes by performing the parables of the Sun on street corners. They were naïve, and spent much time in front of the cracked mirrors they had brought with them, refining and adjusting their costume. Poseurs, he thought, amused. But they were harmless and happy to share their wine with him, their jokes and stories.

The other occupants of the tenement included an old man whose mission was to flood the streets with tracts that proclaimed the celibacy of the Lord. He returned to his room each day fired with enthusiasm. No one took him seriously.

A woman who sold herbal remedies soured the third floor with her concoctions, and an elderly man seemed to have an inexhaustible supply of strong liquor which he guarded jealously from everyone else. Blythe watched him, clutching the stone jars fast to his thin chest, taking several a day up to his fifth-floor room. But he never seemed drunk, and no one saw him taking the empties away. . .

There was a young boy with a fine clear soprano voice and his elder brother who accompanied him on the lyre. They at least were professionals, and Blythe estimated that they would not stay for long among the losers and eccentrics.

On the ground floor lived a poet. Blythe knew him only by repute, for his door was always firmly locked. 'He's a good sort,' said the lyre-player, 'but depressive. . .'

'He's degenerate fool,' said the man with the pamphlets. 'Drinks too much.'

Blythe shrugged, and passed by the locked door.

Katriana and Dion Gillet, he assumed, would be more centrally based. Gillet would want to be close to the Temple. It would not be fitting for a man of God to be lodging amongst the gaudy and unwashed. He had no desire to meet them again, to involve himself in what he knew would be dangerous and distasteful affairs.

He wanted nothing to do with Dion Gillet. It was not simply cowardice. Blythe had no doubt at all that the Priests of Peraldon would be more than capable of assessing the value of such dubious skills. They would know how to evaluate Gillet, were properly equipped to do so.

For all he knew, Lefevre/Weard would be in control already. Gillet's exotic talents might be of interest to the Great Mage, but that was doubtful. He would have other things on his mind: regaining his position, acquiring power. Ordering the worship of the Sun God.

Running the Emperor.

Phinian Blythe supposed that, sooner or later, he might have to play a part in that volatile situation. It was not, however, his first priority. What he needed to do now was to find out how his family was: how his mother was managing, if his sisters had married. If they were all right, happy and well.

No one had recognised him. He had grown a beard on Massiq, allowing his hair to fall untidily to his shoulders. He still wore a battered straw-hat. But he had exchanged the black clothes for jeans and shirts, just like any other impoverished visitor. He was no longer interested in appearing immaculate. Blythe had come a long way since the days when vanity had mattered.

He walked through the familiar streets and squares of his youth and no one gave him a second glance.

Strangers lived in the house on the quayside he and Karis had shared. Late one morning, from further along the street, he watched an elderly couple emerge from a comfortable carriage. A liveried servant opened the door for them. He caught a glimpse of the chequered marble floor, and it mattered to him not at all.

Houses were not homes, possessions carried no significance. The elderly couple looked content and unflustered. The man held his wife's hand as she descended from the carriage, and retained it as they entered the house. He hoped they were happy there. He wished them well.

His memories of Karis were calm now. The Shadows had blunted the sharp edge of his grief. When he saw her face, in dreams and memories, she was smiling and loving. The Shadows had left no stain.

He felt no regret, no anger or sorrow. The past was gone, and he was free.

Sometimes on these long walks through the city, he watched women. He saw them looking at shop windows, busy and preoccupied. Working girls carried washing and groceries, or ran errands. Others sat at cafés, laughed with their men, talked confidentially to each other. They walked their dogs, and pretty voiles and silks stirred with their movements. Their wide, frivolous hats gave protection against the sun.

He saw street-walkers, hands on hips, glossy hair braided with ribbons and jewels. Their long, slow stares passed over him. He was too poor and shabby to be of interest. He wondered if light hands would ever again run over his skin, soft lips press to his mouth.

He thought that probably he had no love left to give another woman. And he certainly had nothing else to offer.

Every day the posters were changed. They gave an approximate guide to each day's events. Parades, displays, feasts, plays, concerts, sporting fixtures. The lists were frequently inaccurate, for there were always last-minute cancellations and changes of programme, and the posters failed to make any mention at all of the chaotic bustle that actually dominated the life of the city.

No one could predict the impromptu gatherings and parties that overspilled on to the streets. Or the numbers of enterprising musicians busking at every corner; the pavement artists underfoot; the jugglers, fire-eaters and fortune-tellers performing on every spare patch of ground.

The only events described with any accuracy on the poster were listed at the top. There, each day's main religious ceremonies were printed in impressive gold script.

The ceremonies always took place at noon, either in the main, glass-roofed Temple to Lycias close to the east gate, or at the mirrored bowl in the centre of Solkest.

Phinian Blythe would not be attending the rites of the Sun Lord. He watched with disillusion the crowds pressing towards the Temple, and then felt his attention caught. There was something unusual in the way they moved, in the way they dressed.

An air of freedom. At last he realised what it was. The women's heads were uncovered, their hair tumbling loose. There was a new fashion that summer, and every layer of clothing was slit, the skirts to the hip, shirts and blouses slashed to the waist.

The older women wore delicate, lacy petticoats: the younger ones were happy to reveal glimpses of smooth, golden skin. A pleasant and harmless style, curiously frivolous to someone who was accustomed to the discipline of the Stasis under Lefevre.

As Weard, he was clearly running things differently.

Dion Gillet, invited back to Peraldon to restore 'standards'?

On the spur of the moment, Blythe joined the drifting crowds.

With them he moved slowly towards the Temple to Lycias.

Chapter Twenty-nine
Ceremony

A fire burnt on the altar. Flames leapt from torches set in brackets. Scented smoke choked in the already stifling air. Sunlight beat down through the glass-panelled roof.

The Temple was an amphitheatre of sharply raked benches facing a wide, almost circular dais. The crowds seated there were animated only by the movement of fans. They sat in patient silence, waiting for the ceremony to begin. The light from above was reflected from their darkened visors, then bounced off the prisms set at every angle on the walls to focus and concentrate the lancing rays into sweeps of rainbow colour.

Blythe had forgotten how uncomfortable it was. How clothes stuck to the flesh, how the hot air seared the throat. Most people were wearing white, but there was the odd flash of colour, borrowing the hues of the rainbows. Rose-pink, turquoise, violet, emerald. But although the brilliant white sunlight seemed to dazzle everywhere, there were areas of darkness.

Stains of sweat showed on every garment. The grey, twisting, laurel-scented smoke could not disguise the smell, could not hide what the sunlight revealed. Black hair hung heavy with perspiration and grease. And on the hard benches close to the altar, men and women dressed in black were decisively separated.

On either side of the altar, heavy curtains draped two great thrones. On the right, a sunburst of jewels decorated the high, golden back. This was the Emperor's chair.

To the left of the altar, the Empress's throne had been vacant for a very long time. In fact, Blythe remembered that throughout the Stasis it had been hidden away behind the curtain. The woven strands of silver and of white gold framed an empty space, but at least it was now on show.

The trumpets blared and the doors from the Palace of Solkest swung open. A squadron of the Palace Guard, uniformed in purple and gold, filed into the area and faced outwards to the congregation.

Seated near the top of the raked benches, Blythe had a clear view of the neat, elegant figure who bowed low to the altar before taking the golden throne:

Xanthon. The Emperor whose election had taken place on the day of Karis's funeral. Blythe had met him once, long ago, when he still worked for the Warden's Watch. An intelligent man, he'd thought, subtle and sophisticated. From that distance he looked small and doll-like, but he moved with dignity and assurance.

The Warden was there, too, sitting amongst the officials on the other side of the Temple and far away from the common crowds. He was unmistakeable in the silver-grey uniform Blythe himself had once worn. There were other faces; other names that Blythe recognised and remembered. He pulled down the brim of his battered straw-hat. He doubted very much that anyone would pay him any attention.

In this he was wrong.

As the second burst of discordant sound from the trumpets throbbed through the heavy air, he felt a touch on his sleeve. He looked away from the display of priestly dignity being enacted around the altar. He missed the tall figure of Weard/Lefevre, leading the other priests in their courtly ceremonies. Instead, he found himself looking at a figure dressed entirely in black, a dense veil dropping from her wide-brimmed hat to cover her face.

'I must talk to you.'

The precise, cool tones were familiar. Katriana Lessure.

'Hush!' An irate aside from the woman next to Blythe.

'Please!' Her hand on his sleeve trembled.

Without a word, he took her arm and steered her towards one of the exits.

The burning midday sun seemed blessedly cool after the heat of the Temple. He sat with Katriana in the shade of the Temple walls and said, 'What's the matter?'

She was sitting bolt upright, her hands twining together. 'You must help me. I have to stop him.'

'Do you mean Gillet?' Blythe had not noticed her guardian among the other priests. He sighed, entirely reluctant to become involved with these two again. 'Sorry. It's nothing to do with me.'

'Please, it's not a lot to ask. It won't be difficult. I just need to get a message to him.'

'But why me? I hardly know you, or Dion Gillet.'

'Listen!' Her voice was compelling. 'Father Gillet was banished from the city yesterday. He had an audience with the Emperor's advisor, Weard, but he was turned away at the last minute. Weard wouldn't even give him a hearing. There was no reason for it. Then, only then, was he given notice to leave the city within twenty-four hours.'

'But what is this to do with me, Katriana? Gillet is quite capable of fighting his own battles—'

'You don't understand! Weard is totally corrupt! Someone has to stand up for the religion of the Lord, and in Weard's hands every distortion is rife! Even the Emperor is in his power.' She lowered her voice. 'He keeps a woman in Solkest! A priest, living with a woman!'

Edine, he thought sadly. Caught in a spider's web, taken in revenge.

'Father Gillet is determined to expose Weard. He says he is a great evil in our lives, that he conceals more than he tells. . .'

'Why have you come to me, though?' Blythe was almost holding his breath, hoping against hope that she would not say it.

'There's no one else. Father Gillet has told me to trust you, he's good at assessing character. That's why he left you with me that first time we met. Please. . .there's no one else.' she repeated.

She gestured towards the Temple. 'I think he's going to challenge Weard today, now that the Emperor is there. *I* think it's too early, too dangerous. He needs to get the support of the priests first. I have to get him out of there, but I need help. All it needs is for you to take a message to him.'

'If Gillet is ready to take on Weard in public, he's not going to give it all up on the strength of one message.'

'If it comes from me, he will.' She had turned towards Blythe, and he thought once more how difficult it was to talk to her. The veil did so much more than conceal sexuality. It forbade any chance of real communication on any level. Katriana was an enigma to him in her strange self-confidence. Perhaps she would manage to divert Gillet, after all.

She was still speaking. 'Tell him that. . .that the fruits of the Sun have been tasted. He'll know what it means.'

'You've a code?' I don't like what I know of Dion Gillet, he thought, and nothing Katriana says makes it any better. A code now, passwords. Her voice was soft, and Blythe recognised the artfulness of it. Does she know who I am? he wondered suddenly. How far was our meeting an accident?

'Katriana.' He stood up and placed his hands gently on her shoulders. She made no move to get away. 'I cannot involve myself in this. There are people in the Temple who would recognise me if there was any disturbance. People who knew me long ago under – difficult – circumstances. I would probably be arrested the moment the Warden saw me.' This was no exaggeration.

'Arrested?' It barely halted her. 'Whatever for?'

'It was all long ago, and is nothing to do with what happens here. . .but I would be no use to you or Gillet. Quite the opposite.'

As he spoke, the clamour of trumpets from the Temple was broken up by the sound of shouting. Blythe found himself drawn to his feet and moving back towards the Temple doors. Other people from the surrounding square were looking up, alerted by the noise.

Blythe got there first. He was reaching up to open the doors when he felt something cold creeping over the leather soles of his sandles. He looked down. From beneath the firmly closed doors to the Temple a stream of liquid was staining the dust of the square. Water. Seeping from the furnace of light, heat and smoke that was the Temple.

A sudden crash as the doors burst open. The trickle of water became a torrent: a rush of brackish, sour-smelling liquid spilling on to the pavement.

The people in the square began to gather around. At his shoulder, Katriana said something under her breath, trying to push past him into the Temple.

Blythe grasped her arm. 'No! This way.'

He took her hand and together they ran along the wall of the Temple, round the corner that cut it off from the square. He knew where the back entrance, the pathway from the Palace itself came out. He led the woman through the dappled Temple gardens, the forest of oleander and jasmine, until they came to the fence which barred them from the walkway and the Palace of Solkest. Iron bars separated the path from the flourishing garden. There was a gate there into the Temple, and such was the confusion within the amphitheatre that it was unguarded.

Blythe and Katriana edged close to the railings, hidden by the heavy scented frangipani. No one from the Temple would notice them there.

Through the gaping gates they saw a scene of utmost chaos. Crowds of people were pushing, screaming and panicking as they tried to escape the torrents of muddy water that spewed from every extinguished torch. Water fell from the walls, welled up from beneath the altar, cascaded down the rows of ranked seats.

Xanthon was on his feet, staring at the torrents in disbelief. Behind him, robed in cream linen, the Priests stood and watched impassively as their long robes became heavy with water.

There were two figures still beside the Emperor. Emile Blanchard, the Warden, watching the crowds cramming themselves through the double doors. And Weard, Lefevre in the stolen body of Weard.

His eyes were searching the ranks of those who were pushing and scrambling to get out. He was entirely calm, and even amused by the spectacle. As Blythe and Katriana watched from their hidden vantage-point, they realised that only one other person was unmoving.

Far over the other side on the Temple, high up on the benches, a lone figure still sat, a dark cloak pulled forward to conceal the face.

The Imperial militia had closed the main doors after the last of the congregation had left. Although the Temple was now almost deserted, the sound of water, still rushing, still falling, blotted from their hearing the few words that the Emperor spoke to Weard.

Weard's voice, however, was built to carry. He lifted his head and spoke to the silent, seated figure on the other side of the Temple.

'Why have you done this?'

The figure said nothing.

'Dion Gillet, why must you exhibit your small skill in this place of worship? Whom do you hope to impress?' As there was still no answer, Weard/Lefevre turned to the militia. 'Arrest that man,' he said.

'Oh, foolish. . .' Katriana's whisper at Blythe's side sounded more exasperated than anything else.

The cloaked figure stood up, at last.

'I challenge you, High Priest and Mage. I challenge you to prove your worth as advisor to the Emperor. For I have skills to equal your own, and knowledge of the Scriptures beyond your understanding.' And as the figure spoke, in an evenly spaced voice that confirmed Gillet's identity, it raised its hands gently and the flow of water began to slow.

The approaching soldiers were very close now. But the water on the stairs and benches had stopped falling, and something else was happening. The surfaces glinted strangely, the waterfalls became rigid. . .slippery cascades of ice covered the stairs. The soldiers' boots began to slide. Cursing, they backed away from Gillet.

The temperature had dropped, suddenly and shockingly. The Temple of the Sun was now an ice-house, and the air around them was freezing. Their breath rose in great clouds.

Weard laughed. 'An heretical Priest,' he mocked. 'There is no challenge here, Your Highness. With your permission. . .?'

Dazedly, Xanthon nodded. And Weard raised his writhing staff, and pointed it at the hooded man.

Blythe and Katriana did not hear the muttered words, could not see from Gillet's face what was happening, but the effect was immediately obvious.

The silvery falls of ice were shifting, sprouting and swelling. Clawed shapes. Needle-sharp lances of ice shot upwards and outwards towards the silent man standing among the raised benches.

He moved, his arms drawing strange shapes in the air, and for a
moment the lances of ice seemed to waver and lose volition. But
Weard's words droned on, and the ice sprang towards Dion Gillet.

Between one breath and the next, the icy slivers halted their
movement. The tips of dozens of ice-lances touched Gillet's throat
even as his hands were lost in the growing web of ice, and they could
see from the stillness of his shaven head that there was nothing he
could do.

At Blythe's side, Katriana's hands were clenched against the iron
bars of the gate.

'Ah, Dion Gillet,' she said half under her breath. 'What now?'

Nothing, thought Blythe. For even at that distance he could see
blood beginning to colour the shimmering necklace of pointed ice.

There was nothing that he and Katriana could do, either. Blythe
put his arm round her shoulders and tried to draw her away from the
iron fence.

A hooded figure stepped out of the shady forest behind them.

'Phinian. . .?' A woman's voice spoke very softly, tentative as a
whisper.

He looked over Katriana's head.

He saw standing there Weard's lover, Edine Malreaux.

She rested her hand on the branch of a tree, and with shock he saw
that although her eyes were still washed by tears, she had changed.
Edine had lost all her beauty: her cheeks were sunken, her eyes
red-rimmed. Her hair was scraped back harshly: she appeared now as
a wasted icon to grief.

'Phinian Blythe, please help me.' Her thin hand was reaching
towards him. 'Please. . .free me. Get me out of here.'

'I can do nothing for you, Edine.' Blythe did not wish to sound
cruel; he felt nothing but pity for someone in Weard's power. But he
knew that he had no way of challenging the High Priest's authority.
He felt the pressure of events enclosing him as surely as ice now
enclosed Dion Gillet. Edine was trying to involve him. . .

'I have a proposition.' She drew in her breath, striving for some
semblance of control. 'If – If I can release Dion Gillet, the challenger
Priest, perhaps you might be able. . .'

'*Who* are you?' Katriana had listened to all this. 'How do you know
his name?'

But before Edine could answer, there was the sound of opening
doors. Looking along the walkway, they saw Gillet being escorted
away by the Palace militia. A necklace of icy thorns still dug into his
skin. His hands were held in more conventional chains behind him.
He was frowning, his head was unbowed. Following behind, walking
slowly and confidently, Weard/Lefevre and Blanchard attended the
Emperor.

'I have to go now.' Edine's hand clasped Blythe's wrist, her voice again only a whisper. 'But if I can get him out, will you—?'

'I will try,' he found himself replying before there was time to reconsider.

A faint scent of perfume, a rustle of dark silk, and Edine had disappeared among the flowers.

Katriana paid no attention. She stood watching the figure of her guardian disappear into the palace.

Her knuckles were white, grasping the thin railings. Automatically, Blythe drew her away, back through the Temple gardens to the city. He accompanied her to her lodgings, and saw her taken in by other women similarly swathed in black. They fluttered around Katriana with care and concern, firmly closing the door against him.

Blythe walked back through the city to his home and all the time he thought only of Edine, her face pale and no longer beautiful, her tears shining like crystal ice.

Chapter Thirty
Travelling

Days of travelling. Eleanor and Matthias passed the assembled armies of Javon, the forests and plains of the central kingdoms. Hoel and Eldin became realities in Eleanor's mind: complicated, wide-sprawling cities; neat farms; villages set amidst vast areas of farmlands; plains; forests; moors.

They avoided the cities, but allowed Amery to put them down only a little way from the villages. The Arrarat hawk caught rabbits and hares for them and, while Matthias waited, concealed in woods or among the haystacks, Eleanor ventured into the villages to trade. Sometimes she was greeted with suspicion and dislike, once even accused of poaching, but usually she found a market for Amery's prey.

Some of the villages were primitive. Dirt-tracks ran between damp, stone cottages roofed with turf. But each cottage, no matter how run down, how crowded and stinking, had its own narrow strip of land. Potatoes, cabbages, onions. . .a few herbs perhaps. The poverty of her markets was no disadvantage to Eleanor: she was not, after all, offering exotic fare.

She had quickly lost the superficial city-gilt of Shelt. She had never felt at home there anyway. Silks and satins were inappropriate to prolonged journeys on the back of an Arrarat hawk. She traded the fine clothes given her at the Castle without regret for coarse wool and tough denim. She no longer looked much different from the peasants she encountered in the villages and farms. Most of the time she covered her hair and its unusual brightness.

Her hands and face were weather-beaten by the daily flights on Amery. Sun, wind and rain took their toll. She and Matthias existed in the open, washed in streams and lakes, and sometimes it was just too cold and wearisome to make the effort. Her hair was long and straggly, and she knew that her figure was changing. She was thinner, almost wiry. No one would make the mistake of thinking her a pretty, pampered young woman now.

The days were spent flying high, usually above the clouds and out of sight. Clear, warm sunlight there, the endless cloudscapes of tumbling white imitating castles and beasts, and figures and faces. In the sudden gaps in the cloud, Eleanor looked down on a heavy, dark countryside of black forests and lonely plains. The few straggling villages and poor farms were almost lost in the swelling grey-green ocean of land.

She preferred to look out and ahead, into the endless blue. In her own world, Eskimos had hundreds of words for snow, she remembered. Surely there should be as many for the shades of blue in the sky. She round herself listing ways to describe it: azure, turquoise, sapphire, aquamarine. The terminology of precious stones. Peacock, cerulean, midnight, lavender, robin's egg, light, pale, dark, deep . . .There were probably others. They were all there, all shades subtly changing in the course of the day and blending into one another, streaking, tinting and colouring her vision.

She had no mirror, and thought that probably her eyes were still grey, but she would not have been surprised to find them reflecting the wide blue; as Lukas's eyes always seemed to. . .

She began to wonder if the experience of travelling on an Arrarat hawk would be the essence of her time on Chorolon, the most remarkable and extraordinary thing of all.

What would she remember, back in her own world? Among all the horrors, the Desert Rose, Lycias, the black-eyed fisherwoman. . .all that really mattered to her was what it felt like to fly, and Lukas.

That lift, that feeling of soaring over ordinary appearance, ordinary life. To love is to see the world transformed: every colour vivid, every experience significant and powerful. Flying was the same. A different perspective on the world: one that revealed the frailty of humanity and its context of wide open spaces. Each precious fragment of memory, experience and hope surrounded by the world, the stars, the universe.

Both experiences would be beyond her reach in her own world. She would have to find a way of living alone, self-sufficient, with only the memory of love and flight. It would be difficult and lonely, unquestionably drab, but she thought now that she would manage it.

She did not belong here on Chorolon. There was no place for her, no home. Even Phin would by now have returned to his home, would be back with his family and friends. But Eleanor had nothing here, no Arrarat of her own, no one to love. She had even outlived her sacrificial rôle as scapegoat.

Here, now, flying with Amery through the endless skies, her ordinary life might seem meaningless – but at least she had been part of the framework. Or so it seemed, looking back. She had a rôle, she was reflected in the eyes of other people. She had a reality in their lives: her parents' daughter; a friend to Lewis, Pat, Caro, Joe and Debs . . .She would find work, she might even return to her old job, and she would slot back into the systems and networks that formed the web connecting everyone. Here she felt far outside any network.

Perhaps individuals only exist in their relation to the people around them. Perhaps that was why the lonely are so often desperate. How can they survive, unreflected in the eyes of others?

Matthias had no eyes to see her, and not much companionship to give either. Better than anyone else, he knew just how far she was not part of Chorolon. It was as if he had brought her into existence, just as a man might make a tool, a god create a person. And in his deep, withdrawn silences, she knew that he was preparing to bring her life on Chorolon to an end.

She was glad to do their trading; to enter the villages and make contact with other people. For a while, living on her wits, reacting to strangers with their difficult accents and their unknown homes, her own strangeness became insignificant. She was just another traveller, passing through.

Each village and homestead was different, but invariably there were stalls, shops and private houses that she could approach. She traded her pathetic little corpses for bread, fruit, cheese or a change of clothes.

Sometimes she drew thumbnail-portraits, rough likenesses of children sketched with charcoal. In cartoon-fashion, a skill learned from watching Felicia, she gave permanency to fleeting expression and experience. People were curious, and prepared to pay. It bought them the odd luxury, and more than that. Eleanor found herself watching people's faces, the play of light and shade, the marks of other, varied lives. But there was little in the way of paper or canvas. Most of the time she had to rely on Amery's prey.

Survival skills, she thought wryly, returning one day to Matthias after a successful day's trading. She did not dislike the process. Bargaining was simple. She was prepared to point out the meat's freshness, the quality of the fur. . .the familiar language of financial transaction. Anyone could do it, she thought. Estate agents, fishermen princesses, Mages. . .

But Matthias never joined her on these jaunts. She thought he looked tired and ill although he never complained and there was no recurrence of the nightmare vision he had experienced in Shelt.

She was walking through a wood at sunset one evening, returning to the clearing where she had left Matthias and Amery. Although the sun was low, slanting through the trees, the air was still warm, fragrant with wild garlic. She smelt woodsmoke, and wondered if Matthias had already started a fire for the evening meal. She was hungry, thinking of the potatoes and eggs in her rucksack. There were leeks left from the day before and a small lump of cheese.

Vichyssoise, she thought. Cheese omelettes, scattered with the herbs that grew alongside the path. She even had a surprise for him: a small cake, sold cheaply at the end of the day's trading.

He was sitting on a log, close to a small fire in the centre of the clearing. He lifted his head at her approach. 'Eleanor?'

'Warming the pot, Matthias? I've found us a chocolate cake. How's that for enterprise?'

He smiled faintly and moved along the log a little, making space for her. 'I think I should start telling you a little of what we will have to do.'

'To send me back?' Suddenly she was not at all hungry.

He nodded. 'You seem to me calmer, now. Do you feel ready?'

She laid her bag down, and took a deep breath.

'Yes. Let's begin.'

Traditionally, the aspiring Mage went through many years of formal learning. A number of teachers would lecture, examine, instruct and guide. Enormous self-discipline was required in a life of austerity and hardship. Demands were made on stamina, on loyalty, on every area of the Mage's life. The pursuit of magic was an ultimate test. There was no room for anything else in the life of a Mage.

A Mage has to be ruthless, said Matthias. Personal considerations must not weigh at all. Feelings are out of place. They muddy the clarity of thought, distort the subtle priorities.

'I don't think I can manage that,' said Eleanor.

'No, I'm not asking it of you. I only want to explain that what I will be teaching you is in fact nothing to do with becoming a true Mage. We don't have the time—'

'Or the inclination.' She frowned. Unwillingly, she recalled her last conversation with Felicia and Mittelson. 'Matthias, have you ever known any *good* Mages? Any who were not avid for power?'

He seemed disconcerted by her question. 'Blaise did not look for power, although it came to him. And the other Mages at the Cliff, Thibaud and Aylmer, were good men – loyal to Astret.'

'Nerissa didn't like them.'

'They did their best under appalling circumstances.'

'What about Imbert and Edine? The Mages at Smintha?'

He paused. 'Edine was no more than Imbert's assistant, of course. Women can't become full Mages. Strangely enough, at one time I thought that Imbert might avoid the pitfalls, the temptations of power. . .'

'Goodness! Whatever gave you that idea?'

'He loved Edine. He was not quite so – single-minded as the rest of us.'

'And there are no female Mages. . .' Long ago, Matthias had told her of the different rôles for men and women on Chorolon. He had seemed aware of the inadequacy of his explanation then, and did so now.

'No. Generalisations are always inaccurate, but it often appears that women are not naturally single-minded in the same way as men. The Priestesses maintained that women have a wider, deeper understanding and that men pursue the paths to power and ambition from a narrow base, cut off from the profound echoes of being.'

'Do you believe that?'

He frowned. 'I think generalisations are useless. Perhaps for some women it is so, but others don't touch the mystic areas. Some men are undoubtedly obsessive, but others are not. We each of us make our own world, our own choices. We are responsible across a wide scale which graduates from masculine to feminine, and back. Our gender is no excuse. . .And we are about, now, to destroy this world. . .' His voice was still steady, but Eleanor saw his hand clench on the damp wood.

'I don't understand—'

He swept on, as if unwilling to dwell on the subject. 'Think of light, Eleanor. Think of the quality of brightness, Sun and Moon. Candle-flame, lamps, the flashing of a mirror against the sun. Think how glass affects light. Think of a prism, separating light into rainbows, concentrating it to a cutting edge.

'Think how light, focused through glass, can become fire. And how fire, anywhere and anyhow, gives light. Think of that particular circle. The conjunction of glass and fire creates a pattern in the same way that the universe hangs together. The speed of light measures all distance. The heat of light initiates all life. Using glass, we can make an impact in the great circle: fire, light, life.

'The resonances that are set up in a glass over fire-Rite are immeasurably strong. And if they are duplicated, matched exactly, anywhere, at any time, then – for that given moment – a door opens between realities. Between states of existence.

'That is the extraordinary circumstance which connects the different worlds. That is the extraordinary circumstance that first brought you here.'

'Impossible for us to bring off now, surely? How can you manipulate events back in my world? Who will light the fire there, and throw the glass shapes?'

'There is no one, of course. Something has happened, you see. A resonance, not dependent on chance, now exists between our world and yours. We discovered it, Imbert and I, when we decided to try to bring you back. The path of the Benu, taking you home, was unmistakeable. It was as if the light had shattered, as if there was a mosaic of light – a path, a tunnel which we could follow. It took us to you.'

'But they brought me back by using the Rite. They lit a fire, and we drove over it.' She was remembering that terrifying taxi, and the leap into the sun. . .

'The path goes one way only. If you take it, Eleanor, there will be no way back. I am not going to teach you anything at all about the Seventh Rite. You will have no need for it. You will go home, and never return. And no one from here will ever follow you.'

'How can you be sure?'

'Imbert is dead. Edine has not the skill to do it alone. I am the only one who now knows the way.'

'Well, then, you could—'

He carried on as if she had not spoken. 'And I will soon die.'

'What! How do you know? Are you sure?' She looked at him with painful anxiety. There was no real need to ask. Pre-vision, clairvoyance, prophecy and dream. Always accurate, but open to misinterpretation. 'You might be wrong, you've been wrong before!'

'But not about this. Blaise knew the hour of his own death. So do I.' He was calm. 'We don't have much time. We should start very soon.'

Think of light. Matthias's only instruction. Shut your eyes, or wait for a midnight with no moon. Feel light flooding through your mind, watch where it comes from and how it fades. Hold your concentration steady until you feel the pressure of light on your eyes. Stay with it. Think of light, that is all.

'Is that what you do?'

'Yes. When I fly with Amery I share her vision. I can see through her eyes, and experience light in that way. But at other times I try to remember light. Try now, Eleanor.'

It was dark, and the fire was low. She turned away from the glowing embers, leaning back against the log, her cloak wrapped tight up to her throat. For although the day had been warm, the nights were still cold.

She could no longer see the fire. There was no moon, and her eyes quickly adjusted to the dark. She could make out the black silhouettes of tree trunks. Eleanor shut her eyes.

And heard the night-time wood. A world of busy noises: the wind in the trees, the rustle of leaves, of twigs moving. The occasional cry of an owl. A stream, running not far away. The fire, still active enough to cause a disturbance.

She tried to shut out the sounds. They were irrelevant. She tried to remember light.

She saw the face of Lycias laughing at her. He no longer looked like Timon or a beautiful youth. He looked like no one and nothing she knew, but He *was* light, battering down her thoughts and identity. All notions of light led directly to the God of the Sun.

'I can't do this.' Her voice was shaking. 'Lycias. . .laughs when I try to concentrate. He's waiting there.'

'Moonlight, then. Think of Astret.'

'No.' A flat refusal, this. A physical wave of hate, supplanting the panic. Black-eyed fisherwoman, beguiling and deceiving, destroying her only chance of peace. 'This is no good, Matthias. Evil gods run this world. They live in light, and wait for us there. . .We trespass on their territory.'

'Go beyond Them. Take it further.' There was a huge tension in his voice. He was willing her to take dangerous chances.

'No.' She stood up, turning back to the fire, and leaned forward to put more wood on it. The flames flared brightly and the dark retreated. 'This won't work, Matthias. Don't They wait for you, too: How can light exist *without* Them?'

'They are facets of light, not the thing itself.'

She didn't believe him. 'Well, I'm not going on with it.'

'You have no choice. It's your only way home. Think of light.'

'There's no way past Them! Whatever They are, whoever They are, they wait at the end of the tunnel. They're there at the heart of every experience, waiting there!' Her voice was rising. 'I can't do this!'

'You must.' He had moved towards her in the dark, and she felt his hand on her shoulder. 'There's a long way to go, Eleanor, and not much time. There is no hope for you here, you know that. Death might be preferable. . .'

'Don't talk to me of death! They lie about death, too. Lukas wasn't dead. They lie all the time!'

'And so you must go beyond Them.' His grip on her shoulder tightened. He swung her round, away from the fire, making her look out into the dark again. 'Shut your eyes, Eleanor. Think of light.'

Chapter Thirty-one
The Lake

They travelled south for two more days, and Eleanor watched the sky, her eyes reflecting the varied, subtle blues.

She thought about light. She kept her eyes open, and the Gods' faces became lost in the empty colour. Ideas took Their place, ideas and memories. She found herself thinking of her parents, wondering how they were. She thought that probably they would not have worried too much about her. They had been going on holiday, she remembered: the start of a second honeymoon, a trip round the world, beginning in the West Indies.

How much time had passed? She had lost track long ago. A month in the Red Desert, perhaps longer: a further week travelling north to Shelt.

Five weeks in Shelt. Five terrible, nightmarish weeks of frustration and despair. It had seemed even longer, a lifetime of regrets and bitterness stretched on a rack of hope.

And now the only thing left for her was to go home. She thought about light, and still the Gods' faces were there, behind the blueness.

At length, Amery put them down at the top of a craggy hill, where a cave was concealed behind a rocky outcrop. A small pool reflected the sky just outside the cave. The hill was part of the Carald Range, Matthias told her. They were in the far south of Stromsall, and she recognised the countryside. Serethrun Maryn had found her somewhere like this.

It was desolate, but Matthias said it would be ideal. A jagged band of hills surrounded a wide valley. In the centre of the valley was a lake dotted with islands. It was calm and quiet, and unutterably lonely.

Only birds lived there. She saw a heron once, lazily skimming from island to island, kestrels and buzzards hovering high. She waited with Matthias in the lonely cave overlooking the empty valley, and concentrated on light. She watched the reflections in the small pool and the clouds scudding across the surface of the wide lake below. Sometimes she cried.

She went walking much of the time, over the marshy land around the lake. For amusement, she built a dam, blocking one of the streams that ran from the hillside. It was warm during the day, and she often swam in the cold clear water. She remembered a sand-castle shore, and a game of chess. She listened to the cry of small birds, sometimes harsh, sometimes fluent as nightingales.

At sunset she would go down to the lake, making stepping stones across the shallows between some of the closer islands.

She remembered a poem by Yeats, learned long ago to pass an exam:

> I wander by the edge
> Of this desolate lake
> Where wind cries in the sedge:
> > Until the axle break
> > That keeps the stars in their round,
> > And hands hurl in the deep
> > The banners of East and West,
> > And the girdle of light is unbound,
> > Your breast will not lie by the breast
> > Of your beloved in sleep.

A long, hot day. She was sitting by the little pool at the top of the hill, polishing the glass shapes until they shone. She no longer wanted to explore the lake and its surrounds. She held it in her mind: water, and the light reflected therein.

Her eyes ached from the glare of sunlight on glass and from the effort of concentration. In her mind, now, she could see the clear blue light of sky reflected in water whenever she wanted. She thought she would be able to hold it steady. During the Rite, she would manage to steer a straight course.

Through the chaos of flame and earth-created glass, she would add the element of water. The four ancient elements of fire, air, earth and water would form the basis of the Rite. A dramatic and daring act, fusing the four into one, and she could go home.

'Ready now?' Matthias spoke softly as always, but nevertheless he made her jump. Sometimes she forgot his existence for hours on end. He sounded depressed and tired.

'Are you ill, Matthias? Is that what's wrong?'

'Nothing's wrong. I'm not ill. But there is not much time, and I don't want us to fail.' There was an edge to his voice.

Eleanor turned away from the sparkling glass globes and stared at him. He had grown very thin, although Amery always brought them plenty of food. The shape of his skull was uncomfortably clear beneath the skin. His blind face showed lines of suffering and worry, and she felt a familiar rush of compassion for him. But his mouth was hard, compressed and unsmiling.

She had always looked to Matthias for kindness and support. She saw only will expressed in his face now. She wondered why she had never seen it before. She knew he was determined to send her home, keep her safe. His motives were honourable. She trusted him, she always had, even when there had been little reason. He was Lukas's brother.

Eleanor turned back to the calm valley, the deep rings of hills and cool water, and prepared for the Seventh Rite.

He told her to build as large a fire as she could. She scoured the hills and lakeside for wood, but there were no trees at this height. Amery took her on short flights into the lower valleys and she found forests of birch and larch. She tied great bundles to the Arrarat's broad, acquiescent back, and sent her back to Matthias while she gathered more. In this way, two days' intensive labouring brought them enough wood. Eleanor stacked it high at the top of their calm mountain-side and waited for instructions.

She watched Matthias draw from his shoulder bags the strangely constructed glass shapes he had brought from Shelt. His hands moved swiftly and confidently. She almost forgot that he was blind.

'Matthias!' Sudden panic. 'It won't work. It can't work, you can't *see* to throw the glass! We'll never get them to clash.'

The thin lips smiled. 'Have all my teachings been for nothing, Eleanor? When you look inwards, following the light in your mind, what are your eyes doing!'

'Nothing. . .blank, or shut. Oh, I see. Of course!'

'I'm glad you asked, because it reminds me.' He paused. 'Do you remember following the light of the Moon when you first came here?'

How could she forget? A compass-point of clarity, undeniable and distracting. It had always seemed to beckon just beyond the edge of vision.

'If you find it again, calling to you during the course of the Rite, Eleanor, you must ignore it. Use all your strength, all your concentration, and turn aside from it.'

'It brought Lukas to me. . .'

'And took him away again. It is ruthless, Eleanor, passionate and obsessed.'

There was sweat on his brow, although it was no longer hot. She saw the sun setting far away over the western line of hills.

'All the evil in this world derives from the struggle between Astret and Lycias. You must ignore that struggle now, and fight free of it. Turn your back on it. You are going home, and nothing must distract you.'

It made sense. The black eyes of the fisherwoman still gleamed through Eleanor's thoughts. At night she felt the touch of Lycias/ Timon flaring down her nerves. She was not free of Them here, and never would be.

She was longing for home.

In the middle of the brief moonless night, Matthias spoke. 'Eleanor.'

She rolled over, immediately awake. She could not see his face: the domestic fire at the mouth of the cave was nearly burned down, but there was a strange serenity in his voice. He told her to prepare for the Rite.

She hesitated. 'Will you be all right, Matthias? When I've gone?' She looked at him with anxiety. 'What will you do?'

'Return to Cliokest, I think. To Stefan, Margat, Aylmer and the others. They'll be wanting to move back to Sarant. They'll need help. I'll be all right, don't worry.'

'And what you saw, that night at Shelt; that vision of death, what of that?'

'It will come. There's nothing that you can do about it. . .' His voice was calm still. 'But now, Eleanor, you must return home.'

If they left it any longer she would cry. She was glad that he was unemotional and distant. She understood him better now. Emotion clouded concentration. She took a deep breath and lit the fire.

Chapter Thirty-two
Earl of Shelt

Felicia dreamt of wings that night and knew that something was going to happen. She trusted neither the peace within the Castle, nor the frail signs of returning prosperity in the city. It could not be that easy, running Shelt. She felt like a caretaker, waiting for the crisis to break. Waiting for the Earl to return. . .

Later, she felt that it ought to have happened after dark. That Astrella should have come back to Shelt at one with the blackness of night, with the wind blowing and the moon glowing. Felicia would be waiting on the battlements, drawn there by something in the air. . .

Actually, she was at breakfast, and there was a deposition of city traders waiting for a consultation down the corridor. She heard the shout from the guard on the battlements, and was aware of a certain confusion on the balcony outside her dining room. She was already on her feet when the door from the balcony burst open, and Serethrun stood there.

She hardly recognised him. His clothes were hanging in rags, layers of them, all torn and filthy. His hair was wild and wind-swept, his skin dark and weather-beaten. But what really shocked her was the expression in his eyes.

Instantly, he had crossed the room, taking both her hands in his own. 'Felicia, you must be brave now.' His hands were like ice.

'What do you mean?' She could not think what he was implying, his eyes so haunted, his voice so intense.

'He's alive, but only just. . .Where's Mittelson?'

'*Who*? Who are you talking about—?' Unbidden, her hands flew to her throat, her heart jumping.

He looked past her to the maidservant who had just come in. 'Get Olwyn Mittelson immediately! The Earl is injured—'

'*Rosco*? Rosco's here?' Felicia felt the colour flood to her face, and as quickly drain away.

'Felicia, come with me.' He took her hand, was guiding her towards the balcony. 'Be prepared. He is not conscious.'

But Rosco's eyes were open, and seemed to observe her approach. . .

She fell to her knees beside the unmoving body and brushed back the dark hair from his face.

Serethrun was beside her, watching as she tried to find some response. But although those blue eyes were indeed open, they betrayed no flicker of awareness. They gazed peacefully past Felicia's face at the clear morning sky. And then she saw that there was a bandage around his head, stained with blood, and that the dark hair was matted and stiff with it.

'I thought – I thought he had gone somewhere else. . .What happened, Serethrun?'

Before he could answer, there was a sudden flurry of activity from the room behind. Mittelson was there, and several of the guard. Unceremoniously, he pushed Serethrun and Felicia aside. He took Rosco's pulse, and stared into his eyes. Then Mittelson touched the head wound and said, 'How long has he been like this?'

'Ten days. We've been travelling for ten days, without pause. Astrella brought us—'

And at last Felicia tore her eyes away from the man on the floor and looked at the shadow at the other end of the balcony. An Arrarat hawk, dove-grey with dark, liquid eyes was drooping with exhaustion in the early morning sun.

'What are you waiting for? The Earl needs medical attention!' Serethrun snapped at Mittelson.

'But should he be moved?' Felicia could barely think straight.

'If they've been travelling for ten days on hawksback, moving him now won't make any difference.' Mittelson signed to the guards behind them. 'Take the Earl to his apartments. Carefully now. I'll come with you. Serethrun, you can tell me later what's been happening, but Lady Felicia needs to know *now*. I'll join you as soon as I can.'

Mittelson seemed to be the one in charge now. Felicia stood up, and made as if to follow him, but Mittelson held out a hand.

'Forgive me, Lady,' he said. 'But you will be in the way.'

Helplessly, she watched them carry Rosco from the balcony, her thoughts in complete confusion. Fear, because he was so ill and had not recognised her; and joy, because he had not left Shelt to be with Eleanor Knight.

★   ★   ★

Serethrun was standing by Astrella, his hand on the feathers of her shoulder. They were both in the spreading sunlight now. He raised his head, as if drinking in the warmth. Man and bird were framed against a background of blue skies and sparkling sea.

He looked like death. Felicia took in for the first time how thin and worn he was. Gently, she held out her hand. 'Come and sit down,' she said, leading him to the table. She ordered food and coffee, and asked him what Astrella would need.

Nothing, he said. She would fend for herself, would soon leave the Castle. She just needed to rest. . .

'Unlike you and Rosco, who look to be in need of considerably more than that.' She smiled, aware suddenly that she was no longer alone.

He said nothing for a while, and she was content to watch him attempt the steaming dishes of fish and rice that the servants had brought.

He pushed the food away, having tasted little. 'You must prepare the Castle defences,' he said. 'It's urgent, Lady. You'll have to warn the surrounding countryside. Shelt is in great danger.'

'We have heard nothing from my father—' She could not imagine what else he meant.

'Not your father. Gawne.'

'But he's dead! Isn't he?'

Serethrun shook his head. 'We – the *eloish* – rode north, and for a while everything went well. But there were signs, signs and portents that something was wrong in the far north. A Mage died. There was dissension between us, things were not going well. . .

'We met Gawne, and his creatures, on the edge of the tundra. He touches them with ice, and then they are his. Animals and humans all fall to his will as the ice spreads.

'The *eloish* fell to his will.' His face was shuttered from her, withdrawn and hidden. 'Not all. . .a few, those of us with the swiftest horses, managed to escape. Luck was on our side, we found bridges in unlikely places, fords where none had been before. There was a child with us and some said miracles accompanied him. . .We tried to halt the pursuers at Dallon Cliff, but under the weight of ice there was a rockfall. That was when Rosco was injured.

'Gawne's ice flowed down the crag, and left a glacier behind. It ran through the forest, touching everything living, petrifying it with frost. I saw ice creep along the ground, leaping up the trunks of trees. . .it moved like fire, like a forest fire, and we could find no way of halting it.

'My sister Irian said that I should bring Rosco back to Shelt. That the Mages here should be informed of what was happening, because magic can only be fought with magic. And so Rosco's hawk Astrella brought us here.'

'What happened to Irian and the others?'

He said nothing, staring blankly ahead. She knew then why his eyes were so bleak.

Felicia found that her hands were tightly clenched together. 'How fast is Gawne moving?'

He shrugged. 'It depends on the terrain. The ice seemed to blow through the forest, like a wind. On the plains, the grass did not impede its passage, but it seemed to move more slowly, as if the grass did not feed it. . .There is a chance – just a chance – that some others may have escaped. There was another Arrarat hawk with us, and a man called Haddon Derray was not without ideas. . .The child, too. . .But I think, Lady Felicia, that you can not afford to look to the *eloish* for help.'

'I was not thinking of help for me, but rather of sanctuary for you.' Her voice was mild.

'Forgive me, Lady.' He stood up, wearily. 'You understand the position, now, and must act. Call your advisors and build up the defences, Felicia, for the chill touch of winter comes in summer now and Gawne will soon be here.'

She nodded and called her servants.

There were guards outside Rosco's room.

They barred her way. 'I'm sorry, my Lady, the Mage Mittelson has requested that you do not enter.'

'His request is noted,' she said thin-lipped, and stared at them, chin raised, until they stood aside.

The room was in darkness; except for a sick green spiral of light which hung over the bed. A shadow stood at its side.

'Mittelson.' Her voice was sharp. 'What do you think you are doing?'

At once the spiralling light died. She heard a step on the floor, and then the curtains were ripped away from the window. Light flooded the room, and she looked into the furious eyes of Olwyn Mittelson.

'You should not be here, Lady!'

'You are not to use magic on him!'

'He suffers from no simple concussion, Lady.' He sounded calmer, but she knew he had not given way. 'There is ice in his mind, ice in his heart. Simple medicine will achieve nothing—'

'More pacts with dragons, Olwyn? Or the equivalent?'

'Magic can only be fought with magic!'

'So Serethrun says. . .' she murmured, approaching the bed.

Her husband lay there unmoving, the blue eyes still open and gazing at nothing at all.

She looked for a long time into his eyes, and found a cold centre there. A dead, empty lack of life and warmth. And although the room was bright with sunlight, and a fire burnt vigorously in the hearth, she suddenly shivered.

'You see, Lady. Simple warmth and comfort will work no miracles here.' There was a suggestion of satisfaction in Mittelson's voice.

'But is he stable at the moment? He's not going to get worse?'

He paused, and she knew what he was thinking.

'Don't lie to me, Mittelson. I warn you now, I will not be lied to.'

He sighed, the pale yellow eyes shifty. He hunched his shoulders, raising his hands, palms upwards to the ceiling. 'I – truly – do not know, Felicia. He will take food and water, his pulse is stable, although a little slow. The wound to his head is not serious. But consciousness is absent. I do not understand it. . .There is no concussion and yet it is as if he is in coma. There is some evil here—'

'Go and talk to Serethrun,' she said shortly. 'I will sit with him. I will call you if there is any change.'

For a moment it looked as if he would argue and then he smiled suddenly, ironically, and sketched a bow.

'As you will, Lady. . .'

She hardly noticed the door close.

Three days later the wind changed. It brought with it ice and snow. Felicia saw, watching from the window of Rosco's room, that the herds of eldeer were flying southwards. Birds screamed overhead, skimming over the Castle in black clouds. She saw wild horses, and foxes and wolves running. . .

And in their wake came four riders: two *eloish* plainsriders and one of the far-north reindeer tribes. The fourth rider was Irian, Serethrun's shaman sister.

They were accompanied by an Arrarat hawk, carrying Haddon Derray and the baby Coron. The hawk did not pause at Shelt, pressing on towards the far south, but the horsemen did. They stumbled into the city just before the gates were bolted one cold, clear evening, and were brought to the Castle where Serethrun was reunited with his sister.

They warned that horror was very close.

Chapter Thirty-three
Xanthon

A secret stair leads from the High Priest's private rooms to those of his Emperor. Lefevre has not used it for a very long time. It is locked, he knows. The Emperor holds the key. It is up to the Emperor to make the first move.

Lefevre has been waiting for three days. Only three days have passed since the ceremony of invocation and for all of those days the new High Priest has been enrapt in private prayer and meditation. On the fourth day, the initiating service of the Midsummer Festival will take place. Everyone understands that the High Priest is preparing to preside over this complicated and elaborate ceremony.

But the prayers that are repeated in Lefevre's quarters bear no relation to the conventional rites of the Sun. He is a man who has bargained once with the God, and does not hesitate to do so again. He knows what issues are at stake. The deep and humble obeisances made to the shining golden face over the marble-topped altar are in supplication.

Lefevre is in search of mercy now. There are Shadows held quiescent in his staff, and he knows that they will not be content to remain there for long.

For long enough, perhaps. . .That night, waiting for Xanthon to arrive, his mind is at rest. The High Priest lies at full length on the narrow bed, staring at the ceiling.

In the borrowed body of Weard he does not even glance at the woman standing motionless against the wall at the side of the room. He knows that she still weeps for her lover, that the wound to her soul remains unhealed, and her tears give him a continual, minor, frisson of pleasure.

It is why he keeps her with him. For that reason, and one other. But, staring at the whitewashed ceiling, he is not thinking of Edine or what he will do to her later that night.

He waits for the tread on the stair, the sound of the handle turning. And then the Emperor will be his once more.

At last Xanthon mounts the stair. He does not knock, and Lefevre knows why. It is partly because there is no need for the Emperor to ask permission to go anywhere within his own palace, and partly because Xanthon is not that kind of man.

There is a blaze of light in the High Priest's room, although it is close to midnight. Candles have been lit on every surface, a clustered concentration on the golden altar. The face of Lycias is illumined in glorious splendour. The Emperor bows his head briefly to the calmly smiling face and then turns towards the High Priest.

Lefevre stands by the window watching his Emperor. There is no sign of Edine.

'I am honoured by this visit, Your Highness,' he lies.

'Hm.' The Emperor abruptly walks to the window and pulls back the curtains. He looks out into the deep night, as if for relief. 'Why do you keep so many candles burning?' he asks. 'It's far too hot in here.'

'The ceremony tomorrow will be both hotter and brighter yet. . .'

'So you're getting into practice. Very conscientious.' He wanders over to the bookshelf by the bed and takes down a volume. He holds it unopened in thin, sensitive hands, looking round the glaring, stifling room.

He seems uneasy and uncomfortable. For a moment Lefevre wonders whether he will blow out some of the candles, but instead Xanthon pauses.

'I am puzzled, Weard,' he says. 'I must confess that there is much about you that I do not understand.'

'In time, Your Highness, you will know me well.'

'No doubt. . .' Xanthon looks directly at Lefevre for the first time. The Emperor is a handsome man, Olive-skinned, with fine, aquiline features and surprising eyebrows that arch at their outer corners, giving to his features a faintly saturnine slant. But his skin is unlined, his mouth set in a generous curve, his eyes calm and considering. Lefevre is interested to note that he is apparently unmarked by the Stasis.

The Emperor is also something of a mystery to him. The Stasis was created by Lefevre long ago, and he feels rather proprietorial towards the few who were born during that strange period. He alone chose who should die, and who give birth within Peraldon. The children of the Stasis were his gift to those he favoured. He governed the balance of life and death more ruthlessly than any god.

Xanthon was born into the family of Lefevre's Governor of the Militia. During the immeasurable length of the Stasis, Xanthon grew through childhood and adolescence following unremarkable patterns. There was no reason to pay attention to his quietly ordered, highly respectable family.

He completed his education at one of Peraldon's colleges, and it was at that time that he first became prominent in the life of Peraldon. Xanthon was lively, charming, cultured. He composed and painted, and if his music and art showed no originality, neither did anyone else's. He was well-read, eloquent in debate and subtle in argument, sociable and naturally courteous. Everyone liked Xanthon.

After the death of the Emperor Dorian, he seemed a natural choice for the citizens of Peraldon, and Lefevre was happy to let it go ahead. The High Priest suspected that Xanthon might be easily maniuplated;

certainly he had never shown any inclination to meddle with magic or religion.

The other candidates for the position stepped down gracefully after the election, and swore allegiance to their new, elegant and clever Emperor. During the heatwave and its attendant drought that succeeded the Stasis, he proved himself a capable leader of vision and determination. He has become more popular than Dorian ever was.

Xanthon has put the book down again. He sits on the chair by the window. 'Tell me what really happened at the West Gate,' he says cordially. 'In your own words. . .'

And Lefevre recounts it all, from the strange miracle at the boundary of the city to his acceptance by both the College of Priests and the College of Mages. His voice makes it seem simple.

Amongst the pressing, swelling crowds at the city gates, a man fell to the ground, his body marked by swelling, blackened lumps. In horror and sickness he vomited over the dusty stones and the smell soured over the noisy masses pushing through the West Gate. The chatter of the crowd became a scream, the pushing a stampede.

Plague.

Only two figures did not move. Lefevre, inhabiting the body of a well-built man with large heavy hands, moved a step closer. And at his side there was a woman, cloaked in drab grey, the hood pulled down over her face.

'Get out of there, you fools!' A frantic voice from the crowd. 'Can't you see? *Plague!*'

The tall man took no notice. He approached the body and the fleeing crowds paused, turning to watch. Only then did they notice that he carried a spiral staff.

'It gave them confidence,' says Lefevre. 'They moved closer to watch me. I gave the staff to my acolyte.'

(He had been glad to see that she had held it far from her body, as if it too might be contaminated.)

'It was not the plague, of course. A simple case of marsh-fever, that was all. One scarcely needed to use magic – but I felt it advisable to prevent panic. I am – acquainted with the plague. In Smintha, my home town, it has decimated the population. The survivors left the city in panic and disarray, trying to escape its curse. I fear that they may have perished in the Red Desert. But I remained, Guardian of the Temple to Lycias, and I worked with those who stayed behind.' He pauses, looking only at the face over the altar. 'By the grace of Our Lord, I was granted the gift of healing.' He shrugs. 'The incantation worked. The man at the gates made a speedy recovery. You know the rest.'

'What arts did you use, Weard? In your great healing exploits at

Smintha and at the gates to my city? Those of magic, science or miracle?'

For Xanthon, this is the problem. His new High Priest seems more powerful even than the Great Mage Lefevre had been, and takes no trouble to disguise it. So Xanthon, a wise and intelligent Emperor, clearly feels the need to assess the extent of this power. He is no longer the naïve aesthete Lefevre knew during the Stasis. He has steered the Empire through the devastation of the heatwave, he has given instructions to contain plague and forest fire. He has protected his people, and feels a continuing duty to them.

Lefevre can see that he does not wish to be dominated by his High Priest. 'Magic, science and miracles. . .all depend on different perspectives, which I have been granted the opportunity to explore. I have been greatly honoured by the Lord.'

'The Mage Lefevre was talented in such ways. . .' Xanthon does not look at the High Priest. His voice is very soft. 'He, however, was chaste.'

This is what the man with the borrowed body has been waiting for. He has prepared a reply.

'Our Lord is Lord of all Love. He does not necessarily require chastity of His priests.' A slight pause. 'Nor of his Emperor. . .'

A longer pause, now. The Emperor Xanthon returns to the window and looks out at the frail slither of light hanging in the black sky.

'Get rid of her, Weard. It is neither fitting nor sensible to undermine your position in this way. It is potential disaster. The College of Priests will never countenance anything less than purity in the High Priest. Our Lord requires absolute devotion in His Priests.'

'My devotion to the Lord is undivided.' He speaks nothing less than the truth.

'It is nevertheless dangerous.'

'But no one knows.' And this is the truth, too. The High Priest and his Emperor live alone in the centre of Solkest.

Of course, the Emperor is attended by guards, servants and courtiers, but they do not often venture into the central tower. And no one approaches the High Priest. But the Emperor has noted another's presence in the cool corridors of Solkest's central tower. He has heard a quiet tread over the quiet carpets, sensed a faint perfume in the air.

He knows, both from experience and intuition, that Weard is not a man to exist for long in solitude.

'Who is she, Weard?'

'Her name is Edine. She lived here some time ago, with the Mage Imbert Cupere. . .you may remember him.'

The Emperor nods. He does indeed remember Imbert. He even holds in his mind the picture of a laughing, charming girl who accompanied him everywhere.

'I worked with Imbert and Edine to contain the plague at Smintha. He taught me much. . .this was his staff.' Lefevre points to the spiral staff, half-hidden behind the blaze of the massed candlelight. A darker shadow yet stands beyond the staff, but that is well hidden by the flames.

'Imbert died of the plague. I was not skilful enough then to save him. Edine was also infected, and she survived. But she is disfigured-. . .scarred. She will show her face to no one, would abhor any contact with the outer world. She trusts – only me.

'And I respect Edine. In the last days of the drought at Smintha we meant much to each other. . .And although my love is given only to God, I do not want to abandon her, friendless and scarred, in the city of her former happiness.'

'It does you credit. It is nonetheless unwise.'

'No one need know. We – Edine and I – rest our fates in your hands. There is no alternative.'

In this way, of course, Lefevre hopes to give the Emperor the illusion of power.

Xanthon says nothing. His eyes still follow the subtle fragment of silver hanging over the lagoon. He hears a bell chime for Veneration Mass. From tomorrow, the High Priest will preside over that cere-mony. Tonight, a senior Priest will burn laurel leaves and waft the smoke over the reflection of the Moon.

Xanthon will be there. 'I shall attend Mass,' he says. 'I leave you to – your devotions.'

He turns and leaves the room by the secret stair. Lefevre watches the door close, listens to the steps descending. He hears the key turn in the lock. Then, smiling faintly, he blows out all the candles and calls to the woman who guards his staff.

'Well, my dear?' he raises one eyebrow. 'How do you like your new rôle?'

'You are taking a very great chance, my lord.' Her voice is distant.

'That's what you think.'

Chapter Thirty-four
Rite

The dangerous paths of clarity.

The fire was alight, burning high into the midnight sky. Eleanor held in her left hand a glittering crescent, a quarter-moon shape of diamond-bright, cloudless glass. In her right a globe, coloured gold and brilliant.

On the other side of the fire, hidden behind flames and smoke, Matthias held a blue diamond, sharp-edged and fine-cut, and a transparent cone.

The cone was etched with a spiral, winding upwards like the inside of a shell.

She could hear him muttering, chanting. She had asked him what he would say, but he had refused to tell her. It was unnecessary for her to know, it would be confusing and distracting. She had not pressed him.

Now she heard words writhing through the smoke, words that reminded her of the Mages she distrusted. Reckert had used such words, Imbert had directed scurries in such terms.

H'ryonil mereia riannorrhil. . .

Blue light, blue water. She dragged her mind towards the cool deep spaces and closed her eyes.

A tunnel of light, plunging deeper and deeper. A vanishing-point beyond her comprehension. Her inner vision was drawn towards it. . .

On her left, black eyes became silver; on her right, green eyes became gold. Eleanor felt impelled by fire and heat and remembered water, deep water into which she might fall.

Or was it sky, blue sky, and was she about to fly?

Her hands moved and released the earth shapes that bound her to this world.

Streams of light, rivers of light, pathways of light.

Doors flung open on blazing rooms, on brilliant hallways.

She saw a Man and a Woman moving through the many rooms of a great house. Unseen, she moved with Them. Each room was different, each held a store of sparkling delights and marvellous treasures.

The Woman paused, now and again, to examine the textures and colours in the rooms. She ran Her hands softly over the velvet grasslands, through the silken waters.

Eleanor saw deer start, a bird rise fluttering from a tree. The Woman bent and stroked the head of a sleeping child.

The Woman was searching. An eternal quest, a quest for courage, for loyalty and for the passive acceptance of faith. Sometimes, Eleanor saw Her act. In cold clarity, She took a hand in the disposition of events within the rooms. She would direct and guide, and when She found submission to Her will, as happened here and there, She knew triumph, and moved on to the next room.

Eleanor saw lives alter and change. She saw the patterns fall into place again, settling like a flock of birds on a ploughed field.

The Man swept after Her, wildly disrupting each peaceful scene. He trampled over the carefully carpeted forests, upturning the carved and ornamented mechanism of the cities. Sometimes He splashed the walls in glorious, dazzling colour, carelessly and generously. At other times He scorched the quiet hangings of mountain and glacier with flame.

He loathed the calmly controlled paths of submission. With furious impatience, He tore through the gently changing landscapes of the Woman. And because He was prepared to destroy, to lose everything in the heat of His passion, He seemed to prevail.

Turn and turn again. Day followed night, night followed day. Death and life alternate. Winter spring summer autumn winter. Through the long ages, the long corridors of light, the alternation of creation and destruction endures.

Who creates, who destroys? The Woman builds an ordered environment, somewhere of peace where new life can grow. It is a construction to contain the hearth and the home. To trap the Man. He splashes it all over with the colours of lust and violence.

The Man ravages each room with His desire. He uses science and magic to force a different order, one far divorced from the quiet pacings of the Woman. He constructs unnatural and sometimes beautiful symbols of His power. He takes everything He wants, rapacious and greedy. He builds walls around Himself with pride.

It is all to escape the Woman. She dances in deep, slow counterpoint, unravelling His creations, destabilising and subverting. She hides herself away behind walls of secrecy.

She turns to bitter and devious resentment, He to violence and force. And because They are of equal power, of equal ingenuity and conviction, battle is enjoined.

They meet, sometimes. On stages set by mortals, in the rôles played out by ordinary men and women. In dreams and nightmares, They fight it out at the concealed centre of human understanding.

In the spreading corridors of the house, spinning down light-begotten pathways, Eleanor heard Voice answer to Voice. She looked for the clarity of clear blue light and found instead the Man and the Woman. Passion to passion, brilliance to brilliance. Like magnetic poles, positive to positive, negative to negative, They repelled each other.

Eleanor saw the Lord of the Sun swirling in dangerous delight, pulling at the strings of fate, watching the puppets in each room dance to His will. A tweak here, a jolt there. Some He let fall, others He held up to the mockery of the stars.

She watched Him play. He was cruel, sensual, inventive; childlike in his desires and passions. And although He was deeply terrifying, powerful without limit, wildly destructive, brilliantly creative, she felt only contempt.

It is easy for women to feel contempt for men, for their crude tactics and unsubtle blandishments. Women smile secretly, even as they wait in fear. It is easy for men to use violence against women. What else can they do, powerless as they are against that hidden, secret knowledge? Violence is the only possible answer to the secret, the knowledge which every woman contains within the patterns of her own body, reiterated with every passing phase of the Moon.

All must die. In a fall of blood, life is washed away, and whatever the passion, whatever the struggle, in the end blood falls and life is ended.

In furious revulsion and hatred, the Man raged against such acceptance. He wanted more than that. He flung Himself against the boundaries of each room, against the walls and ceilings and quiet, quiet earth. He was striving, always, to fly free of the trap.

Eleanor, who was also the Woman, watched through black eyes. She was weaving desperate strategies, cruel bargains, designed to one end only.

She wanted to make Him submit, so that He might at last look at Her, and recognise that She was offering a deep wisdom.

He raged and fought, so that at last She might recognise that he was offering a flame of hope.

That one must try to fight back. That life can only be lived to the full if one risks everything.

That death is only acceptable after a life of passion.

Chapter Thirty-five
Home

The intensity of light was impossible to bear. The dazzling images of disrupted landscapes and eternal corridors, the blazing force and passionate desire of the Man and Woman fighting, and the hatred of it all, became confused into a jumble of shapes and feelings and colours. She was buffeted by emotion, torn apart by conflicting and savage excess. . .

This was a crescendo of power, a conflagration of passion, that could only end in death. There was no other future; nothing else possible. The Woman had always lived with death and now the Man sought it, too. She knew now why Matthias had been so terrified.

Remember light, he had said. But she thought only of death. Remember light, said his voice in her mind, think of light and do not be diverted. . .

Whirled round between the brilliance of light and the promise of death, she tried to remember the blue depths of the sky, the blue depths of the sea. She felt as if she were being dissipated, fragmented, blasted to smithereens by immense forces and then scattered wide over far and various horizons.

Who was she, where was she, what was she?

What was she, who was she, where was she going?

Home. A word took shape. *You're going home.*

Something seemed to snag, to catch, to pull back. An ultimate shock, then, jolting her out of a whirlpool of light.

And all at once the spinning stopped, the colours quietened, the light died. Was this death? As if emerging from deep water, she lifted her weightless hands, brushing the legacy of light from her eyes. Brushing the flakes of snow from her face.

Snow? *Winter?* Where was she? Why was it so cold?

She was standing in a wide space of grassland. A sprinkling of snow lay between the harsh blades of rough pasture. A field, and an oak tree to her right.

Shivering, she slowly turned round.

In the distance she saw a hedge, bare of leaves, and the roof and chimneys of an old house. Pat and Caro's house. She recognised it immediately.

Home. Her head ached with the memory of light and although the recognition held steady, she could not quite comprehend where she was. Another room in the house, another door off the endless corridors. . .

Did black eyes watch her here? Did green eyes laugh through the feeble light of a clouded late afternoon? She knew now that They did. She had watched, and laughed with Them. They had taken her innocence from her. She was bereft in every way. There could be no illusion of free will, of morality, or justice.

No concept of order. There was only death. It was all just a game, a sterile, destructive, meaningless game. Futile.

She was cold. She looked down at thin hands, and saw them shivering. Should she do anything about it? The body, after all, was the ultimate treachery, the illusion that led humanity to assume that there *was* order. It followed patterns, the spiralling double-helix of genetic order. The beat of the heart, ingestion and digestion, the busy pathways of the blood. The gradual passage from birth to death: slow, measured and inevitable.

Meaningless as scribble. Empty of significance, except to the deluded creatures who exist within the rotting frameworks of flesh and bone, thinking that things make sense.

They didn't. Nothing made sense, nothing mattered. Nothing had any kind of enduring existence. Only the battle between Man and Woman was real, spun out on an infinite fabric of light, leading to death.

She had lost that one. That particular, unfairly doomed attempt to love Lukas and to be loved. She had thought him dead, and it had been no lie. He was dead to her. For ever, Matthias said. For ever and always.

She knew what was going to happen now. *Déjà vu* had nothing on this. She would walk back to the house, nails digging into her palms, mourning.

There was no reason to stay here, in a snowy wasteland. There was not much of a reason to move, either, except that it was cold and her hands trembled.

She was destroyed. She could not even mourn now.

She began to walk, and did not notice the other footprints in the snow.

There was no one in. It was a relief. She didn't know how to begin to explain where she'd been; why she was wearing such strange clothes; why she was so thin; so changed.

The back door was open. With an effort, she recalled that Pat had always been careless about such things. He could never find his keys, she remembered.

She stood in the quiet kitchen, staring blankly at the shining surfaces. There was an electric kettle on the side. Perhaps she should make herself a cup of tea. It was always recommended for shock. She couldn't face it.

Eleanor wandered through the house, pausing in the hall to pick up the newspaper on the doormat. The date showed 23rd April. Four months had passed. The headlines said that the economy was in trouble.

Nothing had changed.

There was a mirror in the hallway. She saw a bedraggled stranger, eyes dark-pupilled in the dull, late afternoon shadow. Wearing a full, gathered woollen skirt down to her ankles and a coarse, greying blouse. An absurd anachronism against deep pile carpets and pretty papered walls. Although she supposed she was probably authentically dressed for the date of the house. Pat and Caro had even made a conscious feature of stripped beams. The irony failed to amuse. She could go nowhere dressed like this.

She would have to borrow something. Caro wouldn't mind. She would need money, too. She had no idea if there was a bus service to the village, but she doubted it. She would phone for a taxi. . .

She didn't know if she could face that, either.

It was getting dark. Soon, she supposed, they would be home from work. She didn't want to meet them. With fingers that still trembled she picked up the telephone directory. In a voice that felt strange and unused, she ordered a taxi as soon as possible.

They argued; it was snowing heavily and the roads to Hatfield Greenoak were likely to be blocked. She found herself pleading, promising double, triple rates. . .In the end, the irritable voice gave in. The taxi would be there in half an hour.

This small victory gave her a little courage. Quickly, she chose some jeans and a jumper from Caro's wardrobe. They were too big, but it didn't matter.

There was a small pile of notes and money on the bedside table. She helped herself to it, scrawling an *IOU* on the pad by the telephone. She'd repay it later, when she'd had time to invent some kind of explanation.

Through falling snow she watched the road, waiting.

She went home. To her flat in North London, the upper half of an Edwardian house.

It was locked, and she had no keys. The old man who lived downstairs was out, and she knew no one else in the area. She knew no one would lend her a ladder to break in, no one would trust her.

Her keys were in her handbag. And that, presumably, was still at the house of those people they'd had dinner with before she had been kidnapped. What were their names? She didn't know them well, they had been friends of Lewis's. . .

Lorraine and Steven. Steven Finlay. She looked them up in the telephone directory at the hotel over the road and found the address. She called another taxi, and went visiting.

Lorraine was at home. She opened the door to Eleanor and her mouth dropped.

'*Eleanor?*' She was seeing visions.

'Hello, Lorraine, I just wondered if I left my bag. . .'

She trailed off. It seemed ridiculous, one would hardly fail to notice the loss of bag complete with purse, chequebook, credit cards and keys for over four months.

'Where have you been? Where did you go, that night? Christ, what did Lewis do to deserve *you?*'

She was unprepared for this attack. She stared helplessly at Lorraine.

'You never even visited him, did you? Didn't it matter that you'd run him over?'

'It wasn't me, I tried to make the taxi driver stop—'

'Oh, sure. And where were you, when Lewis was in hospital? Couldn't you even be bothered to see what you'd done?'

'What do you mean?' Her voice was only a whisper now.

'He *cried* for you. He died, wondering where you were.'

'*Died?*'

'Didn't you know?' A sneer in her voice, but her eyes were puzzled. 'Hey, don't do that. . .look, you'd better come in.'

She took Eleanor's arm and pulled her into the house.

Eleanor leant against the wall, and felt her knees give way. A hand forced her head down, and for a moment she thought that the nausea would win. But then the hallway stopped whirling round, the pale gold carpet steadied, the sickness subsided.

Reality restored.

'He's *dead?*' Again, her voice was only a whisper.

'You didn't know? Oh God. Where have you been, Eleanor?'

She could say nothing. It was madness, all madness.

The hand on her shoulder disappeared. From a far distance she heard liquid being poured into a glass. It was put into her hands, a stiff measure of brandy.

The aroma made her feel worse. She put it down on the floor, spilling a few drops onto the carpet.

'When did you last eat?' A cool voice over her head. She couldn't remember.

'Lewis is *dead?* I didn't think. . .'

'An internal haemorrhage. Two days after the accident. He got out of bed, trying to find a phone. He was worried about you. . .'

'I never knew. I was. . .somewhere else. I couldn't get back—'

'*Where* were you, Eleanor? What happened that night?'

She pushed herself to standing, and looked out of the still-open door to the dark night outside.

'Far away. . .I never wanted to hurt him, I didn't want him to *die!*'

'Okay, okay.' Lorraine's voice had lost some of its hostility. 'Can I get you anything? Tea? You're very pale.'

'What?' She couldn't think. She remembered why she was there. '*Is* my bag here?'

'Yes, it's upstairs somewhere. We didn't know what to do with it. . .we left a message at your flat and asked round, but no one knew where you were.' She looked closely at Eleanor's face. 'Have you been ill?'

'Can I have the bag? I don't want to hold you up—'

'I'll get it. But I think you owe us an explanation.'

Eleanor sat on the bottom stair, waiting for Lorraine to return, and tried to think of some story that wouldn't brand her as insane.

'I went to see my parents,' she said at last, holding the bag in hands still unsteady. 'They were setting off next day on a cruise. . .I went with them. A spur of the moment decision. . .'

'Didn't you even go home first, to get packed? Didn't you need *money*?'

'Dad paid. He was feeling generous. A complete new kit.'

'I wish I had parents like that.' Lorraine was still staring at her, and Eleanor wasn't at all sure that she was believed. She moved towards the door.

'Thanks for looking after this for me. . .' She lifted the latch, and walked swiftly down the street back to the main road, not looking back. She didn't see Lorraine still staring after her, her face creased with puzzlement.

She could think of nothing but that other death. Lewis. The violence on Chorolon reaching out and touching her own world.

He had cried for her, Lorraine said. And then Eleanor began to cry, for Lewis and for everyone.

Chapter Thirty-six
Parents

The door to her flat was difficult to open against the quantity of piled-up mail. She pushed it aside and walked through the hallway.

In the kitchen, she made herself black instant-coffee. There were tins in the cupboard, complete meals in the freezer, but she wasn't hungry.

She took the mug of coffee through to her untidy, musty-smelling bedroom and lay on the bed. The flat was warm; the automatic time-switch to the heating must have been dutifully turning itself on and off for over four months.

She thought of Lewis, casually murdered by an ambitious Mage from another world. Of the hostility and curiosity in Lorraine's face.

Eleanor had thought that to return home would be a relief, an escape. That she might begin to forget, that the wounds would heal. Foolish optimism. Instead, it seemed as if her experiences on Chorolon were leaking through to this world. As if the distress of it all would surround her until she died, wherever she was, whatever she did.

She drank the coffee, and turned out the light.

Next morning she defrosted the fridge and opened the windows. She went through the flat, picking up things, listlessly tidying and sorting. She loaded the washing machine. She filled in time.

In the afternoon, she went through the post. Advertisements, prize draws, catalogues, bank statements. An unsurprising letter of dismissal from the estate agents who'd been her employers, a couple of late Christmas cards. Several notes from Lorraine and Steven that she couldn't bear to read; one from Debs; another from Caro, assuming that she'd gone away with her parents after all. Her impromptu lie to Lorraine was, it appeared, common currency before she'd even uttered it. No one seemed to have missed her much. Even the bank wasn't complaining; her bills were all paid on standing orders, and there was still a credit balance.

She was glad she hadn't switched on her Ansafone.

Two postcards from her parents, detailing sights seen, temperatures endured. Back in April, the last one said, see you then.

She wrote, with terrible difficulty, a letter to Lewis's parents, explaining that she had only just returned from holiday, expressing shock and regret. It seemed inadequate in the face of his wanton, untimely death.

Lewis had died because of his involvement with her. It was, at one level, her fault. Her responsibility, just as it had been her responsibility that Lukas had died. Only that hadn't really happened.

The past was muddied with images of the lies she'd been told, the illusions she'd been shown. She sat on the sofa in her flat, and screwed the letter into a tight ball. There was no room for illusions in her life now. She knew exactly what had happened. Lewis had really died, Lewis had paid the ultimate price for her actions on Chorolon.

She thought that she ought to go and see Lewis's parents, that at the very least she owed them the emotional cost of a visit. It was a gesture towards truthfulness.

She had met the Pritchards once before, on the occasion of their thirtieth wedding anniversary. A large garden-party, complete with marquee on the lawn and a jazz trio. She had not been in party mood last summer. It belonged to that strange, dreary time after her first visit to Chorolon. She had thought Lukas was dead. They had found her sulky and bad-tempered.

They lived in an affluent suburb, in a comfortable, half-timbered house set in formal grounds. She remembered neat rosebeds and paths dividing newly mown lawns. Generously stocked herbaceous borders.

She parked some way up the road, leaving herself with a short walk. She could change her mind that way, leave before they knew she was there.

She stood across the road watching the house for some time. Although it was not actually raining when she arrived, the lawns looked damp and soggy, the laurels dark with moisture. The rooms were unlit.

She wanted to say she was sorry, but that was not all. She needed to see what Lewis's death had meant in the eyes of others. She wanted to see that he was mourned, missed. That his death had not been as insignificant, as casual as it seemed. She wanted to know that it had mattered.

Perhaps they would allow her to share a little of their grief. It was simple enough. She took a deep breath, crossed the road and walked quickly up the drive to the front door. Without pause, she rang the bell.

Nothing happened, no movement, no sound. With complicated feelings of regret and relief, she started to walk away. Halfway down the drive, she heard the door behind her open. She turned round and found herself staring at Lewis's mother.

She saw recognition flicker. Puzzlement and distress in equal proportions.

'Eleanor Knight,' the woman said slowly. 'What are you doing here?'

'I came to say. . .how sorry I am about Lewis. I've only just found out, you see. I've been away. . .'

She trailed off into silence. The woman was still watching at her. 'I didn't want to disturb you, I just called to see if you were all right.'

'Come in.' The woman stood back, holding open the door. Slowly, Eleanor passed through. It was not noticeably warmer inside. She shook her head when Mrs Pritchard offered to take her coat. 'Do you want something? Tea, coffee. . .?'

'No, thank you.' How to begin, what to say? Your son died because of me. . .She said, struggling, 'Mrs Pritchard, how are you? Are you managing all right?'

'Day follows day. Time passes. What do you think?'

She was plump, wearing good, stylish clothes. But her lipstick had been carelessly applied, and the front of her blouse was stained. Her eyes, an indeterminate hazel, were red-rimmed.

She spoke again, before Eleanor could reply. 'Anyway, what does it matter to you? I expect you've got another boyfriend by now, you're young and pretty. You've got a lifetime ahead of you, I expect in five years' time you'll hardly remember who Lewis was. . .'

Eleanor could say nothing. This was an anger that needed expression.

'He really loved you, too, did you know that? It really mattered to him, that you didn't visit those two days in hospital. Where were you, anyway? What happened?'

'It's – a long story.' Should she try to justify what had happened, make some kind of excuse? What would help? 'I had no idea Lewis was seriously injured—'

'Your car never even stopped, did it?'

'It was a taxi, I wasn't driving. I tried to get the driver to stop—' This was hopeless, and irrelevant. She tried again. 'Mrs Pritchard. I'm sorry, so sorry about Lewis. I won't forget him, in five years or fifty. It was a terrible thing, a terrible accident—'

She took a step forwards, wanting to touch her, wanting to make contact.

Lewis's mother said nothing. Her lower lip was trembling. She turned away, and picked up a leaflet from the hall table. She handed it to Eleanor.

It was an estate agent's blurb. The house was for sale. Eleanor stared at it, uncomprehending.

'You're moving?'

Mrs Pritchard nodded.

'Perhaps that's a good idea, to get away.'

'Do you think so? A good idea, to leave the house where we were happy, the garden we planted, the neighbourhood where all our friends live? Do you think you can leave sorrow behind in some other world, some other place? Oh no, young and pretty Miss Eleanor Knight, it doesn't work like that. No, we're selling up for one simple reason only. Divorce. And don't look so shocked, haven't you read the psychology books? You're damned lucky if bereavement draws you together, it's much more likely to do the opposite.'

She snatched the leaflet from Eleanor's hands. 'So you can add that to the account, too, young lady.'

For a moment they stared at each other, and then Eleanor turned back to the door, opening it on the dripping garden.

'I'm more sorry than I can say, Mrs Pritchard. I'd give anything to have Lewis back.'

'But you didn't want him, did you?' A short laugh. In the dark, unlit hallway, the pupils to her eyes were large and black. Black eyes gleamed at Eleanor. 'It was written all over your face. You didn't want him. Go on, get out of here. I don't want to see you again, ever.'

Her mother came for coffee. She wandered round Eleanor's flat, obsessively tidying the piles of magazines, adjusting the hanging of pictures, the fall of the curtains. She smoked and talked all the time.

'Well, yes, I suppose you could say that we gave it a good try. Even *he* behaved himself for the first two weeks. But you know what he's like, it didn't last.' Her words were brittle-hard, falling like broken glass from thin lips. She took another drag on the cigarette. The smoke formed eddies around her. '*She* was travelling alone, going to meet someone in Rio, so she said, but she'd lost the key to her cabin or something. . .Galahad to the rescue, the avuncular shoulder, the pulling of weight with the ship's crew . . .you know.' For a moment she paused, staring at the untouched, cooling coffee.

'I knew it as soon as I saw her. So bloody *obvious*. I was just waiting for it to happen, and so it did. Paper-thin excuses, late-night walks, just a breath of fresh air, dear, oh, I've left something in the cabin—'

'What did you do about it?'

Eleanor remembered other rows, other acts of revenge. China smashed, cars scratched, food uneaten or deliberately burnt. At Christmas, her father gave her mother money. She gave him tonics to promote hair growth, or books on diet and exercise. Once she had given him a box with air vents. He had been suspicious opening it but she had laughed. The small grass snake inside was semi-comatose, clearly harmless, but the resulting row had endured throughout the holiday.

'I cleared his clothes from the cabin. All of them, dirty washing and all, and put them in *her* cabin. I thought she might appreciate a turn with the smelly socks.' She smiled, a genuine amusement in her eyes.

'*Why* do you stay together?' Everyone had asked this, for years.

'Oh, you know. . .' Her mother shrugged, taking a long drink from her cold coffee. A pause, and Eleanor waited for the usual excuses: where could I go, what would I live on? So many pathetic widows and divorcees around, and single women are such second-class citizens. . .

'There's no one else, you see.' Her mother was not looking at her, staring instead at the dull rainy sky. 'No one else that matters. He notices what I do. He reacts. It matters, what we do to each other. It makes me – feel alive. Vivid.'

She smiled again, half-embarrassed by giving away so much. She stood up. 'Must go, sweetie. We're meeting for lunch in half an hour. I'll give you a ring next week, and you must come and tell me what you've been up to. . .bye, darling, take care. . .'

A waft of cigarette smoke, a brief hug and she was gone. Eleanor emptied the ashtrays thoughtfully.

They hadn't missed her at all. They never had.

She wondered about finding work. In a desultory fashion she looked through the 'Situations Vacant' pages, and even jotted down a few telephone numbers.

It was too soon. She heard the cool professionalism in the voices of the women she rang, listened to their questions and queries. She had a story to cover the four-month gap in her cv, she was free and unencumbered and could start tomorrow. . .Apply in writing, they all said. Have you any experience? Or, the position's been filled, sorry. . .

It was a dreary process and Eleanor could find no enthusiasm for it. What was holding her back from returning to this particular fray?

There was nothing she wanted to do. She was aware that if she persisted she'd probably find work before long, but there was no urgency about it. She was not seriously short of money, she could always sell her car or flat if cash became a problem.

She rang her old friends and made arrangements to meet. No one was unfriendly, but neither were they particularly enthusiastic. She thought, I've been difficult for too long. I've been far away for such a long time that they've forgotten who I am. I need to start again, to show that I've still got something to offer, something to give.

It was an effort. She gave a party, and although everyone came and complimented her on the food, and drank a fair amount and stayed rather late, she wondered what it was all for.

They talked; they had too many cars and too few holidays. Their mortgages, houses and the M25 were all impossible. Films and television, music and sound-systems were of passing interest; scandal and sex more absorbing. She watched mouths move and heard voices speak and it was like watching automata through a wall of glass. They belonged to her past. She had nothing to do with them any more.

Perhaps it was time to move on.

Chapter Thirty-seven
Wandering

Eleanor told everyone that she was going travelling, and for a while it was the truth. She had lost the taste for settled, ordered life. She went to South America, to Japan and Russia, and found a curious satisfaction in being unknown, outside the system.

She did her best to learn the language wherever she stopped, but was not naturally adept and always moved on before much progress could be made. It made sense, in a way. The fact that she could barely communicate the basics seemed more honest than any amount of talk with her friends at home.

A shared language implied shared experience. But no one could understand what had happened to her: there was no point in even trying to explain.

Once she did try. On a long-distance bus, going from Chicago to Washington, she found herself sitting next to a young man.

It was stifling hot. The air-conditioning, if that was what it was, blew irregular blasts of freezing-cold air round their ankles.

The American was confident and friendly. At first they played travel-scrabble, and then he suggested that they told stories to pass the time.

He began. He told the story of a girl whose hair was made of 22-carat gold, of a dream that was stolen by a friend and held for ransom. Of the death of a mermaid and an end to dreaming. . .

She told him about hawks that could carry people, of spiralling enchantment, of love and infidelity and a magician who turned into a rose.

He offered her a can of Coke, but she had never liked it much. He stood up when she had finished her tale, swaying with the movement of the bus. She saw that they were pulling into a filling station. He steadied himself against the seat in front, regarding her. Although he smiled, his eyes were serious. He was older than she had at first judged.

'I have to get off here,' he said, although though they were still miles from Washington. 'Someone's waiting for me. But I think you should know. My story is true.'

'So is mine,' she said, but he was already out of sight.

She never saw him again.

It had been a mistake, going so far afield. The restless travelling only increased Eleanor's sense of displacement.

She returned to North London and her flat, but it felt as if it belonged to someone else. It was like a waiting room, somewhere in between, a place to pause but not to stay.

She thought, but it's people who matter, not places. The flat doesn't count at all, it's family and friends who are important. I need to pick up the pieces again. . .

She took the phone through to her bedroom and spent the afternoon with her feet up, working through the list. There were few surprises.

Her parents were at the solicitor-stage again, virtually an annual event. Eleanor listened to a tirade from her mother, but her father was in a meeting and couldn't talk. . .She put the phone down thoughtfully and decided to keep out of the way. The continuing acrimony was too depressing.

She rang some of her old friends again, but most were at work. The others showed distant friendliness as before, and told her gossip about people she didn't know. She made one or two arrangements to meet, but it felt strange. Again she wondered if she'd been away for too long. . .

It hadn't been *that* long. Other people went abroad for years, came back and picked up the threads again. Why was it so hard for her?

She wondered if Phin was finding the same, returning to his home. Had he found work again, were his family and friends still around, still relevant? She could not imagine that he would be finding it as difficult as she was. She'd recognised a calmness about him, control-. . .He'd be making a better go of it, she thought, although she would never know for sure. He had just dropped from her life as if he had never existed, although they had shared so much. . .She wished that she'd had a chance to say goodbye to him. She had said goodbye to no one, not even Lukas.

And that was where the real problem lay. Things on Chorolon felt unfinished.

And no one in this world mattered as much to her as Phin, and Lukas.

Her money was almost gone. She'd already sold the car, so she would have to find a job or sell the flat.

'What are you doing with yourself now?'

She had run into Debs in the local M & S, and it was a shock to realise that Debs didn't even know that she'd been away again.

'Job-hunting.' Eleanor shrugged. 'What about you?'

Debs blushed. She actually blushed. 'I'm pregnant,' she said, smiling. 'The baby's due in December.'

'Oh, congratulations, how lovely! I need to hear all about this, have you got time for a coffee? Lunch?' Perhaps this was just what she needed, a nice ordinary chat about ordinary life.

'Not today, what a shame. I'm going to meet Joe at Giovanni's in half an hour and I've said I'll collect the car on the way. . .' She must have seen something in Eleanor's face, because then she said, 'Look, why don't you come, too?'

It was an impulsive invitation, a small show of warmth. And Eleanor thought, yes, I could do this; I could go and have lunch with them and discuss baby names and whether they should get a nanny, and they could suggest where I might work, and ask me if I am seeing anyone. But I don't *want* to do any of it.

I'm not fit for this, I don't want to be part of it.

She looked regretful. 'Oh, I'm sorry Debs, I've just remembered. I've got to call in at the estate agent's—'

'Are you moving?'

'Possibly,' she said, and then, more strongly, 'Yes, I'm moving.'

'Well, good luck with it,' Debs said. 'It's been nice seeing you, keep in touch. . .'

And then she was gone.

★ ★ ★

That summer, using some of the money from the sale of her flat, Eleanor rented a house on the Yorkshire coast. She took several boxes of books, a whole stack of records and tapes. She took writing paper, and wrote to her mother saying that she was perfectly all right, working on a book about her travels. She implied that she didn't want to be disturbed.

She really intended to write an account of what had happened. The American man had opened up a pathway for her. Perhaps one day she would meet someone else who would understand. Perhaps she just didn't want to forget.

She found it so difficult. To pin people down in words was to limit the choices, of necessity a process of exclusion. How could you really describe what someone was like? How could you describe the look in Lukas's eyes, the way he stood, the tone of his voice, the touch of his hands? Sometimes she tried to draw the people she'd known, and in some ways it worked better. But it was both uncomfortable and disconcerting to find the faces of people she had lost forever caught on paper. And when she was tired, or unwary, all too often her drawings became perverted and she saw only the likeness of Lycias, or of black-eyed Astret. She tore up page after page, and went walking instead.

She read voraciously and found a thousand stories of transfers to other places. It was commonplace, after all.

She listened to music, all kinds. She bought bread, cheese and vegetables from the local shop, fish from the quayside stalls at Filey. She thought that perhaps she should be deciding what to do with the rest of her life, but somehow it seemed irrelevant. An empty page or a dead end? She didn't know which.

At nights, a voice rang through her memory.

'You're going home.'

The voice repeated the words. She lay awake and remembered it so clearly. After that terrible baptism of fire, that final purging of illusion, the Rite that had returned her to her own world, she had heard a voice saying, 'You're going home.' At the time she had not questioned it. Now she lay awake, wondering.

It was not the voice of her own thoughts. Neither was it a far-reaching valediction from Matthias. She recognised the timbre of the voice, the clear, merciless logic of it.

Once, long ago, Matthias had told her that she would not be alone on her passage back to her own world. He had not told her who her companion would be, only that it would not be Lukas.

She remembered now that there had been other footprints in the snow, leading to Pat and Caro's house, and at last she knew whose they were. There was someone from Chorolon running loose in her own world. Someone she knew as an ambitious, unbalanced, destructive Mage.

She was in a waiting room, and now she knew why.

She had been there three weeks when her visitor arrived. She heard
the car sweeping over the uneven, half-gravelled track to the cottage.
She heard the stereo as the car pulled up, and the click of the door
catch as it opened. Eleanor went into the kitchen and looked out
through the net curtains.

A woman stood there, regarding the cottage. And although tinny
laughter still rang from the car radio, the woman standing there wasn't
laughing at all. She was staring at the sky, and beyond that to the cliff
paths and grey waves.

Eleanor took a deep breath. Then the woman turned and looked
straight at her through the opaque curtains. A different expression
curved her lips now. Tears no longer fell from her eyes.

Edine looked straight at Eleanor and smiled.

'So sorry to disturb the artist's retreat,' she said coolly. 'I'm afraid it's
quite deliberate.'

'I didn't think you just happened to be passing.' What did you do,
thought Eleanor. Light a fire and spin glass bottles over it? Or do you
have a spiral staff tucked away somewhere? 'How did you find me?'

'I met your mother. She wasn't very interested, but she told me
where you were.'

'Oh, I see.' That forwarding address, Eleanor thought numbly.
Mum has passed it on to a complete stranger. It was amazing she
hadn't lost it.

'I thought I'd come and give you a surprise. You don't mind,
do you?' Edine had taken her arm, steering her towards the
cottage.

Eleanor pulled herself free. 'I think I'd prefer a visit from just about
anyone else in the world. What do you want?'

'I have news for you. And I mean you no harm, impossible though
that may be for you to believe. May I come in?'

An old, unreasoning superstition prompted Eleanor. 'No. If you've
got something to say, you can say it out here.'

'Very well.'

Eleanor began to walk down the straight path towards the dunes.
She wanted to get Edine away from her house. For a while the two
women walked in silence. The flat fields on either side of them were
quiet. The sound of the sea surrounded them.

'Why are you here, Edine?' She could not keep the antagonism
from her voice.

'I've escaped from Chorolon. This is my home, now.'

There was a lot more to it than that, of course, but it could wait.
Eleanor said, 'Why have you come to find me, then?'

Walking through the sand dunes in the twilight, for a while Edine
said nothing. On the edge of the sea, watching the calm waves, she

said slowly, 'You may find this hard to believe but I feel. . .that I owe
you something. Imbert and I did you a great wrong. He paid the
ultimate price for it, and I too – have endured punishment. But now I
am free, and I want to do something for you.'

'What can you mean?' Eleanor stared at her in the dimming light.
Edine was pale, her eyes large and dark, her beauty gone. She looked
drained and exhausted, as if in the grip of some enervating illness.

'There will be a crossing to Chorolon very soon. I set it up, with
help, so that I could return if I wished. I shall not be using it. But you
could go, if you want. . .'

'Why should I? There is no one for me there.' Her voice was very
bitter.

'No one?' Edine was very quiet.

'I was too late. It was partly because of that Rite. Lukas was no
longer free when I got there.'

'Lukas Marling is not the only man in existence.' Her voice was
dry. 'There is someone else there who would be glad to see you.'

'Matthias? He couldn't wait to get rid of me.'

'No, not Matthias.' She paused. 'Eleanor, haven't you – don't you
miss Phinian Blythe?'

'Phin? But. . .' He'll be all right, she thought. He'll be managing
things better than I, he won't need me for anything.

'He's changed, you know.' Edine was watching her, although the
light was very dim now. 'He's back in Peraldon. Active. Making an
impact.'

'You sound as if you know him well.'

'He helped me escape from Lefevre. I would not be here now
without him.'

Eleanor frowned. 'It doesn't sound very likely.'

'Maybe not. Nevertheless it is true. He asked me to tell you – that if
ever you needed a friend, or somewhere to go, he would be there. He
sent his love. That was all.'

It was finally dark now. A small point of light above the horizon
picked out the pale foam of the turning tide. The wind lifted through
Edine's hair.

How could Eleanor trust this woman? Everything she knew of her
was tainted by the memory of betrayal, treachery, manipulation,
ambition.

'Think about it,' said Edine calmly, as they walked together back to
the cottage.

Eleanor invited her in, and began to make supper.

There was so much to say.

Chapter Thirty-eight
Edine's Story

Eleanor made pasta, and opened a bottle of wine. They ate in the
kitchen, elbows on the oiled tablecloth. And although Eleanor was
still wary and disinclined to trust, during the course of the dinner
Edine imperceptibly crossed the barrier between enemy and friend.

She understood so much. All about dislocation and loss and grief.
Eleanor found herself telling Edine all about what had happened in
Shelt, and how impossible it all was. She described her return, her
parents, her travels, her futile efforts to settle. And when at last,
Eleanor had brought everything up to date, Edine asked her what she
would do next.

'I don't really know.' It seemed rather weak, but there was no clear
direction to Eleanor's thoughts. 'At first, I simply felt in need of time
to assimilate what had happened, to find some way of holding
Chorolon safe in my memory, so that it wouldn't upset things here too
much.' She laid down her fork, looking directly at Edine. 'Did you
know that Lewis is dead? When Imbert kidnapped me, he injured
Lewis, the man with me. He died. People here are affected by what
goes on over there, they even lose their lives because of it. And now
you're here again. Is it always going to be like this, trouble-makers
slipping backwards and forwards from Chorolon?' Her voice had
slipped back into antagonism.

'I think – I really believe that the crossing tomorrow will be the last
such event.'

'I've been told that before, and yet you're here now.'

'Eleanor, may I ask you something? You spent some time with
Matthias, did you not, before coming home?'

'Yes. Some weeks, travelling, and then preparing. . .'

'Eleanor, did he still dream of things to come? In the future for
Chorolon, what did he see?'

'He said. . .death. Destruction. The end of the Gods, the end of
everything. He did all he could to help me escape. He said—' she
swallowed, '"—don't tempt me to use you again." *You* did well to get
out, according to Matthias. Do you know what he meant? Is that why
you're here now?'

'I have heard this from someone else. Chanted in prayer by a priest
who is more than half-Mage, a man with unusual insights. . .' Edine
ignored her second question. 'Dion Gillet, someone known to both
Phinian Blythe and myself, saw very similar visions. And to him they
represented an ultimate terror. He saw the death of the Gods, like
Matthias, and for a priest it was worse than anything.

'His aim is to avert this. His whole life is directed to that point, his every act. He says we will be abandoned, left without power to influence our own fates, because of the actions of the being which calls itself Weard.

'*Weard*? Surely not!'

'The Weard you knew no longer exists. His body is now controlled by Lefevre. . .the Desert Rose, remember?'

'*What?*'

'Think of those other transformations, Eleanor. Remember what the Desert Rose was, remember its power, its obsession. All that is now contained within human form, the form of Weard. And Dion Gillet, alone in all Peraldon, recognises the full horror of what inhabits Weard's body. He thinks that if he can only destroy this aberration, this vile distortion, then the Gods might stay.

'To ordinary people, it may not be so terrible. What Gillet and Matthias both saw was parity, at last, between all people.

'An end to the gods. The end of magic.'

Silence. Eleanor sat back in her chair, staring unseeing into space. At last she spoke. 'That's what we have here, and there's no such thing as parity. People always manage to find ways of being cruel to each other.'

Edine said, 'it may not even be a true vision. You see, a Mage, like a Priest, trespasses all the time upon areas more properly controlled by the Gods. The Mage's magic is his entrée to that world and his defence against it. I think that Matthias is so terrified of losing his magic that he can only see it in terms of the death of the Gods. . .'

Eleanor thought about this. 'What happened, Edine? Who is this man Gillet? You'll have to tell me what's been going on, all the details, if I'm to understand.'

Edine pushed away her plate. 'Have you any coffee? It's a long story, but you're right. You do need to know.' She smiled. 'It's just that it's not easy and we don't have long. . .'

Eleanor made coffee, and they moved out of the kitchen, into the sitting room where she lit a fire. It was still summer, but the winds on the north-east coast were unkind.

Edine sat curled up in the winged armchair close to the grate and began.

'I don't know whether you realised this, but Lefevre did not die when we burnt the Desert Rose. Somehow, he contrived it so that his essence was transferred into the body of his henchman, Weard. Weard's own soul or persona, whatever you want to call it, was lost in this process, destroyed. In this new guise, in this stolen body, Lefevre held the staff that Weard had made from the Rose, and Shadows flickered like smoke round the spiral. . .

'He sought me out. He took me, as a punishment for my rôle in burning the Desert Rose.' Her voice was very dry here, as if telling the story of someone who had lived a thousand years ago. 'We travelled to

Peraldon, in the company of a Fosca baron. And there, Lefevre took
on his old rôle as advisor to the Emperor.'

'Sun priest and Great Mage?' Eleanor remembered the stories,
learned long ago, of Lucian Lefevre, the architect of the Stasis.

'Oh yes. He has spoken with God, has performed all the Rites of
Lycias. And no one can match Lefevre for skill in the arts of magic.
No one can manipulate the appearance of the world with more
imagination, more infallible virtuosity.

'Lefevre – or Weard, as he is now known – staged a pantomime at
the city gates, healing a man who appeared to have the plague. It was
only marsh fever, but the stunt brought him to the attention of the
Emperor. He was accepted into the college of Mages, and quickly rose
to prominence.

'I lived with him in Solkest, the Emperor's palace. I saw him
encourage Xanthon's trust and good will. He seemed all set to take
control, but something happened.

'There was a challenge. A priest, Dion Gillet, from the provinces,
dared to threaten Weard. . .'

Edine paused. 'Gillet is very much more than a simple priest. When
he lived in Peraldon, he was Lefevre's deputy within the Temple. He
was a man of knowledge and great sanctity, of such holiness that
during the Stasis he left the city to live as a hermit. No one heard
from him, he disappeared from all our lives. He was held as an
example to us all, a man who devoted his life to God. In retreat,
he devoted himself to something else. . .' Her voice trailed off into
irony.

'Dion Gillet is without compare among the world of priests.
Single-minded, pure in his devotion. But in retreat, he learned
mysticism. Not the magic of illusion, which is taught in the
Peraldonian college, not the wild magic of the *eloish*, but something
else.'

'A gift from God, he calls it.' She hesitated momentarily. 'I have felt
it, I know what this "gift" is. More ruthless, more dangerous than
anything I've ever experienced on Peraldon with Imbert. Weard –
Lefevre – is the only one who comes close to it.

'He can *change* things. Change them into something else. Other
Mages have often used the physical world, and distorted its appearance. Think of the Parid, scurries; loops in time, even, so that events
are played out of sequence. But those are tricks of the imagination,
and depend on people's perception of them. They do not exist
objectively.

'Dion Gillet can alter the nature of something. He can create the
supernatural from the mundane. Make a god of a human. He can
make things greater than himself. . .his ward, Katriana, is one such
creation.

'He has come to Peraldon in order to challenge Weard/Lefevre
for primacy. I even saw it happen: Weard apparently triumphed,

but I think it was part of the plan. Dion Gillet was held prisoner in the Solkest dungeons, and his ward, his creation, wept behind her veil. . .

'But I also saw that Phinian Blythe had become involved: through some freak of chance he had become acquainted with Dion Gillet and Katriana Lessure. Chance may not be the word for it, I suspect that Gillet knew who he was all along. It was a connection I – sought to manipulate. I promised to release Gillet, if they would help me to escape from Weard/Lefevre.'

Her voice halted, here. She still stared into the fire and, unconsciously, her hand rose, and wiped something from her mouth.

The story that unfolded told of danger and subterfuge. Of wild, unstable magic and uneasy, untrusting alliances. . .

Edine was powerless to leave Solkest. She was Weard's prisoner. But within its ringed walls, she was free to move anywhere.

She went to find Gillet in the dungeons of the fifth ring. He stood naked in a cell lined with shafts of ice. Diamond-hard, these shafts pierced his skin wherever he stood, wherever he lay. He could not move without impaling himself on splinters of freezing ice. He was blue-white with cold, shivering, his eyes dark-hollowed with lack of sleep. His skin was streaked with red. Small specks of blood dropped on to the glassy surface of the floor as he breathed against a thousand needles.

He stared at her through the grill in the door as if she did not exist. His green eyes were withdrawn, the only colour in a face of ice and bone. Pale lashes and brows softened nothing.

Edine said, 'Father Gillet. . .?'

He spoke then, his words hard and contemptuous. 'And what do you want, unclean woman? Have you come to interrupt my penance?'

His mouth began shaping words, as if released. A constant flow of prayer: *forgive my sins*, he said, over and over again. *Do not leave us. Do not abandon men, do not leave us*. . .while his eyes saw that tears ran from Edine's eyes, that blood distorted her mouth.

She opened the door (the key stolen from the gaoler), and regarded him.

He stood with bare feet on the dagger-tips of ice that rose from the floor. He held himself just above their sharp points, but as he spoke to her, she saw him sag, saw his feet lower on to the tips.

'He wants you to cry, doesn't he?' she murmured. 'To beg, and give way and be his creature, as I am. . .How long have you been here?'

'Three days and nights. . .' Gillet spoke wearily, and she saw the soles of his feet pierced again by ice. A breath, which pushed his thin chest against the needles around him. Very slightly, very painfully, he lifted himself above the daggers of ice. 'I cannot talk to you.'

No, she could see that he could not. But she still had some skills left. She traced, in her mind, a spiral unwinding. Leftwards, she unwound the spell, and released the hallucinogenic wave-patterns which led Gillet and herself to believe that he was standing on ice. Which led Gillet's flesh to bleed and hurt as his concentration failed.

He fell against her, stumbling forward out of the cell.

Edine had come prepared. From the folds of her cloak, three scurries fell, stolen days ago from the palace guard. She had not known at the time what she should do with them, but this was the answer.

Three words of power, and the scurries assembled themselves into the simulacrum of life. They wailed softly as she pushed them into the cell. She looked deliberately from the collapsed figure of Dion Gillet on the ground at her feet, to the indeterminate mass of transparent matter in the icy chrysalis. She shaped them like a butterfly is shaped from the soup of its earlier being, and imprinted them with the shape of Gillet's head, the look of his face, the anguished tension of his stance. It was not hard. She had watched Imbert, a Mage of Peraldon, create such simulcra. She remembered her lover, the look of concentration in his eyes.

It was only temporary, a small deceit. She had not power enough to make such a thing permanent. She shut the door, carefully and soundlessly, on the disguised scurries.

She turned to Gillet, and helped him to his bleeding feet. He was virtually unconscious, heavy with exhaustion. She could not herself leave the palace, bound as she was by the deep enchantments of Weard/Lefevre, but she knew where the illegal exits were. With difficulty, for he was a tall man, she half carried Gillet through the corridors further into the dungeons.

'There were barriers all round the dungeons, not merely physical ones. Various spells, constraints and blocks. . .But I had learnt a thing or two over the years, and Gillet was himself powerful. There were a number of cells opening on to the fourth ring, the moat where the fish play.

'We planned a difficult escape. Dion Gillet said that he would shatter the thickened glass holding the sea back, if I could keep the door into the corridor shut against the weight of water. He would be prepared to hold his breath while the cell filled, and then swim through the window into the moat. I was then to cause a diversion, something to call the guards from the bridge over the moat. He would take his chance with the fish. . .

'He was still weak, desperately tired. His words were slurred. I doubted that he had the strength for such an ordeal.'

Edine stared into the fire. 'But, but. . .Dion Gillet is not an unworthy challenger to Lefevre. I have never seen such a display of naked will. The window shattered as lightly as the finest bone china. I did not see what happened next, naturally, because I was out in the corridor, keeping the cell-door in position. It was difficult but not impossible. I heard the water level rise, I heard his brief shout, that he was now swimming. . .

'I left the dungeons and went up to the level of the bridge over the moat. There were only three guards there, and they came running when I showed them the slithers of ice I had found outside Gillet's cell.

'I stood on the bridge, listening to the alarms ring, the whistles blow, the clang of gates shutting. I saw Dion Gillet haul himself through the water towards the gate to the sea. He remained there for one moment, looking at me. He would not forget. . .and then he dived into the sea, and I did not see him again for a long time.'

Edine's voice was so cool, so calm, that the desperate risk she had run seemed minimised. Eleanor said, 'But surely there were guards in the dungeon corridors? It could not have been so easy!'

'I used words and concepts you might understand. There were dreams and distortions, visions and deceits. And truth to tell, Dion Gillet hardly needed my help. Once he was free of the ice, the ice of his own making, remember, he could do virtually anything, go anywhere. There were guards, it is true, but he caused them to sleep. There were bars and locks, but they fell open at his touch. Wounded and exhausted though he was, the world arranged itself around him.'

'He sounds terrifying.'

'Yes. I think he is truly terrifying, just like Weard/Lefevre—'

'Surely it was a dreadful risk, freeing someone like that?'

'No one else would be able to release me.' She looked at Eleanor from the depths of the shabby armchair. 'Of all people you should understand the horror of being possessed by the one you hate above all others, the one responsible for the death of your love. And there was no forgiveness between us. Weard desired only to punish me, and I endured. . .too much.'

When you really looked beneath the superficial friendliness, thought Eleanor, beneath the cold dry words, there was nothing but emptiness at the back of Edine's eyes.

'Have you come here to forget?' she asked gently.

'Yes. But it doesn't work, does it? You've said so yourself. There is too much to put it aside. I thought—' and here Edine smiled, painfully, 'I thought that if I came and made some kind of peace with you, that perhaps the pain would ease. But it's no good. There is no peace for me here, no peace anywhere, for Imbert is dead.'

Eleanor crossed the room and put her arm around Edine's shoulders. She felt the other woman shiver, and then the smooth cap of

dark hair leaned towards her. Edine raised her hand to clasp
Eleanor's, and sighed.

'I wanted to bring you a choice, a way back if you wanted it. You
had no choice last time. But now you can take your fate in your own
hands, if you wish.

'And there is someone there, waiting for you. . .'

Next morning they went walking again. Eleanor had not expected to
sleep that night, but strangely there had been no dreams she could
remember, no weary hours of wakefulness.

She awoke early, and dressed quickly. The sky was clear and
bright, the wind still. She saw that the blackberry bushes lining the
path through the fields were beginning to colour. The berries were red
shading to black, the hips orange among them. There was an
unaccountable lift to her spirits, a spring in her step.

She looked at this familiar world, washed clean in the clarity of
bright morning light, and felt no allegiance to it. There was clear
morning light on Chorolon, too. . .And so much else that had
changed her life. People and places and events. The Arrarat and
Lycias and Astret. And Coron. A sudden, fierce, aching desire to hold
him again.

She had tried to forget Chorolon, had tried hard to fit back into life
here, but it was drab. Drab and without comfort. Was she always
going to be on the outside, wherever she was?

Perhaps the fault lay with her. Perhaps she was simply inadequate,
and always would be. . .She shook her head, and turned back to the
cottage.

Edine was waiting for her. 'Have you made up your mind?'

'No. When is the crossing?'

'At midday. We need to travel south from here, about a hundred
miles. We should leave within the hour, if you have any intention of
travelling.'

'I want to know more about Phin. And how you got out of Solkest.
I need more information, Edine.'

And so, against the clock, Edine's story continued.

Three days had passed after the escape of Gillet, three days in which
Weard/Lefevre had questioned her, over and over again.

Usually, he could read Edine's mind. But she found that just by
thinking about Dion Gillet there was a channel for Gillet's immense,
alien, powers. He surrounded her with his thoughts, and Weard/Lefe-
vre heard only the answers her empty words gave.

Weard had sighed with frustration. He did not trust her, but that
was nothing new. Edine had learnt survival tactics during her time
with him. She was used to lying, he to being obeyed. He did not
suspect her complicity in Gillet's escape.

And Gillet's presence in her mind grew. It reminded her very clearly of the way Imbert had shared everything with her. They had never needed words, either.

She felt nothing but revulsion for Dion Gillet. She knew him to be cold as the grave, driven by an icy will that was not far from obsession. But he could get her out, she knew. He was gifted; endowed with powers that went beyond the usual limits of magic. She welcomed his thoughts into her mind, and listened to his instructions.

Mage-power. Matthias had been unwilling to tell Eleanor what it involved, how it worked. She had seen it in action many times, had even participated in the Seventh Rite herself, and yet she had no real idea of the processes used.

Edine, with experiences and knowledge usually forbidden to women, hesitated only briefly before sharing some of what she knew with Eleanor.

There are two main divisions in the use of magic, she said. There are the tricks, the theatrical effects: flaring lights, sudden fires, levitation, the control of the weather, the removal of obstacles. All needing years of training, all requiring dedicated practice and fine concentration. But anyone could learn those, said Edine, shrugging. They were nothing special, routine.

The extraordinary skills of a full Mage lay in the science of mind-manipulation. This covered many areas, a subject so vast that it struck at the heart of everything. The talent for this was acquired genetically. 'You can either do it or you can't,' she said. 'If you can, then all you need is the knowledge that the skills are there, and the training in their use. Those without this inherited talent had no hope of learning.

'Clairvoyance, telepathy, illusion and delusion. How can we know anything, but through the apprehension of the mind? The senses are the pathways through to the mind, but they are frail and easily deceived. The skilled Mage knows how to trap the senses, to direct them so that they understand things to be real that are not in fact so.'

'What skills do you have, Edine? Can you deceive the senses, create illusions?' Eleanor looked curiously at the calm woman walking beside her.

Edine stopped. 'I have never told anyone this, anyone apart from Imbert. . .but yes, I can. All of it. Imbert told me how to direct it, how to use it efficiently, but I have always hidden it from everyone else.

'Woman are not permitted to use magic. It is usually denied that they are capable of it at all.'

'But you. . .?'

'Yes, and I'll tell you someone else who can, too. If you give me a little time, the story will come to her. . .

'I found that Dion Gillet's mind was mixing with mine, and that he was showing me various concepts, various insights that might be useful.'

It went beyond the extent of the magic she knew. His mind was extreme, she said. Brutal. Lined with images of horror, of eyes squeezed shut in agony and hands clenching, nails digging into the skin, blood dripping, blood falling, and nerves flinching, exposed to the Sun. . .

The judgement of the Lord, he called it. The rewards of sin, the rewards of a life spent in ignorance of the will of Lycias. He tempted her with promises of violence. Bring me Weard's staff, he said. Then you will be free and I shall defeat him, easy as winking, expose him to the workings of retribution.

'I could not easily touch the staff,' Edine admitted, 'although I tried.' Sometimes Weard demanded she carry it, but there was something about the shadows, writhing through the spiral carving, that stripped the strength from her limbs.

'I could hold it for perhaps three, sometimes four seconds before the sickness would start. Like water, my fingers would uncurl and it would fall. Sometimes Weard made me hold it for as long as possible. He would watch all the time as the sickness spread from my fingers up my arm until I had to drop it. Then he would order me to pick it up again, and I would have to try to hold it.'

Eleanor saw the sheen of sweat on Edine's upper lip.

'He wanted to make sure, you see, that I would never be able to steal it from him. I think he suspected that I knew forbidden secrets.

'I took his staff, one night, with Gillet's help. Weard was asleep, and I was lying on the floor at the side of his bed, as usual. His hand, falling from the bed, lay on my shoulder.

'In my thoughts, Gillet told me that he was now strong enough to override the sickness from the staff. If I would allow him to control. . .' Her voice failed.

'Control? Control what?'

'My hand. My body. If I let him in, then he would control all my actions, and the sickness would be bypassed, and I would be able to hold the staff for him.'

'It sounds horrible.'

'Yes.' A pause. 'But you have to understand that I would do anything to escape Weard. . .see the world disappear in flames of hatred, see all humanity tear itself apart, and the oceans boil, *anything* to escape him.' She stopped again, breathing hard, her eyes far and distant.

Eleanor, without thinking, took a step away from her. This was the old Edine, the ruthless, ambitious, cruel companion she had seen partnering Imbert. And then Eleanor saw the tears falling, falling as if they would never stop.

'I – have been mad. I don't know if you'll ever understand, or forgive. . .but it has been like a madness, everything to do with magic, everything to do with such arcane skills.

'I let Dion Gillet in. I let it happen. I saw my hand move, and take the staff. I still felt the sickness washing over me in waves of weakness, but it made no difference for my hand still held the staff and my feet crossed the floor to the door.

'There was a guard outside, but the staff caused him to fall. I heard Weard awake and roll from the bed. I heard him call my name and crash around the room, looking for the staff. . .but the staff, and Gillet, were taking me far away, whisking me along the corridors and over the bridges as swiftly as thought.

'Weard followed me. There was a rush of wind behind me, doors slamming, lights flickering. He did not need a staff to travel. He was very close, the air cold on my back. I felt his hand on my shoulder, I saw his face, grinning at my side, as the walls of Solkest were forgotten beneath us.

'The staff had grown wings of its own, lifting me far over the city, and Weard was flying at my side, reaching for it. . .

'I did not at the time wonder how he could fly, but there was a stench hanging round him, the stench of the Fosca, and I heard leathery wings. He was the Fosca King, after all, flying at my shoulder and reaching for the staff in my hand. But the staff had wings of black, drawing me up to the stars.

'It was a struggle between daemons and I was their battleground, my hand the weapon, my breath the fuel. Gillet was fighting back with violence and passion and Weard was smiling, causing the stars to waver, the night to bend, and braided thorns tore at my hand.

'The winged shadows of the staff shifted. Gillet was drawing them down, pulling the staff towards him. In clouds of black the wings infolded, and I began to fall, discarded, irrelevant—

'I fell into the sea. Into the wide lagoon that lies beyond the palace of Solkest. I was almost unconscious, but the sea was cold, the waves moving slowly. I found that I no longer held the staff, and that the sickness was gone. . .'

Edine stopped. She looked up into the sky, into the clear crystal depths of it, and sighed.

'There was someone on the shoreline, watching. And above, in the stars, I thought I saw a dark angel, augmented by other wings. . . A winged creature soared over the city of Solkest and its voice wailed.

'The watcher from the shore was in the water, swimming towards me, strongly. I was weak, and shocked, my face barely above the waves. But I no longer held the staff. . .'

'It was Phinian Blythe who guided me to the shore. He helped me to the lodgings where Dion Gillet waited, and left me there.

'I recovered, and met Katriana once more. We spent time together, but I could not say that I came to know her. She is always concealed, always covered by the deepest veils and robes. It seems perverse, to limit someone in that way, but her disguise was not the strangest thing about her.

'She was a revelation to me, something extraordinary and unexpected. She is a Mage, untrained, untaught, but wildly powerful. Even then, she knew more than a little of Dion Gillet's art. More than he realised. Katriana is the only woman I have ever known with a true instinct for magic. She is Gillet's creation, and has inherited much. She is certainly more powerful than Imbert. But it was unacknowledged, and I think all the more dangerous for that. I wanted nothing to do with it. I wanted to leave magic behind, and Mages, and staffs and most of all I wanted to be free from Weard.

'I was not sorry to leave. This feud between Gillet and Weard filled me with horror, for I knew that they were implacable rivals, and that neither would give way. Each feels that he has the voice of the Lord, and will be prepared to act on it, at no matter what cost.

'And there was something dreadful about the staff. Gillet questioned me about it all the time. He was fascinated by it. He spent hour after hour studying the drawings I made of its carvings, the shape of the spiral itself. He made me remember what it felt like to hold the staff. He put his hands on my head, and shared those memories. He was sick and trembling, just with the thought of it, but he could not leave it alone. Gillet was experimenting with it, and more than that. Almost as if he would find his own fate there. I wanted to get far away from this, and from Katriana Lessure, whom I do not trust. . .'

'I came here. I left the doorway open, so that I could return if there were horrors here I could not face. And there is horror. There is the knowledge of what I have done to you and others, what the past has meant to you. I wanted to do something to help; I wanted to make some recompense. But all I have to offer is my passage back to Chorolon. I shall not be taking it. But *you* can go, if you want. If we leave now.'

Eleanor could not reply.

'It may sound as if Peraldon is infested with ambitious Mages, but you need have nothing to do with them. Phin said that you could travel with him far away, he would take you somewhere innocent of magic, where you need not be involved at all. And if Matthias's prophecies are correct, there will soon be no more magic on Chorolon anyway.

'Blythe said there would be no pressure. No commitment. You would be free to go where you like, with whom you like. He was offering friendship, a base, if that's what you want.'

Edine paused. 'I would not disdain such an offer. I think Phinian Blythe would be the very best kind of friend to have.'

'If you were me—?'

'I am not. It's your decision.'
'Will you leave me for a while? I have to think.'
'There's no time. We must go now.'
'Where do we have to go?'
'Not far. Come on, Eleanor, make up your mind.'

Chapter Thirty-nine
Sundial

I'll just go with Edine in the car, she thought. I'll keep her company, and think about it on the way. This time tomorrow it will all be over, really over, and I'll be able to get on with my life.

But what kind of life will it be? Will I ever make a go of it, here?

Of course you will, she told herself. You're young, healthy, you've made a success of one career and could doubtless find another. But she found herself flinging clothes, a couple of books, some jewellery (in case she needed cash, in case she found herself somewhere strange) into a bag, unwilling to examine her motives. Her heart was beating and her hands trembling.

'Where are we going?' she said as they got into the car.

'The crossing takes place over a hundred miles away from here. At the place where the taxi went—'

'Damnit, we've not got to drive off that cliff again?'

'No. There are other procedures, this time. You will have to stand in a designated place, at the designated time. But getting to that place will hold peril. You will need courage, and determination. But no more jumping off cliffs.' There was a pause. 'So you are going back?'

'Oh God, I don't know.' Eleanor stared at her hands. 'No,' she said at last. 'I can't bear all that again. There's never been anything but pain and misery on Chorolon. Who's to say it would be any different this time?'

Edine did not answer. She was driving rather fast, paying little attention to other traffic and none at all to speed restrictions.

'How long have we got?'

'The crossing takes place in about two hours. But you won't be needing it, you say.'

'I feel. . .not. But I'd like that time to think about it.'

Edine nodded, her eyes steady on the twisting road. She said nothing for a while, leaving Eleanor to her thoughts.

Eleanor's mind was in turmoil. Here she was lonely, an outsider

whom no one would ever understand. There she would still be the
outsider, but Phin would understand.

Phinian Blythe. What did she really know of him?

Only the essentials. Only that he always acted with courage and
humanity. That he was kind and tolerant she had no doubt, but what
did he feel for her? She liked the warm darkness of his eyes, the black
hair that curled at his temples, but she had only ever known him in
circumstances of extreme danger and stress. What would he be like in
ordinary, everyday life, even supposing that such a thing were
possible on Chorolon? Would he get a job?

Would she? What could she do with herself in Peraldon? She
doubted that there would be a career structure for estate agents. She
wasn't a bad cook, and her dancing was better than average, but
nothing up to professional standard. The eternal dilettante.

But what was she doing with herself here? Nothing had got any
easier, the trauma had not lessened in any way. She had virtually lost
contact with all her old friends, and her parents meant as little as ever.

'Stop the car.'

'There's no time, if you want to keep the option open.'

'I have to make a phone call. I have to know—'

'You'll miss it!'

'Look, there's a phone box. It won't take a minute.'

The car squealed to a halt.

Eleanor ran across the road and wrenched the door open.

Phone cards only. She cursed, rummaging through her bag.
Nothing. Back to the car.

'Go on,' she said. 'We'll have to try somewhere else.'

Another village, another box. Another try.

Success.

'Oh hello, darling—' Her mother's voice, distant and preoccupied.
'Look, can't stop now, I have to rush—'

'Mum, this is important!'

'I'm seeing the solicitor, I'm late already.'

'I must talk to you!'

'Later. I'm going all the way this time, it's gone on long enough.
Tell you about it one day. 'Bye.'

'Mum! Please!'

The phone went dead.

She ran back to the car, and fumbled with the door handle. She felt
her eyes prick with tears.

Edine said nothing. She just put her foot down, and the car left the
village.

They were approaching the hill from a different direction, from the
East. For a moment, Edine stopped in a hairpin bend at the top of the
road.

'There,' she said, pointing. 'That's where the traveller will have to stand.' And from the top of the hill, Eleanor could see a pattern in the trees of the forest below.

A spiral path, marked by swathes of dead wood between the fresh green leaves, leading to a central clearing. She saw the glint of something metallic catching the midday sun.

'What's that?' she asked.

'A sundial,' said Edine. 'At twelve, when there is no shadow, then anyone standing immediately to the South of the dial will be transferred. Are you going to try it?'

No. Her thoughts gave that automatic answer, and she knew why. Only fear. That was all that held her back.

'I must make another call!' My father, she thought. It mattered what he thought. She needed to know how far he relied on her.

How far she relied on him.

'There's no phone box for miles. No way round it, Eleanor. Now or never. It's up to you.'

No one else to blame, no one else to ask. Her decision, alone.

Chorolon was not her world, not her home. Full of danger, and warring Gods and difficult people who no longer loved her. And Phinian Blythe, who would be a friend. . .

And what was there to keep her here?

In the clarity of bright midday sun, she knew the answer.

'Let's go,' she said.

There were only minutes left. Edine put her foot down hard, and the car swooped around the next corner, skidding into the straight slope to the base of the hill.

And then there was an explosion, a tyre blowing. She knew what it was immediately, and at the same time the car swerved, crazily, violently. Eleanor felt the wheels spin, failing to grip. She heard, over the roar of the engine and the squeal of the tyres, the breath hiss between Edine's teeth. In strange clarity, Eleanor saw Edine's knuckles whiten as she struggled to control the wheel.

The car left the road, and began to spin.

A whirling tumble of branches and sun and metal.

Eleanor was thrown against the door, hurled against the windscreen. She'd had time to bring her arms up, clasped over her face, and the seat-belt held her back from the worst of it.

She smelt petrol, even as the car fell.

A jolt, thrusting her neck back against the head-rest. Her body slammed against the sharp constraints of the seat-belt, all her breath viciously expelled. She was aware, although everything was chaos, that Edine's body was still moving. . .

Silence. The car had come to rest, impossibly tilted between two trees on the forest floor. In the sudden stillness she heard the birds begin to sing again. There was a crackling sound, like the rustling of paper, as the car shifted on the branches.

There were sharp pains in Eleanor's shoulder, the sticky feeling of
blood. Unfocused, grinding pain everywhere. Her hands still covered
her mouth.

She did not want to look to her right. Instead, she turned to the left.
The pain in her shoulder came from the thorny branches of a tree,
pushing through the open window into the car. Painful, but not deep.
Experimentally, she moved her arms and legs, and took a deep breath.
Aches everywhere, stiffness and soreness and throbbing, but every-
thing was working, moving.

Edine.

At last Eleanor looked to her right. Edine's head had gone through
the windscreen. There was blood everywhere as the jagged edges of
glass cut into the neck. Edine's body was held there, half-stand-
ing, clasped by the necklace of glass. Through the shattered clouding of the screen, Eleanor could not see Edine's face. She did not need
to.

Shuddering, with hands that shivered uncontrollably, she struggled to release her own seat-belt. It had jammed, or she was too
feeble. . .Her fingers slipped against the metal, the plastic webbing
seemed greasy with blood and sweat. The scent of petrol was
everywhere.

The door catch wouldn't work either. She reached out her left
hand, pushing away the branches that jutted through the window.
There was smoke coming from somewhere, and the smell of
petrol. . .

Eleanor brought her legs up, on to the seat, and began to wriggle
out of the belt, out towards the open, branch-filled window.

Twigs caught in her hair, grazed against her skin. The seat-belt only
tightened as she moved, entrapping her knees and then her ankles,
but in a frenzy of painful movement she managed to get her arms and
shoulders free. She grabbed at the branch, and hauled herself out of
the car.

She did look back then at Edine's head jutting from the windscreen.
The front of the forehead was crushed completely, dented inwards
in a pulp of flesh and bone. There was blood everywhere, masking the
face and neck and running down over the windscreen. Edine was
dead.

Smoke, and the smell of petrol. There was no point in even trying to
get the body out. Eleanor had to get away from the car, quickly.

Half-dazed, she scrambled through the tangle of branches, her hair
and dress caught and torn. It seemed to take for ever to get free of the
trees, but her watch, still working, showed that hardly any time at all
had passed since Edine had showed her the spiral path at the top of the
hill.

Five to twelve. Five minutes to find the place, if she was going to
travel back. . .

The air behind her exploded. She was thrown to the ground, as a

plume of fire leapt into the sky. The petrol had ignited, the car
disintegrating in the force of the detonation. Flaming shards began to
fall through the branches. Aghast, she saw the summer-dried trees
around her begin to catch light. A flare of bright flames blocked her
path.

She turned, and tried to run, but the undergrowth was thick, and
everywhere she looked she saw the forest covered in sparks of flaming
matter.

She was in the midst of a forest fire, with no idea which way to go.
She blundered forward anyway, away from the enormous heat that
was consuming the trees.

She tripped, falling awkwardly over a strand of bramble thorns. She
saw, bizarrely, the bag she had packed, half open, spilling into the
path of the flame. Her purse, her driving licence, her diary and keys,
all spewing out on to the forest floor. It was lying on a wide, clear
path, winding through the flaming trees, deep into the forest.

A spiral path.

Three minutes to twelve, her watch said.

She stared from the bag to the flaming wreck of the car, at the
blackened skull just visible through the pluming smoke.

They would think her dead. They would grieve, feel sorry for a
while, but as far as her parents were concerned that part of their story
would be over. Their own conflict would soon return to centre-stage.
She had always been superfluous to it, and them.

In the furnace that was the car, she saw her way out. Edine was her
height, and only bones would be left. Everyone would think it was
Eleanor who had died in the crash. Another crossing, another death.
But this time no one was going to grieve, not for long.

She was free to go.

From above, the path had seemed to bend in dizzying, close curves,
but on the ground the distances were greater. She could not tell how
far from the sundial she was, she could not tell how far there was to
go. She ran, while the forest flamed around her. The wide, flame-
breaking path, so clear of debris or fuel for the fire, was both a shelter
and an escape. She ran, her breath burning in her throat, her feet
stumbling and unsteady to the centre.

An open clearing, now encircled by fire. As she stood there, her
eyes smarting from the smoke, she heard a crash behind her. A tree
had fallen across the path, and fire leapt from it to form an
impenetrable barrier behind her. She could not go back.

One minute. In the centre of the clearing she saw the rough wooden
column, the hasty, impromptu plinth that held the sundial.

She walked towards it.

The Sun, overhead, heavy as iron.

The forest, a context of fire.

She was at the centre of a burning spiral, at a point of transition.

She laid her hands on the face carved on the sundial, and flame blazed.

She was the traveller.

PART TWO

Chapter One
Winter in Summer

The ocean surrounded them. They stood alone, each to a separate island fastness, and watched the sun and sea for presages of change.

Dederic waited on Lisfay, far to the North of Shelt at the end of the chain of islands. He had no staff, no books, no companions. No dragon answered his summoning now. Only one servant, a deaf mute, attended his personal requirements. Six soldiers were stationed there, to guard the supply boat when it called once a month with food and water. It also brought six more men, the next shift. No one apart from the mute stayed for more than a month, lest the Mage Dederic, first Sea Lord of Shelt, should suborn and subvert those set to guard him.

These islands were deserts of rock and sand. They had no water of their own, apart from the transient gift of the sky, and nothing lived there beyond the reach of the tide.

Dederic paced the highest cliff on his kingdom of rock and looked towards Shelt. It was invisible from this distance, and the horizon was hidden in cloud and mist. He felt the chill in the air, and although the sun still shone on his island, he recognised the cold as something unnatural.

He had ruled the weather of Shelt, he had protected its fisherpeople from storm. He was used to noting the direction of the wind, the pressure of the air. Sometimes he felt as responsive as bladder-wrack sea-weed, his skin dry and cracking in the sun, soft and supple with moisture.

Perhaps that would be his fate, enduring on this barren island. He would become a dry flaking husk of empty skin, drifting in the wind, helplessly reaching towards the dampness of the air.

He was resentful, frustrated, furious. He had done his best by the city of Shelt, he had brought untold wealth to its coffers, he had brought it fame throughout the northern continent. He had endowed the Great Temple to Astret with every glory, honouring the Lady in all Her rites. He had neglected nothing in Her name, caring for Her people.

Dederic had saved life after life from the clutch of illness and old age. He had bargained with a dragon to stave off death.

At last, alone on this barren island, he recognised what had defeated him. He sensed in Felicia Westray the feminine, black power of the Moon. The dark side to Astret: the side that Mages everywhere tried to divert or deny, even those who followed the Lady and attended Her

Rites. Felicia personified this dark aspect, she had denied the people of Shelt the possibility of eternal life. She had defeated Ladon. She had brought death to Shelt.

He was himself very old now. He felt things slipping away. He wondered which he would lose first, his magic or his sanity. He could feel the edges of his concentration fracturing now, and assumed that this was a function of his great age. But sometimes doubts arose as he looked at the Moon, so dead and cold, its darkness waiting for them all; another doubt arose as he looked towards the Sun. He thought, what if magic is leaving us all? Now that the Lady had abandoned us—

The Sun, so bright and forceful, the rigid chill in the air. . .

Dederic looked at his fingers, swollen with rheumatism, and traced a small spiral in the empty, sun-drenched space before him. He imagined that the wind had become caught up in the spiral, that he had created a vortex of power, unseen and unfelt, beyond his fingertips.

The Sun threw the shadow of his misshapen fingers on to the rock beyond him, and he watched, fascinated, as the shadows flickered against the stone.

He remembered words that were etched on his soul.

The shadows began to move of their own volition.

Their own, or someone else's? Spirals often had a life of their own, he knew. Every spiral had the potential to draw in other minds, other thoughts, other forces. These sun-shadow spirals had caught someone's attention. There was someone there, playing with shadows. . .

He knew who it was. He acknowledged the debt. His guards were out of earshot and so he spoke aloud. 'Well, well, old friend. What do you want now?'

And the presence in his mind, the presence revealed between thought and spiral, answered.

The whirlwind of snow brought ice to the city. Shelt was encased in frost. And when the snow ceased, blowing clear of the ice into great drifts, the Sun shone coldly on gleaming levels, on slippery staircases and brilliant roofs. On sparkling turrets and chimneys and spires. The city glittered as if made of glass. At first the children whooped and sang, and skated everywhere, and their shouts were wild, out of balance, a little disturbing.

Soon, they fell silent. No supplies were reaching the city from Stromsall. Beyond the ice, a blizzard still raged, and no merchants or traders would venture through it.

Mittelson gave orders for a cut in rations, and for the great houses to be searched for illegal stores.

Proclamations were issued, the frozen city showered with dryly composed leaflets: to survive, we must be moderate. . .fair shares for all. . .central distribution points. . .further rationing. . .

It was not yet desperate, for Shelt did not have to depend only on what it had hoarded. The sea was still open, for this was summer. It was true that the jutting rocks of the two briggs were now slippery with frost, but the cold could not endure against the pressure of a warmly moving tide. The empty curve of sand, the shallow bay of Shelt, could be fished and plundered. There was a clear channel between the briggs, out to the ocean. Daily the fishing cobles were hauled across the cold sand to the tide, to the accompaniment of the prayers and good wishes of all the citizens of Shelt. Once again, Shelt depended on the fisherpeople for its livelihood.

This was an irony not lost on Olwyn Mittelson.

Messages were sent further south once more, this time to Javon Westray, requesting aid. As yet there had been no reply. And summer was drawing to a close.

To the West, the blizzard was barred from the city only by a line of massive, Mage-enhanced fires, constantly attended, constantly burning. Ferant and Alex Aldrich sank all their skills, all their knowledge into the business of burning. The silvery gleam of ice over the western region of the city was coloured grey by black smoke. No winter wonderland here, but a dirty wash of smoke-stained slush.

Felicia passed by the door to Rosco's apartments. Since his return she had been spending an hour or so sitting by his bed after each day's work, watching for any sign of life. She told him what had happened each day, what she felt and thought, all her hopes and fears. She held his hand, and scanned his face. There was never any flicker of response. The cold centre held.

And yet she went back, day after day, increasingly depressed by the blankness on his face.

Outside Rosco's door, Serethrun took her by the hand. 'Felicia, this does no good.' His voice was kind. 'You need to rest, and Rosco can hear nothing you say.'

'I know.' She sighed. 'But I find my thoughts falling into order, when I speak to him. It gives a kind of distance to everything, a perspective which I value.'

'Could I not help?' Diffidently.

She paused, looking at him. She had always trusted him, always liked him. He had rescued her from Gawne, had taken messages to her father. She liked the slant to his eyes, the straight black fall of his hair, the way he moved silently and with elegance. . .He disturbed nothing by his presence. He stood out in no crowd, made no mark in empty rooms. It was a special skill, to blend oneself with the surroundings, a peculiarly *eloish* grace.

'But you are not neutral,' she said softly. 'You are *eloish* and have a stake in what happens here. I would read thoughts and influences in your eyes even if you said nothing.'

He was silent, waiting.

She walked on, past Rosco's door, along to her rooms, knowing that he would accompany her. She thought, and what do I know of the *eloish*, of these people who roam the plains of Stromsall? Why have I not taken into consideration that it is they, with those other tribes of the North, who assault this city with ice?

'But I would welcome your presence now,' she said. 'Sit with me, and tell me about the *eloish*. . .'

It was easy enough, to begin with. He told her about his family. His father Renferell, who had lived as a cripple within Shelt, in the hope of a healing which never came. He told her about his sister Irian, the black Lady of their clan, and how she had exiled him from the *eloish* when he had attempted to save their father's life.

'When a person is deathwards, with no hope of returning to a full life, then he or she is no longer part of the clan. We move on and we know that one day it will be our own turn to watch the *eloish* ride away.'

'That seems very hard.'

'It is necessary. And inevitable, for us. The difficulty comes in making the decision to move on, and that is Irian's rôle. She decides who will ride and who stay behind. Sometimes, she will grant a quicker death to those who desire it. . .'

He was silent for a long time after this, and when he spoke again it was about something so strange that Felicia hardly dared believe him.

He told her about a baby, a small child who had joined their clan during the last ride to the North. Serethrun watched her carefully as he spoke. Coron was like water in the desert, like laughter in springtime, he said. He'd been brought to them by Haddon Derray, who was a Caver like Rosco. And who had known him once. . .

'Tell me about the baby,' she said with unexpected longing and, because he smiled then, she knew that he had wanted to divert her, that this was part of an instinctive, natural courtesy.

'It's difficult to describe,' he said. 'He – made things better. It was impossible to be angry or frightened when the baby was there. He even seemed to dismay Gawne for a while, and that is how Irian, Rosco and I managed to get away. He gave us the strength to escape. Jerr Morrelow knew something about the child, I think, but he would never say and now it is too late.'

'Where is the baby now?'

'Haddon did not want to stop here. He said he was going home, that he knew where the child belonged. . .

'They were going south to Sarant. It is the place where Haddon Derray, and Rosco and his brother, came from. An island in the Malith Channel, between north and south.'

'I should like to see this child, one day. . .'

'Lady, you will have a child of your own to care for soon.'

'If we can escape winter—'

'And if the ice halts. . .'

Chapter Two
Seashore

Next day, there was more bad news. One of the fires had got out of control, and a large area of the poorer quarters by the western walls had caught fire.

Nine people lost their lives, including two children. It had been the responsibility of Ferant Aldrich. A desperate, reckless attempt had been made to defend the western gate, and Ferant had augmented the inadequate flames with unwise spirals.

His brother Alex had tried to drag him away, to interrupt the flow of words, the flow of fire. Ferant had pushed him off, offering all of himself to the spiral while saying, and Alex heard every word of it, 'Take me, take my life, take this power I offer—'

There had been a modulation in the wind. Ferant saw the spiral of flame lean towards him, and stepped forward. He found himself touched by flame, singed and charring at the extremities. He screamed then, and felt himself drawn up towards the vortex, caught in it, caged within it and whirled round about. He exploded in a catherine-wheel shower of light, and sparks and flaming debris flung themselves wide over the wooden shacks. . .

Alex Aldrich had worked through the day to repair the breach in defences, helped by the Castle guard. There was no time for mourning, no time for grief. The survivors sought shelter at the Castle, and Felicia refused them nothing.

Mittelson waited until the food began to run low before he moved. As autumn approached he gave the orders for further rations to be imposed and went to find Felicia.

As usual, she was in the state apartments, in one of the smaller reception rooms. The Countess of Shelt held open court every day, and people brought their requests, complaints, grievances and disputes to her.

She never failed, never missed a session, although she was now entering the final stages of her pregnancy and moved with slow heaviness. She listened carefully to every complaint, and asked pointed questions. Witnesses would be called. Sometimes the plaintiffs were sent away while she discussed their case with Gereth Hallan, the Lord Chandos. He was often at her side, the slight, clever man with his aquiline features, his darting eyes. It rarely took her long to come to a decision. Usually, she would give the answer straightaway.

No, you cannot evict your tenants without warning.

No, we cannot reserve supplies of wood to heat private houses, no matter how much is paid for them.

Yes, the refuge for the homeless should have extra funds.

No, you cannot expect your goods to be returned to you after the crisis, for no one knows how long it will last. Every effort will be made, but no promises given. . .

Secretaries wrote down every word, and sometimes Mittelson requested transcripts. They were never refused, for Felicia trusted his judgement in these matters and asked his advice in many cases. Like Gereth Hallan, he knew the people of Shelt better than she, and could tell her when one was lying, one exaggerating, one genuinely suffering. As time went by, she began to match the knowledge of the two men.

But it was all a constant weight of worry and responsibility, and although she was so tired every night, physically exhausted by the effort of dragging round a sluggish, unfamiliar body, she found sleep elusive.

It was partly the difficult decisions forced upon her every day, the lives that depended on her will, combined with this deadly threat of winter. And partly the fact that Rosco still lay unmoving and unresponsive in his room, and that nothing anyone could do seemed to make any difference.

She lay awake in her chilly bed, watching the cold ice gleaming, feeling the small movements in her abdomen which reminded her that her body was not her own. And then she would feel fear: fear that she would fail this child by being weak and preoccupied; and fear that she would fail the people of Shelt.

This was the only time she allowed herself the indulgence of her own feelings. Never had so much been demanded of her. As the days passed, she was vaguely aware that she was changing. Differing pressures required differing strengths; she found in herself a dogged perseverance, a vivid sense of priorities and the will to carry them through. Some might have recognised this as courage, but Felicia herself never thought in such terms.

She just knew that there was work to be done, and that she was the one to do it. And if at the daily courts there were violet shadows under her eyes, the heaviness of her gaze seemed to draw honesty from her petitioners.

Looking at her, sitting small and alone behind the wide, ornate desk, Mittelson wondered how far she would resist him.

'Lady, may I talk to you?'

She sighed, and looked at the list on her desk.

'There are people waiting to see me of course, but then there always are. Very well, Olwyn.' She looked at the Lord Chandos. 'Gereth, would you tell those waiting outside that there will be a delay?'

'Certainly, my lady.' Chandos went to the door, and bowed to her before leaving. She nodded dismissal to the clerks and scribes, and leant back in her chair with a sigh.

'Is it necessary to drive yourself so hard, Lady?' Mittelson had brought forward a chair and sat beside her.

'I see no reason to abandon these people to their pain. It's little enough that I do.'

'Felicia, I have had to cut the rations today. There are indications that the sea is beginning to freeze beyond the briggs and the temperature is falling. There is no sign of help from Javon, no effort we have not made to push back Gawne and his followers—'

'What are you suggesting, Olwyn?' She was sitting upright once more, anxiously scanning his face.

'The only way to fight magic is to use magic.' He paused. Then, 'Lady, I seek your permission to bring back the Sea Lords.'

'And have them join up with Gawne, as they did before?'

'No one could face Gawne's army and want to become part of it. They are men of Shelt, this is their city. If there's any loyalty left, if not to you, then to the place, they'll help us now.'

Every day, now, the ice warriors fought against the blazing fires that defended Shelt from the wintry plains. Through the smoke and flames, the people of Shelt saw shapes of grey and white moving with slow precision. The eyes of the ice-bound glowed with a dead luminescence. They never spoke, never acknowledged the people on the other side of the flames. Sometimes they attempted to break through the line of fires and then there was horror indeed, as the ice melted and their bodies writhed in the flames.

'Felicia, we need help, and the sea will soon be beyond our reach.'

'*Not* Mages, Mittelson. Not those Mages.'

'Alex Aldrich is useful, but he's more than occupied with the fires. And I can't defeat Gawne alone, I've tried before. I need help, Felicia. And there's no one else.'

'The Sea Lords are self-seeking, ruthless, hungry for power, and I will have nothing to do with them!' She was on her feet now, gathering together her papers, refusing to look at him. She was flushed with anger.

'I would trust them to act correctly in this matter.'

'*Correctly*? Why should they help us? We incarcerated them on those damn islands, comfortless and powerless, as a reward for their actions. They're not going to want to help now.'

'They might if their exile is ended.'

'Bring them *back*? Back to Shelt? Do think, Mittelson! There's some degree of trust here, some working together of people, and you want to reintroduce the ultimate distortion of magic to Shelt!'

'Felicia, I can think of nothing else. If you can, I'd be only too glad to try it. But the sea is icing over, and the sun does nothing to help us.'

'Go away, Mittelson. I don't want you here. Go and play with your spiral charms and see what results. I will consider what you say, but I must say that I think you are wildly astray in this. There must be an alternative!'

'I hope you are right, Lady.' He stood up, stretching long legs. 'Shall I cancel the other consultations for the afternoon?' He saw how white she was, how tired. Her skin was pinched with fatigue.

She hesitated. 'Give me five minutes. Send in some tea. Then they can come once more. . .' She looked up at him suddenly. 'They need me, Mittelson. I can't betray this trust.'

'They won't thank you when they're starving.'

He crossed the floor and left the room.

That evening she did not even attempt to rest. She went to her own rooms, and put on her warmest cloak, her strongest boots. She told her servants to delay the evening meal, and that she was going walking. To satisfy Mittelson, and everyone else, she took Annis with her. Then she went to find Serethrun Maryn.

She knew where he would be. Down on the seashore, gathering driftwood to fuel the fires. There was little enough of it by this time, but still the tide brought in the ruins of old wrecks, old tragedies. Serethrun was there most days, she knew, as if he could not bear the claustrophobia of the Castle and the city. Here the wind blew the snow in white clouds away from the sea, and the waves broke with unabated vigour.

She saw him in the distance, walking along the line of debris where the tide turned. His hands were in his pockets, his shoulders hunched against the wind. He looked not at the tangle of weed, old rope and shells at his feet, but instead out to sea.

'Annis, wait here for me, please.' She smiled brightly at her companion, who was already stamping her feet on the damp sand, her cheeks rosy with cold. 'I'll try not to be long. You could walk up and down, swing your arms. You'll keep warm that way.' It gave Felicia a small malicious pleasure to express concern about others. It was but slight recompense for all those years of unwanted attention.

Annis sighed. 'Very well, Lady. But it's getting late. . .'

'I know. And dinner waiting.' Although her words were light, she was distracted by the swirls of snow which eddied around them both. It seemed predatory to her, attracted to their warmth. 'I won't be long, Annis. Patience. . .'

Serethrun looked up as Felicia approached. She never managed to surprise him with her occasional appearances on the seashore.

'Serethrun—' she said quickly, before he could greet her. 'I need to talk to you. I want some advice.'

She waited for him to say, you shouldn't be out, why aren't you resting, it's too cold, but he merely nodded.

'Is Mittelson pushing for something?'

How did he always know? 'Yes, he wants to bring back the Sea
Lords. He says he cannot defeat Gawne, and that the sea is beginning
to freeze.' She shivered suddenly, as a gust of frosted wind buffeted
them.

'He's right about the sea. Look.' He held her arm, and pointed
out along the line of the south brigg. A glassy smoothness was
reaching out into the waves. The tide kept breaking into it, and
sometimes it fragmented, but the small channels between the
rocks were iced over, and a glaze of frost was spreading over the grey
water.

'I don't want them back, Serethrun, whatever the cost. Whatever
Mittelson may say. Nothing could make me trust them. They are
purely ambitious, purely vengeful. They will not forgive what Rosco
and I have done.'

'No, they won't. But we need something. . .'

'Evacuate the city? While the sea is still clear?'

'Gawne will pursue us.'

'What does he *want*? The city, his old position back?'

'No, not that.' He was studying her face, his eyes deeply serious. 'I
think he wants you. You defied him all the way, you and Rosco. Rosco
is already half under his power, under the touch of ice, but you are
free.'

She was very pale. 'If I gave myself up?'

'No. Don't even think it, Felicia. That would be an ultimate
failure for us all. Gawne wants you because you are powerful.
You're our one hope against the ice, our only chance—' There
was passion in his voice, and his eyes were locked on hers in a kind of
fury.

'I? What could I do?' She could not imagine what he meant.

'What have you ever done, what did you do before?'

'Nothing. . .it wasn't me. All I did was—' Felicia stopped.

'What? *What* did you do?'

'The tide turned, once. Rosco was rescued from the dragon, by the
turning of the tide.' The words were almost inaudible, but he heard
her.

'Come with me, Felicia!' He took her hand, and began to walk
swiftly across the sand to the sea's edge. 'Look at that, look at what's
happening.'

The growing ice, battered by the tide, crushed and shattered by the
force of the waves.

'Put your hand in the water, feel its strength.'

She crouched down, taking off her gloves. The cold air stung her
skin, but the water was of a higher temperature, seeming almost
warm, swirling around her fingers.

She straightened, slowly. 'I don't know how it happened. I don't
know if it can be done again. . .it wasn't quite real, somehow.'

'And that is how all magic is made,' said a different voice, coolly.

Felicia looked round. Serethrun's sister, Irian, stood there, dressed in grey like the sky. Neither of them had heard her approach.

Felicia had only met her once before, when she had first arrived in Shelt. Irian had stayed in the Castle only long enough to inform everyone what had happened. She had told her story with a strange mixture of contempt and loathing for her listeners. When she walked out, very soon afterwards, she'd left a trail of offended and frightened people behind her.

She seemed to despise the city, to hate the limits of bricks and mortar. To be besieged in a city felt like the strictures of death to an *eloish* shaman, Serethrun had explained.

Felicia saw desperation in Irian's eyes, and thought she knew why. 'Could *you* help against the ice, Irian? Against Gawne?'

Irian smiled, but there was no humour in it. 'Why should I? I owe nothing to the people of Shelt.'

'To save your own life?'

'It is worth nothing now. Now that my people are dead.'

Serethrun said, 'Not dead. It's not that. They are gripped by ice, but might be released—'

'Only in flame. We've talked about this before, Serethrun. A few, terribly burnt, might survive for a short time. That price is too high.'

He was silent, and Felicia, looking from one to the other saw that the divisions between them ran deep.

Irian had turned away, was walking over the damp cold sand. Felicia ran after her.

'Irian, please wait. Tell me, what is this about releasing those taken by the ice? What does the fire do?'

'Come and see, Lady.' Irian's voice was sharp. 'Come and see why my people are as good as dead to me.'

She grasped Felicia's arm almost painfully, and began to walk swiftly towards the rocks of the north brigg.

Felicia was half running, trying to keep up with her.

'Irian!' Serethrun spoke sharply.

For a moment the shaman paused. She looked at Felicia, who was almost breathless, and shrugged. But when Irian started walking again, her pace was slower and Felicia no longer had to run.

Serethrun took Felicia's hard. 'You don't have to go with her,' he said. 'You can hear about this at second hand. It is distressing, you will have seen nothing like it before.'

She stared at him for a moment, and then said calmly, 'But I have to take these decisions, Serethrun. I need to see for myself just what the risks are.'

'It's not pretty, Felicia. . .'

Even with this warning, she was not fully prepared.

The sound of soft moans filtered through the air, mingling with the wash of the waves. Irian's cave in the brigg was almost entirely dark, but not quite.

One torch hung in the entranceway, and its light gleamed redly on the naked flesh of those living within. Few were moving. They lay on ledges and on the floor, and their whimpering cries pulsed in Felicia's mind with a weight of unendurable distress.

They looked so nearly human, she thought. Even those without eyes turned their suppurating faces towards her, and their finger-less hands fumbled in the air. The muttering voices were in a language she didn't know. She heard Irian reply in cool tones. She heard her own name mentioned and that of Shelt, but she understood nothing else. It didn't matter. How could any words matter beside such torment?

'Oh, you must bring them into the Castle!' It was a relief to look away from them to Irian. 'We have beds, nurses—'

Irian stared at her, implacably, silently, and Felicia turned to Serethrun, her hands outspread.

'It would do no good,' he said gently. 'The *eloish* would find their sufferings far worse within walls.'

'What could be worse than this!' Her voice was shaking.

'They are free here. And the sea air is salty and cool.' Irian did not look at her. She was on her knees, lifting her hand to touch the raw red shoulder of a woman on the ground. The slit that had once been a mouth moved in a mockery of speech, and Irian bent closer. As Felicia watched, her hand nerveless over her mouth, she saw Irian draw a small slim blade from beneath her cloak.

The woman was still talking, quietly chanting or intoning. . .The shaman leaned forward suddenly, so that the woman's face was shielded from Felicia. But still in her view was Irian's hand, and the knife, and the exposed, charred skin of the woman's breast.

A quick, sure movement and the quiet stream of words from the woman was cut off. Felicia saw the thin dribble of blood slow and stop. The rasping sound of breath was gone.

She stepped forward, trembling, but could find no words. It had been an act of mercy.

Then her thoughts found shape, inappropriate and shocking. 'Why kill her, and not the others?'

'Because Brianne asked it. In the end, I will kill them all.' Irian spoke flatly.

Other voices around the cave called out, and the shaman passed from one to another, saying a few words here, smoothing tears from smoke-ruined eyes there.

She returned to the mouth of the cave, and nodded to Serethrun. He moved forward and with infinite gentleness lifted the ruined body of the woman. He carried her out of the cave and beyond Felicia's sight.

'And Serethrun, where is he going?' she asked Irian, surprised at the steadiness of her voice.

'The dead are taken by the tide. No dragon lives there now to give them the semblance of life. They become food for the fishes, who in their turn are food for the people of Shelt.'

I can accept this, thought Felicia. The sea seemed a kinder place of rest for tortured flesh than the harsh ground. 'You must of course judge what your people need,' she said calmly. 'But if anything from the city may help, it is yours for the asking.'

She moved suddenly, uncontrollably, and left the cave.

Outside, the swirls of snow struck her exposed face with stinging frost. She saw, as in a dream, Annis approaching over the sand.

'Lady, it is getting late. . .' Her eyes noted that Annis was shivering with cold. 'It cannot be good for you to be out here in all this.' Annis waved at the swirling snow. 'The Mage Mittelson said you should rest in the evenings.' She looked past Felicia towards the cave.

Felicia took her arm and steered her away from it. 'Yes, let us return.'

As they walked back to the Castle, Annis kept up a flow of inconsequential chatter to which Felicia replied automatically.

At the steps to the harbour she paused and looked back towards the cave. In the far distance she saw two figures outlined against the falling snow. They were both dressed in drab grey, but the snow was falling thickly and their shoulders were stained with white. Predatory, she thought. Battening on to heat and warmth, Gawne's cold would soon devour them all.

She ate very little at dinner, but that was not unusual. And when she claimed that she was tired, and needed an early night, no one tried to dissuade her. It was self-evident that the Countess of Shelt was feeling both her condition and the weight of her responsibilities.

Alone in her room, Felicia stared at herself in the mirror. But she did not see the familiar thin face, the unfamiliar bloated body. Instead her eyes saw a shape not quite human, moaning softly, its skin hanging in blackened red rags.

The Sea Lords could help, Olwyn had said. And the bay was freezing over. Probably they would use fire, like the Aldrich brothers. Cauterise the growing ice, burn out the creeping horror that gave Gawne mastery over living creatures.

Except the only cure, the only defence was to burn beyond bearing those afflicted with ice. That was what the Mages would do, in order to defeat Gawne.

And Rosco? Would they burn the life along with the ice from him, too?

We must fight evil with whatever means we have, Mittelson would say. This is to preserve an ultimate peace. And whatever the suffering,

whatever the cost, it will be worth it in the end.
She did not believe it.

Chapter Three
Firelight

That night, Felicia's dreams were filled with the faceless forms of the
hideously burnt. She struggled against the sheets and blankets,
whimpering. She heard echoes of their groaning, smelt the charred,
sickly scent of fire-eaten flesh. Burning wounds throbbed to the
rhythm of her heart, blunted fingers waved feebly around the curtains
of her bed. And all the time the only relief, the only comfort and
possible way out, was the promise of cold steel waiting to slide
through the agonised flesh.

In her abdomen the baby fluttered softly. It drew her to waking.
She thought of it, blunt and hairless like the burnt ones, its hands
without strength, its eyes unseeing. It bathed in the enclosed sea that
was her womb, safe from harm, safe from evil. No fire could touch it
there, no light from moon or sun. She did not know whether it was
male or female, and did not care. . .

So long as it was safe. So long as it swam in salty water until it was
strong enough to face the world.

To swim in salty water. . . .

She rolled over and swung her legs over the side of the bed. It was
an effort. The room was bitterly cold, unheated now to save fuel for
the fires outside. Her wrap and slippers were on a chair nearby. She
put them on, and then went to the window. She pulled back the heavy
curtains, and opened it.

The snow beat at her like blows. She pulled a blanket from the bed,
and masked from the wind all her face but the eyes. She was
shuddering with cold, but she had to look.

She saw, at the end of the brigg which lay beneath the Castle a sheen
of ice, glinting in the reflected light from the partially hidden moon.
The ice seemed to stretch further than she remembered. It curved out
across the bay, stilling the movement of the waves.

The bay was over eight miles wide, and as yet the creeping ice jutted
only a few hundred yards from the north brigg. She could not tell how
far it extended from its southern twin. But still, she thought, it would
take time for the barrier of ice to surround Shelt.

She looked down, and drew her breath in, suddenly, sharply. Dark
shapes moved there. The ice-warriors were scrambling over the

tumbled strata beneath the Castle itself. She saw them clinging to the foundations of the tower where she stood, and everything they touched shone with frost.

They were filing silently over the shining rocks, moving along the brigg and out into the waves. There were so many of them. She saw their shadows passing beneath her. Tall figures moved with clear-sighted precision over the dying waves and wherever they trod, the ice thickened.

She could see it happening. The reflected light of the moon moved more slowly, sluggishly. It was a heaviness over the water, a dead hand. . .

Quickly Felicia moved back into her room, taking matches and candles from the mantelpiece. Out into the corridor. Her first instinct was to rush to Mittelson's room, to tell him what was happening. But Mittelson would want to call the Sea Lords, would try to make her change her mind. There was one other thing she could try.

She ran, cursing the inefficiency of her laden body, along the corridor to Rosco's room.

There was an attendant sitting with him, as usual. She dismissed the woman and locked the door after her. Then she went round the room, lighting every candle, standing them on tables and chairs, on book-shelves and windowsills. She touched one to the small, dead fire in the grate and blew it to life.

She took hold of two candelabra and moved across to the bed. Through the dazzle of flames she looked at the unmoving, unknowing face.

'Rosco!' She was shouting. 'Wake up!' She moved closer, putting the candelabra down on the floor. Then she slapped his face, and his head lolled on the pillow. The skin on the cheek reddened slightly, but his eyelids did not flicker. 'Rosco, I *need* you, come *on!*' She pulled back the sheets and blankets so that he lay there, naked before her eyes.

With her hand to his face, she pushed his heavy eyelids back. Blue and unseeing, the familiar eyes stared past her. She stroked the reddened skin, stroked all his body. There was no answering response, no tightening of muscles or shiver of nerves. Like a weight of dead meat, he lay there, unreachable. This time, human warmth was not enough.

She sat beside him, and thought. She had mourned him when he left Shelt. She had thought him lost for ever, because he loved Eleanor Knight and was gone from Shelt.

He was lost for ever. Even if he awoke from this chill coma, he would always love Eleanor Knight. His heart would be, as ever, frozen towards herself. The ice would always live.

Felicia deserved better.

She had managed to rule Shelt without him, to keep up a positive show for everyone around her, and they had not noticed any lack, she was sure.

It's no good sighing after stars. She would do without him, in every way. She would do this alone, too.

'All right, Rosco. I'll leave you in peace. I'll manage without your help. And perhaps I don't need you, anyway. Perhaps this, like that other thing, I can do by myself. . .'

The candles were burning down.

Then she leant forward, beyond the dying flames, and kissed the cold lips, once. Slowly she blew out each candle, until the only light in the room came from the fire in the grate.

She drew the sheets and blankets over the inert body.

She left the room without looking back.

On the way back to her own room she wondered how many others were awake in the Castle that night. The corridor seemed not quite silent, not quite calm. A faint whisper of icy wind played round her ankles. And somewhere, at the edge of sound, she thought she heard the sibilant hiss of words.

She opened the door to her room and went straight to the window. She heard, slightly below her and a long way to the left, the sound of some other window opening. From above, she saw the foreshortened, familiar figure of a thin man move out on to the balcony. She recognised the shape of his eloquent hands, held palm-upwards to the Moon.

She heard the words he chanted out over the waves, and sudden rage gripped her.

Mittelson was calling the Sea Lords. She had never learnt the Mages' words of power, knew little of the way their thoughts could be projected, but she was in no doubt of this.

He was calling the Mages back to Shelt, before the ice kept them apart for ever.

She wondered whether to call the guard and arrest Mittelson immediately. But it occurred to her that she needed him almost too much. He was still her central contact with the citizens of Shelt. He was trusted by the fisherpeople, respected by the aristocracy. Olwyn Mittelson might yet prove a useful ally, even if he could not be trusted.

She rang instead for Annis, who was more than an ally. It took some time for her to arrive. Felicia spent the interim pacing her room, forcing herself away from the window.

A knock on the door. Puzzled, yawning, Annis stood there, half-flushed from sleep. 'What's wrong, my Lady? Shall I call the guard?'

'No. No need for that. Can you get a message to Serethrun Maryn? I think he'll be with the other *eloish* camped on the beach. Ask him to come to the Mage Mittelson's quarters as soon as possible. Say that the message is from me, but that he is not to tell anyone else.'

Annis was no longer yawning. 'Now? Outside?' Her back straightened and an air of importance brightened her eyes. 'I'll get Kes, if
that's all right. He's on Castle duty tonight. He'll find Maryn for you,
and keep his mouth shut.'

'Good.'

Felicia watched the retreating figure of her friend until it was out of
sight. Then, quickly, she flung on her warmest clothes.

'Why are you here, Lady Felicia?' His pale gold eyes regarded her
unblinkingly. She had not even time to try the key in the door. It had
opened as she approached. Olwyn Mittelson was waiting.

'You are calling the Sea Lords, in defiance of my orders. I should
have you arrested, Mittelson.'

'But you won't.' He did not trouble to deny her accusation. 'Where
are your soldiers, Lady Felicia? Your guardsmen with their sharp
weapons and battle skills?' He smiled at her discomfort, but she
thought his eyes were serious. 'I'm sorry, Lady. I do not disobey you
lightly. But come with me. See what is happening.'

He took her arm, pulling her into his room.

She hung back, shaking him off. 'I know just what's going on.
We've all been window-watching tonight, and I tell you, Mittelson,
that you have gone too far.'

'Too late, Lady. The message has been received. They're on their
way.'

He spoke so coolly, so mildly that at first she did not believe what
she was hearing.

Then she pushed past him, running across the bare boards to the
balcony.

The bay of Shelt was calm, too calm. There was moonlight glinting
over the sea, but at the ends of the two briggs it slanted strangely,
harshly, where the ice was. Dark shadows moved there, bending and
dipping, like waves breaking. She knew what they were doing,
reinforcing the ice with their breath and their touch.

Within the two arms of ice, the waves were almost quietened. Only
a narrow channel still tossed in the restless, snow-laden wind. A mile,
she thought. Only a mile, and the ice was moving so fast that by
morning it would be too late.

But further still beyond the spreading line of ice, she saw the
minuscule, fragile outline of a square-rigged ship coming towards
them.

'Damn you, Mittelson, you take too much on yourself!'

He said something, standing just behind her, something about there
being no other choice, but she hardly heard him, because pain had
seized her.

She leant forward against the balcony, her hands clenched on the
cold stone, her breath gasped in the silence.

'You must not blame the garrison on the islands,' Mittelson was saying. 'I sent them instructions in your name. . .'

'How *dare* you, Mittelson?' The pain gave her words a colouring of violence. 'Were all your professions of loyalty lies?' It seemed to be passing, and she managed to uncramp her fingers. He had not noticed, she was sure.

'Not lies, no. But you are in no condition to govern Shelt on your own. I felt that your judgement was awry in this case.'

'You never even asked. You sent word to the garrison long before you spoke to me.'

'I was aware of your mistrust of Mages, Lady. I knew what your answer would be.'

'This is treachery, Mittelson! When this is over you can leave Shelt—'

'If we are still alive and free when this is over, you will owe it to Mages, my Lady.'

No. There was no need to say it aloud. She saw Serethrun Maryn standing at the door, waiting her instructions. 'I have more urgent things to do than to squabble with you, Mittelson. Go and join your precious Mage friend at the west gate.'

'Your danger comes from the East, now!'

'But you have forfeited your rôle at my side. You cannot be trusted, and I don't want you here. Serethrun—' She looked at him. 'See that Olwyn Mittelson is conducted to the west gate. And then return here, as fast as you can. I shall need to talk to Cammish too, and Chandos, and the other members of the Council. This is very urgent.'

Mittelson's eyes, glaring at her, were piercingly angry. She felt the force of his will directed along the line of his sight, augmented by the patterns he was drawing in the air, and she had no difficulty ignoring it.

She could ignore the power in his eyes, the shapes of his eloquent hands, because the pain was starting again. She turned her back on him, deliberately, so that neither he nor Serethrun could see the sweat beginning to prick her upper lip.

She heard Serethrun hustle Mittelson from the room. He knew enough now to resist the creeping spirals of magic. It was something to do with his *eloish* background, she thought. But then the cramp tightened over her abdomen and she gasped, losing the thought. Her hands were pressed to skin which felt tight and solid. Her body was gripped in iron.

It was too early. The baby would not survive this.

There were tears in her eyes, watching the ice. The ice was coming, and so were the Sea Lords. Shelt would be overrun by horrors, frozen with evil. . .

Her baby would die.

Chapter Four
Flood

His hands were spread wide over the bay. He held Shelt almost
entirely within his clutch of ice, and now only a narrow channel
remained open for the tide.

Far out along the bridge of ice extending from the north brigg,
Gawne crouched at the edge of his kingdom. His shoulders were high
and hunched. Under his fingers, crystals of ice grew and flew on the
wind. To his left, the grey sea still surged and broke against the ice.
He did not care. His attention, his will, his desire were all focused
inland.

To his right a sheen of ice covered the city, ready to receive the Sun.
Bright winds flew down the alleyways and avenues of Shelt, draping
every house, every tree, with ice. Those who were unwary, those who
strayed outside, were touched by the chill breath of freezing wind, and
their blood slowed and froze. The newly possessed moved down to the
sea in their hundreds, towards the growing wall of ice.

They lifted their heads and let the ice settle over their eyes. Moving
blindly, they found the pathways of ice. They crossed the beach,
reaching out to the briggs. They were spreading slowly across the
glistening bay and under their touch the waters stilled and the waves
failed.

Shelt was almost within Gawne's clasp. Only the small, insistent
movement of moon-driven salt water defied him. The ocean had
rejected him once before, and now it did so again, strengthened by the
woman's travail.

He sensed the waves resist him, the liveliness of the depths, and
pale anger flickered in his bottomless eyes. He would not be defeated
by her. He would break her, this woman so beloved of the Lady. He
knew now which was the stronger, where his best hope lay. He had
lived at the far north of the world in a shroud of ice and the Sun had
burned through his captivity, had burned through both day and night
revealing all its power, all its force. In Shelt he had been betrayed by
the Lady, and now he would return to the source of life.

As all true Mages must in the end acknowledge God, he gave his
allegiance to the Lord of the Sun. This was why he had come back to
Shelt. He would transform the city into a mirror for the Sun, and the
Lord's brilliance would dazzle in the lives of all who named Him
King.

His strength would crush the Lady, confound Her servant.

In the Castle, he sent a spiral wisp of frost to his sleeping enemy. He
laid the dead finger of his will on the unconscious man. The blue eyes
were open, blinded by ice. The figure did not move, merely waiting.

All around him candles stood, dead and cold.

Gawne sighed. All was well. He had no rival there, no warrior to aid the woman. She was alone, and had no defence. He turned and looked away from Shelt.

Out to sea, he saw the ship approach. Old friends, old alliances. . .He considered the ship, tossing like driftwood on the violent waves, and knew it for his own. It would pass through the channel just as he was ready to make himself known. He estimated its slow, difficult progress an omen of success.

At first, she kept moving. She paced her apartments, moving between balcony and fire, her hands constantly adjusting the position of flowers in a vase, the lie of the covers on the bed. Felicia was restless and anxious, and could not settle anywhere. On the balcony, the wind blew snow at her, and frost and ice clung to the railings. And although the wind was so strong, the waves no longer crashed beneath the Castle walls. They moved with sluggish insistence under the increasing weight of ice.

She was drawn to watch the drama unfolding outside. But it was bitter and impossible to endure for long in those freezing conditions. She moved unwillingly back to the fire, and held out hands blue with cold. A short time there, to regain the feeling, to stop the uncontrollable shivering, and then back to the balcony. A constant oscillation, a peregrination between ice and flame.

As time went on, as dawn approached, her steps became slower. She paused more often, and for longer, holding the back of a chair, or the railing outside. She caught her breath as the rigid wall of iron around her tightened its grip.

The Sun began to rise.

On the ship, eyes were glittering. The Sea Lords were returning to their domain, summoned in supplication by someone who had defeated them long ago. This was indeed a pretty irony. To be courted, invited back to their former home, was nothing less than superb.

Quass turned to Dederic, their former leader. 'So. We lend our skills to help Olwyn Mittelson. . .'

Dederic looked at him sideways. 'Is that what you think we're doing?' They were within sight of the icy claws clasping the bay of Shelt, close to home. Dederic continued softly. 'We return to Shelt, dear friend, in order to defeat the usurpers. And then all shall live under a greater mystery than that of the Moon.'

'What can you mean?' Quass was very pale.

'It will be sweet, will it not, to defeat Felicia Westray and her upstart husband?'

'Indeed. We are all behind you in this. But what mystery greater than the Moon?' This was a test, a leading question.

'Mittelson has summoned us but lately. He wants us to give our help to Felicia Westray in the Lady's name. But I at least have already given my allegiance elsewhere.'

'And I. . .' Quass said softly.

Dederic smiled. An old Mage, with hooked nose and bushy eyebrows, and treachery in his eyes. He was confident now, knowing that they were all comfortably back in the train of their old master.

He looked at the claws of ice reaching out from the city and noticed how the rising Sun was reflected there. The brightness of it was quite extraordinary, and his eyes began to ache with the glare.

He did not look away. He did not even notice the figure who sat in the bows of their ship, dressed in the black clothes of a fisher-woman.

She sat there in silence, waiting.

Look to your new master then. Unheard words. She regarded the elderly men through eyes that shaded between silver and black.

Dederic caught Quass's arm, and pointed to the ice. 'It's the Sun!' he said, his voice curiously unguarded. 'Look how it shines, look at its brilliance!'

His companion turned and stared towards the city. He was still very pale, his hands now beginning to shake. He thought, are we right to do this? There was doubt growing in his mind. 'But our families . . .Can we really do this to Shelt, to our families, our homes? Can we afford to deny the Lady, like this?'

'Ah, Quass, you are not thinking. What considerations of family have ever weighed with you or me, or any of us? We left them behind long ago. And what has the Lady done for us? How has She rewarded our years of service?' He stared intently at his colleague. 'What can defeat the Sun? What can stand against such brilliant power!'

Quass felt a pressure at his back, something that called to him, something black and dark. 'The *Sun*? Dederic, what are you saying?' Quass stepped away from him, looking round for the others.

'Just look, look. . .!'

And without thinking, carelessly, casually, all of the old men on the ship looked towards Shelt.

They saw a dazzle of light, a brightness that burned through their eyes, through their brains, through their souls. Their hands, raising to shield their sight, were stilled, fingers outstretched. They were held there, staring, rigid and immobile until there was no process of cognition left. Nothing left to appreciate the final irony of their life.

The truth that brightness of day is always followed by the darkness of night.

Felicia watched by the fire, willing her breathing to steadiness. Hours had passed, the long, slow time before dawn, and now the sun bathed her city of ice in brilliance.

She had not managed to stay standing during the last onslaught of pain. She sat now, and tried to think how to defend Shelt, while every fibre of her body wanted to concentrate on the coming birth. She saw everywhere about her dazzling ice and stilled waves; while other waves, waves of pain, washed away at the edges of concentration.

Serethrun found her, alone, in the blessed interval between contractions. He had with him three people. Philp Cammish and Gereth Hallan, as she had directed. The other was Irian, his shaman sister.

Felicia told Cammish to put all the boats out to sea. To fill them with men from the Castle guard, and take them to the edge of the ice. She told him to sail the fishermen's boats back and forth through the narrowing gap, and to resist the attempt of the Sea Lords' ship to enter the bay.

She said that Shelt would die if the ice enclosed the city. They must look only at the sea, and shade their eyes from the glare of the Sun. That this was their last chance, their only hope.

She told Gereth to organise blankets, stretchers, medical supplies. To prepare beds, and alert all with any knowledge of healing and herbs. . .

And then she turned away, shaken by the tide of pain, and her teeth clenched again with the effort of containing it.

Serethrun took her hands, and let her fingers curl around his. She thought her nails might draw blood, but he took no notice. His voice was soft.

'Felicia. Irian is here. She will help. . .'

She looked up at him. He knew what was happening to her. He must have seen it when she had first called for him. It was why he had brought his sister. 'There's nothing that anyone else can do.'

'I don't want you to be alone.'

'She won't be.' Another voice from the door, one she did not want to hear at all.

Olwyn Mittelson stood there, leaning against the door jamb. His clothes were hanging in rags, blackened with smoke and charcoal. She saw that his hands and wrists were shiny-red with burns. His eyes glowed fiercer yet amidst the charred skin, twin pools of burning gold.

Felicia heard Serethrun exclaim, and knew that the colour had drained from her own face. Her first thought was fury, that Mittelson should still thwart her. And then she began to listen to what he was saying, his light voice trembling with passion.

The ice-warriors had broken through. The fires had failed, and they ran through the city, down to the sea. They were breaking into the houses, where the people of Shelt crouched, frightened, behind barred doors. They had crashed through windows, battered down doors and their breath was like death. Everything they touched, they contaminated with Sun-reflecting ice. Everyone they touched became puppets moving at the will of Gawne. In their thousands, the people of Shelt were making straight for the sea, and the waves were freezing over. . .

Felicia had watched Mittelson enter the room and had heard him saying these things. Now, he was standing in front of her and his mouth was shaping more words: something about the Sea Lords, about spirals of protective magic; about bargains and deals; about the necessity for swift action and, she thought, you are irrelevant here. This is nothing to do with you.

'Serethrun, get him out of here,' she said.

He moved across the floor and she saw from the flash of steel that he had drawn his sword.

Mittelson's hands began weaving helpless, exhausted, spirals. There was another figure behind him, similarly shadowed in black smoke. Alex Aldrich, come to support his master. . .

The circles of light strengthened and daggers of silver darted through the air: to Serethrun, to Irian, to Felicia herself. . .

The sword flashed, a swift ballet of unlikely movement. There was a crash as Alex Aldrich fell to the ground, folding over the wound to his heart. The knife in his hand ran skittering across the floor. And then another sound, something dreadful, as Serethrun's sword flashed again, with delicate accuracy.

Felicia did not see Mittelson collapse. The wave of pain had broken, casting her into some other realm, far beyond the reach of these events.

A new intensity, a different response to the pain. An effortful desire to lose herself in it, to run free through the Moon-governed tides of agony.

This was a reality stronger than anything around her. No one else existed there. She was opening, widening, to embrace the waves of pain and welcome what they brought. People were shouting, moving, fighting, but they were so far away. Everything was so far away.

A wild freedom, beyond constrictions, beyond iron walls of labouring flesh, the iron walls of enclosing ice. She was released now, a wanton beyond the reach of desire or will, cut loose at last from conscious thought and decision.

She lived at the extreme end of experience, where only truth exists.

Only this matters, only this has priority.

And at last, although the water was deeply cold, the grip of ice gave way. A wave broke, and then another. The seawater moved gently, and the jagged edges of ice became first clear and then frail. The channel between the briggs widened. With slow and easy warmth, the water washed over the ankles of the possessed, and the glistening crystals of ice could not hold.

Gawne turned away from the Sun-blinded men on the ship. They were useless to him now, empty husks carried along by the hostile tide to their final destination. He saw their ship run on to the rocks of the brigg. He saw it tip and tilt, the waves dashing it against the spar. And he thought, they will be drowned. Nothing will save them now. . .He did not care. He had other concerns. On the edge of the ice, he held his hands out to the Moon.

'Lady of all mercy, preserve Thy servant—'

It was a blasphemy, a mockery. Too late and all wrong. There was, of course, no reply. Instead, the waves of warm salt-water played round his ankles drifting through the rags of his clothes, and ate into his skin like acid. He stumbled; fell. Received by waves. Fishes, called to this strange catch, circled warily and came no closer.

Across the bay the fishermen's boats, called to another unusual catch dipped their nets.

Fishers of men and women. Freed from ice, blue with cold, a thousand souls were brought from the waves. *Eloish* and tribespeople, citizens and soldiers. Where the ice had clutched, salt water healed. They lay in the bottom of the boats, and blankets were wrapped around them, and in relays were brought to the Castle, where warm beds waited.

All day and all night, the fishermen trawled the bay. By morning, those brought from the waves were dead. By midday, only fish moved beneath the waves.

Shelt was a city for the drowned, a city for the released.

A city for the new-born.

Chapter Five
Roseland

The Emperor Xanthon awakes to the scent of roses. He lies on silken sheets and watches the misty, autumnal, sunlight filter through the leaves and thorns of the climbing roses outside his windows.

Servants bring him breakfast, and put out his clothes. He dismisses them. He prefers to shower and dress himself, an independent, controlled man. After breakfast, he crosses the walkways from his central tower in the palace of Solkest to his office and the public rooms. There he consults with ministers, with Council members, with the Warden and other civic authorities.

It does not take long. His staff is very efficient. His seal is required for certain letters, his consent for various proposals. Formalities. He does not have to initiate anything, although he always listens attentively to his advisers, and reads each document with care.

Lunch he takes with friends, in one of the reception rooms in the second ring. The blinds are drawn against the streaming sunlight, and the conversation flows with ease and grace in the shaded room.

In the afternoon, he confers with Weard, his High Priest and Great Mage.

And Weard tells him of a plague in the city. Of a blight, a spreading stain of evil. The Mages are dying, he says. Slowly, one by one, they are being eliminated.

'Good God!' The Emperor is shocked. At the centre of his palace of Solkest, it seems he knows very little now of his city, Peraldon. He is like a spider in the centre of a web, but a spider deprived of all its powerful senses, locked in an illusion of control.

'Who is doing this, why? Why have I not been told?'

'The time was not right. I needed to be sure that the path being followed was the correct one. I did not wish to burden you before it became necessary.'

'Who is responsible?' The Emperor is too dismayed to notice the way Shadows are writhing around Weard's spiral staff.

'I am,' Weard says, watching.

'*What*?' Stunned, unwary, the spider trapped, Xanthon looks into Weard's eyes, unable to believe this.

'Magic has become evil,' Weard says. 'It has become the tool of heretics. The Mages are in the grip of a dangerous religious idealism, and are starting to use magic to further the cause of this heresy, to further their distorted faith.'

'What form does this "heresy" take?' Through the shock, Xanthon is determined to understand what is at stake.

'It is that Man is sinful, naturally born into sin. And that Woman is the source of sin, to be shunned. . .'

'And Priests should be celibate, and women covered from sight.' Xanthon is quick to understand the implications. 'You would not like that, of course. . .'

'And neither would you, Highness. It is attractive to Mages, of course, who by tradition have little to do with women. Dion Gillet speaks with passion to illegal gatherings, and inflames his congregations.'

'But Weard, whatever the heresy, whatever the influences, we are talking about murder here!'

Xanthon is white with fury, white with the horror of it all.

Weard's voice drops as he comes close to his central point. 'But the Mages are plotting against your life, Highness.'

'Nonsense!' Xanthon turns away from Weard, pacing the room. Weard stays silent.

The Emperor is on the verge of calling in the guard, on the verge of arresting his High Priest, but something holds him back. There is more to this, he thinks. Weard is up to something, or he would never have admitted to these murders. There must be some dreadful reason for it all. . .

'Who has died? Which of the Mages?'

Weard lists a handful of names. They are all Mages within the College, administrators and tutors.

'What proof have you of their treachery?'

Sighing, Weard shows Xanthon transcriptions of conversations overheard, of letters intercepted, of signs and portents and secrets.

'These could all be forged.' Xanthon is dismissive, letting the sheaf of papers fall to the floor.

'And this. . .?' Weard guides the Emperor to a table where a candle is burning. 'Watch the flame,' he says, 'And I will show you the truth.'

In the flame, the Emperor sees a number of men meeting. One he recognises as the upstart Priest, the elderly man who challenged Weard in the Temple and was then imprisoned. They are all crowded around a table and the Emperor hears Dion Gillet say: 'We should elect the new Emperor from our midst *now*.' And the others all agree, and they all turn to him, saying: 'Dion, Emperor of the Sun, to you we owe all faith and honour and loyalty—'

Weard leans forward and blows out the candle. 'Do you understand now, your Highness? At the centre of it all Dion Gillet is always to be found, but they are all implicated. You can trust none of them now.'

Xanthon is not looking at him. He gazes instead at his own thin hands, his breathing untroubled, his brow clear.

'Weard,' he says at last. 'What is the point of these dreadful games? What do you want?'

What more *can* you want, he meant. Living in Solkest with the ear of the Emperor, in control of the Priesthood, at the centre of the world – what more can you want?

'It is not enough to be powerful,' said Weard/Lefevre in a strange moment of honesty. 'Mages will always betray, will always lie. They can never be trusted, and should be destroyed.'

'And yet a Mage must run the Priesthood, must befriend the Emperor—'

'But I, my lord, am faithful and true. As a rose is true to itself, so am I loyal to my ideals.'

In doubt the Emperor walks back to his rooms in the central tower. He is deep in thought, his gaze abstracted, as he passes through the rose-covered walkways. He absorbs the scent of sweet perfumes almost without realising it. He lifts his hands without thinking and strokes the velvet petals.

And the Fosca purr as he touches their flower-faces, although he cannot hear them. They sheath their claws, so that his clothes are not snagged by thorns. They do not move much, as the light sea-breeze disturbs the rags of their flesh, and so the leaves and stems barely stir about the Emperor as he passes through their careful embrace.

They cling to the walls of the central tower and peer in at his window, nodding petal faces and the Emperor is reassured by the scent of roses, by the bright sunlight and the flaming candles.

He is still worried, but not unduly so. He knows that ultimately he can trust Weard. Weard is his faithful and loyal servant.

There was never any serious doubt about it.

Chapter Six
Peraldon

Under her fingers, the sundial blazed. Light shone from the image of a face she knew well.

Her fingers rested on the carved eyes of Lycias, God of the Sun and she knew, at last, that this was where she had to be. His face was set in a pattern of stone-etched flames and she thought, flames have brought me here, flames have concluded my life there. This is the only place left to me.

Eleanor looked up and found herself standing in a garden. Gravel paths ran in geometric patterns between dark trees and shrubs. In the distance somewhere, she heard the faint splash of water. A fountain, she thought, bewildered. Where am I? It was warm, the air dusty, glowing with an autumnal haze.

She lifted her hands from the sundial and turned round. Phin was there, just as she knew he would be, standing in the shade beneath one of the taller trees. Light, slanting through the heavy foliage, passed over him. As she watched he walked forward, out into the sunlight.

She took half a step towards him, but her knees were unreliable, and she reached out to the sundial again to steady herself.

At once his arms were round her, his hand smoothing back the hair from her eyes. 'You're hurt – Eleanor, what happened?'

Blood on her shoulder and arm, and behind her eyes the blackened stump of a head, thrust blindly through the windscreen of a burning car.

She was clinging to him, her hands gripping his arms. He was warm from the midday sun, but still she shivered.

'Edine's dead,' she said, somehow. 'An accident. . .'

'Can you walk?' he interrupted her. She saw his eyes consider her, judging whether she was seriously hurt, seriously disoriented. 'I'm sorry Eleanor, there's no time—'

'The car exploded, and she'd gone through the windscreen, I think she was already dead.' Muddled words, muddled thoughts. He was wrapping a long cloak around her, hiding her jeans and jumper. Where did it come from? She hardly heard what he was saying.

'Listen, Eleanor. We have to get out of here, and quickly. We'll talk at home, later. Come on.'

His arm was round her waist, insistent, taking much of her weight. She stumbled beside him along the straight gravel paths, unaware of the curious glances from the other people walking there.

She did not understand why he was hurrying, and could not bring herself to ask about it. She thought, where am I now, what have I done?

He took her through streets utterly strange, utterly foreign, filled with people she didn't know, shops and signs and places she did not recognise. It was a jumble of colour, movement and sound that meant nothing to her. A filter of heat stood between her and everything else, beating down from the high midday sun, bouncing off the sand-coloured paving stones, stifling the air. Phin's arm round her waist was tanned a deep golden brown, slightly sweaty. . .Eleanor glanced up at him and saw that he was preoccupied, his eyes watchful, scanning the crowds.

At one point their path brought them face to face with a cordon of grey-uniformed men, heavily armed, marching quickly. He pushed her into a doorway and stood next to her, flat against the wall in the shadows.

She caught her breath. 'What's wrong, Phin, what's going on?' she whispered.

'There's been a clampdown. We don't want anyone to start asking questions. Things have changed since Edine left.'

And then he looked away from the street, directly at her for the first time.

'You should never have come back,' he said steadily. 'There is danger everywhere now, Fosca on the loose, soldiers, curfews. There was no way to warn you. But Eleanor, even if I had managed to get a message through, I could not have told you to stay away. Lives such as ours need a sense of resolution.' His hand touched her cheek. 'Do you know what I mean? We never even said goodbye, did we?'

She felt tears in her eyes, and could say nothing. For a while they stood there, locked together in the shadows, and the grey uniformed men passed them by.

He lived in a boarding house on the northern side of the city, close to the docks. She was too bewildered, too dazed, to take in the surroundings. They climbed what seemed like a mountain of stairs to get to his room. She sat at a table while he bandaged her arm, and tried to give him a brief outline of her meeting with Edine. She was almost incoherent with exhaustion.

At last he told her to go to bed. 'You need to sleep, Eleanor. We can talk tomorrow.'

There was a camp bed on one side of the room, a mattress behind a curtain on the other. 'Take your pick,' he said, smiling. 'There's not much to choose between them.'

She sagged down on the mattress, and he pulled a blanket over her. She held her hand out to him. 'Phin – you won't go away, will you?'

'No, I won't leave you. I promise.'

'Don't draw that curtain.'

'No. Don't worry, I'll be here.'

But that night she tossed on her narrow bed, somewhere between nightmare and fever. She woke once, confused and anxious, and saw him standing at the window, watching dark night shadows flying over the city beyond.

'Phin. . .?'

He turned and moved to her bedside. 'Can I get you anything, Eleanor? Something to drink?' His hand was on her shoulder, an imperceptible assurance.

'Those shadows. . .What are they?'

'Fosca, I think. Trouble, certainly. But nothing to do with you, or me. We'll move from here. Go somewhere calm and peaceful.' He sat on the floor beside her bed, leaning back against the wall. His voice ran on, quiet and slow, telling her about his childhood home on a small island, an idyll of canals and orchards.

She held his hand, drifting back into sleep. And forgot, for a while, the Fosca flying in the night, the grey uniformed men, the watchfulness in Phin's eyes.

The morning sun hurt her eyes. The scratches on her arm were sore and inflamed. Irritably, she pushed the blankets back, and struggled to her feet.

'Hello. . .' He was standing across the room by the window. 'How do you feel?'

She grimaced. 'Coffee might help.'

She could smell it, freshly ground, sharp and aromatic. There were rolls too, and nectarines, but she wasn't hungry and didn't even really want the coffee when it came. 'It's so hot here,' she complained. 'Is it always like this?'

'For most of the year, yes. This is nothing out of the ordinary. But it's beginning to get cold at night now. . .' He laid his hand on her forehead. 'You'll have a thousand questions, of course, so much you'll need to know, but right now I think you should go back to bed.'

Her head was thumping, her limbs heavy and uncomfortable. She had no intention of arguing. 'All right. But, just, don't go away,' she said, and then wished she hadn't because it sounded so pathetic.

He was patient with her, endlessly attentive throughout all of that long first day. She dozed on and off, and fits of shivering alternated with a wild nightmare of flames and burning.

Phin was always there, never failing. He brought her water, wiped her clammy hands, held her close when the shivering was at its worst. She wondered, as her thoughts cleared towards evening, if he ever put himself first, if he would always be so calm and gentle.

'What are you really like?' she asked. The shadows of late afternoon were lengthening now, the sky a darkening blue, tinged with violet.

'Don't you know, after all this time?' He was amused. 'Or are you still dreaming?'

'No, it's not the fever talking. Only, why are you so—' *Good*, was what she meant. *Virtuous*. Impossible words. '—kind? And I don't mean, why are you nice to me, I'm not looking for compliments or reassurance.'

'What else is there?' He was sitting in the chair by the table, a book open on his knees. Carefully he closed it. He did not look at her. 'However you live, wherever you go, whatever you do, there is always suffering. Happiness never lasts, love always loses because people are frail and self-seeking, and there is only one end to life. We're caught in a spiral, and death is the only way out. At the very least we should be kind to each other, smooth the path a little. . .'

She thought she understood. 'Does ending the Stasis give you nightmares?'

'No. I don't dream now, or at least I can't remember dreaming. And even if I did, ending the Stasis was almost the only unequivocal thing I've ever done.' He looked at her then. 'At least there's a way out now. It won't go on for ever.'

A half-smile, a minute shrug. He returned to his book.

Eleanor lay back on the mattress, and closed her eyes. Sleep had never been further from her. She thought, Death has returned to this world, partly because of the actions we took. How can we survive it, what can we build now?

As night fell, she saw that Phin still sat there, the book open, untouched on his lap. In the twilight, she could not see his expression.

'Do you want to die?' Was it fever or dislocation which made her ask?

He was silent for too long. 'It doesn't really matter,' he said at last. 'But I hope to be here for as long as you need me.'

She pushed the blankets free, and stood up. The room stayed steady, and she reached his chair without wavering. 'Not me,' she said. 'Don't put all that on me, or any other one person. It's too much. You have to find something else.'

'I know.' He stood up, and put his arm round her. Her head dropped against his shoulder, heavy as lead. 'And anyway it's nowhere near over, not with Lefevre back in place at the Emperor's hand. And there's plenty enough to do, cities to build, lives to reconstruct, a living to be made. I expect to be busy for a while yet.'

'Count me in on it?'

'Any time. Always. Whatever you want.'

Next morning, she felt better. The scratches on her arm were sore but nothing more. She drank coffee with enjoyment, made an attempt at the fruit and rolls. She leant back in her chair, considering Phin's home.

'It serves,' he said. 'No one asks questions, and there's plenty of time to prepare for visitors. The stairs are usefully creaky. How do you feel about staying here? Are you up to a day on your own?'

'Why, are you going to work or something?' It seemed as likely as anything else.

He smiled. 'No. I'm going shopping. And to find out if we really do need to leave Peraldon. The situation changes from day to day.'

'What *is* wrong here, Phin? What's going on? I need to know.'

'Yes, of course you do. It happened soon after we released Dion Gillet and Edine from Solkest. To be expected, I suppose. There's a price on both their heads, there have been searches everywhere. There's a curfew, and movement between the various sectors of the city is through checkpoints. No one can leave Peraldon without authorisation. Edine found the only sure way out.' He paused briefly. 'It's illegal not to have papers, not to register with the Warden's office.'

'Are you registered?'

'What do you think? No one knows I'm here. I've been working as a casual labourer at the harbour, but even that's getting difficult. I'll need papers, now, to get a job. If it goes on like this, we'll need them to buy food. It'll be difficult, getting out of here.'

'Was Edine so very important?'

'I don't think it's about Edine at all. Dion Gillet is the quarry. A rival to Lefevre. . .'

'Is he really? Is he in that league?'

'I don't know.' He stood up. 'It hardly matters. The point is that he is perceived as such, and that's more than enough to turn the whole city upside down.'

With misgiving, she watched Phin slide a knife into his boot. 'Where are you going?'

'To pull a few strings.'

'What do you mean?' She didn't trust these evasions. 'What do I do if you don't come back? Phin, you'll have to tell me where you're going!'

'Yes. . .It's not quite true to say that no one knows I'm here. There are in fact a number of people who know where I live. One is Katriana, but I would not recommend that you approach her, far less her guardian Dion Gillet. Another is the man in the ground-floor flat here. He's an old friend. I brought him home one night when he'd had one too many. He's called Harren. You can trust him, even when he's sober.'

'Do you mean that?'

He grinned. 'I told him that I might have a visitor. He knows who you are. He'll help you get away if I'm – held up.'

She let that pass. 'Is that all, though? Don't you know anyone else?'

'Oh, many. A hundred or more, family and friends. But I'm in no position to go public yet.' He put his hands on her shoulders, and lightly kissed the top of her head. 'Sorry, Eleanor,' he said. 'I'm not being much use, am I? It'll be better when we get away from here.'

'It's okay, don't worry. Just come back.'

'Sure. Make yourself at home. Till sunset, then—' A half-grin, and he was gone.

She stood staring at the closed door for a moment, a thousand words and questions dying unvoiced. An exhalation, of combined frustration and unease. She turned slowly around and regarded Phin's home.

Her home, for a day or two. The only one she had now. Phinian Blythe her only companion, her only friend. She was massively apprehensive. Sooner or later, one thought, I'll meet other people, there will be networks of acquaintances and friends, and Phin will not be the only person in my life.

But it was still so far away. The flying shapes of Fosca, the marching soldiers in the streets, the problems of living in Peraldon: everything seemed to stand between Eleanor and any kind of calm.

Not yet, she told herself severely, it's not your turn yet for the quiet life, the easy chair. Just as well, you're not even middle-aged. . .And it was better here than back in her own world, because Phin was here. And she knew, if there was any truth anywhere, that she belonged with him.

But, Lukas, she thought. Still there, still at the centre of everything in her mind. Nothing's changed, nothing ever will.

She put it aside. It was an indulgence, nothing more, thinking of Lukas. She was in Peraldon with Phinian Blythe, and it was still such early days. She shrugged, and returned to her inspection of the room.

She could make no sense of it. It was an attic, the ceiling sloping sharply to meet the floor. There were two gabled windows, looking over other roofs to the harbour.

There was very little furniture, no carpets and only the one curtain, green and white stripes, screening her bed. Just plain honey-coloured wood, all very simple and unadorned. Impoverished? she thought. But there were sudden splashes of colour, touches of a strange exoticism that she couldn't imagine coming cheap. There was a circular painting of sea creatures, framed in a gilded wreath of seaweed. The yellow cloth over her bed was silk, the emerald green bowl holding oranges looked very old and was finely etched with golden dragons. There were scarlet poppies in a clear glass jug on the table by the window.

She was glad to have time on her own. She needed to recover some degree of equanimity, to find her balance, her centre. A little space, she thought, to come to terms with what has happened. It was a kind of delicacy, she realised, leaving her here today. No pressure, no demands. . .

With reluctance she explored. It felt intrusive, opening doors, examining Phin's possessions. There was other food, bread and cheese, in a shady cupboard by the door. A shelf along one wall, with a few books and some crockery. Nothing matched, everything had been acquired from markets or second-hand, she decided. But the chipped cups were made of fine china, and the bowls glowed with deep colour.

She sat at the table, and considered the poppies. Phin had waited for her, she thought. He had talked to Edine, long ago, and had waited in the garden with a cloak for her to wear; waited for her to return at the appointed time. He had put flowers on the table to welcome her, although he could not have known for sure that she would ever sit there, touching the delicate vermilion blossoms.

From the windows she could just see the lagoon, glimpsed over the warren of sun-baked buildings. The ships were faint in the heat-haze, approaching the harbour from far horizons. Coming from Stromsall, she supposed. And from the East and South. Peraldon was a centre of trade, she remembered, and its wealth was founded on the skill of its goldsmiths.

They might not be here for long. She wondered whether Phin would decide that they should leave, and how they might escape if it came to that. Eleanor was curiously passive about it all. She felt she had taken the last decision in her life, deciding to return. She had no will for anything else.

Chapter Seven
Nightflower

He came back at sunset, footsore, hot and sweaty, dumping various packages by the door as he came in. He told her what had happened as he unwrapped meat from the market, ready cooked, spicy and still warm.

'There's a possibility of a crossing next week.' He looked at her carefully. 'To Sarant.'

'Sarant?' The name was distantly familiar. 'Isn't that where the Cavers came from originally?'

'That's right. It's being resettled. You may meet old friends there. . .'

'Matthias, do you mean? Or—?'

'The rest of Lukas's family. Perhaps. Or would that be too difficult?' He was concentrating on the wine he was pouring.

She paused. A difficult subject, but one she needed to talk about. 'I liked Lukas's family,' she said at last. 'There was an elderly woman, some kind of stepmother. . .She was called Letia, and was lovely when I first came here.'

Phin raised his glass. 'To Letia, then. May we meet soon.'

He had brought flat bread-cakes, rather like pitta and a bag of tomatoes and herbs. While he washed, she laid out plates and glasses, and made a salad.

She was stupidly flustered. This was all too domestic, too soon.

'This is very beautiful,' she said awkwardly, putting the dragon bowl down in the centre of the table.

'Family heirloom, liberated from the ancestral home,' he said lightly. 'Not that they know I'm here yet.'

'Why haven't you told them?' What do they mean to you, she meant, your parents, your family? Have you left them behind, too?

He was swirling the wine round in his glass, not looking at her. 'In truth, it's not easy. They thought me dead. Any sudden resurrection would be an undoubted shock.'

'But you can't dodge it for ever.'

'No. Neither will I. You see, I didn't know for sure if you'd come back,' he said. 'It was difficult to plan, not knowing that. . .'

He had left his hair long, although the beard had gone. Out of doors he habitually wore a battered straw-hat, pulled down to shield his eyes. He demonstrated, and she laughed. He looked oddly unremarkable, the hat softening the effect of the hook nose and deep lines. He said that occasionally he saw people he knew, but that no one gave him a second glance. He was faceless, shabby, undistinguished. Just an anonymous figure, part of the landscape like a million others. He was not short of money; he worked because he liked it. He dressed in rags.

'Why wear anything else?' he said. 'It's hot out there on the quayside, and dirty. It would draw attention to dress otherwise.'

He talked to her about life on Sarant, and what it was like. She found it hard to imagine, hard to believe that they would ever get there.

'They're making a whole new community,' Phin said. 'The city there was razed long ago, during the War.' He leaned forward across the table towards her, tracing a map on the table with his fork. 'The lagoon's here, Jeren, Arrarat Isle. . .Sarant lies beyond them. It will be exciting for everyone, starting it all again.'

'Rising from the ashes. . .'

'If you like.'

He stood up, and brought over a parcel which he had left by the door when he came in. 'I have a present for you, Eleanor. I nearly forgot.' He put it on the table beside her. She opened it, and saw what lay beneath the layers of gold tissue-paper. The folds of fabric were diaphanous, slashed in multiple layers of rainbow colours. She held the garments up to the light.

'How did you know my size?' She ran her fingers over the fine gauze, the delicate panels of shifting colour.

'You're not unlike Karis in height and weight,' he said gently. 'I guessed that these would fit. . .'

She laid the clothes down again, thoughtfully folding the tissue around them. 'Did you ever think that I might not come back?'

'Well, I don't know much about your life in that other world, what ties there are there. But at some level, yes, I did think that probably you'd return.' He shrugged, looking at her with dark eyes. 'Where else could you go?'

And at last she knew why she was there. It was not because she had any hope of seeing Lukas again, because there was no hope in a world where the Gods lied and fought. But, here, Phinian Blythe understood everything about her. He had known that she needed a resolution. He gave her a context, a companionship that she might never find again. He, too, had nowhere else to go.

Later she stood at the window watching the pattern of lights over the city. The attic was some distance from the harbour, overlooking a warren of small, winding streets. To the East, a massive black silhouette rose high above the rest of Peraldon. Phin had pointed it out earlier. Solkest, where the Emperor lived, together with his High Priest and Mage. There were lines of lights there, outlining the span of bridges and walkways that united the seven rings.

It was still hot, although the sun had set long ago. The attic was stuffy, and she'd gone to open the window.

Had he chosen to live here because of its view of Solkest? Eleanor was about to turn to ask him, when the breath froze in her mouth.

A petal face bloomed from the night, staring in at her, the stink of decay befouling the air. . .

She slammed down the window, and for a moment the glaze of glass hid what she'd seen, and when she looked again, it was gone.

'*Phin!*'

The attic was in sudden darkness. He had put out the candles. 'Yes, I saw it too.'

'Fosca, here? Do they often come this close?'

'No. Never. . .it looked straight at you, didn't it?' In the warm night, his voice was strangely flat. 'They'll be back. All this week there have been rumours of death, that the Mages are being struck down at night, ripped by claws. . .Nothing is publically admitted, nothing published, although most people have seen Fosca flying now, and some have heard screaming. They're getting too close. We'll have to get away from here. I think we should leave immediately.'

He was pushing clothes into a bag, and she saw the blade of his knife catch in the starlight.

'That's fine by me.' She remembered the expression on that grey petal-face, the mouth that almost smiled, the gleam of small eyes, the way it had dipped and swerved away from the window. 'But. . .we're not going outside, are we?'

'With Fosca all over the place? No. Better get changed: we'll go visiting.'

'Who?'

'Harren. On the ground floor. Time to widen your acquaintance here a little, Eleanor. He'll give us a place for the night.'

'You think they're after *you*?' The man at the door was derisive. 'Well, yes, I can see why you might not want to stay up there. A bit too close to the sky, that flashy penthouse. But what makes you think you'll be better off here?' Nonetheless, he stood away from the door and let them in.

A blast of heat hit them. There was a fire burning in the grate, a chair drawn up to it. A heap of handwritten papers overspilled from the table, littering the floor. There were books and papers on every surface. The place stank of tobacco and sour wine, like its occupant. Eleanor smelt it on his breath, saw the stains on his clothes. His eyes were deep-set, his skin flushed rosy with heat. His brown hair was tied back with a greasy scrap of velvet ribbon. He hadn't shaved for days.

He turned to her suddenly. 'And this is Eleanor Knight. Well, well. A most becoming outfit. . .' He was grinning appreciatively. Eleanor frowned. She was not sure that she wanted her identity revealed to this man. 'Such a ladies' man, Phinian Blythe. Always knows what will suit. Did he give you some scent, too, or am I thinking of someone else?'

'Take no notice of Harren, Eleanor, he lives in a world of his own, and it's long past his bedtime.'

'Nonsense, the night is yet young, and I was just getting going.' He sounded offended, but Eleanor could see he was delighted. He's glad we're here, she thought, glad to have company. She found herself smiling at him. Perhaps it didn't matter, him knowing. . .

'As a matter of fact, Blythe, it's not just Fosca who are looking for you. Those comments about the fairer sex are distinctly apposite. How you do it, that's what I'd like to know. Perhaps you could give lessons, charge a small fee. I *think* she was beautiful, but it was difficult to tell under all the veiling. Her voice. . .' All humour had vanished. He was suddenly vulnerable, too much emotion trembling in his mouth.

Phin had wandered into the room over to the fire. He picked up one of the papers from the floor. 'Book burning, my friend? Why?'

Carefully, Harren took the paper from him. He let it drop, and it swayed through the warm air into the fire, lifting in the updraft. 'No, not today. Not that particular story. Aren't you interested in your visitor?'

Phin sighed. 'Katriana, I would bet. You fobbed her off?'

'The phrase is not adequate. I said you'd gone to work, as instructed. The lady was – well, I don't think she believed me.' He looked at Blythe hopelessly. 'She – but forgive me, I neglect our honoured guest from wherever it is. Some wine, Eleanor? There's nothing else worth drinking here, unless you want to try the water.'

'Thank you. . .But Phin, she'll come back.'

'Perhaps. . .perhaps not. If she thinks the Fosca are on to us, she won't come anywhere near.'

'You're serious about this, aren't you?' Harren had removed papers and books from the other chairs in the room, motioning them to sit down. His eyes looked from Blythe to Eleanor and back again. 'Come on now. Let me in,' he said softly.

'You know the score. You know who this is. There was a Fosca right outside our window this evening, and although it could have been a coincidence, I wouldn't like to bet on it.'

'Was it looking for *me*?' This was something Eleanor had not expected.

'I don't think so.'

'It's you, isn't it?' Harren said, leaning back in his chair. 'Phinian Blythe: ex-Captain in the Warden's guard, turned renegade and traitor, and incidentally responsible for Dion Gillet escaping his prison, for helping Edine Malreaux to desert her mysterious lover. . .'

'Lefevre knew we would meet again. He implied as much when we met on Massiq.'

'Is this the resolution you wanted?' Eleanor asked.

Phin shrugged. 'I sometimes wonder if there will ever be anything else. Cycles of revenge and retaliation. . .Lefevre said that we were like lovers, fated to meet.' He paused, and she saw the lines of his face deep-etched, severe. 'It is not a prospect which pleases.'

'A drink, that's what you need.' A flurry of activity as Harren uncorked bottles, laid out glasses, poured wine. 'It's true that these fancies belong in the small hours of the morning, but only when well lubricated.'

'Harren's philosophy, Eleanor.' Phin smiled at her, but there was little enough humour in it. 'You don't have to go along with it.'

Eleanor took a glass from Harren. 'Tell me about Katriana. Am I ever going to meet this woman?'

'I can't think of any good reason why you should. She and Gillet are trouble all the way. But it has to be acknowledged that they are quite – extraordinary. There's something about them both which I don't like.' Phin paused, his eyes running over the heap of handwritten papers on the table. For a moment he glanced at Harren, and then turned back to Eleanor. 'Gillet is a man with a mission, his mind attuned to what he imagines the Lord Lycias might want. It makes him entirely blind to human considerations, puts him entirely beyond the ordinary claims of action and reaction. And Katriana. . .she is also outside humanity. It's pride or arrogance, something that keeps people at a distance. And she is always dressed in black, always veiled, hidden from the eyes of the world.'

'What is Gillet planning? Will he make use of Katriana?'

'Gillet does nothing without reference to his beliefs. Somehow Katriana is part of a scheme to appease Lycias, or destroy Lefevre. That is all Dion Gillet cares about. Edine imagined that Gillet had created Katriana, but I think it's unlikely. She seems all too human- . . .manipulative, devious. It hardly matters. They are hunted, and feared. Pariahs, if you like. I very much doubt that they'll be able to evade Lefevre for long. Trouble, all the way.'

Harren put his wine glass down, 'There are so many sects these days, so many little tin-pot creeds in Peraldon, each with their own Messiah, their own prophets and mystics. Gillet could probably pick up a following without too much trouble.'

'He's halfway there already,' said Phin. 'He was invited back to Peraldon, probably by some of the priesthood. Katriana told me so when I first met her, and although she's not renowned for her veracity, I've no reason to believe otherwise – Gillet has friends here, friends who are hiding him from Lefevre.'

Eleanor heard Harren answer something about charismatic leaders, and Phin reply, but her mind made little sense of the conversation. The wine and the heat were making her drowsy, and she'd not met either Gillet or the woman. . .

Her eyes closed.

Chapter Eight
Harren

When she awoke, Phin was gone. There was a smell of coffee, the
sound of crockery from behind a curtain. Eleanor looked round the
untidy room. Sunlight was streaming in from the window over the
piles of papers ringed with wine stains, mug stains. . .Motes of dust
sparkled in the air. She remembered where she was.

Someone had put a blanket over her. She stood up, stiff and
uncomfortable from her night in the armchair, and said, 'Harren? Is
that you?'

His face, unprepossessing in the clear light of daybreak, poked
through a curtain at the end of the room. There were dark shadows
under his eyes, and he moved with caution.

'I'd wish you good morning, Eleanor Knight, but the light's too
bright for sincerity. . .Blythe will be back soon. He asked me to give
you his apologies.'

'Where is he?' A sudden anxiety, a lifeline snapped, broken?

'Gone to find a way to Sarant for you both. Don't worry, I shall do
my best to entertain you in his absence. Do you take sugar in coffee –
cream?'

He cleared a space and put down a plate and cup for her. He sat
down opposite her, elbows on the table. She was aware of being
studied. She looked up, met his eyes.

'Ah, Eleanor. What are you doing here? A dream from another
place, a wisp of some Mage's enchantment imprisoned in frail
flesh. . .No, don't attempt to answer—' although there was nothing
she could have said. 'Instead, tell me, what do you make of your old
friend Phinian Blythe? Has he changed since last you met?'

She looked at the tired, worn face and wondered why she liked
Harren so much. There was something restless about him, something
unformed and vulnerable. He has warmth, she thought, and has made
mistakes. She wanted to trust him.

'I don't really know, I've not been here long enough. Essentially, he
seems much the same. But it was all so different, last time we met. I
do wonder—'

'What?'

'How he'll adapt. . .whether he will ever get back into life here
again. Friends and family, all that. I—'

'Left all yours behind?'

'Yes.'

'Don't look so tragic. It happens, you're not unique.'

She thought, yes, people leave home and lose touch all the time, but
not like *this*. I've never known anyone else who has managed it quite

so thoroughly. 'What will he do? Phin, I mean. He talks about taking me to Sarant, but I don't know if there's any future there for him.'

'No, probably there isn't. I expect that sooner or later Blythe will find his way back into society here. It's where he belongs, after all. He won't want to leave it alone. I don't think he'll wait long.' He paused, looking at her speculatively. 'And how would you like that, the life of a well-dressed lady about town?'

She frowned. 'I can't imagine it at all.' With Phin? For a moment, she played with the idea. Not unpleasant, not thrilling, just unlikely. She looked up and caught Harren's eye.

His head was on one side, observant as a bird. 'Well, perhaps we'll just have to wait and see.' He stood up, went to the window, and rubbed the corner of his jacket against the grime. It made little difference. Sighing, he pushed the window open, and the room was filled with smells and sounds. Eleanor heard the rumble of a cart, a dog barking. Voices, and a baby crying. The smell of frying onions, and fresh-baked bread. She drank coffee, more relaxed than she could remember for some time.

'Tell me, what do you think of our fine city then? You've not been here before, Blythe says. Does it appeal?'

'I hardly know. All that I've seen so far has been full of uniformed men and Fosca.'

'Forget the Fosca. They're an aberration, an artificial construct. Briefly fashionable, they'll last only as long as their master does.'

'Well, that could be for ever, judging from Lefevre's past record.'

'We might only be talking about Weard, of course. We've only got Blythe's word for this strange reincarnation idea.'

'You've only got Blythe's word for who I am, and yet you seem to take that on trust.' She considered him as he leaned back against the window frame, patchy morning sunlight behind him. 'Why?'

For a while, Harren said nothing. She watched his small hands take a pencil from the dusty windowsill, and start playing with it, pushing it end to end between finger and thumb. Outside, two women chattered, arguing over the price of something. . .

'I knew him before. Phinian Blythe, Captain in the Warden's Watch. Before those reports of his death, before Karis died. We weren't close, but we lived in the same quarter, went to the same parties. He was different then, extrovert, confident. . .he was elegant, always dressed well. It was a shock, meeting him again.

'To disappear like that, just to vanish.' There was more than a touch of envy in Harren's voice. 'To leave everyone thinking him dead. It must have been something extraordinary, something bizarre.' He looked at Eleanor seriously. 'And I see the same scar on your face, the same look in the eyes.

'And the Stasis *has* ended, after all. . .' It was almost an internal thought, an expression of something that had no inherent existence. His voice was light, ephemeral, secret. 'I'm willing to believe what

Blythe tells me. And although he looks different, in one respect he has not changed. People trust him. Have you noticed? People think he'll make it all right, that he's competent, when no one else is.'

Eleanor crossed the room and looked out of the window. The square outside was filled with market stalls and people, an untidy and colourful rabble, vigorous and noisy. 'What do they imagine happened at the end of the Stasis?'

Together they regarded the crowd, framed by the window. Harren's words were unstressed. 'There are a thousand theories, a thousand experts on the matter. The Mages say it's a secret not for the uninitiated, and priests never tell anyone anything anyway. But everyone knows that a Caver Mage was at the heart of it, that it was a Caver scheme. And they also know that a stranger was involved, someone from outside. From Stromsall, they think, or the far east. The story Blythe told me would be way beyond their wildest dreams.

'So, you see, there's no one here to back up what he says about Weard.'

'Edine Malreaux knew about Weard,' she said.

'But I never met Edine, and hardly anyone else will remember her. Imbert kept her well tucked away when they were on Peraldon. There is no actual evidence beyond hearsay. Have you never thought that Blythe might be mistaken?'

'Not about this, no,' she said. 'We've been together through so much, you see. I was there. And I know the Desert Rose, I know what it's like.'

'It – or he – is just another Mage. An illusionist, a superior kind of trickster.'

'There's more to it than that. Edine told me once that magic and religion were unalterably connected. Think what you were saying about Dion Gillet last night. And Lefevre. Lefevre was both High Priest and Great Mage, wasn't he?'

'Couldn't that be just coincidence?'

Eleanor was leaning her chin on her forearms, nose almost touching the dusty glass. Just outside the house she saw a woman bend over a pram to touch the cheek of the child lying there. 'No. No. It's all connected. It's almost as if the Gods are still active *because* of the Mages.' She struggled with difficult concepts. 'The Mages use all the unseen skills, they manipulate those fuzzy areas beyond reality. And that's just where the Gods walk. . .'

'Where dreams drift and faith lives,' he completed for her. He was thoughtful. 'Do you mean that the Mages, through their actions, give the Gods a pathway through to our world here?'

Long ago, she had questioned Thurstan's mother about such things. Martitia had told her that people create the Gods they deserve through their own imaginations. She had said that the priests and ceremonies merely serve to distance people from their Gods.

It's too dangerous, Martitia had said. The area where Gods meet humans, the area where Mages operate, should be sacrosanct. For the Gods are already too close, closer than any kind of formal worship acknowledges. Under the rule of Astret, Mages and priestesses were in conflict. The Caver priestess Nerissa had accused the Mages, including Matthias, of heresy.

But on Peraldon the two rôles went hand-in-hand. The divisions between Mage and priest were indistinct. Dangerous, she thought. The Gods walk vividly through our lives because of the corridors through to Their own realms, routes created by the Mage/priests. . .

She was trying to frame an answer for Harren when the door was flung open.

'You lied to me! How *dare* you!'

Standing there, rigid with fury, was a woman shrouded entirely in black.

Chapter Nine
Katriana

Eleanor stepped back against the wall, away from the intruder. It was an instinctive action she could not explain.

The woman was impossible. The layers of black cloth shifted around her, and nothing could be seen of her shape or size. But although she was entirely hidden, she gave an impression of massive, inappropriate, shattering power. The trappings of submission and discretion were wildly misleading. It was something to do with her voice, something in the ram-rod straightness of her back, something to do with the air around her. She seemed to fill the room, to fill their senses.

Harren was on his feet, his mouth dropping, his face entirely colourless.

Eleanor found herself wondering if she could edge past this woman, if she could get out of the door into the bright market outside. No one had prepared her for this.

'Phinian Blythe was not at work yesterday, and he's not there now. What is he hiding and why did you *lie* to me?'

She was turning round, searching the room, as if Blythe might be concealed somewhere. She halted on seeing Eleanor, who was transfixed against the wall like a hare caught in a searchlight.

A cool exhalation of breath, a soundless whistle. The voice dropped, the power reined in. 'So that's it. And does the Moon still shine brightly for you, Eleanor Knight? What is your great mission this time?'

'How do you know who I am?' This was too much. Eleanor's precious anonymity had been shattered twice in twenty-four hours.

Katriana's hand moved and touched the Moon-scar on Eleanor's forehead. 'It's written all over your face. Literally.'

Without thinking, Eleanor knocked the hand away.

Katriana said, 'Yes, it's still there, still active. . .' There was a tinge of pity in her voice, or was it contempt? 'It doesn't matter, it means nothing. That story's over, that tale's done. And now Blythe approaches, and something else will start.'

'What do you *want?*' But as Eleanor spoke the door opened. Phin, stopping on the threshold.

Katriana said, without turning, 'Now. The only chance, for us all. . .'

'So, Katriana. And what can we do for you?' Phin was considering her, his hand on the lintel. He was entirely unexcited and it seemed that the emotional tension in the air had subsided.

There was silence for a moment as Katriana looked from one to the other. 'I need help.' She spoke slowly, as if unused to petitioning. 'I need a refuge. A way out. There's no where else to go.'

'Why? What about your guardian?' Blythe walked past her into the room, raising an eyebrow at Eleanor, who shook her head, bemused.

'Are the Fosca after you too?' Harren said. Eleanor saw that his hands were clenched so tightly on the chair-back that his knuckles shone white. He was staring at Katriana, a pulse in his throat jumping.

'It's Gillet I need to escape. And the Fosca don't make anything easier. . .'

'What's wrong?'

Suddenly she seemed smaller, helpless. Eleanor saw what was happening, she recognised the artifice of it. Fine hands, white as wax were upturned as Katriana turned from Harren to Blythe. 'He's no longer sane. He has some idea of a bargain with the Lord Lycias, a deal that will give him power.'

'How could he? Ridiculous!' Eleanor thought of Lycias, that cold mockery, that wild passion. She could not imagine how anyone would wilfully tangle with such a being.

'It's been done before,' Katriana said simply. 'Lefevre himself made such a bargain. And he too sacrificed a woman. . .'

'Sacrifice? *You?*' Harren pushed the chair aside with such force that it fell crashing to the floor. He went up to her and took her shoulders. 'How could he?' He repeated Eleanor's words, but in tones of tenderness and concern.

Katriana leant back against him. 'Please help me. . .'

'The passage to Sarant.' Harren looked at Blythe. 'Any luck?'

'A waste of time. All ships leaving the harbour are subject to minute examination. Without papers or authorisation we'd have no chance at all.

'Katriana, what exactly is Dion Gillet proposing?'

'My guardian is a visionary. He follows in the footsteps of the Lord, and knows the will of the Lord. He's trusted by so many. . . . But Weard knows he's dangerous. Dion Gillet has his own band of disciples, men from the Peraldonian priesthood. They think he's some kind of Saviour. They preach austerity with a fine old passion, and everyone flocks to the banner. But more than that, he's been talking to the College of Mages. They were all so interested, so entranced, so pleased, they wanted to know all about him—'

She was contemptuous. 'They are frightened of Weard anyway, they don't trust him, shut away in the centre of Solkest with the Emperor like that. The Mages have wondered about deposing Weard, there were all sorts of plots and plans, but it's far too late for that now. Weard's authority, I would say, has been unassailable for some time. . .Somehow, he found out about the conspiracies. There are always traitors, of course.' She paused. 'And now there's death everywhere. You may have heard rumours, seen shadows, although the Mages are trying to keep it quiet. At night, flying death visits them, one by one, and six have died now. The assassins come from Weard. Haven't you heard? The Mages are dying, because of Dion Gillet, because Weard will do anything to destroy his rival. . .'

'And so Gillet wants to buy safety from the Lord Himself. What has this to do with us?' It sounded cold. Eleanor thought that Blythe suddenly looked older, stern lines about his mouth, his eyes hard. He doesn't want to be involved, she thought, no matter what Harren thinks. He'd rather just get out of it. . .

'I don't know anyone else here. No one I can trust. You will help me, won't you?'

Eleanor frowned. She saw Harren pick up the chair, and help Katriana into it, pouring her wine. She glanced down at the papers littering the table, and picked one up. She read:

> Kinship with the world is something others seek,
> And if I never love again, it would almost be enough
> To know your face, your form and style.
> Revenant dreams assault my frail peace,
> Illicit and unseen, I witness only shades—

Katriana's name was spelt out in initials, the whole thing scored through with heavy black. Eleanor looked at the other papers, and recognised the shapes of poems, quatrains, sonnets, devoted to one subject only.

Harren caught her eye, and blushed. Eleanor sighed. She had thought him sensible, someone with a little understanding. . .

'How did you get away from Gillet?' Blythe said. 'I'd have thought you'd be more or less under lock and key if that is really what he's attempting.'

'He has never understood what I am.' It was a bare statement, unquestionably honest. 'He does not know what I can do. But this is ridiculous, wasting time. Don't *you* want to get out of here too?'

'Not without knowing more.'

'There are Fosca flying every night now, hundreds of them, flying through the air, searching, smelling out people who—'

'People who use magic? Dion Gillet and his followers?'

'Yes, and anyone else who is perceived as dangerous.' Katriana waved her eloquent hand towards Blythe and Eleanor. 'And don't tell me that you have been left to run free throughout this city?'

Eleanor remembered Edine saying that Katriana Lessure held more power, raw and untrained, than anyone else she had ever met.

'They scent us out. Anyone with magic in their blood, anyone who weaves the mind with strange shaping. Anyone who has spoken with the Gods. . .' Her voice was purely contemptuous. This was not untrained power, Eleanor thought. Either Edine had misjudged it, or Katriana had been taking lessons.

'The only way out would be to steal a boat.' Blythe said with finality. 'And I've never seen a heavier guard round the harbour.'

'Shouldn't we at least *try* it?' Harren spoke heatedly.

'Harren, what's this to you? You don't have to leave Peraldon in a rush—' Blythe was sharp.

'Oh, but he does!' Katriana was holding out a hand to Harren. 'He's implicated in our lives now, all the way. You'll come with me, won't you?'

His face was lit up, transfigured with joy. 'Anywhere, dear lady,' he said. 'To the ends of the earth and back again.'

'Sarant will do, I think.' She looked at Eleanor and Blythe. There was no triumph in her voice, no sense of victory. She sounded merely cool, almost bored. For a moment, Eleanor nearly forgot the sense of power that had hung round Katriana when she'd first arrived.

'Tonight,' Katriana said. 'It'll be easier at night-time. I can help, a little. . .'

I bet you can, Eleanor thought. And I don't believe a single word you say.

Chapter Ten
The Garden

It was an endlessly difficult day. Katriana withdrawn and cold; Harren pathetically eager to please, fussing around in what Eleanor considered a very tiresome fashion. Phin stayed at the window, watching the constant stream of people across the square.

Eleanor wondered how long it would take before they all became cross with each other. Waiting was never easy.

'Won't we be followed? Won't we be vulnerable, out on the open sea?' she asked at one stage. 'Even if we do manage to get a boat?'

'The Fosca are concentrating on the city. They know that Gillet is still here, possibly planning some kind of counterattack. With any luck, they won't waste time patrolling the coastline.' Phin spoke calmly.

'What will we do on Sarant?'

'I don't intend to be there long.' said Katriana. 'This battle between Weard and Gillet will soon be over.'

'How can you possibly know that?' said Eleanor.

Katriana sat unmoving, her small hands quiescent in her lap. 'They are made for each other. They are obsessed with God, and will risk everything for His sake. And there is only room for one High Priest, one Great Mage on Peraldon. It will be a swift and certain death.'

'For whom?'

'That is in the hands of God.'

'What will you do?' Come on, thought Eleanor. Give an inch or two, show us who you really are, what you're doing here. . .

'It lies in the hands of God,' she repeated. A convenient answer, thought Eleanor. Meaningless.

'And it is not fit to speculate on such matters. Even you, Eleanor Knight, who has spoken with the Lord Lycias Himself, should know better. It is for us to accept and endure. That is all that is required.' For a moment she was silent. Then she raised her head. 'I'll go to Stromsall,' she said quietly. 'That's where the followers of Astret live. I think there may be a place for me there, one day.' She turned to Harren. 'Would you like to accompany me there?'

'If it would give you pleasure, lady.'

It was infuriating. On and off, Eleanor dozed in the chair by the fireplace. She found the room cramped, uncomfortable and stifling. She was glad when the market closed down and the stalls were packed away. The rapid approach of dusk was a relief.

They waited until it was completely dark, until the mid-evening patrol had passed.

The streets were silent. The festivals of summer were only a memory. No late-night revellers sat at the tables and chairs still littering the pavements outside cafés and bars. Doors were closed, shutters drawn.

Their footsteps were the only sound. They kept to the shadows, avoiding the larger squares and piazzas which offered no concealment from the platoons of uniformed men.

They heard, behind windows barred with iron, the constant chanting of prayer. Voices were raised, echoing the words of the priest with fervour. Occasionally, a blaze of light flooded the pavements where the devout performed the Rites of the Sun. Light and heat. Fire and flames, burning through the sins of the ungodly. . .

The evening air was chilly, now unmistakably autumnal. As Eleanor, Blythe, Harren and Katriana moved down the long avenues, black leaves fell from the trees and stained their path with patches of dark. The flaring illuminations of the righteous were left behind in the city centre.

They were following Blythe: their few, whispered words matching the sibilant leaves, whisking over stone.

They were beyond the wide avenues and elegant crescents now, crossing one of the many parks in the city. The fountains no longer played and the surface of each pool was slightly ruffled by the cooling wind. Shrubs and trees cast shadows around them. There were further drifts of leaves here: broad flat shapes, black leaves, turning in the wind.

Eleanor jumped as a peacock cried out suddenly, very close to them, a fading scream. But Katriana had stopped, was standing motionless in the centre of the path. 'Too late. . .' Her voice sounded peculiar to them all, tense and vibrant. 'Watch!' she said, pointing into the night sky.

They looked up. The sky was crowded with fleets of flying black creatures. Their wings were jagged against the stars, and their smell was unmistakable, putrid, sick, rotting. They raced along, riding on the wind, swooping and swerving.

As they watched, the Fosca dispersed and flew in fragmenting formations widely over the city. And Eleanor remembered why they were leaving Peraldon. She looked at Blythe and saw that his thoughts mirrored hers.

'Come on, Katriana, we shouldn't be out in the open.'

'Closed doors do not stop Fosca.' Her voice was unrecognisable still, a sharp, grating tone to it, something that was neither fear nor anger.

Harren had taken Katriana's arm, pulling her onwards. The stench of Fosca was massing in the air and Eleanor knew that they did not have long to find shelter.

They were almost at the quayside when the attack came. There was no warning, just a whirl of air over their heads and the sudden, choking stench.

A claw ruffled Eleanor's hair, tore at the cloak she was wearing. For
a moment it caught, and she was surrounded by threshing, leathery
wings, and the air in her lungs turned sour with panic. The wings
battered round her head, tangling in her hair. She felt the sickness
rise, her limbs weakening, the darkness closing in even as she tried to
protect her face.

But none of the sharp thorns raked her flesh, no claws tore her skin.
The Fosca had moved on and when she looked again she saw it
swooping towards Katriana.

Her naked hands were moving. . .

A dislocation. It was as if air had instantly solidified around the
Fosca. It hung, motionless over Katriana's head, and the woman's
strangely fluttering hands spun an invisible cocoon to wrap it in
immobility.

The gashing mouth was stretched wide in an enraged grimace, its
pale eyes void and staring. The curved claws were halted, hanging
empty on the dark air.

Suspended above the ground, it was a black flowering of the night:
a dead shadow rising from the stars, blooming in folds of violence over
their heads.

It was calling, a thin high note intermittently edging into inaudibil-
ity.

'Get help. . .!' Katriana's harsh voice cut through the wheeling
noise and Eleanor saw Blythe and Harren running, running faster
than she thought possible across the empty lawns to a line of trees.
Through their thinning branches, she saw the outline of a small
pavilion.

She saw Katriana's hands hesitate, and the creature hanging in the
air stirred. The deadening eyes swivelled, and the mouth began to
move. And then Blythe was there again, a long-handled scythe in his
hands and, ludicrously, a rake thrown for Eleanor's use. They closed
in together just as Katriana staggered, and the Fosca began to drop.

In its first swoop it avoided their weapons, dodging between them,
its claws flaring out towards Katriana. But she had collapsed sideways
into the shelter of the shrubbery, and its claws caught in the earth.
Harren fell to his knees beside her.

The Fosca was up and away, wheeling round, ready to attack again.
Eleanor and Blythe stood together as its great weight plummeted out
of the sky towards them. 'Ready!' he shouted, and at the last minute
she lifted the rake towards it.

The Fosca was going too fast to stop. The winged mount fell on to
the spikes of the rake. The handle broke in Eleanor's hand with the
weight of it and she found herself off balance, sprawling in dirt,
making a desperate effort to get out of the way of its tumbling bulk.

The scythe bit. The grimacing petal head was lopped, tumbling into
the thick foliage of the shrubbery, to be lost amongst other, more
fragrant flowers. The claws and hooks flailed uselessly. The body lay

on the ground beside the dark angel, and still the claws scraped against the gravel, sending up sprays of small stone.

Katriana was lying on the ground, her head in Harren's lap. Twigs had caught in her hair, snagged in her clothes. At last they were able to see her face, dead white in the moonlight, sculpted like marble. Perfect lines, classically balanced features, an exquisite, untouchable beauty.

Her eyes were closed.

Blythe went over to Harren. 'Is she hurt?' His friend shook his head. His face shone oddly pale under the moon, his breathing uneven. 'Just exhausted, I think. Come, wondrous silver lady, time to move on. . .' He stroked the side of her face.

The dark lashes fluttered softly, and at once her hand went up to pull the veil forward, hiding her eyes. She nodded slowly and held out her hand to Harren. He helped her to her feet.

Blythe was scanning the sky. 'They've moved on,' he said. 'They're heading for the city centre.' The sky was empty of Fosca, the moon shining clear and undiminished. He looked at Eleanor. 'Okay? To the harbour?'

'That's all right by me,' Eleanor said. Katriana was silent, hanging virtually unconscious between the two men, her arms round their shoulders.

'But not by me.'

A figure stepped forward from the shadowy lines of trees. He was tall and straight, dressed in plain black robes.

She had never met him before, but Eleanor had no trouble identifying Dion Gillet. She saw a closely shaven head, gleaming deep-set eyes, a heavy brow. Like Katriana, he filled their thoughts with his presence.

He was not alone. Beneath the arching tress, Eleanor saw other shadows, other shapes. She heard murmuring voices.

'What have we here? Katriana, are you hurt? Damaged in any way?' He came closer and grasped his ward's shoulders. Harren and Blythe were pushed out of the way, and other men from the shadows took their place. Dion Gillet lifted Katriana's veil, roughly turning her face this way and that in the clear moonlight.

There was something proprietorial in his action, something halfway between brutality and sensuality. He was neither gentle nor careful. She moaned faintly, her eyes still closed.

Harren cursed, suddenly and furiously, and lashed out, knocking Gillet's hand aside. The priest glanced at him. He spoke one word, something Eleanor did not catch, and Harren screamed, the sound high and out of control. His eyes were wide, staring: he clutched at his own right hand, holding it out far in front of him as if it no longer belonged to him.

No one had touched him, no weapon had moved, but Eleanor saw it plainly. The flesh of his palm split wide, as if stabbed by nails, and blood gushed out, a great fountain of bright crimson, pumping and spurting with every beat of his heart.

'No!' Eleanor was shouting at Gillet, and Blythe was already moving, making a dash towards the discarded scythe.

He had no chance. A brief scuffle, some fairly vicious and desperate manoeuvres, too quick for Eleanor to follow, and then she saw one of Gillet's followers raise a club and wield it forcefully at Blythe's unprotected head. He was already dodging, and it caught him only a glancing blow, but that was enough. He crumpled on the gravel, lying motionless at Eleanor's feet.

'Eleanor Knight.' She dragged her eyes away from Blythe, unwillingly compelled by something in the cold voice which summoned her.

Dion Gillet held out a hand to her. 'Come with me,' he said. 'You have no other choice.'

'What about them?' One of the men nodded towards the Harren and Blythe.

'Leave them. Blythe at least will be useful yet. He's worth more to me here.'

He turned back towards Eleanor. 'And Woman brought death into the world with Her act, and thereafter shall all men suffer. Come with me, Eleanor Knight. You shall know what you have done.'

And without control or volition, her feet began to move. She looked frantically round for help, but Phin was unconscious, and blood still poured from Harren's hand.

'Come with me,' said Dion Gillet, and so she did.

Chapter Eleven
Lukas

The baby was too small to cry: his little lungs gave no howl of outrage, no shrill protest when she laid him down. He fitted like a jewel between her breasts, nestling in the soft warmth of her skin, and he was rarely moved from that place of safety.

Felicia wrapped him round in silk and lambswool, and held him fast all night and all day. She watched fearfully each struggling breath. He made only the smallest of movements, shifting elbows and knees, sharp with meagre flesh, against her.

She knew enough to keep him close to her heart. To express milk and guide it patiently between lips too weak to suck. She almost dared not sleep, in case she should miss the slight beat of his heart. She was helpless with love, overwhelmed with its passion. Nothing mattered to her but the slight rhythms of his small life.

She was not there when Rosco regained consciousness.

Serethrun said, 'And they're all recovering?'

'All.' Philp Cammish was most unusually flushed, moved by an excess of emotion. 'Some ten deaths – those who were injured or very old, those not found until dawn. But everyone else, even the strangers from the North. . .There's no trace of ice, Maryn, it's as if it had never happened.' He ran his hands through wiry grey hair, shaking his head with disbelief. 'Even those from the far north, those who lived for the longest with winter in their blood can remember little of it. A dream or delirium, it seems, nothing more. An icy wind blew them to the South and then abandoned them. A miracle, nothing more or less. A miracle. . .' He paused, and his voice softened. 'The Lady, how is she?'

'Gaining strength, rejoicing that the people of Shelt are free.' Serethrun disliked the formality of his own words. He wanted to respond to Cammish's warmth, wanted to share the relief and happiness. But he could see a quagmire ahead, an ordeal as onerous to him as the onslaught of Gawne's ice-warriors.

Serethrun had injured Mittelson more seriously than he had intended during that crisis before the birth of Felicia's baby. The Mage's lung had been punctured, a wound slow and difficult to heal. But worse than that, he had fallen awkwardly when Serethrun's sword had found its mark, his head striking the marble mantelpiece.

After three days of oblivion he had woken to a world of blackness. Mittelson's pale gold eyes registered nothing but darkness. And with the loss of his sight, Mittelson lost the power to weave spirals between hands and eyes. He had trained himself to do without a spiral staff by concentrating on the magic augmented by the glance of those pale gold eyes. But his eyes saw nothing now, and his magic was gone.

He kept to his sickbed at first, silent with bitterness, with anger and despair. He was suddenly powerless, had no way of influencing the world, of changing its shape or form. He had nothing left now, but his humanity.

And intelligence. In the enforced idleness of illness, this active and acute mind began to stir once more. Mittelson knew what the options were: he could live out the rest of his life in solitude, trading on past reputation, on past connections. . .or he could make a place for himself in the new world, this world where magic was dying.

He had fallen to his knees in front of Felicia, begging for forgiveness. He had intended only to save Shelt. Next time, if she allowed him to remain in the Castle, he would be guided by her. He would never disobey again. . .

Preoccupied, she saw that he was powerless and felt pity. Stay here with us, she said. But do not blame Serethrun, who acted on my orders.

Serethrun watched Mittelson recover. The Mage would find another path through to influence. Blindness has never stopped Mages before. He remembered Rosco's brother Matthias, unquestionably potent in his blindness. This is only a hiatus, he thought, a calm before Mittelson returns to power.

He was deeply suspicious. He regretted the death of Alex Aldrich, but the apprentice Mage had been about to throw a knife at him. It had been self-defence. Magic gives men the illusion that they can act without reference to anyone else, he thought. It denies their relationship to the world around them, they start thinking in terms of the supernormal.

Mittelson's presence was felt throughout the Castle, drifting down the cold corridors from the state rooms, to Felicia's side, to Rosco's room. Servants constantly attended him, supporting, guiding, opening doors, clearing his pathway. But Mittelson was alone in his omnipresence, shadowing each room. The breath hissed between his teeth like a wind from the sea.

Felicia was concentrating on her child, and on the affairs of Shelt, and did not realise how much Mittelson had changed. He dominated the Castle in subtle ways. He was driving himself far and hard, tracing the patterns of life there, learning the boundaries of each room, each passage, each stairway. He was often to be found within earshot of private conversations, concealed in window-seats, on the other side of hangings. He was always just round the corner in the corridor, walking the battlements at dusk and dawn.

He behaved with punctilious courtesy to everyone, including Serethrun Maryn. But Serethrun knew this for a lie. He had not been forgiven. The memory of his act was burning beneath Mittelson's sightless eyes, and was part of the impulse that drove Mittelson to pace the corridors so obsessively.

There were other matters of urgency. While Mittelson's presence pervaded the Castle, while Felicia nursed her tiny child, and did what she could to assist the city's return to ordinary life, a ship was observed beyond the bay of Shelt. It came from the far south and carried complex and difficult messages from Javon Westray, Duke of Eldin, to his daughter Felicia. Javon was on his way, and Serethrun knew that it meant trouble for them all.

But there was something more disturbing than all these things to Serethrun, more immediately disruptive.

Serethrun had seen that morning the fluttering auguries of life in Rosco's eyes.

The ice had thawed, after all. Lukas felt a tingling, near-pain in his limbs, a heaviness in his muscles. It did not happen all at once. There were drifting moments between comprehension and dream, a gradual awareness of light and dark.

Around him, he felt unaccustomed soft sheets. He heard a voice talking, close to him. It was familiar; he had listened to it for a very long time. It rang through his blood but he could not at first remember whose it was. Someone of authority, he thought, someone he used to like and trust.

He felt strangely reluctant to open his eyes. Instead, he let the rapid words run through his mind, and all too soon they began to form the shapes of sense and comprehension.

'—and if they don't, it will be necessary to reclaim most of their horses and ban them all from the surrounds. The far north is safe once more, and there is no reason for them to stay near Shelt. And when Serethrun Maryn is apprehended, as you will surely agree is essential, only then can we afford to start trading with the West—'

'Mittelson?' His voice seemed suddenly loud, harsh in his hearing.

'Ah. . .' A long sigh. 'So you are awake, after all. Welcome back, Rosco. Your city of Shelt waits for you.'

He opened his eyes, and saw the Mage sitting at his bedside. Mittelson had changed, and it was partly to do with the way he was now dressed in grey robes, more like a Sea Lord than one of the fisherpeople. But more disconcerting still was the blankness of his eyes, staring at a point some inches to the left of Rosco's own face.

He thought of the words he wanted to say, and somehow it happened, his voice creaky and unreliable as a broken thing. 'Mittelson; what's wrong? Your eyes. . .'

'Our young protégé, our dispossessed *eloish* Serethrun Maryn, decided to take matters into his own hands. We – disagreed over a matter of policy. I fell. It was – almost – an accident.' He saw Mittelson shrug. It was difficult to comprehend the meaning of these words, his brain was unused to understanding. But Mittelson went on, and the salient facts found their way through. 'The sight may even return in the end. But more important that that, I must first of all congratulate you on the birth of a son. Felicia and the child are doing as well as can be expected, considering the extreme risks of such a premature birth. . .'

This was too difficult to take. 'Just a moment.' His mind flailed around the sums and calculations, and gave up. 'She's had the baby? How long have I been here?'

'Months, Jolin Rosco. For three months you have lain under a pall of ice, and no one has been able to rouse you. And during that time we have been under siege from Gawne and the ice-warriors, and have been defeated them. The Sea Lords are all dead, and the Lady Felicia is a great heroine. She has saved us all, and Shelt rejoices.' The irony in his voice was shockingly out of place, even to Lukas, hearing this news for the first time.

'A child. . .' He did not want to consider Mittelson's ambivalent words, or the strange timbre of his voice. He was trying to comprehend all this implied. This new rôle: father. A son, an ultimate responsibility. It seemed not to fit at all. He tried to pull himself to sitting, but it was too difficult. He was dismayed by the weakness of his limbs.

'Take care,' said Mittelson. 'I'll ring for help—'

'No. Never mind.' He heard Mittelson continue talking, more about the Sea Lords and the *eloish* and all sorts of things, and he suddenly said casually, as if it didn't matter at all, 'Eleanor? Is she all right?'

Mittelson frowned, and the flow of words stopped. 'She left Shelt with your brother the same night that you disappeared. We all thought you'd gone together, but when Serethrun Maryn brought you back here we realised our mistake.' Mittelson's voice was acid.

Lukas raised his hand from the sheets towards the bedside, where the bell-pull hung. Even such small movements made his heart race, his head swim. He let the hand fall back to the bed. He took a deep breath, trying to focus his thoughts. She would be all right with Matthias. He need not think of her now. 'Okay, Mittelson. I'm back once more, ready to go. Send word to Felicia. I would like to see her. As soon as possible.'

The Mage rose calmly to his feet, and slowly crossed the room to the door. He carried a cane now, plain and unadorned with distracting spirals, and felt his way at each step. And although Lukas watched him, and one part of his mind felt pity and regret, he was really only concentrating on a portion of what Mittelson had told him.

He was thinking, a child. Felicia has had a son. And I am his father.

And Eleanor has left Shelt, and I don't know where she is.

Felicia came at once, but he had sunk back into an exhausted stupor and knew nothing of her presence at his bedside, the child at her breast.

Next day he managed to sit up, and Mittelson ordered a programme of massage and exercise. Again, he sent for Felicia. But because she moved slowly, he wondered if Mittelson had lied, or if he had dreamed that a child had been born. . .

She knocked on the door, but waited for no answer. She crossed the room to his side, and sat in the chair Mittelson had used. Her eyes barely touched his face. Instead he could see that she was concentrating on the small bundle at her breast, gently unfolding the wrapped silk, gently nudging the heavy head free from its nest.

'See?' she said. 'Rosco, your son. I think – really think that he is gaining strength. It was too early, but he is beginning to suck—' She looked up suddenly, and met his eyes. It came to him that she was nervous of him, and distant too, as if he were some stranger.

'If you want to, I think you could hold him for a while, but it might be best—'

'No, let him sleep.' He viewed the little, hairless head and its delicate, peaky features, with misgiving. How could one hold such a being, or take care of it? For surely the least touch would bruise, the quietest noise shock and terrify?

'He won't bite, you know.' She was amused, watching him, and in relief he reached out and stroked the baby's head. He had never touched anything so soft before. He rested his hand on hers.

'Was it very hard?' he asked.

'There are worse things,' she said honestly. Courteously, making it look natural, she withdrew her hand from his, tucking the material around the baby's head once more.

There was a pause. He thought she looked better than ever before. Her cheeks were delicately coloured, her eyes clear and sparkling.

He owed her so much. He could at least start with an explanation. 'Felicia, I did not run out. Astrella took me north, I did not intend to abandon you and Shelt.'

'Yes, I know.' She looked directly into his eyes at last. 'It was necessary. You delayed Gawne a little, delayed the grip of ice a day, two. . .Enough to allow the child to live, perhaps. Without that little grace, he would have come too soon. He would not have been strong enough. I understood none of it at the time. But you're back now, Rosco. What are you going to do next?'

'That rather depends on you.'

'And Mittelson?' she spoke seriously.

He shook his head. 'No. I think. . .I think that Mittelson is out of it now. The Mages have had their day.' It was a strange knowledge, an unlikely intuition. Garulf had seen it, had warned that this would be so. Lukas had woken to a world where magic was slipping away. He remembered the unpleasant timbre to Mittelson's voice, the way his words had skimmed acidly over momentous events. He thought, all the Mages I've ever known have weakened, or have died. Matthias, Gawne, Mittelson, Blaise, the Sea Lords. Aloud, he said, 'I think it's up to us, now. To ordinary men and women to shape their own fates. And here in Shelt, it is most particularly up to you. A great heroine, Mittelson said.' He smiled, but it was an effort. He suddenly felt extraordinarily tired.

She stood up, unhurriedly. 'You should rest, Rosco. It will take some time to regain the strength lost over three months.' She was looking at him, but he could see that her mind was elsewhere. 'I'll come back tomorrow if you like, but I shan't be able to stay for long. My father Javon is due to arrive within the week.' Her mouth dropped a little. Irony, he decided, not fear or apprehension. 'And for that little encounter, Rosco, I would really rather that you were out of the way. There are certain things I want to say to him.' She smiled quickly. 'A sickbed is such a convenient excuse. . .' Absently, her fingers continued to stroke the top of the baby's head.

Soon after, she left the room as quietly as she had entered it. He lay back against the pillow and wondered at the change in her.

He knew what had happened. She didn't need him any more. The child required strength from her, and so did the city, and she knew that she could provide what they wanted. She had already done so. She no longer needed anyone else to take responsibility, to make her decisions.

She no longer relied on him.

Lukas was free.

Chapter Twelve
Shelt

Over the next few days Lukas Marling regained strength. By degrees, he left his bed, got dressed, began moving slowly around the room. He still slept a great deal and when he awoke Mittelson was usually there.

The day after he had spoken with Felicia, he found Mittelson sitting in silence by the bedside, hands resting on his cane. He turned his head as Lukas moved, waiting.

'Tell me what happened, Mittelson. There's so much to fill in. Gawne, the ice-warriors, all those people from the North. . .Haddon Derray, and that other child. Where are they all now? And tell me about Felicia and her father Javon, and this extraordinary birth.' He was out of bed, reaching for clothes and boots. Mittelson was still silent. 'But first, before all that, I want food. Not slops, but proper, steaming hot food to chew. . .'

'It's waiting for you.' Mittelson pulled the ornate braid by the bed. 'Don't overdo it. You'll need every resource when Javon Westray gets here—'

'Felicia says she can handle him.' Something unknown made him say it. He had absolutely no intention of leaving Felicia to encounter Javon on her own. He could see that Mittelson was strung-out with tension. The hands on the cane were clenched tight.

'You cannot, for one minute, take that seriously. She's in a dream world, has been ever since the birth. Javon won't take the slightest notice of her. A woman, with a baby at her breast! Absurd.'

Perversely, he wanted to argue, although to some extent he could understand Mittelson's point of view.

'She should be allowed to try,' he said calmly. 'You should not underestimate Felicia Westray.'

'I have never underestimated her.' The voice was sharp. 'Right from the start I knew she was fated to bring peace to all Stromsall. The Lady Astret shines in her eyes, has named her for Her own. She is of mystical significance, and is worthy of reverence. But it's nothing to do with politics, or armies, and Javon Westray thinks only in such terms. She needs you, Rosco, to handle such aspects. That was why your marriage was fated. It is a matching of archetypal forces. The mystical feminine, and the practical masculine.'

Lukas was saved from answering by the arrival of servants bearing trays. He began to eat, and let Mittelson's voice run on, telling him all that happened.

He heard that many of the northern tribes had already left Shelt, taking advantage of the mild autumnal weather to travel back to their homelands. The *eloish* were regrouping in Brenet Forest. Haddon Derray and the baby had left, long before the siege, travelling south. . .

And Felicia was obsessed by her child, seeming to pay little attention to affairs of state.

'How do you know?' Lukas looked up suddenly. Mittelson appeared much older to him, now. His greasy hair was iron-grey, thinning across the forehead, his tight-clenched hands flecked with brown.

Mittelson shrugged. 'You've seen her. The baby is everything to her. It's only natural. You shouldn't expect her to take part in things which are not essentially a woman's concern.'

Mittelson was missing the point. He saw women only in terms of archetypes. Mystical significances. Lukas could not take such terms seriously. Mittelson had never loved, as far as he knew, had never joined with a woman in passion. How did he know what women were like?

Unbidden, another picture filtered into his mind. Inappropriately and disturbingly, Lukas remembered smooth skin; silky, red-gold hair. A mouth that lifted in laughter, and grey eyes that challenged and matched his own.

The practical masculine. He almost laughed. He was the Earl of Shelt, married to Felicia Westray, the father of a son. He could not afford to go on thinking of Eleanor Knight. She had left, she was far away. Probably Matthias had sent her back to her own world, as he had himself suggested.

He did not know why she still lived in his heart, why he could not manage to put this love aside. In every other circumstance, the mind learns new habits, new patterns. Gradually, sooner or later, it becomes full of other images, other concerns, and those who are lost, those who have died, or have travelled far away, lose their power to influence thoughts and even dreams.

Other people and events take priority. Forgetfulness is a blessed relief, a loosening of the chains.

He liked Felicia, and admired her. . .There was no logical reason why he should not forget the past.

Except a vow, sworn so long ago on a dark seashore. It meant more now than he had anticipated. It was as vivid, as binding now, as it ever had been. The sense of time passing since then was artificial construction. His emotions were still all tied up with a stranger from a strange world.

He pushed the food away and leant back in his chair.

He did not notice that Mittelson had left the room.

Later that evening, he had another visitor. He had been sitting at the window, the curtains flung wide, watching the restless waves and racing clouds. Astrella was there, somewhere, circling the Castle far above. Disturbing messages came from her, a feeling of displacement, an uncomfortable sense that it was now time to move on. . .

Move on? How could he, with Felicia and the child and Shelt, all waiting for him?

A knock on the door. Lukas was too tired for visitors, heavy-eyed, and yet unwilling to sleep. . .

He said nothing.

The door opened. The figure that stood in the doorway was both familiar and unexpected.

'Esmond. . .?'

A slight smile, a contained and graceful walk across the carpet from an exquisite person he had last seen grovelling in the mud. He had been pulled from the waves with the other *eloish* and tribes from the North.

'I bring you a message, Jolin Rosco. You needn't stand up, or ask me how I am, or offer me wine. I am no courtier, no friend of yours. However, I have something to tell you, something you may find of interest.'

There was a sly slant to his face, a gleam in the beautiful eyes. Lukas said nothing, waiting.

'My father spoke to me, just briefly, before he died. Did you know he was dead?' He swept on before Lukas could speak. 'No, of course you don't. The ice came, but it was not ice that killed Garulf. Flames took my father, flames ate at his skin and flesh and cauterised the creeping disease that is life from him.

'We tried to protect our home. My father had seen that the ice was coming, and said that fire would halt its movement. And then riders swept through the forest, a shaman called Irian and others of the northern tribes. They confirmed it. The ice would take us all, but fire might delay its spread.

'I helped with the fires, cutting trees, encircling our home with flames. For a while, I even forgot my love, my poor dead love

. . .Fire purifies, you know.' Esmond looked severely at Lukas. 'It demanded that I tend it, build it up, take care of it, and when, just for a while I stood back from it, resting, trying to breathe clear air, it flared suddenly and caught the edge of my father's robes.

'We wrapped him in blankets, and beat at the flames with branches, but there was no real chance of saving him. He lay in my lap, moaning in pain. He was shivering with shock, and I could see his hands loosening. I said to him, had he foreseen this? Was this expected, like everything else? He didn't answer, but he did say something. He said he'd misled you. He said, he'd lied to you.'

Esmond leant forward. 'Lies and flames, you see. They go together, Moon and Sun, kiss and tell, lies and flames.'

Slowly, delicately, he kissed Lukas's mouth. 'Now,' he said. 'Who are you going to tell about this?'

Lukas had no interest in such games. 'What did your father mean, Esmond? Have you any idea?'

Esmond shook his head. He stood up, looking down at Lukas, the same faint smile curving his lips. 'Sweet dreams. . .'

He left then, and Lukas was too tired even to take off his boots. He lay fully clothed on the bed, his eyes open against the dark.

With an effort he tried to recall his brief conversation with Esmond's father. Garulf had been mysterious, to say the least. And Lukas had been preoccupied, had not paid much attention. He remembered only one, very clear, prediction. *You will return to enjoy your rôle, to protect and care for the City of Shelt*, Garulf had said.

And he was here now – alive and almost active – and no one had questioned that he was rightful Earl of Shelt.

And then he remembered something else. Javon Westray, Felicia's father, was due to arrive next day. Javon of Eldin, whose armies had conquered all of Stromsall. Javon, who might have his own ideas as to who should be the Earl of Shelt.

Chapter Thirteen
Welcome

The Castle was immaculate. Every inch of metal was burnished, every piece of furniture polished, each corridor swept, flowers everywhere. Sweet-scented candles burned in the dark inner rooms, fragrant logs fuelled every fire. The kitchens were encouraged to extraordinary feats of culinary endeavour. Specialities were imported from far and wide, bonuses given to fishermen who brought in particularly prized delicacies. New livery was issued to all the public servants.

The guard was drilled into automatic, knife-sharp order, their weapons inspected, their uniforms cleaned and pressed.

Felicia spared no expense. It was all for show, but she knew her father. She ordered Feltham, the Captain of her guard, to call irregular inspections. And although her baby still nestled quietly between her breasts, her voice was cool and sure.

'You must make sure the men are immaculate. That there is no flaw in appearance or demeanour. Because if they appear slack, or ill-disciplined in any way, my father will take it into his head to lend us aid, and troops, and commanders, and that is the last thing I want.'

'You need not worry, Lady. We are all aware of the situation.'

Feltham had trained under Javon long ago. He was too well disciplined to betray his pleasure, but Felicia knew that he was enjoying this. He was in no danger whatsoever of underestimating her father.

Over breakfast, she visited the Great Hall. She had given orders for it to be opened up, for the cold stone floor to be polished, and a thousand candles prepared. The dais at the end was carpeted in scarlet, the Castle musicians already rehearsing fanfares in the gallery.

'Not your usual style, Felicia.' Serethrun was amused.

'It's all for effect. My father will think we're doing it properly, so long as the trumpets are bright and the uniforms pressed.'

'It won't make any real difference. He'll see beyond the ceremony.'

'I know. But it will set us off on the right foot.' She smiled at him. 'And if he cares to probe further, he will find an efficient and loyal populace. I have not been idle, these last days.'

He knew she had not. While Mittelson had drifted through the Castle, wrapped in distant dreams of revenge and returning power, Felicia had been practically involved in getting Shelt back in working order.

She had drawn deep on the Castle stores and coffers, distributing her resources widely throughout the city. The Castle was rich, if the city was not. The Sea Lords had ensured that. The fees charged for the healing ceremonies had been enormous, and to a large extent untouched. Felicia was generous but circumspect. She gave money freely to various projects. A school to be built one day, hospitals. She loaned the fisherpeople money to refurbish the fleet, and said they could return it as a proportion of the catch.

She wanted to talk to Javon because she intended to re-establish trading routes with the rest of Stromsall. She wanted Shelt to be independent of her father's control, but allied to Eldin. She wanted, deep down, for the people of Stromsall to share the same ideals, the same common aims of justice and basic standards. She wanted to break down the divisions between people.

She was, after all, her father's daughter.

'No, Felicia, I am not going to pretend to be too ill to receive your father. I will, of course, keep out of the way while you speak to him privately. Naturally. The reunion of father and daughter must be respected, but I am certainly going to take my place in the Great Hall and at the banquet, and at all discussions to do with the future of Shelt.'

She sighed, feeling suddenly harassed. Rosco was indeed looking much better, more than capable of standing up to her father, but she knew what would happen. If Javon liked him, he would take Rosco aside, and they would begin to talk about running Shelt as if it were nothing to do with her.

'Just don't try to cut me out, Rosco; no secret discussions, no deals without my permission.'

'Of course not.' He raised an eyebrow. 'What is this, Felicia? Paranoia, or don't you trust me?'

'Don't be melodramatic. It's just that Father has only ever seen me as a potential breeding machine, and you've only ever known me weak and feeble, and pregnant—'

'And you've changed. Yes, I can see that. It's all right, Felicia, no one's ever going to ignore you again.' He was laughing at her, she thought resentfully. She handed him a piece of paper she had been carrying.

The smile vanished, as she expected.

'A *seating* plan? For Lady's sake, Felicia, your step-mother and Serethrun Maryn? Is there no other way?' His dismay was almost comical.

'Unavoidable,' she said. 'And besides, I think it's time you made it up with Serethrun.'

'I've always liked him. Nothing would give me greater pleasure,' he said. He was looking frantic.

'Liar,' she said mildly. 'And something else. While my father is here, it might be a good idea formally to invest our child as heir to the Earldom. What do you think?'

'Fine. Of course. Go ahead and make the arrangements.'

'But haven't you forgotten? He has no name yet.'

Rosco looked at her. There was a long pause. At last he said,
'Whatever you like.'

She nodded, and left the room.

Ceremonies, receptions, banquets. Everyone behaved themselves, and
the arrangements went without any untoward crises. After some
deliberation, Felicia had decided to welcome her father on the
quayside, thus side-stepping the question of precedence. She could
not envisage herself seated on the throne in the Great Hall with her
father approaching across the yards of scarlet carpet. It would not be
appropriate.

She stood on the quayside, her cloak fluttering in the wind. Rosco
was at her side, Serethrun, Cammish and Feltham. Other members
from the Council and their wives. A line of uniformed soldiers
stretched from the quayside to the ceremonial carriages.

Javon's ship was anchored out beyond the brigg, flags
and pennants of white and orange were brilliant in the crisp
breeze. She saw the small boat tossing on the sparkling waves, and
thought that her father's temper would not be improved by such an
advent.

A deep curtsy for her father. His eyes were sharp, watching her.
She held her head high, and smiled at him.

'My Lord, it is with such happiness that I greet you today! Our city
of Shelt is honoured by your presence.'

He gave his hand for her to kiss, and then pulled her close
in a formal embrace. 'You're looking well, girl. And a child. . .'
Already his eyes were casting around the assembly, searching for the
baby.

'He's in the Castle, sir. Too small yet for the autumnal winds.'
Rosco stepped forward.

Felicia watched them meet, saw the way that neither man would
bow, saw that both were cynically prepared for a show of friendliness,
but knew that it would go no deeper than mere show.

Depressed, she thought, there will be trouble. This is not going to
work.

Merield greeted Felicia in a cloud of scented kisses, with every
evidence of affection and delight. There were more introductions and
reunions, and slowly the party moved towards the carriages.

As they crossed Shelt to the Castle, the newcomers politely
commenting on the voyage, the weather, the architecture of the city,
Felicia felt further presages of unease. But, although her father's voice
was unstressed and his words cool, and although Rosco replied with
distant courtesy, when she looked down at her hands, she was
surprised to see that they did not tremble.

'Your first concern, of course, must be to dismiss the *eloish*. Only then
will you be able to re-establish the trade routes to the rest of Stromsall.

Drive them north. My brother initiated such a campaign when he first
came to this throne—'

'I see no reason to follow his example.' Rosco spoke coolly.

'The *eloish* will always refuse to deal with those they consider
mereth.' Mittelson sounded detached.

It was as Felicia had feared. There were only five of them
round the table, and already the disagreements were surfacing, and
the antagonism becoming obvious. Mittelson was confident, reassured by Javon's mistrust of the plainspeople. Cammish, to her left,
was looking uneasy. Felicia was being ignored. She took a deep
breath.

'First of all we should consult with the *eloish*. We may be able to
come to some kind of an agreement with them.'

'They are not trustworthy. They do not understand the value of
property and have no respect for authority. And even if they did fight
to depose the Sea Lords, even if they were loyal to Torold on that one
occasion, it would be the height of foolhardiness to suppose that his
successor would now command a similar loyalty.'

'Of course. Loyalty has to be earned.' Felicia stared owlishly at her
father.

'And the most efficient way of earning it is through strength. They
must be brought to acknowledge the rule of Shelt in these regions, and
force is the only way. I'll send three divisions. It's late in the year now,
and besides it will take some time to get the merchant houses running
efficiently once more, so a series of spring campaigns would be the
answer—'

'We must talk to them first,' Felicia said.

'Well, you'll have all winter for that, won't you?' Javon barely
glanced at her. His attention returned to Rosco, Mittelson and
Cammish.

'The fleet should be replenished and expanded. I'll want to see the
accounts here, and if necessary I'm prepared to make a loan.'

'That won't be required. The fishing fleet is in good order.' Rosco
indicated Cammish, who nodded shortly.

'Nevertheless, I will make my own decision about this.'

'We should of course be glad of any advice you may wish to offer.'

'You may be glad of a damn sight more than that!'

'Why don't you wait until you've seen the state of the boats?'

'I intend to!'

The discussion continued, in varying degrees of antagonism. So
many points to be proved, positions to be defended. Felicia spent
more time listening than talking, and it seemed to her that the main
problems lay between Rosco and her father. Neither would give way,
and both were suspicious of each other.

At length, it came to the problem of governing the city itself.

'We have in mind an assembly, elected by the adult populace, to
undertake most of the decision-making.' Rosco was speaking.

'Opting out already? What will you do, as a figurehead? Open hospitals?'

'It's not a new idea. The Sea Lords were elected to begin with.' Felicia joined in.

'You seek to emulate the Sea Lords, Lady? Surely you have better things to do?'

Stick to your child, his tone meant. Keep out of this.

And so it went on. Javon offered money and men, so that Shelt should be run under his terms. Rosco, resisting and refusing, trying to introduce other ideas. Cammish kept silent, waiting to see the outcome. Felicia was discounted entirely.

She did not walk out. She stayed present at all their discussions, and observed.

Felicia missed very little, and it came to her that her father was proposing an extreme position, almost as if he wanted to turn Shelt into a military outpost for his empire, with little or no autonomy. At first she was flushed with anger, outraged that he should try to hijack this city.

And then she saw that he didn't mean it. She saw him weigh up Rosco, and then propound an even more outrageous tyranny. He sweetened each step of the way with bribes, and waited to see how his son-in-law would take it.

It was all a test. And then she saw that Rosco's mobile face was alight with mockery, his words fluent as ever, undisturbed by anger. She knew that he was playing games too.

There were of course rows and disagreements. And at every stage Felicia herself was ignored. But it didn't seem inappropriate, as their visit drew to a close, to hold a celebration, a ball in honour of the understanding that might yet exist between them all.

However, there were a number of loose ends to be untangled before her father left Shelt. Felicia went to her own quarters, and called for Serethrun.

He was never far away. When he walked into the room, she scented fresh, salt air hanging in his clothes. His black hair had grown long, and was tangled by the wind. He had been out on the battlements. The slant eyes were wary, and he stood very still just inside the door, waiting to assess her mood, her wish.

'I need to talk to the *eloish*,' she said abruptly.

'Now? What about the party?' He looked at her quizzically. 'Have you forgotten what happens tonight?'

She sighed. 'Very well. Afterwards. At midnight.'

'I'll wait for you here.'

'Will you?' She raised her face to him. 'Don't be late. . .'

'I'll never be late for you.'

He never lied, she knew. For the first time, she began to look forward to the evening.

But there was one more interview to be sought before the party began. Felicia went to Merield's room, and knocked on the door.

The room was scented with pot-pourri and fresh cut flowers. The lighting was muted, focused on a small table by the fire.

Her stepmother was in the process of choosing which jewels to wear that evening. A number of ornate cases lay open in front of her, their contents spilling out on to the polished wood.

'My dear! How well you're looking, you should always wear pale colours. . .and the little fellow, how is he?'

Merield stood up, and approached Felicia. She peered at the baby still clasped at Felicia's breast. Her beringed fingers plucked delicately at the silk shawl. A drift of perfume accompanied every movement.

'He's fine, now.' Felicia was watching her stepmother's face for signs of insincerity. She could detect nothing, but it made no difference to what she was determined to say.

'Merield, there is something I must ask you.'

'This is most mysterious, my dear. Come and sit by me, here.' Merield went to the chaise longue by the fire, and settled herself, patting the rose brocade.

Felicia stayed where she was. 'I would like to know if it was with my father's knowledge and permission that you and Yerrent conspired against me in the spring.'

'Conspired? Whatever are you talking about?'

'In order to induce a miscarriage. Medicines, magical smokes and smells. . .'

A silvery laugh decayed into silence. 'Why, I believe you're serious! Felicia, my dear, how can you say such things?'

'I'm not asking you to prove that you're innocent or anything like that. There is no evidence, after all. I threw away every pill and potion you gave me. There will be no recriminations whatsoever. And anyway, it didn't work; my son is well and thriving. I have no intention of pursuing this any further.' She paused. 'I only want to know if my father was involved.'

Merield said nothing. Even in the subdued lighting, her face seemed drawn, no longer round and pretty. The make-up seemed overdone and unsubtle against the pallor beneath.

Felicia said, 'You must tell me. Or I shall have to ask my father himself whether he knew what you were doing.'

Merield's eyes closed, momentarily. Her voice was distant. 'There's no need for that. Javon knew nothing of it. It doesn't matter now, anyway. As you say.' She sighed, and stood up, absently taking a necklace of pearls from the casket on the table. She began to twist it between her small hands. 'I wanted to be the one to give Javon his heir, you see. Not you. I wanted to ensure that his line should continue through me. Yerrent was in my confidence, of course, and it was he who brought in the Aldrich brothers. They wanted to return the government of Shelt to the locals.' Felicia watched the milky pearls running between the manicured fingers, and waited for the string to break. 'But it doesn't matter, now.'

'Why not?' Felicia spoke sharply.

'Javon will never father a child, on me or anyone else. He is ill, you see, and has been for a long time.' She looked at Felicia directly, meeting her eyes. 'I don't know how to tell you. He. . .will not live for long. Six months, a year perhaps. He didn't want you to know, he was worried that it might upset things here.

'Felicia, are you all right?'

Strangely, it was no surprise. Frightening perhaps, to hear those words on someone's lips, saddening certainly. But no shock, not at all. Her father, mortally ill. . .that influence and energy and overwhelming ambition, to end? The world would change. She could contemplate it now, for she had already changed. She was in control now, and had a part to play. If the world changed too, it might well be for the better. . .

She had not needed Rosco here in Shelt. . .

Her hands moved, and tucked the warm silk more securely around her child's head.

Merield was speaking again. 'Felicia, I must ask you to keep this secret. He must not know that I have told you. He would never forgive me.'

Felicia thought, and you are nothing but trouble. I owe you nothing. I nearly lost this child, because of you. She saw anxiety and fear in Merield's countenance, saw the network of fine lines beneath the make-up, the carefully concealed shadows beneath the older woman's eyes.

Merield said, 'I am in no position to beg. But I ask you, in the name of the tie that binds father and daughter, to consider his. . . happiness. His peace of mind. . .' She looked at the pearls in her hands, and laid them gently on the table. And for once Felicia thought that she could read what lay in those bright eyes. Merield *loves* him, she thought. She genuinely wants to spare him. It was a revelation.

She lay her hand over Merield's. It was not difficult. 'Don't worry,' she said. 'I won't let you down.' She turned then, not wanting to prolong this interview.

There was so much to consider.

It had not gone badly. Rosco had even consented to dance with Merield: one of those formal, distant dances where people circle each other warily, as enemies. Javon had smiled benignly over them all, revealing nothing. The aristocracy of Shelt had relaxed, reassured that there was no open animosity. They applauded the pretty display of conjuring tricks by Yerrent, Javon's court Mage.

Mittelson was not present at the ball. Instead, he haunted the corridor leading to Felicia's private quarters. He waved away her servants, dismissed his own attendants. He was frowning, his staff tapping with irritation against the stone floor as he paced up and down.

Felicia found him there at midnight. She had made her excuses and was returning to her own room, where she had arranged to meet Serethrun.

Olwyn Mittelson turned to face her, barring her way along the corridor. 'Lady Felicia, where are you going?'

'To my room.' She was mild. She was used to him greeting her by name whenever they met. His blindness never prevented him from recognising her. Tonight he was looking desperate, highly strung. As he did not stand aside, she continued. 'Where were you tonight, Olwyn? You were missed.'

'I have no desire to be present at the abuse of the arts of magic. Neither have I any desire to stand by while the Countess of Shelt becomes enmeshed in *eloish* matters.'

'The *eloish* are not our enemies, Olwyn.'

'They use wild magic, untaught, untamed. They abandoned Shelt when we asked them to stay. They are *not* to be trusted.'

'Your loss of sight was an accident, as you know.' She spoke with compassion, unerringly perceptive, all her intuitions particularly sensitive today. 'Serethrun acted on my instructions. You must put these ideas out of your head.'

Mittelson hardly seemed to hear her words. 'A party of *eloish* plainsriders were seen approaching Shelt an hour ago. They will not be allowed to enter the city, of course, but you should take care. Do not walk these corridors unattended—'

'I might find my way barred by unreasonable people lurking in alcoves?'

He ignored it. 'Will Annis be attending you?'

'Of course. Let it be, Olwyn. There's no need to worry. The *eloish* are our allies.'

'That's just the problem.' Nevertheless he stood aside and let her pass.

Outside her quarters, Serethrun was waiting.

'All honour, Lady,' he said. 'I attend your pleasure. . .' He was smiling. 'I think that it would be better if we returned to the Hall, Felicia.'

His eyes were sparkling, his voice very quiet. He had changed out of his city clothes. There was silver ribbon threaded through his cloak, a fine gauze webbing along his arms. His hair was swept up and back, away from his face, framing those dark slanting eyes like a black halo. She had never seen him like this before.

'Why? What are you planning?' She felt a thrill of excitement quivering in the air around him. It sparked dangerously between them, subtle and mischievous.

He was vivid with laughter. 'Let us say, that we felt there was no need for you to risk the health of your child by leaving the Castle tonight. The *eloish* have come to the party, Felicia. They wait to greet you.'

Lightly, she laid her hand on his arm. He stroked her cheek, and she gazed at him steadily.

'This is for you, Lady,' he murmured.

Together, they returned to the ball.

Yerrent was approaching the culmination of his act. Strange music drifted from the mouths of a hundred faces, suspended in the air over each candle, each lamp, each naked flame. Over the chandeliers a choir fluted in uneasy, thin harmony. In the torches burning at intervals round the walls, wide mouths with rosy lips opened and sang. It was a bizarre, surreal effect. Disembodied faces, not male, not female, distressed the air with their noise.

Felicia halted on the threshold, all good humour in abeyance. She was unsmiling at this unsubtle show. Automatically, her hand had flown to the child at her breast, stroking and soothing.

Abruptly, the sound died. The faces vanished.

The air changed. A breath of coldness, of woodiness and green fertility cut through the heady scents of perfume and food.

She could not see them at first. As usual, they blended with their surroundings, even these highly artificial surroundings, waiting and watching, assessing the situation. In a crowd of people standing by the door, she caught a glimpse of slant-eyed derision.

She smiled. 'Welcome, friends.' And although Felicia's voice was quiet, everyone heard it.

No one had dared fill the vacuum left by the vanishing choir of Yerrent's creation. The people of Shelt, her father, Rosco, everyone turned towards her.

And so the *eloish* stepped out of the crowd, and stood before her in the centre of the ballroom floor.

They were none of them strangers to her, now. She had watched them recover from ice and drowning in the Castle wing nearest the seashore. She had visited them often, and commanded that the windows be always left open, the doors never bolted.

She saw Irian and Lara, Mir, Enthor and Jerr Morrelow, and many others, all walking towards her.

Ceremonial clothes. She had never before seen them so dressed. In shades of white and grey, embroidered by silver and black, they shimmered in the crude candlelight. They had braided their black hair with gossamer ribbons of light-spun silver. Their eyes flew upwards at the corners, gleaming with ebony shadows.

All at once, all the windows in the long room were flung open. No

one had touched them, there was no one outside. But the noise of the
sea and the wind swept through the room, and women of Shelt pulled
their wraps close. There were one or two faint wails, a rustle of deep
disturbance. The sound of swords being drawn.

Her father was on his feet. Felicia could see that he was about to
summon soldiers, that the frown on his face heralded action.

She lifted her hand, and he was stilled. He looked at her, and the
frown became one of puzzlement.

She walked further into the Hall, and held out her hands to Irian
and Lara. For just an instant the three women were joined, and then
the two *eloish* stood free once more, regarding her. Everyone's
attention was on Felicia. It was like a wave breaking over her, the
pressure of so many hopes and expectations.

She saw dark slant-eyes, light blue and grey, brown and hazel eyes,
all regarding her. She said to them all, and particularly to the *eloish*,
'My dear friends, I present to you this child.' She unwrapped the baby
at her breast. He was quiet and serene, calmly watching the bright
colours.

She was conscious of her father's gaze, minutely following her every
movement, but something else was taking precedence now.

She looked across the room towards Rosco. For a moment their eyes
met. Then he nodded, almost imperceptively.

'His name is Renferell,' she said.

A sharp movement to her left. It seemed as if Javon was going
to say something, but Merield had taken his hand, pulling him
back.

'I promise now, on the name of this child, that the *eloish* shall walk
in peace throughout Stromsall. That no one shall impede their riding,
or attempt to fence the open plains.

'Go in peace, dear friends. For we are forever united.'

Irian said slowly, 'We have a gift for you and your child. We have a
promise to make, too. No one shall be harmed on the inland plains.
All travellers will have our protection and care, all life shall be held
sacred, *eloish* and *mereth*.

'As you held our lives sacred.'

There was a vivid flash of movement, an alteration in the lighting of
the Hall. A flare and a brightness, all dazzling and deceptive. And
when Felicia's eyes began to make sense of it all again, the curtains
were fluttering, the windows empty of life, the ballroom bereft. The
eloish were gone.

Except for one. Serethrun Maryn paused, standing there by the
wide windows to the battlements, looking at her.

She felt herself crossing the room towards him, drawn by an
enchantment she had no intention of resisting. He put his hands on
her shoulders and although his words were wild and passionate, they
were meant for her ears only.

'And when the full Moon reflects in your eyes, then I'll come back,

Felicia. I will be your Moon-time lover, your gift of silver and blood. . .'

A strange pattern of shadows fell across his face and head. The wind swept the fall of silver-braided hair back and suddenly it looked as if he had horns of light flying away into the night. Then he was gone.

For only the briefest of moments, Felicia thought that she, too, might soar away from the people here and follow the call of the wind and the Moon.

She was flushed with something she had never experienced before. Physical need: wanting and yearning for the dark, hornèd man who promised to visit her with the Moon. She took a deep breath, bent her head towards the baby, so that she might hide her burning cheeks.

Rosco was crossing the floor towards her.

He was to her a stranger. She smiled as he took her arm, smiled as he drew her away from the Hall and back towards their quarters. It did not matter to her what he thought.

Chapter Fourteen
Farewell

'Why don't you leave Shelt?'

The hardest words in the world.

They had walked in silence through the corridors. Torches and candles burned calmly in their brackets. The carpets were deep and soft beneath their feet, and no other words had been spoken.

All the while they were watched by soldiers, and guests and friends and acquaintances. News travels fast. Lukas Marling walked by his wife's side, knowing that he appeared relaxed. And all the time, he remembered the words of a hermit long dead.

You will return to be Earl of Shelt.

That was the lie. He felt that the chains were unlocked, falling. The pressures were dissipating. And while he was inexpressibly moved by his small son, by the wise, all-knowing expression in his blue eyes, Lukas had not yet even held him. Renferell was safer with Felicia, safer kept close to her heart, to the warmth of her body.

Walking through the Castle, they did not touch.

In her private sitting-room, she dismissed her servants. She stood in the centre of the floor, straight-backed, the baby nestling at her breast, her arms curved round him.

'Rosco, I don't know how to say this.'

He said nothing, watching her.

She tried again. 'Shelt will be at peace now—'

'I know. And it will all be due to you.' He saw that she was confident and that, although this was difficult, she was determined. 'I think – I really think that you can do it, Felicia. Nothing has ever been clearer to me. Shelt has its best chance, with you. But what of your father?'

'He's dying.' She spoke very quietly. 'Merield told me this afternoon, before the party. A wasting disease. It will take some time yet, but he is clearly ordering his affairs. It is why he will concede so much. These disagreements have been little more than an elaborate test, as you know.' So Felicia had seen it, too. It all made sense to Lukas now. The pattern was falling into place.

'The child helps. . .' he said.

'Yes. Renferell will make a difference to him, I think. There will be something of himself to continue. He's starting to let things go, gradually. In the end, he'll let me have my own way. Javon doesn't know that Merield has told me. And no one else knows.'

'What will happen to the Empire of Eldin?' he asked, although the answer was clear, held in her curving arms.

She smiled. 'The line is safe.' She may have other children, he thought, his imagination caught. She probably will. . .

Felicia shrugged. 'My father will appoint advisors and councillors, but I will inherit. He has ensured that the female line will hold, in Stromsall at least. This is acceptable because I have a son.' Her voice was dry. 'Regional assemblies are already operating in Eldin and Trey. We may decide to move to somewhere more central.'

She sat down by the fire. 'You can stay here in Shelt, as Earl of course. He likes you, he thinks you can do it.' She paused. 'I see no need for it myself. Long ago it was governed perfectly adequately by assembly. So, if you want to leave, there's little to hold you back—'

'Except for the fact that Renferell is my son, too.'

She was unwrapping the bundle at her breast, peeling back the layers of fine cloth, so that the little, feeble limbs were able to move freely. He began to cry, a thin high sound, and she waited for Lukas to pick him up.

He raised the child to his face, and lightly kissed the furious, screwed-up face. For a while he held the tiny person in his long-fingered hands, wondering. A gift, this child, promising the future. But not for him.

Then he passed the baby back to Felicia. 'Keep him warm, my dear. Keep him safe, and yourself also.'

'Of course.'

A silence lay between them, undemanding and unstressful.

She said, 'Goodnight, Rosco. Goodnight, and goodbye. . .'

'It's not for ever,' he said suddenly, severely. 'I'll come back to see

him, and you. You are unique in my life, and in the lives of all who
surround you.

'All honour to you, Lady. Lady of the tides. I can leave him, and
Shelt, in no better hands.'

'You do not mind about Serethrun?'

'How could I? I can only offer you debased currency. He is gold,
gold and silver. I wish you well.'

She took his hand. 'I hope you find her,' she said. 'I hope it's not
too late.'

'But Felicia, don't you know? There are no second chances. . .'

Mittelson drifted down the corridors like a lost soul. Lukas said,
walking alongside, 'You'll have to help her. She's strong, but she'll
want friends. You'll be needed now as you have never been.'

'What use am I without magic?'

'She has magic enough. That's not the point.'

'I don't know whether I can live without it.' The words were abrupt
and harsh.

Lukas stopped walking, and put his hands on Mittelson's shoulders. 'Don't think like that. Let go, Olwyn,' he said softly. 'The day
of the Mage is almost done. It's fading, all that influence and illusion.
There will be only people left, men and women, and that's the most
difficult thing of all.'

'There is nothing for me to do.'

'You are a healer, Mittelson. Use your knowledge, and whatever
remnant of magic is left, to that end. You will be needed.'

'Perhaps.' He spoke slowly. 'But what about you? I don't think you
should leave, Rosco. She still loves you.'

'No, I really don't think she does. Not in that way. It was a
necessary rite of passage. That was all.'

'She'll not do it alone.'

'Felicia's not alone. She is never alone.'

'That eloish barbarian!'

'He's a dream, a dream of grace to lift her loneliness, to warm her
nights. She'll be all right.'

'I had a dream once, too. I dreamed of you, married to Felicia, and
a child born to give us all peace.'

'Well, it came true, didn't it? What more do you want?'

'What more do you want?'

Saying goodbye to Olwyn was more difficult than the parting from
Felicia and the baby. Lukas saw a long struggle ahead for Mittelson.
He was finding it hard, almost too hard, to adjust to the loss of magic.
Even if his sight returned, Lukas knew that Olwyn's magic would not.
And whether he would be content with the rôle of healer was dubious,
at best. If it went wrong, he would be no use to Felicia, and worse
than useless to Serethrun. . .

Lukas stood on the balcony outside his own room, watching the slight signs of activity aboard Javon's ship anchored out beyond the briggs. They were leaving early next morning, the dying man with his sad little wife and court magician.

Probably Yerrent's magic would remain, he thought, in tawdry rags and tatters. Party tricks and small deceits were not enough to upset the balance. But he'd never get anywhere near the Rites, or Synchronicity. Real illusion would forever lie beyond the reach of small, plump fingers.

Lukas saw, in one of the turrets to the South of his room, a figure come out on to the balcony.

Esmond, he thought. Drawn to the sea, unable to sleep, sad and bitter. Perhaps he would find consolation at the Imperial Court, when Felicia ruled them all. He hoped Esmond would at least find some degree of contentment.

But as he watched he saw someone else join Esmond on the balcony. Slim, slant eyes, young, vague. . .one of the *eloish*, his arm twining around Esmond, pulling him back into the room, stroking his hair.

Consolation of a sort, if not contentment. . .

A movement caught his attention on the beach below. The tide was halfway in, the line of white sparkling and frivolous in the bright moonlight. People played at the edge of the sea, teasing the waves, darting between plumes of spray: a weird and exotic dance of celebration. Other *eloish*, rejoicing in a new freedom.

Lukas felt a warm presence in his thoughts and looked up. Far beyond the anchored ship, way beyond the jutting lines of the brigg, he saw a disturbance in the clouds. Astrella, coming for him. She *was* coming, this time. No refusals, no mysterious missions. It was an added reassurance, not that he really needed it.

He was ready to go.

Chapter Fifteen
Alarm

Through a fog of the senses, Blythe was dimly aware that they had gone. He shifted uneasily against the gravel, and lifted his hand to his head.

In the half-light of dawn he saw his fingers sticky with blood. And then he remembered that other blood, gushing, and Eleanor and Dion Gillet. He forced himself into action.

'Harren?' His friend was still there, kneeling on the ground, bent over a hand which no longer founted with scarlet. He lifted a face whiter than bone towards Blythe. It was a terrible effort.

Blythe pulled himself to standing, impatient with the unsteadiness in his legs, the thumping pain in his head and neck. He saw puddles of blood congealing on the gravel, great stains and streaks stiffening Harren's clothes. His friend was almost beyond words. Blythe took his arm, hauled him to his feet.

'Katriana. . .?' It was the faintest of whispers.

'And Eleanor,' Blythe said grimly. 'Gillet has them both.'

'Where do you think you're going?' Four guards, turning the corner, and finding Blythe and Harren crossing the city in the early hours of the morning. 'Papers? Identification?'

'Ah, such a long night. . .' Harren's words were slurred, slow and uneven. He reached into his breast pocket and withdrew a half-empty flask of spirit. 'Drink?' he said, unscrewing the top, tilting it to his mouth. He lost his footing as he moved, and tumbled sideways against Blythe, spilling whisky over them both.

'What a fool. . .' Blythe shook his head sadly. He took the bottle from Harren, and took a deep and necessary draught. Would he be recognised, now of all times?

One of the guards was giving orders. Blythe and Harren were taken by the arm, roughly hustled along through the streets. The guards were impatient and irritable, at the end of their shift. No point in arguing now, thought Blythe, they're in no mood to listen. The duty officer will be a better bet.

'A day or two in the cooler won't do you any harm.' The guard laughed as they entered the large warren of offices and cells that was the police headquarters. 'That'll teach you to go out without papers.'

'A nosebleed?' The man at the desk stared with disbelief at the blood on Harren's clothes. 'And what about you? Walked into a lamppost, did you?' He frowned at Blythe. 'What did you say your name was?'

'Tourneour,' he muttered. He thought, if they don't let us go *now*, I'll have to tell them who I am. I'll have to start pulling weight, and stop Dion Gillet leaving the city with the two women. Out of the corner of his eye, he could see that Harren was swaying. It was amazing that he'd kept upright for so long.

The duty officer was scanning a list taken from a pile of papers. The sign on the desk between them said *Captain Destaiz, Warden's Watch*. There was a bustle of activity even at this hour. People were being questioned, men in grey uniform were checking lists, examining papers. Blythe saw street walkers herded together in one corner, a tramp mumbling quietly on a bench. Two young men in good clothes were shouting aggressively.

Captain Destaiz sighed. He seemed about to pronounce when a man in uniform approached his desk and clicked his heels together smartly. 'Well, what is it now?'

The man saluted. 'Message from the Warden, sir. Urgent. The Emperor—'

'Just a moment.' Destaiz lifted his hand, indicating one of the guards. 'Two days below for these two. . .' And before Blythe could protest, he had been whisked away through the crowds to the office at the end of the hall.

'Wait!' Blythe shouted. 'I have urgent news—'

'Oh yeah?' The guard smiled unpleasantly. 'And just why should we listen to you?'

'My name's Phinian Blythe. I used to be a Captain here—'

'And I used to sell flowers for fun. Come on, down below with you!'

There was nothing Blythe could do. He had missed his moment. He tried talking reasonably, he looked out for someone who might recognise him, but it was useless. Ironically enough, he had spent so long trying to conceal his identity that now it was impossible to shed the disguise.

No one would listen, no one believe him. Blythe could hardly blame them. Alarms were blaring constantly now, soldiers running down the corridors of the station. Something had happened, something terrible and urgent, and the Warden's Watch was on emergency stand-by. The situation was too urgent to waste time listening to the incredible story of some disreputable drunk and his dozy friend.

At last, driven to violence, Blythe lashed out and dropped the guard trying to hustle him below stairs. It was a desperate and doomed attempt, and in moments his arms were pinned behind him: a fist slammed into his jaw, another into his gut. His head struck against the wall of the stairwell, reopening the earlier wound. He subsided into blackness.

He knew nothing of the day dawning in Peraldon. He lay unconscious beside Harren in a cell deep below the Warden's offices while the alarms kept ringing.

★　★　★

The lagoon was calm that morning, rose- and gold-tinted waters lapping at the moored boats. The harbour was a different matter: there, a company of grey-uniformed guards were methodically searching the quayside, examining each mooring, checking each warehouse, every crate and container.

Dion Gillet and his companions slipped through the shadows, dodging between the warehouses on the west side of the docks. Drifting as in a dream, Eleanor went with them.

The men around her were all chanting, repeating words she did not understand. Prayers? Incantations? They were moving lightly, delicately and deliberately, not in the least worried by the swarming guards.

At first, she could not see clearly, and her thoughts were all confused by the words whispered all around her. Taste, smell and sight were all distorted by pressure of these voices, by the pressure of sounds she didn't understand.

She had no will to escape, passively accepting the decisions Gillet made. Part of her knew that the words were an illusion, that she was being hypnotised in some way, but it didn't really matter how it worked: she could only observe, and if there was a scream soundlessly battering deep within herself, she knew of no way to release it.

In front of her, Katriana was free of restraint. No one took her arms, no one muttered in her ears. She was moving swiftly, almost eagerly, and Eleanor could see no reluctance at all, no resistance. Was she enchanted, too, or was this what she had wanted all along. . .?

As the sun rose higher, the waters of the lagoon shone clear blue, gleaming and sparkling through the narrow gaps between buildings. The freshening scent of the sea was submerged in the haze of sound Gillet had created around Eleanor. She could hear somewhere that gulls were screaming, but their song had no power to rescue her from this strange trance.

A shadow, spiky and jerky, fell across Eleanor's face. Looking up, she saw dark stains against the pale sky. She saw jagged shapes flutter and knew them for Fosca patrolling the city's waterline, augmenting the careful search of the grey-uniformed men.

She saw Dion Gillet move out of a sheltered doorway to stand quite deliberately in the open, looking across the wide quayside to the guard there. She heard the man shout, saw him draw his sword, beginning to run.

'*Now*. . .' A half-muttered word from Gillet. Abruptly the grip on her arm tightened as he plunged through the doorway. It was being held open by two of his men. The others had already gone ahead.

A narrow winding passage, dark, stifling hot, another door. Open sky above them now, high walls all around. A small, stone-paved yard and, ranged against the walls of the yard, Gillet's followers stood waiting.

Although the walls rose high all around the tiny, enclosed space, there was a sundial in its centre. The sun would only reach it for a few hours each day, Eleanor thought vaguely. How ridiculous, what use was that? As she watched, one of Gillet's men laid his hands on the sundial's face, and she became aware that they were all still chanting.

The man's hands were on the sundial, concentration and will radiating from his face. Eleanor caught her breath, suddenly remembering another sundial, a transfer from one world to another.

'Was that how it happened?' Gillet was looking at her curiously. 'Ah, what secrets you know, Eleanor! What knowledge and experience, so far removed from here. And no chance to tell. . .'

'What do you mean?'

'Shhh.' He laid his finger on her lips. 'Heresy is inappropriate at such a moment as this. Now, watch, for you will find it of interest.'

The man at the dial had been joined by three others. Eleanor knew they were priests, although they wore jeans, and not robes. Golden sun-medallions hung round their necks, and their heads were shaven. They were curiously indistinct to her, undifferentiated from each other. She saw the jutting jawbones, the bony outline of skull and cheek glistening with sweat and found them alien and forbidding. She heard the words they chanted, but they made no sense.

Everyone was looking up into the clear sky.

Footsteps suddenly, rushing at them down the narrow alleyway. Gillet turned, dropping Eleanor's arm, his own hands outspread. In welcome, she thought. He's been waiting for this.

A grey-uniformed guard burst into the courtyard. Instantly, the priests around the sundial stepped back, their hands raised in the same gesture as Gillet's, and the Sun hit the gleaming golden face on the dial for the first time.

The attacking guard did not halt, could not. Propelled by forces Eleanor did not understand, he ran on, and then his foot caught. He pitched forward on to the sundial, his hands flung wide. He was stabbed there by its raised point.

Eleanor saw the gleam of bloody silver through the man's back, heard his anguished scream. His limbs were splayed and juddering, his head thrown back with impossible tension. She could see his face, see the agony and the impossible plea for help. She folded over, vomiting on to the dusty stone.

The man's head, still conscious, was slowly turning towards Dion Gillet, as a flower turns towards the Sun. Light was streaming into the courtyard now, towards the sundial. It was caught on the priests' sun-medallions, and focused laser-sharp on the skewered man. His eyes were bulging and his skin reddening. He might have screamed again, but flames sprang from his mouth and suddenly his whole body was alight, burning like dry wood. A vast heat filled the courtyard, forcing them all back against the walls. Black smoke clouded around the sundial, not quite hiding what was happening. There was a sweet nauseating smell of flesh roasting.

The man had not been alone. Two other guards were backing away from the courtyard, their eyes wide and staring.

Eleanor was leaning against the wall, half fainting, turned away from the burning man. His scream still rang in her ears, lancing through her senses.

'Watch.' A cool hand on her arm, drawing her up, turning her towards the sundial. Katriana, still hidden in black, pointing at her guardian.

Dion Gillet was watching the flames, a faint smile on his thin lips. His eyes were serious, abstracted. His hands slowly rose and, between them, the sickly smoke above the sundial parted.

Eleanor saw there another face, someone she half recognised, someone she did not know at all.

Weard looked at them through the flames, Weard, carrying his writhing staff, watching them.

Weard, the Desert Rose, the Fosca King, the High Priest of the Sun and Great Mage, Lucian Lefevre, looked through the black smoke at Dion Gillet. There was doubt in his eyes, doubt shading into anger, and that alone was enough to terrify.

'A blood sacrifice,' said Gillet softly. 'And now meet the justice of the Lord, Great Mage.'

The smoke from the pyre on the sundial became entwined with the smoke on Weard's staff. It began to spread, to grow outwards from the spiral carving, to wreathe around the head and shoulders of the man who called himself Weard.

The Shadows, born of agony, released through agony, found their long-desired victim. As they settled on Weard's shoulders, his voice began to echo the scream of the burning man, and the sound went on and on. Even as the smoke dispersed and the vision of his Shadowed face ended, the scream still rang in Eleanor's ears. She knew the pain would endure for ever.

Chapter Sixteen
Fosca

The doors were barred by Fosca. They were loyal to their King. Let no one in, Weard had said that morning. Let no one in except the Emperor. Bring the Emperor Xanthon to me, and then make sure the doors stay closed until I give the word.

They were his servants, and of limited intelligence. Only the Fosca baron had been gifted with speech, with the remnants of reasoning, and after it had witnessed the Emperor greet his High Priest in the Hall, it took its customary station on the roof of the central tower of Solkest. There, it could survey the entire palace and even have an overview of most of the city. It could ward off any danger from its master, halt the approach of any enemy.

It heard the scream.

A wail of agony that extended beyond the limits of the Hall, up through the roof, out of the open skylight.

Curiously, the Fosca baron edged nearer. It looked down into the Hall, and saw what was happening. It saw that Weard had lit a fire and that he was looking closely into the flames, his face flushing redly in the heat. He was showing something to the Emperor, but the Emperor was hanging back, revulsion on his face. There was something in the flame, screaming.

The smoke from the fire was shimmering, flickering. It looked wildly unstable, and for a moment the baron wondered if the fire would kindle the hangings and furniture of the Hall. It saw, then, that there was a relationship between the wreathing smoke of Weard's fire, and the spiral drift that always streamed around Weard's staff.

The two were attracted to each other, winding together, becoming lost in each other. And then, like some terrible birth, the smoke exploded outwards, for a moment concealing Weard from the Fosca baron's view.

It craned closer to the open skylight. And as the smoke cleared, it saw that the Shadows of the staff were changing. Directed by something the baron would never understand, they sprang free from the wood and settled on Weard's shoulders.

And then the screaming began in earnest. The baron saw the Shadows take on faces, their mouths voicing accusation and pain. The weight of anguish began to bear down on the Fosca baron's master.

The baron did not understand what was happening to Weard, but it knew where its duty lay. It was entirely uninterested in the fate of the Emperor. It took off from the tower, flying through the city.

It was looking for Mages.

★ ★ ★

The Mages of Peraldon were in conference. The Fosca baron flew in through one of the high windows of their library and left its mount there, snapping irritably at the flies and dust motes.

The baron wandered along the dry corridors towards the scent of flesh. There was no one to obstruct it, for only Mages and their apprentices ever walked those labyrinthine passages, and they were all busy.

In conference: discussing the threat to their own kind. The flying death that continued to skim through every night, sniffing out and destroying those with magic skills. They were wondering how to defeat Dion Gillet. Their leader, Weard, had told them that the Fosca were being sent by the rebel priest. In shock and dismay, they wondered how to find him.

The baron halted outside the door. It was powerful, and had been endowed not only with speech and intelligence by its master, but also with some of the Fosca King's more esoteric skills. But assembled on the other side of those doors were all the adepts of Peraldon, and it doubted whether it could withstand a massed attack. It was not brave, because it had no knowledge of fear. It had a message to give, something it wanted. Nothing mattered, except that the message should be communicated.

It paused, its petal face expressionless and vacant. And then, in one oddly fluid movement, it kicked the door open with its two lower limbs and folded all the others above its head into a tulip shape.

Instantly, a hundred beams of spiralling light encased it. Any three of those Mages together would be strong enough to immobilise it. It would have to be very careful. Through the haze, it saw the Mages moving warily towards it, suspicious, contemptuous. The baron felt the immense pressure of light increasing.

It managed one word, before its mouth was blocked. The sound was cracked and straining, an unnatural use of unnatural vocal chords. 'Peace,' it snarled, and the Mages paused in their attack.

It heard them discuss, knew that telepathy was used, and that there was much dissension. It did not fight against the constraints that held it immobile. It assumed that, in the end, their curiosity would overcome their distrust.

It was right.

Its mouth was unclogged and one of the senior Mages, Neque, said with bitter contempt, 'What do you want?'

'Shadows on him. Help.'

'Him? Who, your master?'

'Master,' it confirmed.

'Dion Gillet?'

'No. Weard.' It knew only essentials.

'*Weard* is your master?' They rustled, these Mages, fluttered and stirred like burning leaves. Their minds were leaping round the baron's few words, drawing conclusions, imagining scenarios.

They sent a messenger, a runner to Solkest.

Cautiously, the baron tried to move one of its claws, and found that in the moment of the Mages' disarray it had gained a little freedom. It waited for them to settle.

It heard their words, light and insubstantial as smoke: *Shadows, Gillet, Fosca, Weard* and then, increasingly, *Emperor, Emperor, Emperor. . .*

The baron waited, knowing all the while that its mount would be growing restive. They were unwise, making the baron wait in this way.

The runner came back at last, gabbling that Fosca were barring the way. No one could get into the Hall, where Weard and the Emperor were in conference.

'Call them off!' Neque shouted at the baron. 'Get the Fosca out of the way, we have to see what is going on in that Hall. We can't act without knowledge.'

He was lying, the baron knew. Neque wanted to see what had become of Weard, but the knowledge that Weard was also King of the Fosca might stop them helping. . .

Slow, unaccustomed lines of reasoning began to shift.

The Fosca baron said, 'Yes.'

There was a scrabbling outside the door to the conference room, an impatient scraping at the wood. The baron could see that the Mages were torn. They did not want to trust a Fosca, but had little confidence in their ability to defeat the huge numbers of Fosca guarding the Hall in Solkest.

The Fosca baron did not know how to laugh, but at this point a laugh might have been appropriate. Its mount was becoming aggressive, outside the door. It decided to say one more thing to them.

'Must help. Or die.'

And although Lefevre, the Fosca King, was a master of deceit, his servant knew no artifice.

The Fosca baron did not lie.

Chapter Seventeen
Going Home

Two days and two nights. Blythe and Harren recovered to find themselves shut in a cell at the end of a long corridor. They heard other prisoners rattling the bars of other cells, they heard shouting and pleading. Sometimes they shouted too. No one paid any attention. The guards who brought food and water were hurried and preoccupied. No one took any notice of what Blythe was saying.

'How much longer?' Harren fretted. That first day, he drifted in and out of delirium, dangerously weakened by loss of blood. 'What *is* going on up there?'

Blythe was pacing the narrow cell, his mouth a hard thin line. 'I'd wager the Fosca are attacking. Listen to those alarms. They're probably looking for Gillet and his followers, but God knows if they're still on Peraldon. If they've any sense, they'll have left long ago.'

'Did you see her? Katriana, I mean?' Harren was rambling again. 'Ah, her *eyes*!'

Blythe stood still, arrested by something in Harren's voice. 'No,' he said slowly. 'What about them?'

'Her eyes – ah, my old friend, you may have seen wonders, but nothing like this. Her eyes are pure silver, through and through. Not grey, not white, but silver, although the pupils are black. . .' He half laughed. 'It feels like a dream, but so clear. . .I remember it more clearly than anything in the world.'

Blythe squatted down beside him. 'Harren, *what* did you see?'

'It was in the garden. With black leaves everywhere, those turning black leaves. . .when you were fighting that Fosca. I held her in my arms, and she looked at me, beautiful, beautiful. . .Phin, I've never seen the like! Her eyes are luminous, glowing with light. She is a goddess!' He paused, flushed with fever and remembrance. 'It's the only word for it. A *goddess*. There are Moon scars on her temple, and silver in her eyes.' His own eyes fluttered to closing, as he dropped again into an uneasy sleep.

Blythe's fingers traced the scar on his own skin, his mind racing. And Gillet is a priest of the Sun, he thought. What is he doing with someone who has been marked by the Moon? What bargain does he hope to exact, what reward does he seek?

Eleanor also bears this same scar. She came back to Peraldon because I offered her peace and friendship.

It was the most brutal of ironies.

He moistened a rag from the water jug, and wiped Harren's face. In the distance he heard shouting again, the clash of sirens. How long, he thought. How much longer must we stay here?

★ ★ ★

On the third day, they were turned out into the city streets. Everything had changed. There had been fires everywhere, and many buildings were still smoking. Blythe saw people with shocked faces searching through the rubble, trying to retrieve their possessions. Soldiers were on guard at every corner, on every rooftop, but no longer were they simply watching the people of Peraldon. They were scanning the skies, too. *Fosca*, he thought. Only Fosca could cause such destruction here.

Lefevre's legacy. Searching out those with magic and those unreliable priests who delved into mysticism. They were searching out the Great Mage's most powerful enemy, Dion Gillet.

Harren had revived. Some of his colour had returned and with it a certain clarity of thought. As they left the police headquarters, he looked at Blythe disparagingly. 'It won't do, you know.'

'What?'

'Looking like a tramp. You'll meet the same reaction again, and we'll need the Warden's help to get to Sarant.'

'Yes.'

'A resurrection,' said Harren. 'Whether you like it or not. . .'

'Long overdue.' Blythe regarded himself in the dusty window of a shop.

'Yeah, a resurrection and a haircut.' The faintest of smiles, fading as they pushed through the distressed crowds who filled the streets. The Warden would have his hands full, without listening to wild stories from disreputable strangers. Blythe would have to assume his old persona. It would take an hour or so, but what did that matter now? So much time had already been lost.

It took longer than he expected to cross the harbour quarter to his lodging. Some roads were blocked by fallen buildings and the debris of fires, others were cordoned off while the searches continued.

Back at the boarding house, Harren collapsed heavily into a chair. Blythe considered his friend. 'You should sleep, have a rest,' he said gently. 'I'll see what I can find out.'

'Come back for me. . .?' Harren's voice was like a thread, his eyes bright with the threat of fever.

'I don't think there'll be time.' He paused at the door, looking back at the smaller man. 'Don't set your heart on Katriana,' he said. 'Don't expect too much.'

'Sighing for the Moon. . .' He did not laugh. 'I know. Silver ladies are beyond the reach of mere mortals. I like Eleanor Knight.' Inconsequentially. 'You'll find her, won't you?'

'Yes.' There was no doubt in his voice.

'And then what? Slipping back into Peraldonian life, society parties, a nice house on the quayside again?' Harren answered his own question. 'I can't see it myself.'

Blythe said nothing.

'You know, it's better to live in hope than to want nothing.' Harren raised his head. 'I would not change place with you for all the silver eyes in the world.'

Blythe stepped out of the door. 'Goodbye, Harren. Perhaps we'll meet again one day.'

'Perhaps. . .' Harren stared at the closed door. 'But somehow I rather doubt it.'

Blythe ran up the stairs to the attic, and caught his hair back with a cord. He pulled from a cupboard the clothes he had bought on first arriving in Peraldon. He had chosen them deliberately to indicate his status as wealthy and high-born, in case he ever needed it. In case he ever went home. A silk shirt, tailored breeches and a light grey cloak lined with black. New boots, high-polished, to reflect the sun. He stared in the mirror, and saw a stranger, a counterfeit, a hypocrite.

He looked like part of the old order, of a past life. A figure of authority and power. Such things were irrelevant to him now, these trappings of convention. Too often they indicated a reluctance to question. But it would help the Warden, Emile Blanchard, to believe what Blythe had to say. He did not want a repeat performance of the last two days. He wanted to look credible, worthy of consideration. Blanchard, his old superior, was more than a professional contact. He was a relation, a distant cousin. With any luck, he would find time to listen to Blythe's story.

He had to reveal who Weard really was. This was the essence of it. The Warden had to be told who was controlling not only the Fosca but also, possibly, the Emperor.

And Blythe could see only one way to overpower Lefevre. It would have to be through Dion Gillet. Blythe had to convince Blanchard that Gillet was crucial to what was happening, that Gillet had to be found. He could think of no other way to defeat Weard/Lefevre. Of course, his own agenda was to release Eleanor, but he need not mention that. Again, he found his thoughts returning to Katriana. . .

Silver eyes, black pupils: Harren's dream lady. A strange complication, something out of a vision. . .it could not be a coincidence. Why had Gillet taken them both? Blythe's mind leapt around concepts of bargains and sacrifices, scapegoats and saviours. The strange deal with the Sun God set up by Lefevre. Deals that had distorted so much. Meddlesome Mages, ambitious priests. What was Gillet's plan? But Blythe did not doubt that Gillet was powerful, powerful enough even to challenge Lefevre.

He made his way swiftly through the crowded streets towards the Warden's offices. Preoccupied with thoughts of his friends and of the meeting ahead, he turned a corner into the square by the Temple and saw his sister Victoria. She was talking to someone across the road. If she spotted him, now, she would recognise him immediately.

Victoria turned away from her friend and looked across towards him.

He turned his back on her, walking swiftly away, down the street, not daring to look round. And it was not just because he was in a hurry, not because too much time had already been wasted.

Thoughts in chaos, he walked away. You can't go home, not yet, perhaps not ever. Eleanor had tried to, but it didn't work. There is no home, if there's no one to love. . .

You can love your family, but that's not enough. And there is too much to resolve, too much in the past which gets in the way all the time.

He saw a cordon of the Warden's Watch across the street. Neat grey uniforms; polished boots; swinging, light-weight capes. They were systematically visiting every shop, every café and restaraunt in the small square. Blythe heard the ripple through the crowd, the anxious looks and snatched conversations.

Notices had been pasted on doors, in shop windows. He picked up a leaflet from the gutter. The curfew was extended, it said. Between the hours of sunset and sunrise, for their own safety, the citizens of Peraldon were instructed to keep to their homes. They were also, incidentally, forbidden to gather in groups of more than five.

He looked at a torn poster, nailed to a tree behind him. A face stared at him, harshly drawn and quite unmistakeable.

'Wanted for murder,' ran the text. 'For the illegal use of Fosca mercenaries, for treason to the Emperor and sacrilege and heresy against the Sun God's priests, a counterfeit Mage and heretic from Challet.

To be apprehended, living or dead.

Dion Gillet.'

As he crossed the gardens towards the harbour, Blythe heard the noise of wings beating against the air. Like everyone else in Peraldon, he looked up.

A black cloud was covering the city. The Fosca were flying, running across the face of the Sun. He saw that they were travelling away from the centre of Solkest, in the direction of the academic quarter.

Where the Mages met, and studied, and wove their spiralling enchantments. . .

In fear, he began to run.

Chapter Eighteen
The Warden

There were fences all round the Warden's offices. Barriers of guards, secretaries, officials and clerks. They were not only unhelpful, but also obstructive.

'He's in a meeting.' At last, an almost straight answer from the young man outside the heavy panelled door. He looked up from the sheaf of papers on the desk in front of him. 'It doesn't matter how urgent it is, you'll have to wait. I have instructions not to let anyone through.' He was secure in his authority, bored with the interruption.

'I have information about the whereabouts of Dion Gillet.'

'You and a thousand other crackpots. This is a matter for the Warden.'

'I know. That's why I'm here.' Blythe spoke with control.

There was the muffled sound of raised voices from within the heavy door.

'Who's he got in there?' Blythe leaned forward across the desk, and the man there looked irritated. 'What could be more important than the information I am offering?'

'This is nothing to do with you. You can make an appointment over there.' He pointed across the hall to another desk. 'And if you don't get out of here right now, I shall call the guard and have you thrown out.'

Blythe did not want a fight, but too much time had already been lost. He stepped forward towards the door and at the same moment heard a crash outside, a door flung back, wrenched off its hinges. Other voices were shouting and all at once a man burst into sight, running at full tilt down the corridor to the Warden's office. He was in battle kit, his clothes torn and splattered with blood. The smell of scorching hung around him.

He was wearing Captain's insignia. His cloak had been torn from his shoulder and hung in loose, charred rags almost to the floor. His left arm was gashed open, his face blackened with smoke. The man at the desk was on his feet, but the Captain had already thrown the panelled door open. Without hesitation, hardly looking, he knocked the official out of the way and swept into the office.

Blythe was behind him. There were shouts and movements out in the corridor, but he slammed the door and leant on it. In the office, three men stared at the Captain and himself.

Blythe recognised all of them. The Warden, Emile Blanchard, he expected to see. But the other two were familiar to him from what seemed like another lifetime. Black cloaks and hidden eyes: an indefinable, maddening, air of secrecy. They were Mages, elderly men with spiral staffs.

Aylmer Alard and Thibaud Lye, Cavers both. He had met them long ago, at Cliokest after the breaking of the Stasis. They had worked with Matthias for long hours, long days and weeks to release him from the Children of Night. They had failed of course, but Blythe remembered them well. He would never forget that they had tried.

But what could they be doing here, in close discussion with the Warden of Peraldon? They stared at him with something like – satisfaction? And then Blythe heard what the Captain was shouting at Blanchard, and for a moment his own message was forgotten.

A massed attack of Fosca on the College. Blood and fire everywhere. Deaths. And the Captain had lost near on twenty men already, and there was no defence. . .

'Where do they come from? Who is sending Fosca?' He was shouting, white with fury. 'Why couldn't all those Mages defend themselves?'

'Do you need more men?' The Warden's voice was sharp.

'No. It's too late.'

There was a shocked silence. All at once, all of them turned towards Blythe. He moved away from the door, and immediately it burst open: the man from the desk stood there, surrounded by armed and uniformed soldiers.

He was trembling in agitation.

'Go away, Giraud. Now!' The Warden looked only at Phinian Blythe.

'But—'

'Get out! Do as you're told.' With frustration and incomprehension, the man returned to his desk. The door shut behind him.

The Warden's eyes were still on Blythe, unblinking. 'Phinian Blythe, back from the dead. And at such a time. What have you to do with this?'

The Mages were unmoving, watching. They were waiting, alert, excited by something Blythe didn't understand.

The Captain was staring at the Warden with incredulity. Why was no one reacting to what he had said?

Blythe spoke. 'I know who is sending the Fosca. It's Weard you have to blame for these attacks. Not Dion Gillet—'

'Indirectly, it is also Dion Gillet.' Thibaud Lye, the short Caver Mage who always accompanied Aylmer Alard everywhere, was speaking now. 'Gillet has to be found and incapacitated before there is worse. . .'

Blythe stared at him. 'Gillet is on his way to Sarant. He has taken hostages—' He paused. 'He may be able to control the Fosca. I don't know that anyone else can, apart from Weard.'

'Just a moment.' The Warden spoke with control. 'What possible reason can you have to think that it's Weard rather than Gillet who is sending the Fosca?'

Blythe took a deep breath. 'In a previous incarnation, Weard was the Fosca King. The being you know as Weard has many aspects, many rôles. Great Mage and High Priest, he is not subject to ordinary constraints. He was once a creature known as the Desert Rose. You, Warden, knew him long ago as your old colleague, Lucian Lefevre. He created the Fosca, then. Dion Gillet is a serious rival to Weard/Lefevre's position here in Peraldon; therefore he and his followers and any other potential rivals, are all being discredited or obliterated. That is why the College of Mages has been attacked.'

'Lefevre? Weard is Lefevre?' Blanchard sounded incredulous but Blythe could see that he was more than halfway to believing it. Blanchard looked at the two Caver Mages.

'He's right,' said Thibaud Lye. 'He has the truth of it.'

Blanchard turned to his Captain, not commenting on the rest of Blythe's information.

'Which of the Mages have lost their lives?'

The man was white and stammering. For a moment, he could hardly speak. The words were too hard. 'I don't think anyone escaped. . .not anyone. They were holding an assembly when the College caught fire, and they were all there—'

Appalled shock.

Then, 'Surely, together, they could have made some attempt to put out a fire, a Fosca attack?' At last the tall, round-shouldered Mage Aylmer spoke, his voice arid and spent. Blythe thought that there was more than a trace of disbelief about his words. Peraldonian Mages, unable to defend themselves? The rivalries still existed. As he expected.

'I don't know what happened.' The Captain stared at Blanchard, his mouth grim. 'There was a wind blowing, and there were leaves everywhere. . .'

The College was an isolated building, sprawling over a slight rise, surrounded by the gardens and park-land to the West of the city. It lay concealed between avenues of trees, Blythe remembered, colonnaded, graceful, a repository of books and ideas spread over a mile of labyrinthine passages and hallways. It was also remote from any natural source of water.

The Captain had been on duty there. It had been quiet, calm, apart from a slight breeze. He told them that he had been watching the leaves fluttering in the wind, when he realised that something was wrong. A smell on the wind, something putrid. . .when he'd looked up, there were Fosca overhead.

Their fire-arrows flew in through the windows, scattering sparks amongst the tinder-dry books and wooden shelving. They fell on sheaves of papers, on bunches of dried herbs, on the ancient hangings to beds and windows.

Some of the sparks caught, some flared and spread, others merely smouldered before dying. But the College stood in the centre of a parched city, a summer's-end place, an end-of-season husk, and all around it a forest of trees had shed its leaves in the first winds of autumn.

The picture the Captain gave was vivid enough.

Leaves that were black by night were flame-coloured by day. They were desiccated, crackling together in uneven drifts. They lay heaped against the doors, piled against walls and pillars. And as the small fires inside drew on the warm midday air, they began to blow down the passages and to sparkle in the flames flaring wildly through the dusty corridors.

The Captain's voice was faint, almost failing. In comparison, the bustle of the street outside, the noise of voices beyond the room, was bright and distracting, as if this were an ordinary day, an ordinary event.

An apprentice had left a door open, another broke a window to jump out. . .the wind became coloured by flame and rushed through the College.

The Captain's eyes were wide and staring as he recalled scenes of horror. 'There was nothing we could do. It was almost over by the time we realised what was happening.

'A fire-storm, something that burst through the building. . .' He passed his hand over his eyes as if trying to wipe the memory from them. 'There's nothing left,' he said. 'Only rubble and ash.'

The two Caver Mages were looking at each other. There was a long pause before Aylmer Alard moved. 'Do you still require our services?' he said to Emile Blanchard. 'Perhaps you have other priorities now?' He sounded purely courteous, but Blanchard brushed him aside.

'More than ever we need you! If our own Mages – God, Merreau, Neque. . .*all* of them?' he shot at the captain. 'All of them. . .'

The captain had no need to reply.

Emile Blanchard turned away from them all, facing the window that looked out over the harbour.

In an undertone, Blythe said to Thibaud, 'What *are* you doing here?'

'Waiting for you,' he said, incomprehensibly. 'We – and you – have experience of the Children of the Night, do we not?' His round face was drawn as he looked at Blythe. There was no trace of a smile, although his words were civil. 'I am glad to see that you are no longer – in thrall. The Warden has called us in because of our knowledge of the Shadows.'

'Have they taken someone here? Who is it?'

Blanchard had turned round. He went to the injured Captain and laid his hand on the man's shoulder. 'Go and get that wound seen to. You have done very well. . .' He waited until the man had left the room, and then turned back to the window. 'Haven't you guessed, Blythe? Think what you have just told me. Who bears the weight of guilt now?'

'It is Weard,' Aylmer answered for him. 'The being who originally lived here as Lucian Lefevre. The Fosca will not cease their attacks until Weard/Lefevre has been released. You were only half-right that Weard is sending them. They are exacting revenge on the Mages for what has happened to their King. *That* is why the College has been destroyed. They'll probably start on the priests next—

'The Children of the Night are here, in Peraldon. Shadows exact their price, weighting the guilty with living nightmares. You have endured the Shadows, Blythe, you know what it means.'

'And so Weard bears them now. . .' It made sense.

'Who else?' Thibaud's thin lips were tight.

'The trouble is that he is not alone with the Shadows,' the Warden said slowly. 'The Emperor is in there too.' He was looking out of the window across at the ringed towers of Solkest. 'They've been in there three days. The God alone knows how Xanthon survives there.'

At last Blythe realised why Aylmer and Thibaud were present. 'You've come to get Xanthon out. . .?'

'If we can.' Thibaud regarded him steadily. 'We would like to make a gesture of reconciliation towards Peraldon. . .this may be our last chance.'

'What about the Peraldonian Mages?' It felt like sacrilege, even mentioning them. 'Why didn't you get them in when it first happened?' Blythe said to Blanchard.

'They refused. They said, like you, that Weard was the Fosca King, and had sent the Fosca to murder and hound them. They are proud, our Peraldonian Mages. They said it was a just retribution.'

'But the Emperor—'

Blythe crossed the room to stand beside him, looking out across the quayside.

There were crowds immediately beneath the Warden's office: sailors and merchants; labourers; hawkers and beggars; all thronging the harbour. He could hear the gabble of countless indistinct conversations, the shouts of the hawkers, the rumble of carts and barrows, the crash of lifting tackle and machinery: all the noise of a working harbour.

But further away, further along the wide promenade that bordered the lagoon, the high walls of Solkest dominated the skyline. Its towers and walkways cast long shadows over the surround. The ringed fortifications were as forbidding as ever.

And more so. In the distance Blythe saw a thousand black, spiky shapes clinging to the walls of the central tower. Black creepers, he thought, black roses and their sharp thorns. Strange that even the midday sun should not give them colour, should not reveal them for what they are. . .Every now and then, a leaf would fall and turn in the

violent wind, changing as it flew towards the city. With a shock, he
recognised what the leaves were.

'He's in there? Weard, I mean. In the central tower?'

'Where else?' Blanchard was following his gaze. 'No one has seen
him or the Emperor for three days. Fosca guard the doors and let no
one in.'

'How do you *know* that the Shadows have Weard?'

'We saw them.' Aylmer's gaze was unwavering. 'It was inescapable.
Every time we used magic, every time we tried to see the future, they
were there. They are waiting for us, waiting for every Mage, every
guilty man of action, at some point in his life. There is no way to avoid
them, no way out. And so we tracked them, watching to see who
would be next. Watching to see if it would be us. . .We saw their trail,
north from Cliokest, and followed it. We saw them entrapped in a
spiral staff, contained by vast power, and for a while we rejoiced.'
He closed his eyes momentarily. 'If you wonder why no Mage
exposed Weard's present incarnation, this is the answer. We saw that
Weard had the power to contain the Shadows. It was a way out, for us
all.'

'But then Dion Gillet arrived in Peraldon. A priest who is more than
half-Mage, a dangerous and ambitious man. He sees in himself an
emissary of the Lord, a man of purity and justice, driven by visions.
Three days ago he released the Shadows from Weard's staff. They
found their intended victim.'

'We came to offer our help.' Thibaud Lye said. 'We thought the
Warden should know what was happening here within Solkest.' He
looked at Blythe. There was an appeal for understanding in his eyes.
'We want to make our home again on Sarant. We will need to deal
with the Peraldonians. The breach must be healed.'

He was an old man. Wise in more than magic.

'What about Xanthon? Have they taken him too?' Blythe asked.

The Warden shrugged, but his hands on the windowsill were
clenched.

Aylmer Alard said, 'If he has offended and knows his guilt, then
yes, they will take him too.'

'There is no escape, as you know.' Lye looked at him with the
memory of compassion.

'How will you get the Emperor out?' Blythe asked.

'We'll have to tackle the Fosca.'

'Did you ask them to try this?' Blythe said to the Warden. There
was still something missing in this equation.

Emile Blanchard nodded briefly.

Blythe considered the two Caver Mages. 'And you are willing to
take this risk?'

'The rewards are high for us. We wish to rebuild our home on
Sarant, and the best way would be to show our loyalty and goodwill
towards the Peraldonian Emperor.'

A hand of friendship extended over a pit of fire. They were good men, full of generous intentions.

'Shall we go to Solkest?' Aylmer said to Blanchard. 'There is no reason to delay.'

The Warden frowned. 'I am more grateful than I can say for your offer, but things have changed. I hesitate to allow you to risk your lives by confronting the Fosca.' The Warden's cool, businesslike tone did not conceal his grief.

'We are going to need our Mages now.'

All of them looked towards the window. Black leaves flew across the face of the Sun, a storm of wild, flying fugitives returning to their station, gazing in through the windows at the Emperor. And at his advisor and controller, Weard, seized by Shadows.

'But even if you do get into the place, Weard will be in no position to do anything constructive. Why should he, anyway? His only motive is ambition.' Blythe said.

'We'll have to destroy him. The Fosca will be powerless without their creator.' Thibaud Lye spoke wearily.

'But you can't destroy Weard! Don't you remember? He is surrounded by Shadows!'

He remembered all too well. They would never let anyone release their victim. They would rather kill, and maim, in order to prolong the suffering of the guilty. 'You'll have to lift the Shadows before you can tackle Weard. Before you can get him to call off the Fosca.'

'It's a closed circle. Only Weard can control the Fosca. Weard is in the grip of Shadows. We can't get in to try to lift the Shadows, because the Fosca won't let us.' The Warden lifted his hands, helplessly.

'What made the Shadows leave you?' Thibaud said to Blythe.

He paused. There was an answer, then. 'The child could do it,' he said softly. 'The child Coron lifted them. . .'

'Coron? Who is he? What is he? Where is he now?'

'I have no idea where he is.' Blythe answered. 'I can tell you *who* he is though. His mother was Coronis, daughter of Ingram Lapith, Archon of Bilith. His father is the Lord of the Sun, Lycias.' His voice was steady, although he felt reluctant even to pronounce the name. The other three men watched him, predatory for information.

Blythe continued. 'But the person who actually cares for him is Haddon Derray. . .he married Coronis, and became stepfather to the Child. He is a Caver. You probably know him.'

The two Mages exchanged glances, and then Aylmer nodded briefly.

Blythe continued. 'Coron has divine power. That is how the Shadows were lifted, and if you want to take them from Weard, you will have to find him.' He paused and then said deliberately to the Warden. 'And you must remember that if you free Weard, you will also be releasing the King of the Fosca. There's no reason to suppose that Weard would be willing to call them off.'

Emile Blanchard sat at his desk, staring unseeing at his clasped hands. 'Ah, dear God. And no Mages of our own to advise us.'

'You don't need Mages.' Blythe leant across the desk towards him. 'This is a human decision, needing nothing more than common sense.'

'The priests. . .'

'All those remaining will have been tainted by the Fosca King. They have been under the sway of Weard as High Priest, and you cannot separate Weard from the persona of the Fosca King. They must all have trained with him, when he lived here as Lefevre. You cannot trust any Peraldonian priest.'

'If Weard is Lefevre—'

'He is. And he has been responsible for the Stasis, and the drought, and the Fosca.' How could he make them believe it, what could he say? The room was hot, the Sun pouring through the wide, picture window. Flies buzzed against the glass.

The Warden's voice was thoughtful. 'Some say that the Stasis was not all bad. People die now, they die all the time. . .Your mother is dead, did you know?' He glanced sharply at Blythe. 'It was all too much, your disappearance, the rumours. . .she just gave up.' He seemed almost glad to see the look on Blythe's face. 'So you didn't know. You don't know everything that's happened. How can I trust what you say about Weard?'

'Aylmer can confirm it.' The words came automatically through the shock. But then he realised that the two Caver Mages had gone. The door to the corridor was ajar, and curious faces outside stared in over the shoulders of the man at the desk.

Without hesitation, Blythe closed the door. He stood for a moment facing the blank wood, while his heart absorbed the knowledge of his mother's death.

It was directly his fault.

All those grieving souls, all of humanity, enduring death and separation. He was guilty for all of them, responsible all the way, and he had opted out of this final confrontation. He had known who Weard really was, he knew what Lefevre had become. Since that meeting on the island path, that deadly transformation, he had been deceiving himself. He had been content to live a sheltered easy life, thinking that ending the Stasis had been all that would be required. There was an idea of justice here, something that deserved answering.

Blanchard said, very quietly, 'Why did you come back here?'

'This is my home.'

'Your family believes you dead. Your friends, colleagues, everyone thinks you are dead. I suppressed the rumours that ran wild after your disappearance. The news that you had joined the Jerenites, that you had acted as a traitor. It seemed kindest to your mother, at the time. What do I tell your sisters now?'

How could he answer? 'Tell them nothing. There's no need. My only priority now is to get to Sarant, to find Dion Gillet and his hostages.' He moved towards the door. 'Can you arrange transport for me?'

Slowly, the Warden shook his head. 'You're on your own, Blythe. The crisis here, the deaths of the Mages, the Emperor. . .I can't help you.' He paused. 'I don't even know if I want to.'

For a long moment they looked at each other. Then Phinian Blythe left the Warden's office, walking quickly down the crowded corridors to the busy streets outside.

Chapter Nineteen
Ruins

The city had changed. In the space of a few short hours a pall hung over it. Smoke tainted the air, the smell of burning and occasionally of blood. People were standing in huddles at street corners, at park benches. He saw shock on face after face: shock and grief and fear.

Peraldon's Mages were dead.

He found himself drawn to the ruins, against all logic, all reason. He walked through the groves of bare trees to the College. He saw where the last Mages on Peraldon had met their end. The end of an era, of a giddy, power-driven spiral of ambition. . .

He was not alone there. Crowds stood around him, silently regarding the smoking rubble, paying their respects to the dead. No longer would the quiet parks shelter the home of magic on Peraldon. No longer would serious men play tricks on the edge of unreality.

It was no loss, the death of magic. It was only worth grieving for dead humanity. For men and women, and the whole impossible passage of life and death. He turned away with tears in his eyes.

They were waiting for him. Thibaud Lye and Aylmer Alard, standing a little back from the crowd, deep in the forested shade.

'Are you ready?' Ayler asked. 'Shall we go?'

'To Sarant?'

'Where else?'

'The Warden won't help. There's no transport—'

'Have you forgotten the Arrarat?'

'You have *Arrarat*?'

Wordlessly, Aylmer moved to one side. Standing a little way from them, almost concealed by trees, Blythe saw the gleam of eyes, a whisper of feather.

It seemed significant, something that might at last go right. He went with the two Mages and mounted an Arrarat hawk.

He did not know that they were observed. He did not know that the Fosca baron was beginning to realise what the death of the Mages implied.

It was on the lookout for Mages now. It did not know of anyone else who could lift Shadows.

A last scan through the skies of Peraldon. Beyond the stink of blood and flames, it found nothing. No trace of magic called across the ruins and the rubble, no muttered words straying into the realms of illusion.

The two Mages and the other had left Peraldon, on swift Arrarat hawks. It knows what it must do, it has only one obsession.

Its king must be released.

It returns to its post, high on the roof of Solkest's central tower. Precariously perched, it looks in through the skylight.

His back is to the wall. Xanthon can get no further away. The thing in the centre of the hall is blundering towards him again, its hands extended, while the swirls of black that cloud around it pull and tug at its skin.

Xanthon sees the mouth stretched back, the skin tearing and running with blood as black fingers rake through the flesh. The teeth are bared, the eyes masked and clouded with visions, visions that the Emperor cannot contemplate sharing. Hearing the voices is more than enough.

They come from the Shadows. He knows this. There is no one else there, no one in the whole world as far as he cares. He is isolated here in this prison with something which had been Weard. Once. It seems so long ago, but it can only have been a matter of days. Time has lost its relevance, its shape and order.

The banshee wail rises in frustration as Xanthon dodges the creature, skidding across the floor, almost slipping on the vomit. He finds himself crashing against one of the pillars, almost falling. . .and clings to it, gasping.

They are in the hall at the centre of the Solkest. Vast pillars support a high-arching ceiling, and the structure of the tower above. There is a dais at one end where Weard used to sit, conducting the affairs of state before the Shadows claimed him.

The doors are bolted. Xanthon has tried them over and over again, screaming, hammering, until his throat is hoarse, his fists bloody. No one comes.

The noise is rising. There is always a constant whisper of words, a litany of deeds and sins, of sorrows and betrayals. Xanthon hears them all, is appalled and sickened by the catalogue of horrors. Over it there are other, more varied, sounds: screams and shouts, surging on the edge of audibility.

He jams his fingers into his ears, trying to block it. The cloudy figure stumbling towards him is trying to do the same, but he can see that the Shadows are holding its hands back. The fingers are straining like claws, the bones pushing against the flesh. He knows that soon they will break through, and blood will run from its hands as the nerves hang, exposed. . .

Its movements are less violent now. At first, it hurled itself against the walls in a vain attempt to knock itself senseless. The Shadows cushioned the impact, holding it carefully free from physical harm. It sank to its knees in front of Xanthon, and he could hear, among all those other terrible sounds, Weard's own voice begging for oblivion.

Xanthon had no weapon. And when he tried to smash the candlestick from the desk down on the head of the afflicted creature he experienced, just for a moment, a taste of the Shadows' being. In terror and revulsion he immediately dropped the candlestick, realising at once the futility of such an act.

The thing that had been Weard, the Desert Rose, the Fosca King and the High Priest, Lucian Lefevre, moans throughout day and night. Bright light filters in through the high windows at midday, and reveals the wreckage of the hall. Chairs are tumbled and smashed, carpets rucked up, floor and pillars smeared with vomit and excrement.

At night the Moon and stars give only a slight illumination, and hide something of the chaos. But this is far worse, because the Shadows now have no boundaries and seem to exist everywhere. They scream from the corners: from the high, arching ceiling: from the floor beneath Xanthon's feet. They squat on the ceiling struts and emerge from the pillars to execute a deadly dance round the wrecked thing uselessly cowering by the door.

Xanthon is caught in the crossfire. He knows that nothing the Shadows do relates directly to him. He recognises none of the voices, understands none of the myriad accusations. But he is the Emperor, and this is his world. He feels that there is a question of responsibility here, one he has not addressed.

He is shuddering with terror. He can barely frame thoughts after two days and nights in the hall with the Shadows. He supposes that he ought to feel hunger or thirst, but it is irrelevant. The very idea of food makes him retch. The idea of sleep, surrounded by swooping Shadows is beyond bearing. If they get into his dreams he will never find the way out. And yet, he knows that he *is* tired, on the edge of exhaustion and delirium.

It seems to Xanthon that the creature huddled by the door is failing. Its arms no longer thresh around, it no longer screams vain prayers for mercy. He wonders if it will die, and thus find relief.

He wonders if the Shadows will persist after death. There can be no easy way out of their clutch. Mere cessation might not be enough.

The thing that was once Weard lurches to its feet. He watches bemusedly as it staggers across the hall, disappearing at last behind one of the vast pillars. He can still hear it, of course, but it is now out of sight. He sags to the floor, his head nodding, and tries not to sleep.

Without hesitation the Fosca baron smashes the window. At once, the thing that was Weard, and the Fosca King, leaps up from the floor.

The Shadows still hang round its shoulders, trailing behind it like a black wash of blood. It flies out of Solkest, hurling itself among the stars, so fast that the Fosca baron can hardly keep up with it. As it flies its form mutates, unstable with stress. The memory of other shapes, other incarnations govern it now. And vast as the Desert Rose, potent as the Fosca King, it blots out the stars with its guilt, in its attempt to escape the Shadows.

'Sarant!' the baron screams as the Fosca King wails out of sight. 'Sarant, Mages!'

And from all around Solkest, black leaves spring into the air. All the Fosca of Solkest leave their posts around gates and doors, walls and towers, to follow their King out over the lagoon.

The Warden and his men, waiting beyond the central tower, see them leave.

They rush down that last corridor to the doors which have been barred for so long, fling them wide and instantly halt, recoiling at the stench. The Warden slowly enters the room. At first he can see nothing.

'Your Highness. . .?' he says cautiously, hearing a faint movement somewhere to his right. His men have swords. He motions them forwards.

On the dais, half-sprawled across the table lies a hunched body. Emile Blanchard takes another step.

'Your Highness!'

Chapter Twenty
Sarant

The voyage took so long. The bright sea tossed the boat deep into troughs and high on the crests. Lines of white froth shone in the sunlight. Eleanor's hair was caught in the freshening wind, and whipped round her face.

She spent most of her time watching Dion Gillet and his followers at prayer. It was the kind of prayer that seemed to her closer to magic than anything else. The same chanted words, the same degree of concentration. Spiral staffs or Sun-medallions, what did it matter what the props were?

The effect of this concentrated 'prayer' was to conceal their escape from Peraldon.

Complex distortions wreathed around the small boat. The words of the prayers denied reality as completely as any spell. Gillet's hands wavered and hovered, expressing sound in physical shapes, and delicate wavelengths were adjusted. Light and vision flickered oddly, and the appearance of the waves changed. The boat would not be found.

The danger came during the hours of daylight, when watchers flew overhead.

Fosca. At irregular intervals a fleet of them would skim through the skies, but they never attacked. They seemed to be on the other side of an out-of-focus looking-glass. One of the priests, a man called Cassun, stood in the stern of the boat. Gillet was in the prow and together the two men enclosed the craft within the troughs of turbulent water. Eleanor was close enough to watch it happen. She also saw that although sweat ran from Gillet's forehead, he was confident. He thinks he's infallible, she thought. He thinks he's already won, because Shadows have draped themselves over Weard's shoulders, and his screams still ring in my ears.

This is just insurance, what is happening now: the Sun blinking nervously through the clouding enchantments, the way the Fosca can't see us. . .

Priests manned the oars. They had stripped off their shirts and bent pale, reddening backs to the task. They took it in turns to row. Four of them were on duty at any one time, while the others knelt in the bows, at prayer. Sometimes they lifted their voices in song, and the oarsmen fitted their stroke to the rhythm of hymns. They looked horribly naked to the Sun with their close-shaven heads. There was no way of knowing whether they were also adepts. Certainly it was clear that Gillet was in charge, High Priest and undeclared Mage, and that Cassun was his lieutenant.

They had untied her hands and feet, knowing that there was nowhere for her to go. She sat miserably beside Katriana and wondered what was going to happen next.

Katriana. Out of reach, a lifetime removed from them all. She no longer wore a veil and Eleanor preferred not to look at her.

Silver eyes, black pupils. She was not human. Eleanor remembered coolnesses, arrogance and extraordinary magical powers. Her eyes were silver, and her face perfect, apart from two small scars. Two crescent moons marked the white skin at each of her temples. Proof of divine dedication.

When that veil had first been lifted, just out of the harbour of Peraldon, Eleanor had cried aloud at the sight of the silver eyes.

'She is a child of the Goddess,' said Gillet to Eleanor, a curious victory in his tone. 'My creation, my envoi to God. She will persuade the Lord Lycias of our good intention. She will offer Him all He desires, and leave the world free for men.

'Lycias will unite with the Moon. It has been foretold. In the mystical words of ancient prophets, in the dance of the stars in the Heavens, I have seen this. And it is truly a consummation to be desired.'

He looked at Eleanor severely. 'I tell you this for a reason. You are to bear witness, you are to tell the world how it has fallen out. Your presence here is an omen, a presage of success. You too have played a part in this conflict.

'Our world is divided now, because of this battle between Gods. Male and female, always opposed. And yet They need each other . . .the dissension between the two is destructive, always. But during the Stasis, Astret was defeated. It was possible, then, to swing the balance by human agency.

'That is what I shall do now. I have no desire to reinstate the Stasis: men must live and die as always. But I shall tempt the Lord Lycias with my Katriana. And I think it will work. I think He will take her, symbol of the Moon, because man, fatally, is always tempted by woman. And she is undying, immortal as He is. It was a heavy price to pay, buying immortality for my little sea-child.

'The price was her own humanity. The Lord will take her, and they will live in ecstasy together, and leave us alone. . . .'

He paused. 'That is all I require. That we should be left to run our world without the need of woman. Do you understand? Woman is the source of evil, Astret is the bringer of death and destruction.

'As you are yourself. Think, Eleanor Knight, what you did for this world. You brought death in your train, and Astret came to power through you. I have here the solution to all human pain and your witness to this shall be your punishment. Sun and Moon shall be united, for ever, beyond this tired and tawdry world. For the Moon lives eternally in this my creation, as the Sun shines eternally in the bright midday skies!' There was such triumph about him, such an air of victory.

He turned away from Eleanor. 'Cassun.' Gillet's voice was soft, his dark gaze was eloquent. The man in the stern of the boat raised his hands and intensified his movements. The waves around them rose high enough to disguise the height of the mast.

The boat was tossed to and fro within the deep cradle of water. Eleanor smelt salt and sweat and something far worse. A cold metallic tang, something to do with silver, with blackness.

Katriana's eyes were silver, her pupils black.

The simulacrum of a god sat beside her. Chained within a human body, something dreadful was breaking out through the surface of her eyes. Katriana watched the movement of men, listening to the words they spoke, but made no sound at all.

Eleanor could not handle this. She rejected what Gillet had told her, knowing that he could not possibly create life, not like that. . .

And yet, Katriana sat there, her silver eyes glowing with secrets Eleanor could not imagine.

At one stage, Gillet left his post, moving down the length of the boat to Katriana's side. Familiarly, he put his right arm round those perfect shoulders, and passed his left hand over her face. He made a gesture like a cross over her eyes and at once they closed. She began to sag against him.

With reverence, he laid her in the bottom of the boat. Looking up, he caught Eleanor's eye. 'The Lady demands much,' he said. 'It is a strain, for a poor human body.'

'You said she was your creation.' How to understand this man? 'How can a priest create a person? Or is she a dream or a Parid?'

'Oh, she is real enough. No rough enchantment or distortion. I found her, you know. Long ago, on the wild seacoast where I studied the ways of the Lord. I found her, tossing in the waves like a doll, like seaweed. I took her from the Sea, the chosen medium of the Lady. I rescued her, and nursed her to health.

'Her eyes were clear then, her skin unscarred. I decided to dedicate her to the honour of the Lord. She had no knowledge of what she was, no memory of the past. I dedicated her to God, a sea-child, a child of the Lady. There were certain Rites, certain processes. . .For her life was now mine, you see, because I saved her from the waves. And I have seen visions, I have seen the end. It seems that the breach might be healed, that I might unite our two warring Gods in the person of this woman.

'And it is true that sometimes. . .' His voice was very low. 'Sometimes, I think that the Lady works within her.'

His face was close up to hers; she saw a greasy skin pitted with blackened broken teeth. His breath was foul over her face as he spoke.

'Silver eyes, a black soul. . .A fitting emissary of the Lady, my little Katriana.'

'What are you going to *do*?'

'Ah, Eleanor. Wait and see. There's not long to go now.'

She looked away, over the heaving waves, the empty horizons, and remembered what Matthias had said. The death of the Gods, the end to magic. Would Dion Gillet bring about such a thing, using the person of Katriana?

He had defeated Weard, after all. He had hidden their boat in the force of his will.

She wanted out of this. She wondered what Phin would be doing, whether he'd be on his way. That he would come after them, she had no doubt. He would not abandon her, not turn aside. It was not in his character. He would not fail, not now.

'No, Eleanor Knight. Phinian Blythe is not going to come to the rescue this time.' Gillet laughed at her outrage. 'No, don't worry, I can't really read your mind: but your face is such a giveaway, such a traitor to you. You should be careful with a face like that. No, I'll tell you why I think you can forget about Phinian Blythe. No one in Peraldon will believe anything he says. He may try to see the Warden, to get help, but it will be no use. He is a traitor there, someone who betrayed them all. I'm almost – no, not almost. I *am* sure that he will either be ignored or arrested. It's a sheer fluke that no one recognised him these last few months.'

His face was still too close to hers. She wanted to slap it, to shock him out of these contemptuous words, but again he seemed to know her thoughts. He raised his hand, and she thought with revulsion that he was going to caress her skin, but his fingers merely brushed over her eyes.

Heaviness descended. With a sigh, Eleanor let go, and slipped sideways on the bench.

She awoke to the harsh sound of hawk-song. She looked up into the bright air and saw, wheeling there, a hundred Arrarat, and the craggy outline of a mountain rising from the sea.

Arrarat Isle, she thought, with helpless yearning. Hawks were hanging on the wind, or dancing up against it, buffeted and lifting, soaring high above. She saw the black entranceway to the inner world of Arrarat Isle, and as she watched a great grey hawk leapt out of it, catching the thermal immediately and rising up towards the Sun.

The glare was too bright. She looked away, back to the heaving waves and her eyes were watering too much for her to notice that the grey hawk carried a rider.

They passed by Arrarat Isle to the island that stood some miles from its north face. They kept at a distance rounding its south-east point, and at first Eleanor thought that they were going to miss it altogether.

She saw that the island was on two levels. A high plateau rose above the wide reaches of a plain, too high for her to see more than a purple tinge to the sward of heather.

Towards the sea, the plain was littered with the remains of a city. The blackened shells of houses and other buildings stood starkly in the sunlight. Squinting against the Sun, Eleanor thought that she saw movement, the lift of a great hawk, perhaps, or was it a Fosca? This was not just an island of ruins and empty moors.

'What is this place?' she asked Gillet.

'Sarant,' he said briefly. 'Where the Cavers used to live. Some of them have returned. There has been talk of them resettling there, but we won't be visiting that side of the island.'

'Where *are* we going, then?'

'Over there.' He pointed to a small cove cut deeply into the cliff face. 'No one will find us there.'

'Then what? Are you just going to hide out there until the Fosca break through your defences?' This was pure bravado, and Gillet knew it as such.

'Break through?' He laughed. 'No Fosca will find us, Miss Knight, you need not worry. No, we're going to the Temple of Lycias on Sarant, and there shall Katriana fulfil her appointed rôle.'

'How can you expect to manipulate the Gods, Gillet? You know this is madness, don't you?' Her words were desperately forceful. She thought, this man understands nothing. He's playing with fire and worse than that, and it will surely rebound. . .and who will be caught up in this, who will find themselves scarred by such arrogant meddling?

'So many questions! So many doubts and fears. This will not especially concern you, Eleanor, for you have already acted on behalf of all women. Relax. You'll come to no harm this time. Your rôle here is to lend respectability to our ceremony, and to witness its outcome.'

Respectability? For a moment her mind was diverted by the word. She loathed the implications of what he said, loathed the way his eyes glanced over her as if she were unworthy of consideration. She looked again at Katriana who was sitting on the bench once more, her hands lightly clasped, her face turned away.

Unapproachable, untouchable. Eleanor shivered. They were nearing the cove now, showered by cold spray from the waves crashing against rocks. The two men in the bows jumped into the water, and guided the boat towards the narrow semicircle of sand and stone.

They unloaded quickly, and Eleanor was left standing by Katriana. She looked at her covertly. Both women were damp with spray, their skirts clinging and clammy. The wind swirled around the small, shadowed bay. It was very cold and Eleanor's teeth were chattering.

Katriana seemed oblivious to her surroundings, her silver eyes staring blankly ahead. Tentatively, Eleanor reached out and touched her arm.

'Do you know what's happening?' she whispered. 'Do you know what they're going to do?'

For a moment, the silver eyes looked at her. There was a faint smile on the perfectly moulded lips. 'Oh yes,' said Katriana Lessure. 'I have waited so long for this. . .'

Miserably, Eleanor looked up the cliff. There was a path of sorts, complicated by mud and landslip. And when they all started climbing it, as she knew they would, gobbets of damp clay fell from Cassun's boots into her hair and face. She cursed. They'd given her a rucksack to carry and although it was not heavy, the ascent was steep.

Ahead, Katriana was moving smoothly. Eleanor wondered what she was thinking, how far she was human, if at all.

Lycias, as Timon, had not appeared extraordinary. She remembered the black fisherwoman, who stopped her getting into Shelt's Castle before the wedding. She had been part of a wholly unremarkable crowd. The Gods can do anything, after all.

It took two hours of muscle-aching weariness to reach the cliff-top and then the path continued on a milder, upward slant across high, boggy wastes of heather and bracken.

They walked all day, stopping for dry bread and cheese at one stage. It clearly wasn't worth arguing, or trying to break away; they watched Eleanor carefully. She found herself looking again and again at Katriana, hoping for some crack in the façade. But the perfectly sculpted head was always turned away from her, the terrible eyes hidden, denying any relationship.

They trudged on through the long afternoon, at last over reasonably flat ground. They were on a plateau, a high moor, and at its perimeter Eleanor saw only sky and sea.

As it grew dark, Gillet called another halt. He instructed his followers to build a fire, to cook the fish they had brought from the boat.

Fish over a campfire, the soft murmur of voices. Eleanor sat as far as possible away from Katriana and pulled the cloak they'd given her tight at her throat. The wind was cold, the ground hard and uncomfortable.

But still, she slept.

Eleanor dreamt that she lay on her bed at her childhood's home, waiting for her parents to return from a dinner party. She waited, hoping that her mother would lean over her with a goodnight kiss. She wanted to smell the expensive perfume, to run her hands over the beads decorating the elaborate evening dress.

Her mother did not come. And then she heard voices raised in anger, slurred with alcohol. Her dreams were filled only with this: the sounds of her father and mother fighting. She lay unmoving in the warm darkness, and heard glass smash, heard all the same old lies, knowing that she was quite forgotten.

She didn't think that Phinian Blythe would forget her.

Chapter Twenty-one
Marriage

'A word of advice, Eleanor Knight. Be careful how you speak to Dion Gillet.' They were tramping once more over the lonely moor, and she found herself next to Cassun. She had been entirely silent: searching the landscape for the familiar square-cut figure of Phinian Blythe: watching the skies for the approach of the Arrarat: hoping against hope that *someone* would come for her. She barely listened to the words of the man beside her.

'The Priest Gillet is able to intercede with the God Himself. You should not antagonise him. He walks in the knowledge of God, and has insights vouchsafed to few. He is in addition a master in the appearance of reality. Alone, you cannot trust the evidence of your senses, woman. Your only guide must be to listen to us, with the knowledge of your weakness. It is only a matter of time: Dion Gillet will rule us all, and the righteous will walk once more in the reality he will construct.'

'What a truly appalling thought,' she said unwisely.

He pursed his lips, and strode out so that she was left behind, walking alone once more.

Their path began to climb again, as the Sun rose higher. The clear air became tinged with warmth, and she began to regret the heavy cloak Cassun had given her. At first, they had followed what looked like a sheep-track, a narrow path littered with droppings, but after a while it met the remains of an old road.

It was set with stone blocks, but they were crumbled and broken, and moss and grass grew in every crack. The surfaces were dry and chalky. It seemed to be very old.

'Where does this lead?' she asked Cassun.

'To the Temple of Lycias.'

'Why is there a Temple to the Sun God *here*?'

'Because at one time people thought it would be possible to tolerate alternative paths to holiness. It fell into disuse when the divisions arose, as of course they must. Cavers have not used this road for a long

time. There is no natural meeting place for Moon and Sun in this
world, although people continually try, misguided as they are.
There was a Temple to Astret on Peraldon, of course, long ago. We do
not intend to revive such practices. Compromise does not lead to
peace.'

Eleanor said nothing. This was all part of a desperate philosophy.
Everything Matthias and the rest of the Cavers had ever tried to do
would be distorted or forgotten. Fanaticism was the most dangerous
of distortions. But she was struck by the truth of what she had been
told the day before. She knew what this battle between men and
women meant. It had rung round her childhood home, it clouded her
life wherever she went. This wanting and needing, with so little hope
of peace.

The path wound upwards. She took the cloak off and carried it after
a while, and when it became heavy one of the men took it from her.
Gillet was walking far ahead, just in front of Katriana. Every now and
then he paused and looked back at the woman with the silver eyes, as
if checking that she still existed. They never spoke to each other, and
Eleanor wondered whether they ever had. What could the created say
to the creator?

And Eleanor's own eyes still searched the horizon, watching for a
rescue she hoped would come.

As dusk fell, they saw the jagged outlines of a building on the
summit of a hill above them.

Broken pillars, heaps of crumbled masonry, crushed stonework. An
air of desolation and emptiness about it all. A low wall marked the
boundary of the temple, two broken pillars the entrance. Grass
grew between the cracks, moss swarmed over the mosaic stones.
They were set in a sunburst pattern, the colours still vivid and
strong.

A stone altar still stood by the remains of the west wall. Unhurriedly, the men began to unpack their rucksacks. They covered their
jeans and shirts with robes of fine cream linen. Dion Gillet, with care
and reverence, unwrapped something from dark folded velvet. One of
his companions jammed a wedge of stone into the fissures in the wall
behind the altar.

The last rays of the Sun caught on a gleaming surface. A shining
golden disc, contoured by the outlines of a face Eleanor knew well.

They hung the stern face of Lycias from the Temple wall, and fell to
their knees.

Not Eleanor. Not Katriana either. She stood slightly to one side of
the golden face, her face unmoving, unchanging.

'Come on woman, there's your master.' Cassun's rough words
behind Eleanor.

'Oh no. And anyway, that face is all wrong.' He was glaring at her,
his attention caught.

'And what do you know about it?'

More than you can imagine, she nearly replied. But this was not the time for past lives. She said, neutrally, 'Everywhere else in this world the face of Lycias smiles. That is not the Sun God.'

'You are wrong, Miss Eleanor Knight. This is the other side of our eternal Lord. Revealed at last, through the sacred insight of His servant Dion Gillet.

'Lycias is the God of Flame. Of vengeance and retribution. There is no escaping His justice, no mercy or forgiveness for those who have offended.' He turned and looked at her suddenly. She saw dark light flickering at the back of his eyes, a flaring and unstable passion. His hair was hanging lank with sweat. He was frowning.

'And have you offended, woman?' His voice was cold. All he needed was a long beard, she thought, to look like an Old Testament prophet. He would glare at her in a minute, and say, *Woman, you are sinful. . .through you sin has entered this world. And although your eyes are grey, there is blackness at their centre, as with all women. . .You did entice, you did tempt and destroy and lie. And in pain shall you bear children, and pain will mark the times when your body is your own and not within our control.*

Misogyny.

She turned away from him, and from the others kneeling before that dread face. Dion Gillet was standing now, his arms raised to the Sun-disc. He had lit candles, was pouring something into a wide polished bowl. . .

Images fluttered through her mind, presages of a stern and unforgiving religion. It was familiar. In a moment of great unease, she saw a future path opening up on Chorolon. It would follow, in the end, the inadequate, dreary patterns of her own culture. And the indirect, subtle paths of the Lady would either turn to destructive resentment, to lies and distortion, or they would be lost altogether.

A movement at her shoulder. Cassun was holding out the cloak to her, and she put it on. It was not an act of kindness, rather of propriety, even prudishness. In a minute, she thought, he would say, *Cover yourself, Woman, in the presence of the Lord.*

'What is going to happen here?' She spoke clearly, but no one around them took any notice. All their attention was on the increasingly elaborate ceremony beneath the frowning face of Lycias.

Cassun said, 'This is a ceremony of marriage. The Moon and Sun joined as one. You must be quiet.'

He turned his back on her, looking once more at the actions of the robed priest standing there.

Smoke and flames sprang from the offertory bowl Gillet held. The face of the Sun God looked at them through smoke and the words of Katriana's creator were meaningless lies in Eleanor's ears.

God of justice. Gillet turned to face them, and his voice rang loud and clear, echoing over the lonely moor.

He dwelt on the the the punishment of sin, the fierce, unswerving retribution of the Lord. There was a stern moral law, he said, which they must all obey. It was a hard and narrow path, this way of righteousness, and they must regard themselves as disciples and deny the self. Men must trust in God, and women must be guided by men. . .

She remembered the darting green light of flashing eyes, the wicked amusement and cruel relish of Timon/Lycias. Exotic sensuality, and passionate devotion. Out of place here, surely. She could not understand what was happening. This was a dread, puritan reaction against sensuality, a hijacking of passion into the intolerant realms of religious fervour.

A distortion, a terrible division between men and women. Worse, even, than the original battles. . .Was separation the only alternative to the war between Man and Woman?

She heard the strength of Gillet's voice, the unwavering certainty of the words he spoke, the promises he made.

'I am Yours, Lord. Body and soul, devoted to the Word of Your law. I shall abstain from the pleasures of the flesh, shall put aside women, and all unclean things. I shall fast and strive for holiness. I shall not sleep while I still sin, I shall live only for Your Word, only in accordance with Your will.'

How does he know, she thought? Has Lycias indeed touched his soul, has Dion Gillet the private ear of the Sun God?

And has Lycias changed? Has the Lord of Love lost all His passionate sensuality?

She doubted it. And as she thought about it, one of the hooded figures kneeling before Gillet turned and looked at her.

He threw back His hood, and Eleanor stepped back, hand at her throat.

She supposed that He possessed the ordinary features of humanity: head, hair, body, limbs. But she could never recall afterwards what He looked like in this guise. Certainly not Timon, certainly not the pale, smoothly smiling face on all the other statues and pictures. He was an assembly of negations now, bitter and hard and vicious.

She knew that He was smiling, even so. He did not appear angry. He was enjoying this tawdry ceremony, He liked to see humanity making a fool of itself. There was contempt for her, and every other woman, in the way He looked at her.

There was contempt for men, too. For Dion Gillet's missionary zeal and reckless vows.

His voice sounded in her mind. *Little one. You and I know all about this, don't we? The just vengeance of the Lord, the rewards of sin. . .*

Do you think it is finished? That you have suffered enough, that you paid the price?

She never thought to speak with Him again, never imagined that she would encounter Him, and not like this, in a crowd. The smile on those curving lips filled her sight and the rest of the world faded into terrible derision. She stood alone; Phin was only a dream and Lukas belonged to the past, and the Lord of Terror required an answer. . . .

Eleanor thought her mind would seize up, and her voice never sound again. But still the words formed and were somehow articlated. 'It is not my decision to take. It never has been. I never thought justice came into it much, anyway.'

He laughed. *And you are honest, at least. Something rare, if foolhardy. Well, little one, there is not long to go now. Very soon I shall leave you to your fate. I shall take My beloved companion and leave you to your games.*

And then the smiling face fragmented and like a swarm of wasps fell over the crowd, glittering and glinting falling into their hair, their breath, their hands.

The swarm of light clung to one slight figure, standing closest to the altar. It bathed this one figure in gold, in a caress of sunshine. Eleanor saw Katriana lift her head, the fine spiral of her neck yearning towards that greater warmth. Her silver eyes were closed, her mouth slightly parted.

Eleanor saw it happen. Saw Katriana enchanted by the God, seduced and possessed by His light.

She was overwhelmed with pity, with sadness. It would go on, over and over again, for ever. She wanted to look away. She saw across the heads of the unknowing and uncaring crowd that one other person was watching this acquiescent rape.

Dion Gillet watched the God take his creation, and smiled.

Chapter Twenty-two
Zaeus

The sun had set, taking Katriana from them. In deadly silence, everyone looked at Dion Gillet. He threw back the hood to his cloak and drew himself up, preening like a hawk.

In silence he stared back at his followers, his eyes still reflecting the last gleam of the Sun.

Eleanor saw triumph there, a deep satisfaction. A bargain, successfully concluded. He was speaking, his voice ringing clear and strong.

'It is accomplished, it is done. *Now* we are free, my friends. Free to rule the world how we wish, in the Name of the Lord, the Lord who will no longer trouble us. For now there will be peace between the Gods. The Moon, in the person of Katriana, is united with the Sun and all shall be well. For the Lord has accepted our gift, our offering, and will concern Himself no longer with our affairs.'

The listening men stirred. Their voices rose. A babble of conversation, an excited release of tension. One of the men close to Eleanor began to sing a wild, rough hymn with words she didn't try to understand. Gradually, they all joined in, stamping their feet on the turf. More candles were lit, and placed in niches in the stonework. They were celebrating the success of a Rite of sacrifice, not one of marriage.

Eleanor turned away, tired, depressed, tears on her face. She leant against the dry stone of one of the few remaining walls. No one took any notice of her. No one seemed to remember that she was there.

The words of their song gradually became clear. It was a celebration, a song of rejoicing, because the God had left their lives. Strange lyrics for Priests. Stupid, she thought, it'll never last anyway, because there's still the Lady, meddling in everything everyone does. And who could ever be sure that Lycias will be content with one woman, whether she's got silver eyes or no? Do they seriously imagine they can get away with this? They'll find themselves cheated because of this arrogance.

Trying to manipulate Lycias, the Lord of Lies. What idiocy.

Matthias would know the worth of this, she thought. How would this fit into all those dreams or prophecies, whatever they are. . .The end of the Gods, death and destruction for everyone.

She turned away from the Temple, away from the rowdy singers, intending to creep away into the night, intending to find the Caver settlement at the other end of the island. There would be friends there, she was sure. Matthias might be there.

'Oh no you don't.' A heavy hand on Eleanor's shoulder, another grasping her wrist. Cassun. She ripped herself free, starting to run. She heard the song behind her abruptly cease and knew that all attention was focused on her. She had no chance at all against a dozen men, at least two of whom used the skills of magic.

But she did have a head start. . .she was running fast now over the soggy turf. But then someone threw himself at her and she fell under the weight of his body. She wriggled around, and felt her hand brush against something sharp in the folds of the man's robes. A knife.

She seized it, and found her fingers gripping the blade. The pain didn't matter as she slashed it at her assailant, aiming for his face. So that he can't see, she thought furiously. So that he can't spin spiral spells between his eyes and hands. There was a sprinkling of blood, hers and his, and he cried out, falling back. She was up and off once more, but in the fall her ankle had twisted and now gave way, folding beneath her like a rag, leaving her nauseous and weak. She was on her knees once more, but wouldn't let go of the knife, not even when the men surrounded her and advanced with mockery in their voices.

Still she fought, jabbing out at them. But the only person to get hurt was Eleanor herself, because they pushed her over, and the knife cut a long, deep gash in her own left forearm.

She spat at them, as they took the weapon from her bloody, nerveless fingers, 'What is it *now*? What do you want this time?'

'Look, you've hurt yourself! And all for nothing.' Dion Gillet had taken her left arm, and was winding a scrap of cloth round it, tightly pressing the edges of the wound together. 'We'd have let you go anyway, there was no need for this.'

'Why stop me then?' She wished her voice was not so unreliable, her hands so shaky.

I want you as witness. There must always be a witness. You have to be credible, Eleanor Knight. Your Caver friends will want proof. There's a Mage here on Sarant, Matthias Marling is his name. You'll know him, of course.' It was not a question. He knew so much.

She nodded unwillingly. 'Matthias, then. Tell him, Eleanor Knight, to get his people out of Peraldon. Tell them to go north, to Stromsall. There will be no place for Cavers on Peraldon. The worshippers of Sun and Moon are to be separated, for now and for evermore. I don't want any subversion close to home. The Law of the Lord will be followed in purity here. The presence of the Lady and Her followers will not be required.'

'Why should they go? *This* is their home!'

'If they stay, they will upset the balance. I can't allow that. They'll be hunted down, they'll lose more than their homes. Tell them that, Eleanor Knight. Tell them that there will be no escape in Peraldon, nowhere to hide this side of the Channel. They will be destroyed like vermin. This, I promise, is too important to be cast into doubt by the Lady's dreamers. . .I use the word advisedly. I am generous to give them this warning.'

'Haven't you forgotten something?' She sounded cool, but the pain in her ankle was making her head swim. She hadn't looked at it, but did so now. It had swollen to twice its size, streaked with red and purple. Sprained at the very least. Distracted by pain, her thoughts were running wild all over the place, returning again and again to Katriana, taken by the God, and the implications of it all. She strove to think straight. 'It won't work. You had to run away, Dion Gillet! Where are your followers, your power? A dozen men, here? They didn't want you on Peraldon, the Emperor saw you captured, Weard was hunting you. . .We were pursued by Fosca on the way here!' He was lost in hopeless ambition, she thought. This was unreal, absurd.

Incredibly, he was laughing. 'Weard is out of the running, remember? You saw that happen too, my witness. He bears the mantle of the Children now, and his only course is to suffer. To pay the price of his guilt.' For a moment Gillet's eyes were in shadow and she could not tell what he was thinking. 'And the Emperor. . .well, he is no Mage. He will have few defences.'

'The Peraldonian Mages will find you out. You'll never get away with it!'

'But there are no Peraldonian Mages now, Miss Knight, didn't you know? The day we left Peraldon the Fosca began a systematic campaign. By now, they will have burned down the Mages' College. None will survive. And let me tell you something else to enliven your story for Matthias. Tell him that I have taken the Fosca for my own. That I shall use them against any followers of Astret I find in these territories.'

'Fosca! You! You were hiding from them on the way here!'

'That was then. This is now. Things have changed, Eleanor Knight. You saw it happen. At the Temple to the Sun on Sarant. A sacrifice was accepted, an honour granted.' She did not know what he was talking about, and bent forward over her throbbing ankle.

He was looking down at her still, a faint curl of mockery on that thin mouth. 'You can't walk. And Matthias is some distance from here. You'll need a mount.' He was smiling, as if this was a joke. 'Let me show you how it works, Eleanor.' He held out his hand to the dark sky and called, a high, wheedling noise.

Totally unlike an Arrarat summoning, but still potent and wide-reaching. She held her breath, dreading what might appear.

It did not take long. It could not have been far away. The Fosca's wings were leathery, its scaled flesh slimy and slippery. It stank. It had no rider, and its small red eyes gleamed as they watched it settle on the ground close to Dion Gillet.

'There,' he said kindly. 'Shall I help you up?'

'On *that*? Oh, no!' She struggled to her feet, horrified by the way the Fosca's claws scraped at the boggy grass, by the stench of its breath, by the way its eyes shone blood-red. She was revolted by everything about it. 'I'd rather crawl!'

'But I want my message delivered tonight, not next week.'

'Well, take it yourself then!'

'Don't be silly. Matthias knows *you*, Eleanor Knight, and will listen to what you have to say. Especially if you arrive on one of these.'

And before she could protest further, he had picked her up as easily as if she were a doll and had put her on the Fosca's back.

Before she could throw herself off it had leapt into the air, jerking itself high up into the cold clouds. And then she needed to clutch the horny bone jutting from its shoulder, to stop herself falling to the ground so far below. The speed of the thing was quite dreadful, the rhythm of its wings irregular and deeply unsettling. She felt nausea in her mouth, and her ankle screamed at the movement.

The Fosca did not skim the back of the wind like a hawk. Instead it cut through, seeming to derive energy from the gusts of cold moisture. Its flesh was cold beneath her fingers, cold and clammy. She felt it soaking through her dress, foul and slimy beneath her. She was gagging with revulsion, and thought it would be a relief to fall.

Just let it get over the sea, she thought. Then I'll take a chance with the waves.

But it sped on over the island itself, informed by who knew what urgency. Gillet, she thought. He really is in control of these things, he really does know what he's doing. A rival to Lefevre.

He was a true Mage, a master of Rites, with all the ambition in the world. Prepared to use his creation to appease a God who was beyond any such blandishments. She shuddered.

Sometimes the cloud cleared below them and Eleanor could see the thin thread of white which was the road to the Temple. She watched it as if mesmerised, thinking that however revolting this ride was, at least she would soon be amongst friends. The Cavers would remember her, surely, even if Matthias were not there. And Matthias. . .perhaps *he* would be able to challenge Dion Gillet. Perhaps that would be his rôle.

The Fosca screamed suddenly, a wild swerve to one side, an instantaneous loss of height and then a collision against some other flying creature, something vast and black, covered in the night's own darkness. It happened so fast that she hardly realised that her hands had slipped from the greasy scales.

And then she was falling, all her breath gasped into nothingness, her stomach cartwheeling in terror. Her hands clutched wildly at something, nothing, something. . .

Something brushed against her and she recognised, rather than the touch, the smell of wild sea-salt, of warmth and feathers. . .

Still falling, but knowing now what to expect, she saw the hawk again as it dived towards her. Eleanor braced herself, her arms outstretched and *there* it was, alongside, falling at the same rate, black wings lifting under and around her.

An awkward reaching, a desperate embrace, all breath whipped from her: an alteration in the speed of her descent and she was flying not falling.

Her hands were still covered in slime and she felt them slipping; but then the hawk swerved slightly, a minute movement, and there he was, steady beneath her. Her first thought, crazily insignificant, was that she didn't want to stain the beautiful, black feathers with Fosca slime, but then the relief took over and she felt a presence in her mind, encouraging, triumphant. . .

The Fosca mount was still wheeling round, diving towards them, but the Arrarat used the scything wind as an ally and banked high to one side. The Fosca scudded past, squealing with rage. She almost laughed at it, and felt the amusement in the alien mind which touched her own.

Who are you, she asked silently, and the answer was no picture, no fall of dust or ash, but a blaze of glory, syllables unheard but evident like flame in her thoughts.

Zaeus!

She was laughing and entirely incoherent, but it didn't matter because the Arrarat were never interested in words anyway. The great black wings swept through the air and they were going very fast now, faster than she had ever been on an Arrarat hawk. She saw the red points of the Fosca's eyes diminishing in the distance. Skimming the clouds, swooping on the back of the wind, flying south towards the city on Sarant, they left it behind.

She felt the slime from the Fosca still sticky on her limbs and realised that Zaeus was sharing her revulsion. She sensed consent from him, and their course slightly changed, taking them towards the sea.

He put her down at the tide's edge and she slid to the ground, forgetting her injured ankle. It collapsed beneath her, and she cursed vividly. But she was already in the shallows, and flung herself into the waves, allowing the tide to draw her a little way out. The cold made her gasp, but she rubbed herself and her clothes vigorously, until the slickness had all gone. Her teeth were chattering and her bones beginning to ache with cold before she was done; she knew that the wind-chill of flying with Zaeus would make her colder still, but it was worth it. At least she would be free of the insidious Fosca influence.

There were other benefits to this night-time baptism. Her various wounds were almost numbed by the water, although her ankle still refused to bear her weight. Zaeus was standing in the water close by, a black sentinel.

A gust of wind sliced round her shoulders. Eleanor was shivering uncontrollably. She hauled herself on to his back, hoping that there was not too far to go. For a moment he stood there, unmoving. She felt his thoughts probing, questioning her own. There was a demand there, imperious and urgent.

Mine? he asked, and she could scarcely breathe.

Yours, she assented, and felt the great flooding warmth of his delight smoothing over all her worries and fears.

She could not believe this good fortune. I must have done something right, she thought, somewhere, somehow.

It had been right to return to Chorolon. However it turned out, she would not count it a loss now that she had been claimed once more by an Arrarat hawk.

Faithful unto death. Black, like a fall of ash, black like his forerunner.

Memento mori.

Chapter Twenty-three
Sarant by Night

Zaeus took Eleanor to a ruined city set with only a few, feeble lights. To the South, near the harbour, a number of houses were topped by new thatch, and candlelight and fires flickered within uncurtained windows. But most of the buildings were still only charred piles of rubble, their roofs collapsed, broken spars and beams jutting. She saw that some of the roads had been cleared, that some of the rubble had been shifted to stand in orderly heaps. The Cavers had come home, and were starting to reconstruct their city.

She had no need to tell Zaeus where she wanted to go. He set her down outside a small cottage, and as she was hesitating, nursing her ankle, steadying herself against his shoulder, someone came out.

An old woman stood there, peering uncertainly at her.

'Letia? Is that you?' For a moment Eleanor was unsure. So many changes. So much time had passed, so much had happened. The thin, faded woman who clutched a shawl round her shoulders was both familiar and unfamiliar.

Letia had been so kind to her when she first came to Chorolon. A woman with bright eyes, briskly trying to make the best of impossible conditions, she had struggled to keep the family together. And had welcomed Eleanor with generosity. Her eyes were dull now, her hair thin and straggly. She took a hesitant step forward, and Eleanor could see that there was some awkwardness holding her back.

'Letia! It's me, Eleanor.' She paused. The old woman's eyes were scanning her face, as if searching for recognition. 'Letia, I've hurt my ankle, I can't walk,' she said with some difficulty through teeth that chattered uncontrollably. 'I'm sorry, can I come in and get warm?'

She looked with longing at the firelight flickering within the cottage and thought that unless she got warm *soon*, she would probably start behaving badly.

Letia was looking as if she might cry.

'Please Letia?'

'Eleanor, I don't know what to say. . .Matthias is here, and I'm so frightened—'

She didn't understand. 'Is it something to do with me?'

'He's – depressed, and I don't know what's the matter. He won't tell me anything!' She looked back towards the cottage and Eleanor thought she was going to turn away. But then she seemed to notice Eleanor's condition, the blood on her arm, the shivering, the swollen ankle. 'Oh, this is so ridiculous! Of course, you must come in at once!'

She had taken her shawl off as she spoke, wrapping it round Eleanor's shoulders, taking her arm and some of the weight.

Awkwardly, they began to hobble towards the cottage. Letia was talking all the time, and the ceaseless ramble of care and concern was comforting.

'You're so cold my dear, what have you been doing? And your clothes all wet. . .How did you hurt your arm, it looks like a knife wound? Has there been a fight?' A darting shrewd glance at Eleanor's face, and a hasty change of subject. 'I'm so sorry to have left you standing there so long, but I don't know what to do about Matthias. I suppose he'll just have to come to terms with it, but it's very hard. . .'

They had reached the door, but just outside Letia stopped again. 'He's in the back room,' she said. 'I think he's trying to sleep, so let's not disturb him. Oh Eleanor, *what* are you doing here?'

'Exorcising ghosts,' she said simply. 'I couldn't put this behind me.' She looked back to where Zaeus stood, still watching them.

'Poor Eleanor,' Letia said, following her gaze. 'But an Arrarat brought you here. . .' She sighed. 'Perhaps it's all for the best.' Perhaps.

She helped Eleanor to a seat by the fire, and began to bustle round with dry clothes and towels and hot broth and bandages.

Eleanor leant her head back against the wooden chair, her eyes closing, letting the warmth embrace her.

A hand touched her sleeve. She looked up into an anguished, blinded face that existed at the back of all her thoughts.

'Matthias. . .' She spoke slowly. 'I thought you were sleeping.'

He said nothing, standing at her shoulder and she was glad that he had no eyes, because she knew there would be horrors reflected there.

His hands were thin, the bones jutting, white-clenched on the chair's arm. His mouth had forgotten all laughter, knew only the shapes of fear and despair. His hair hung limp and lifeless.

He crouched down, staring with empty eyes into the fire and she wondered if he would speak to her. 'I had to come back,' she said at last. 'There was no other choice.'

'I thought that at least *you* would be safe. I thought I'd got you out of it, that at last I'd managed to do you a good turn. I hoped, so much, that you would be all right.'

His voice, turned away from her, was quiet as whispers, dry and arid as desert wind.

'There's nowhere else, Matthias. This is all there is. There are lies and flames everywhere, but here at least we know what we're up against.' She paused, and the flames she was watching brought memory with them. 'Matthias, I've got so much to tell you! He, Lycias I mean, has taken Katriana—'

'I know. It's all part of the nightmare, it's the place where my mind lives now. There's nothing anyone can do about it now. Eleanor, for Lady's sake, *what* made you return?' She heard the pain in his voice, and knew she could match it.

'There's nowhere else,' she repeated. She could find no other words for it. 'And Phin is here, and he understands, so do you. . .' She was trying to be honest, trying to drive deceit from her life. 'And the Arrarat live here. I have been chosen by an Arrarat hawk, Matthias, I'm not alone at all!'

Zaeus was not far away, she knew. Playing in the clouds, riding the night winds, waiting for her.

'The hawk makes no difference. You shouldn't have come back. It's at an end here. There's nothing here for anyone. Those fools think they've got rid of Lycias, but they don't know the half of it. . .'

Matthias's words were almost lost in the crackle of the fire. She tried to understand why he was so desperate.

'Do you think that Astret will fight back? That it will all start again, all that violence and cruelty?'

'You can think that if you like. But it's not what will happen. There's only devastation awaiting this world. An end to magic. . .'

She hated the way his words flared, so uneven, so extravagant. 'Come on, Matthias, you've been wrong before. Edine told me all about this. She said that when you saw the end of the world, all that was going to happen was that Mages would lose their power.'

'Eleanor, that *is* the end to everything! The Mages make this world what it is, structure everything about it. There will be chaos and chance and madness!'

'No, there won't.' She struggled on. 'The world will keep going, just the same as usual, and if people try for a little common sense, a little tolerance towards each other, then it will be all right. Adequate anyway. Magic isn't everything.'

'You understand *nothing*! It's what holds all worlds together, overtly or covertly. Our Gods created us, and here the Mages have given them a pathway through to us.'

This was wrong. She remembered other words, and recognised the truth in them. 'But Martitia said that *we* create our own Gods. That they only reflect what we do, and depend on our decisions. She said that it's up to us, all the way, and didn't mention Mages once!' She heard Matthias start to say something, but swept on. 'And what of the priests and priestesses? Surely they've got more of a rôle than Mages in understanding what the Gods want?'

'Have you learnt nothing, Eleanor?' He sounded both angry and bitter. 'Don't you realise that God is rarely found within the walls of a temple? Do you not understand that priests and priestesses exist only to fudge the issue? To keep us, us and the Gods, apart from each other.'

'I don't believe you! What about Nerissa? Dion Gillet, with all his mystic knowledge? Lefevre, when he lived at Peraldon?'

'*Especially* them. Think what Lefevre did. He gave his sister to Lycias so that Lycias should leave him free to run this world how he wanted to. In visions, I've seen Dion Gillet give his adopted daughter to the God, and it's just the same. These are true visions. . .And

Nerissa preached acceptance, passivity, no action. She hated the Rites, hated everything the Mages did. She did nothing to draw the Gods closer.

'Martitia was right in a way, though. The Gods live in the way we behave to each other, in the choices we make, in what we *do*. Especially there. Organised religion does not dare to admit it. Rites of worship imply that the Gods can be placated and trusted, that Gods will listen to our prayers. . .and nothing could be further from the truth.

'The truth is that God, in the divided form of Lycias and Astret, exists on either side of a knife edge. Our lives take place along the edge. And only when we fall through the sky, down the pit into despair, or when we fly into ecstasy and joy, only then do we ever encounter God. Only when we are fragile as glass, smashing. . .destroying ourselves at the sharp edge of experience. For whatever we do, whatever we say, pushes us towards one side or the other, and then there's no escape.'

'So where do the Mages fit in?'

'Our only hope lies with the Mages. Whatever control we have is due to them. The Gods can be induced to appear, sometimes, to Mages. Then we have some true knowledge of Their nature and desire. How will we know how to appease Them, without magic?'

'You'll do just the same as we do in my world. Muddle through, somehow. It's not much different, in the end.'

'You are unduly optimistic, Eleanor. This is not like your world, however well we seem to understand each other. There is an essential, inescapable difference. This world, Chorolon, is defined by Magic, and Magic sets the arena where the Gods exist. The Gods are active here. They walk among us—' For a moment it seemed as if he would say more, but then he stood up and reached for the cloak that lay over the back of Letia's chair.

'Are you going out?' the older woman asked.

'Yes. I have to go. The Gods will walk tonight, and there is death ahead.' His voice was as quiet as ever and it drained from Eleanor every last remnant of comfort or relief.

He moved unerringly towards the door and she thought that he was going straight out into the night, but he paused there, turning towards her.

'You should not have come back.'

The door closed behind him and although she was warm now, dressed in dry clothes, the fire burning brightly not far away, it felt like the death he had promised her.

Eleanor turned towards Letia, and saw the firelight play over her features. Letia was wan with tiredness, her weakened eyes encased by fine webs of lines, her mouth drawn tight.

'Don't mind him, Eleanor, he's not well, he has such dreams . . .There's more food, if you want it. And a bed made up over there.'

She gestured to a pile of blankets and cushions in the corner of the room.

'I can't eat anything.' Eleanor stood up and looked towards the window, staring out over the dilapidated buildings. There were lights further along the street, and the silhouettes of scaffolding and half-mended roofs were rigid against the stars. A cold, bright night; a tinge of frost in the air.

'I've been thinking of you as one of the family,' said the faded voice behind her. 'Matthias told me all about you, and what you did. It can't have been easy. And you loved Lukas, didn't you?'

There was no pressure in her words. It was just an inquiry, Eleanor thought. A simple, concerned quest for information.

'Yes, I loved him.' How natural was that past tense? How true was it?

'And you are welcome here.' Letia smiled at last. 'Welcome home, Eleanor.'

Letia lived alone. Her husband Niclaus was still on Peraldon, negotiating passage for any others who wished to join Astret's followers back at their old home. Other members of her family were here on Sarant. She saw them most days; Caspar and Fabian, Margat and Stefan Pryse.

Margat was pregnant, said Letia, brightening. And although Niclaus was away, and the rest of the family living elsewhere, she was rarely alone. Matthias was often there.

Eleanor could not picture Matthias enjoying comfortable gossip at the fireside. The depression that she had witnessed in him in Stromsall had deepened. She wondered if he were quite sane, if the obsessiveness had gone too far.

Letia looked exhausted. Eleanor put her arm round the bony shoulders of the older woman and gave her a brief hug. 'You're so kind, Letia. You've always been kind.'

'Now you should rest,' Eleanor was told. 'I can see from the shadows beneath your eyes. Come and sleep, there's a long night to get through. I hate the night, don't you?' Letia shivered. 'And there's only the coldness of winter ahead. But at least it changes now. At least it's not always dusk, wind and rain.' The tired voice stopped for a while. Then Letia said, almost as if it didn't matter, 'I don't think that Matthias will come back here.'

But where is he? And what about Katriana? Eleanor wanted to ask. And Phin, he'll be worrying. How can I sleep tonight when there's still so much in the balance, so much that's wrong?

However, she did sleep, beside the dying embers of the hearth, and the face of Lycias did not disturb her dreams, did not echo through her thoughts.

Chapter Twenty-four
Seekers

The Fosca baron saw the ruined city far below and knew that it was occupied. It could smell men and women, could sense their heat through the autumnal night air. There was the odd, small light flickering through uncurtained windows. They were arrogant, these Moon-lovers. They did not even seek to hide their lights.

The Fosca baron's attention was caught by a movement. It flew a little closer. A man was wandering through the streets, peering in at the windows. For a while the baron watched, fascinated. The man was moving quietly, swiftly, and no one on the ground would have seen him at all, so adept was he at keeping to the shadows. He was wearing a wide-brimmed hat, hiding his face from the watcher above. He seemed to be searching for something or someone. Before long he was swallowed in the dark passages.

The baron lost interest. Soon the Fosca would illuminate all these meagre dwellings in flame, and all these little wanderings, these little quests and complications would be over. If the Sun did not touch their lives first. . .

But first the baron needed to find a different quarry. Its servants were spreading through the night behind it. They were avid, excited with lust and the promise of battle. They were not obsessed, as was the Fosca baron, by the black cloud that hid the Moon above them.

The Fosca King, Weard, Lefevre, the Rose, swung through the stars on cloudy wings which were almost all that remained of its magic. It howled at times, trying to drown the voices singing the eternal litany of sin in its ears. Some understanding was left to it; it knew that Mages alone would not be able to help. And as it neared Sarant, it felt a different influence, a different power.

There was a Child somewhere, a saviour, and healing flowed from his fingertips, flowered from the air he breathed.

And although the Shadows filled all its senses with irrefutable evidence of guilt, this finer instinct persisted. With almost tentative yearning, the thing that had been Weard was drawn to Sarant, in search of innocence. It beat amongst the stars, hiding the Moon, forgetting the Sun.

It cared only to find a child, nestling quietly at his stepfather's side. The child would release it. The child would lift the Shadows, and then all would be as it was before. . . .

It had no knowledge of the man below who was carefully avoiding the patches of light, searching for that same saviour.

That night, the child Coron stirred briefly in the snatches between dreams. He did not want to probe the horrors of the night. He knew they waited not far away and that, sooner or later, he would have to confront them. But for the while he was content to rest by the side of his stepfather, Haddon Derray, in their half-renovated hovel down one of the back streets of the city on Sarant.

It would end, this life. He could no longer pretend to be helpless and in need of protection. There was something to be done, a decision was about to be forced on him, actions taken.

Coron whimpered, and Haddon woke immediately, super-sensitively attuned to every movement of his son. His hands gently smoothed Coron's fine dark hair, and cuddled him close. In the dim, shadowed light, he could see that the child's plump cheeks were streaked with tears.

'Ah, little love, don't worry, it's just a dream.'

He laid his head against that of the child, and at length drifted back to sleep.

The city was not quiet that night. Although hardly anyone apart from Coron realised that massed hordes of Fosca were hanging high above with their bedamned King, few people on Sarant slept easily.

Three men dismounted from their Arrarat hawks on the southern edge of the city. They were very close to the sea here. The waves crashed monotonously at the harbour walls, betraying no trace of storm or enchantment. This last act was to be played out between Gods and humanity.

Two of the three were Mages: Aylmer Alard and Thibaud Lye. The other was Phinian Blythe, looking for two women. They walked swiftly through the streets, picking their way over the rubble that still obscured so many paths.

'They'll not be in the city, not Gillet and his men. They won't dare come here. They'll be at Lycias's temple, to the North. . .'

'Couldn't we have gone there straightaway?' Blythe looked towards the hills beyond the city.

'We need Matthias for this. And, if you're right, Haddon Derray and the baby. Come on, let's not delay.'

They arrived at one of the houses, and asked for directions. In minutes they were at Letia's house. They hammered on the door.

The Temple of Lycias was quiet at last. The dancing and singing had died away, and Dion Gillet sat by the fire beneath the altar and spoke quietly to his companion, Cassun.

'And the Lady?'

'Yes. . .'

Both men looked up to the distant Moon, and for a moment Dion Gillet thought he saw a shadow cross its surface. Just a cloud, he decided. 'The Lady, next,' he confirmed.

'Their Temple is not far from here.'

'It could just as well be across the Marant Channel. That's not the way. No. Gods can die, you know.' He spoke the words as if they were a secret. 'Deprive Them of Their believers and They have no existence.'

'You cannot seriously expect to wipe out a whole continent!' Even Cassun was aghast at this.

'Of course not. There has been a boundary between North and South before now. There are only a few followers of Astret now outside Stromsall. Most of them live here.'

He looked up again, and saw the shadows across the skies. Black leaves were flying through the night and, of course, he knew exactly what they were. 'And we won't even have to try all that hard,' he said. 'Help is on its way.'

The leaves were swooping very low over the city of Sarant, and far away Gillet saw that the fires were beginning.

He nodded, satisfied.

There was only forgetting. Nothing else to show who or what she was. She lived in a dream of light and love. She thrilled as golden fire ran through her limbs, and touched with delight every nerve end.

She was swaying through warm air, wrapped about in His sweet breath, held with exquisite care within His all-embracing, all-knowing hands. She felt as if she were made of water, pliant as silk, opening and reopening until she was all revealed, all welcoming and quivering. This was her only purpose.

And then with delicacy and subtlety He invaded her, body and soul. He took everything from her that she was prepared to give, and more. He showed her that there was nothing of her He could not own. There was nothing that could be concealed, for it all belonged to Him. He took what was left of her innocence and joy, and spoilt her for anyone else. He saw that she was magic, so He took that too. And then He held her there, on the high edge of ecstasy, for all eternity. And for the briefest of instants. For the God Lycias can exist out of time, and those He loves join Him there.

He made sure that He was observed. He flaunted His new love over wide universes and unseen dimensions.

Black eyes watched him coldly.

They did not weep.

The pillars of Astret's temple on Sarant were still standing, although the roof had fallen in long ago. It was not inappropriate, Lukas thought, that the night sky should shine over such dead stone. Polished by wind and rain, the stones picked up the dim light and seemed to shine.

The Moon was a thin curve, at the end of its waning. But the night was clear, and the stars flickered behind the shadows of leaves that blew in the wind.

No, not leaves. He received from his hawk Astrella a different intimation, and anxiety filled him. Why had she brought him here, when surely he would soon be needed in the city?

'Lukas?'

A figure stepped out of the deep shadows by the ruined doorway. He could not quite see who it was, but the voice was more than familiar.

He held out his arms, moving towards the sound.

Chapter Twenty-five
Attack

The calamitous thunder on the door happened at the same time as the city caught fire.

Eleanor sat up abruptly, shouting, 'Letia!'

Through the window, she could see the flames licking the new thatching on the house next door. The smell of burning was acrid throughout the room, the rosy glow of firelight flattering the poor furniture.

She almost forgot that there was someone at the door.

She scrambled for clothes, cursing her absurdly weak ankle and then Letia was at the front of the house, and she heard hurried, muttered voices, and the door flew open.

In two strides, Blythe had crossed the room. 'Eleanor, thank God I've found you.'

She was on her feet, clinging to him, tears of relief on her face. He kissed her gently, wiping the tears away. She knew him so well. She had known he would come, that he wouldn't fail. He had never lied to her, never let her down. He was irreplaceable in her life. Her very dearest friend. . .

Amidst this strong conviction, this sudden warmth, there were still tears on her face, tears because she was no longer alone.

'I – oh, Phin, how did you get here, how did you know where to come?'

'Thibaud and Aylmer brought me. Eleanor, what about Gillet? Where is he now?'

There was no time for detailed explanations. Through the door she could see sparks flaring in the street outside. There were screams and shouts not far away.

'Are you all right?'

He had seen that her ankle was unsteady, that there was a bandage on her arm.

'I twisted it, it's nothing, I'm fine. But why did you come with them?'

'Looking for you, of course.'

Prosaic words, calmly spoken. Again, without pressure, without pressure, without stress. She owed him so much.

But the city was on fire. And dreadful things had happened. 'Phin, Katriana has been taken! The God came, and took her. Gillet made it happen—'

He held her close and transmitted this over her shoulder to the men by the door. She turned, still leaning against him, and saw the two Caver Mages, familiar to her from long ago. Two elderly men, dressed in dreary black, who both bent their heads to her.

'Mistress Eleanor,' the taller one said, with utmost formality, 'We are relieved to find you safe—'

'But just now there's work to be done.' The other, round with tiny, sparkling eyes, spoke sharply. 'Where's Matthias?'

Letia answered them. 'He left here some hours ago. I don't know where he was going.' She was looking at Eleanor with a strange expression on her face. Puzzlement, and something Eleanor didn't want to acknowledge. Regret, was it?

It was quickly superseded by brisk urgency. 'Eleanor, keep that cloak, and take this.' She held out a long, serrated knife to her. 'And you. . .' she looked at Blythe, 'must be Phinian Blythe. Look after her.' Letia turned away. hastily clasping her own cloak tight. 'Let's get out of here,' she said. 'I don't want to be fried alive.'

The stones of the wall were becoming warm to the touch. The thatch was smouldering. They ran outside, Eleanor's ankle just holding up under the tight bandaging. The street was filled with people, thronging the spaces between houses. Dark shapes swooped overhead, and there were arrows flying. She could see indecision on every face. To be trapped in burning houses, or stabbed by arrows from the sky?

'Can't you do anything?' Blythe was shouting at Thibaud Lye.

'We have to find Matthias first!'

'Oh no, we don't. We need the Arrarat to help out here, there's no chance otherwise!' And this was true. For although many of them had weapons, there were huge numbers of Fosca circling the city. None had dismounted yet.

They screamed through the air. Eleanor heard the high-pitched wails that trembled on the edge of audibility and smelt the thick stench of rotting flesh. The rain of arrows fell through a light mist, the grey rags of decaying skin falling over them all. She saw people stumbling, and then others would pause, and try to help.

She saw women clutching wailing children to the breast. She saw one of them fall, an arrow jutting from her shoulder. Her head drooped over the screaming baby, her hands beginning to loosen their grip. . .

'Do something!' She yelled at Aylmer as she ran to help. But someone else had already caught the falling woman, taking the baby, pulling her to her feet. Eleanor turned back to the Mage. 'You can't abandon them! Call the Arrarat!'

'Look—' Phin had caught her arm, pointing up to the stars. She saw then that the battle was starting in earnest.

The Arrarat had needed no formal summoning. They swooped down to collect their riders, and then the familiar wheeling dance began. Great hawks soared and lifted, their wide wings pushing at the air, claws extended and braced. With squealing agility the Fosca ducked and swerved, and sometimes escaped. . .

Phin's arm was round her shoulder, his voice in her ear, 'Come on, let's get out of here—'

The Mages had disappeared into the crowd. She saw Letia some distance ahead, supporting a crippled young man. 'Where are they all going?' Eleanor asked, as they pushed their way through the crowds.

'They'll be safer out of the city, I imagine. Sarant burned once before. . .'

And the Arrarat had come to save them. She paused for a moment, looking back into the dizzy chaos above the city. Where was Zaeus? But through the drifting clouds of smoke, through the darting creatures far above them all, she saw that the night was coloured by something else.

Staring upwards, holding on to Phin's arm for reassurance, Eleanor's fingers tightened.

A shape emerged from the clouds. A face yawned out of the sky, obliterating the Moon. Its eyes were screwed tight in agony, and tears fell like torrents of rain over gaunt wastes of flesh. Its mouth was open, a deepening chasm of noise, and its howling filled every register of sound beyond the reach of human ears. The face was known to her, and the claws that raked the sky had nails as long as thorns.

It was swathed in shadows, muffled and blinded and gagged by creeping mists. In agony it swooped down towards them, and the Fosca and Arrarat all scattered before it.

There was panic, a huge rush to escape the lowering creature growing out of the night sky. Blythe and Eleanor struggled free from the movement of the crowd, searching for the two Caver Mages. They found them sheltering in the shadows beneath a stone-built house.

Thibaud and Aylmer did not look at them. Instead, all their attention was focused on the shrouded face in the sky, and their hands were clasped strongly around their spiral staffs.

'The baby, Aylmer, where will we find Haddon Derray and the baby?'

The Mage barely glanced at Blythe. His mouth was murmuring incantations almost unconsciously. A faint nod indicated a road to their right.

'Come on.' Blythe had taken her hand, but Eleanor paused briefly. The Mages, their backs to the wall, were chanting an even stream of words and it seemed as if light were springing from their staffs, into the air, approaching and nudging the tormented creature above them. It winced further away, and the light fell back to litter the stone roads and ruined buildings with fire. . .

She saw that they were trying to ward it off, and meeting with some success.

A multitude of forms flickered over the face. Its own identity was fragile as glass, having passed through so many incarnations, and now the Shadows wreathed about it, expressing a thousand more.

Remember this one? And this? He died like this – and a face would melt and run – and she like this. . .A slow welling of blood and tears, and the face in the clouds could not look away, could not turn aside. Its fate was to share in every moment of every agony.

And yet the Shadowed one was holding off just clear of the city, waiting with terrible patience for relief. It had gathered up the Fosca, and they circled around it like the spiral of a whirlwind.

The Mages had won a little time. . .Blythe and Eleanor started down the street of burning houses. The timber frame to one of them abruptly collapsed in a roar of flame. Further along, a door opened.

A man was drawn from the house.

He carried in his arms a small baby. Eleanor knew at once who it was. She felt her breath catch in her throat, her hands suddenly clench.

The man carrying Coron was a stranger to Eleanor, but she saw nightmare written on his face. His eyes were haunted in every way. Unbearable grief and fear. It was as if he had woken to the knowledge of every horror in the world. As if the monster howling through the city, howling through the wind, had opened the doors to memory.

Blythe was walking towards the man and child, holding out his arms. 'Derray, you have to let the child go. We need him. Coron can release the Shadows, will release the afflicted from their guilt—'

'Why? Why should I do anything for anyone else?'

Eleanor heard a blank hopelessness at the back of Haddon's voice, a despair that Blythe could not reach. The child was frowning, holding out its small hands towards Eleanor.

She took a step forward, and the pain in her ankle lessened. She went straight to Haddon Derray and gently touched her finger to the baby's cheek. 'Let me carry him,' she said. 'Please. For just a little time.'

He looked down at her as if she was entirely insignificant. 'No.

I will never, never let anyone else take him from me. Not for anything.'

'Not to save your people from the Fosca King and his subjects?'

'What use is it? What is the use of anything? My only fault was in loving Coronis, in loving too well. I have been the Stormbringer, I know it now. This – creature is nothing to do with me. Leave us alone.'

'You must help us, Haddon!' Eleanor had moved her hand until it encased his. He was so lonely, so bitter. 'These are your people, and the Fosca will kill them all!'

Haddon bent his head over Coron, as if listening for unheard melodies, while all around them the howling of the creature above shattered the night, shattered their thoughts. There were tears on Eleanor's face, watching Derray look into the child's eyes.

'I only want to be left alone with Coron. I care nothing for anyone else. This is a terrible world, a place built on suffering.'

'But Coron can help!'

'I only want to be left alone with him.'

'Please!' She was passionately trying to break through this despair, her eyes fixed on Haddon's face, and did not see what happened next. But Blythe did see the man step out from one of the houses at the side of the road. He wore a wide-brimmed hat, but even so they could see that his eyes slanted upwards. Blythe suddenly realised that everything they'd just said had been overheard.

'That child is not for mortals to fight over.' The man spoke quietly. 'That child belongs to the tribes of the North, as you know well, Haddon.' He was fitting an arrow to a bow.

'Jerr?' Like a man poleaxed, Haddon Derray swung round, his mouth hanging open. 'What are you doing here?'

'You should never have deserted the *eloish*.' Jerr Morrelow sounded almost kind. He raised his bow.

'Watch it!' Blythe tried to push Derray and Eleanor out of the way, but it was already too late. The arrow burst into flame as it flew through the air. It buried itself in the side of Derray's neck.

At once he began to topple, and by the time he had reached the ground, his face and hair were lost in a blazing flare. A last, effortful action to fling the baby away from him, and then his clothes caught. A tortured scream briefly chimed with those of the creature above.

Eleanor had fallen to her knees, reaching out to the baby without thinking. In dreadful shock, she dragged her face away from the inferno that engulfed Haddon's body. She saw, instead, Blythe making a rush at the *eloish* stranger, sword drawn.

There was the sound of weapons clashing.

Blythe moved so fast that she could not disentangle the weapons or their action. She had seen him fight before, she knew he had been a trained soldier, had fought professionally many times. But this was a bitter, dirty fight; the *eloish* man curiously insubstantial, writhing and twisting, wavering out of the way like water.

There was nothing watery about the way he used his knife. Eleanor knelt there in the dust, watching the whirling steel with horror, and did not think to look at the baby on the ground.

Chapter Twenty-six
Coron

This was deliberate. The child did not want to be observed. Eleanor would not have remembered him, whatever happened.

It was such a shock, such a disruption and a disturbance, thrown through the air towards the stone of the street, that Coron had instinctively removed himself both from his physical surroundings, and from the consciousnesses of those around him. Only when the first trauma had faded a little did he allow himself to return to the scene.

He did not realise what was happening at first. And when at last his anxious baby-eyes found his stepfather, it was already too late. Blackened and charred rags of flesh were all that remained.

Coron stared at the body, helpless with horror. With difficulty he absorbed the fact of Haddon's death. His eyes were dry. It was too late for tears. He was no longer just a little child, able to cry, to scream and wail for comfort. . .

There were wings beating nearby, waiting for him, but he didn't care. There was no comfort. His father was dead. Haddon Derray had been consumed by fire.

Coron was truly bereft, and that, not for the first time. In flames had his mother died. He had been born into flames, he was the son of the Lord of Flames.

This other Father, Lycias, King of the Sun, would be rejoicing. In vengeance had He cursed Haddon with storm. And now the flames lit by the stranger from the North had murdered the only real parent the child had ever known.

With rage, Coron willed himself to maturity, as he had once before. He called on the powers he had inherited from his Father, ignoring the boundaries of this physical world. He stood straight and tall, and looked down at the wrecked body on the ground.

The final death of innocence. This was what all humanity had to face. This was the final baptism of flame, destroying the evidence of the senses and of the flesh.

Destroying love. He dropped to his knees, covering his eyes. This was how love ended. His voice rose, and he cried into the flames, 'My Father, listen now to Your son! Grant this prayer, grant that this man may live once more! Show to me that love is worth something!'

There was only the noise of flames and fighting, the whistle of fire-driven winds driving through the fragile city, the sound of his breath in his lungs.

His tears were falling at last, great sobs choking in his throat. He looked at the salt water falling on his hands, and remembered his mother. Coronis, vowed to the Moon.

'Oh Lady, Lady of soft waters and gentle new life. Remember the suffering of children, remember Your daughter and her son. And if You have any kindness, grant me this prayer, Lady who governs birth and the tides of humanity. Let this man live once more.'

Salt water ran over his face and hands. Through the chaotic violence of the night he saw the Moon fading fast, only the slightest curve of light, remote and uninterested. There was no answer there, for him or for anyone else.

Coron knelt on the ground while two men fought nearby, and a woman watched. He made sure they would not see him. Overhead, the tormented and Shadowed creature still wailed softly in the night. In the distance, other fires still burned and people ran from the city, and no one knew what had happened to him.

He kept himself hidden from the fighting men and the red-haired woman. She, too, had been touched by flames but he felt no kinship. She was wholly human, and he was not like her, not one of them. His stepfather had provided his only way through to the world of men and women. Coron would never be simply human again, never love or be loved again.

Governing his emotion, with hands that trembled only a little, he bent towards the charred bones that were all that was left of Haddon Derray's body.

He lifted the still-warm, black skull with its empty eyes, and stroked the ragged remnants of flesh with his hand. Where his fingers passed, the flesh became smooth and unscarred, gently and perfectly healed.

He paused, watching. His eyes widened, filled with light. And then he let his hand drift over the blank eye-sockets, and lashes closed over eyes at peaceful rest. Flesh grew over the charred bone, and the mouth was there once more, open and unbreathing.

Very slowly he replaced the heavy head on the ground, and then Coron did not move for a long time. Even after the man Blythe had dealt with the *eloish* and returned to the woman, he did not move. He let them approach, let them watch what he did. He knelt there beside the burnt body and the healed head, while the city of Sarant crashed into ruins once more and flames leapt to meet the stars.

His hawk was calling. The man and woman were talking to him, holding out their hands, wanting him. He took no notice. He held himself away from them.

He bent his head towards the mouth of his father and began to breath life into it.

Chapter Twenty-seven
The Temple

All was quiet at the Temple to Astret on Sarant. The fires that consumed the city; the people running; the battling Fosca and their monstrous king: all were far away over bleak miles of moorland. The Moon shone coldly and silently on broken stone, on a deserted arena.

There was one man there. Lukas Marling stood alone between the ruined pillars and turned towards the Woman who had called his name. His arms were spread wide in unthinking and instinctive welcome. She was smiling, still smiling even when his face changed and he stepped back lowering his arms.

He turned away. It was not the hardest thing he had ever done. He walked steadily away from the Lady although it was deadly, like walking through blood. His breathing was uneven, his hands clenched, but he did not look back.

There was no compulsion. The Lady did not have to beg, or coerce. There was no need. Everything would happen just as She had planned.

He walked away from Her and all he heard was Her voice: saying, *You will not reject me for ever. You cannot escape the Moon in your life. I am the beginning and the end. . .*

He did not pause, made no effort to speak. With every fibre straining he dragged his mind away from Her voice, although it echoed everywhere.

He saw far beyond the high moor a glow in the sky, and wondered if the city was burning. But the firelight was feeble beside the cold light that followed him. Still it flowed round him, thick and cloying, and Lukas kept walking, down from the Temple, away from the Moon symbols and the ruined choirs of pillars. He looked towards the city, and thought of the people there, of what might be happening. He tried to concentrate on that drama, and not the one being played out behind him.

The light began to withdraw.

He saw in the distance a frail figure, running towards him. A black silhouette, outlined against the flaming sky. Another dream, another enchantment? He looked around for Astrella, but she had disappeared. And then he realised who it was running across the moor, stumbling, falling. . .

His brother Matthias, guided by unearthly sight, was hurling himself at Lukas, clutching at his shoulders, to prevent himself falling.

'Go back, Luke, go back to Her!' He was shouting, hauling on Lukas's shoulders, as if trying to turn him round.

'No. Never. The Lady is nothing to do with me.'

'There will be no peace, no happiness, no contentment for you. Never to rest, never to know love. . .you cannot reject the Lady! You have no choice, you are bound!' His grip on Lukas's arm tightened.

'No, Matthias. This is *because* I have no choice.' His brother's hands fell away.

Matthias stepped back, his mouth a straight, hard line; his empty face creased with anguish. 'We need our Gods,' he said. 'Don't you understand? They are necessary. They are at the centre of everything.'

There was no answer. After a long pause, Matthias turned away.

Lukas watched his brother walk straight past him towards the Temple, towards the fading light. Matthias was muttering: a worrying, unstable thread of sound.

'Don't leave us Lady, don't go. Stay, for we are eternally loyal, true to You, loving You, needing You. Remember the child, and us. Don't go. . .'

Her voice hissed in the light in reply. It sparked dangerously over the stones of the Temple, running like wildfire along the contours of the pillars and the altar.

She said: *You have nothing I want. . .*

Matthias fell to his knees, his empty hands raised in supplication. His face was marked in grief, drawn with lines of loss. Lukas could hardly bear to watch this. He wanted to go to Matthias, to stop this abasement, this shame.

'Don't go, don't leave us. . .'

You have nothing I want.

It repeated soundlessly, endlessly, a dying echo as the light finally drained away.

Matthias remained motionless on his knees. His hands dropped, hanging loosely at his sides, his head drooping.

Lukas approached slowly. A hand on the shoulder, another beneath the elbow. 'Matthias, we need to get away from this place. Sarant is burning, we have to help—'

'Ah, but Lukas, you don't understand; you don't know what's at stake. This affects all your life, your every desire. You think it doesn't concern you, that this is a mere act of the intellect, of the will. But it's more than that. She's here, you see. Eleanor's here—'

The shock to his heart was like a blow. For a moment he said nothing, and then he took his hand from his brother's thin shoulders.

'She came *back*? Matthias, tell me straight, she's here on Chorolon again?'

'I make up nothing, I create nothing, I deal only in distortions. . .I am empty, I have never loved. I have nothing She wants. . .' He stopped, passing his hand over the scars on his face. 'But it won't make any difference, because of what you've done. There's no happiness now anywhere, for any of us—'

'What have you seen, Matthias? What visions of the future have filled your mind with lies?'

'I don't know!' Matthias's voice cracked painfully, desperately, and his hands flew to clasp his brother's. 'I can't tell any longer! It's all dreams and visions and lies, just as you say, and I don't know what's true any more, but if the Gods leave us there'll be no way out!'

'But Eleanor's here, now? On Chorolon?'

'Yes, yes! The city burns around her, and it's all too late. . . .'

Lukas ripped his hands free from Matthias and ran back up the hill. The glow in the sky above the horizon looked like a false dawn. Beneath the pall of smoke and flames, he could see the city now, its gates flung wide. Crowds of people were pushing through, scattering over the starlit plains.

'Astrella!' he shouted, hurling the word as far as he could. And then the Arrarat summoning, the low, ornate cry that she so rarely ignored.

Nothing. No sign of her, no response in his mind. Looking down at the plain, he saw that there were two groups coming towards the Temple.

From the East, Lukas saw torches blazing, a golden Sun-symbol held high over a band of men, striding over the heath. Coming from the old Temple to Lycias, he realised. And there was arrogance in the way they moved: confidence. It was as if they were coming to display some triumph, some great victory.

This is the cost of it, he thought. Reject the Lady, and the Lord triumphs.

There has to be some other way, he thought. Surely there has to be some answer?

To the South, he saw a larger group. They carried no illumination, content to trust to the night. Cavers, he thought. Friends, relying on the Moon and their own night-vision, as he had. Losers, all.

Black cloaks fluttered about them, people from the city of Sarant. They were walking steadily towards Astret's Temple, moving together. He tried to see who was leading them.

The Mages Aylmer and Thibaud. Spiral staffs, and purpose in their stance. Behind them the figure of a man, tall, well-built. A faint luminescence hung around him, and his face, wide-browed, brown-eyed, was immediately familiar. Haddon Derray: the friend of his youth, the guardian of the child.

Beside Haddon, wrapped around in the same gleaming light, there walked a strange young man whom Lukas did not recognise. Dark hair, dark eyes, a lightness in his step.

There was something wrong there. Something in the way Haddon moved, curiously unfocused. Something proprietory in the strange youth with his hand on Haddon's shoulder. The light that shone around them turned the gaze away. Lukas found he could not bear to look at them for long, that his vision was repelled by everything they did.

He looked beyond them, and saw the faces of old friends, many others he knew. . .Letia, Stefan. . .coming to the Temple. Coming to ask for mercy, for the Lady to stay, just as Matthias had done. And then, to one side, slightly separated from the others, he recognised Phinian Blythe. And beside him, Eleanor Knight.

His breath caught, a moment of stillness. They were close together, Eleanor leaning against Blythe, his arm round her waist.

Time must have passed while he watched them, moving together towards the Temple, but he had no knowledge of it.

There will be no peace, no happiness, no contentment for you, you will never rest, never know love. . .you cannot reject the Lady. Matthias's words repeated in his mind.

They were old friends, and knew each other so well. . .

There was no reason why she should wait for Lukas Marling, not after what had happened in Shelt. He had sent her away, after all.

His instinct was to find out *now*, to confront them and discover immediately the truth of it. But before he could react, before he could run down the hill and tell her that he was free, and loved her still, a howling gust of wind crashed through the night air, forcing him to step backwards into the line of pillars. It raked through his hair, whipping his cloak away from his shoulders. It carried a chill with it, a taste of winter and the scent of roses, rotting. . .

A scream, lancing through all the registers of sound, cutting through every wavelength. He didn't want to look, but his eyes were dragged upwards against his will. Something was drawing him into its train.

He saw Fosca there, wheeling through the curves of a vortex. A spiral of dead leaves circled overhead, dizzying circles over circles, a coiling dance around one still centre.

In the eye of the storm a tormented face, Shadowed by black, gave the wind its voice.

At his side Matthias was braced against the ruined walls to the Temple. He was muttering again, but this time the words were of arcane significance and purpose. Lukas saw that the other two Mages were within the boundaries of the Temple now, joining Matthias in power. A pyramid of light sprang into existence between the three men, and above it the black Shadows swirled in the night.

The other Cavers were ranged over the hill leading up to the Temple, pausing now in doubt, their faces white and upturned towards the horror in the sky.

Lukas took a deep breath. He did not move out of his concealed place. He stood silently in the darkness behind the pillars, out of sight. It was all he could do, to hold back, to wait.

Eleanor and Blythe were still beyond the Temple walls, Haddon and the young man standing with them.

Lukas saw Blythe gently smooth the hair from her face, saw him talk to her softly, with love.

It was unmistakeable. She lifted her head, and his breath caught at the sight of the line of her neck, the curve of her breasts. Lukas saw the Moon mirrored in her eyes as she replied to Phinian Blythe, saw that she was soft and sensuous with it.

See? The cold clear voice sounded in his mind. *You were not faithful and neither was she. You denied Me, and her. You have earned the right to tragedy.*

This is the way it will always go, between those who dare to love and yet deny the Gods.

It was too late. Matthias had seen the truth of it, and the voice of the Lady confirmed it. There was no happiness for Lukas Marling here, or anywhere. *Too late.* He did not move, standing out of sight, but he could no longer bear to watch what was happening beyond the Temple. He looked instead at the wide stone floor between the broken lines of pillars, and his mind barely registered what took place there.

The three Mages were calling. Enticing, beckoning, calling down from the sky the tormented creature wailing there. They were weaving a reverse enchantment, Lukas realised. He remembered other ceremonies, other rites. He had lived with Mages for so long. This was an undoing, a backwards tilt to time.

Their aim was to restore the howling figure in the sky to human proportions. They would try to bring it to earth, to walk among them, to live in the same world. They imagined they could deal with it, manipulate, understand, if only it were standing on the earth before them. It was so inconceivably dangerous a manoeuvre that Lukas knew they would not survive.

He felt the tug of the enchantment yearning into the air. The Fosca were scattering before it, still wheeling through the sky, but at a distance now. The great clouds of black began to intensify, to concentrate. And then, too fast to see, too bizarre to contemplate, the black funnelled down through the stars, a black hole falling to earth.

There, suddenly and shockingly, standing unsteadily on wide-spaced legs, something that was neither man nor flower nor Fosca. Thorns erupted from the skin of its face, petals fell from its skull like scales. Its eyes were barred by the veins of leaves. Its hands, nailed with thorns, draped with trailing stems, were raised in curving claws.

The Shadows still furled around its shoulders, still crawled over its face, and Lukas knew that the creature was barely aware of what was happening. It was still in a state of shock. There was a blessed, brief hiatus while it tried to assess where it was, what it was. Its muffled face blindly nuzzled the cold night air, trying to scent something beyond the pervasive Shadows. It was contained within the pyramid made by the three Caver Mages, but Lukas knew that this was only temporary, a momentary calm before an inevitable cataclysm.

It seemed to draw itself inwards. Lukas saw the petal shapes quiver, the thorns tremble with force. It gathered itself together, and then noise exploded over them all. The Shadowed figure was screaming something at the four people still beyond the Temple. The words were indistinct, reaching up to the stars, but their sense was unmistakeable.

'Mercy! Saviour, release, peace—'

Haddon Derray and the young man at his side moved towards the low wall bordering the Temple

Chapter Twenty-eight
Starlight

'No! Do not approach!' The voice came from someone standing beyond the Temple. He was surrounded by robed men carrying torches, carrying the emblems of the Sun, they had come to Astret's Temple, were waiting just outside the ruins of the east wall.

His eyes were blazing in the torch-light of his followers. His hair was shorn, the bones of his skull plainly revealed. His skin was colourless, gleaming with exertion. His voice held a strange glory, a deep triumph.

Lukas did not know who he was, this Sun priest, but his charisma was undeniable.

He could see that the Caver Mages were beyond the reach of this stranger. They gave him not one flicker of attention. They were concentrating on their steady pyramid of light which just enclosed the Shadows and their victim. The creeping horror within the Temple was still contained, but Lukas could see the tremor of stress running through each of the black-cloaked Mages. They would not be able to maintain this equilibrium for long.

The Sun priest was speaking, his eyes alight and gleaming with knowledge. His large hands were held out towards Haddon Derray and his companion, beyond the boundary of the Temple.

'There is a lie here. Witness. A great distortion. A reversal of more than time, a reversal of death.' He was speaking not only to the Mages, but also to the weight of people ranged around the Temple – the watching faces of the followers of Astret.

He looked beyond the monstrous figure weighted by Shadows. He stared across the Temple to where Haddon Derray and the young man stood. 'It cannot endure.' His voice was now very quiet. 'Your saviour is lost, Moon Mages. Lost for ever. You will suffer always, and there will be no relief to blur the edges of reality. This is the end of magic. The only comfort will be the word of the Lord God. The only comfort will be the knowledge of His rule, and the knowledge which will teach us the path to righteousness. There will be nothing else, no hope of salvation, because this child is lost.

'Because your God does not care.

'Listen to me, and prepare yourselves. Know yourselves by a new name, followers of Astret. Know yourselves to be the fools of Astret.'

A gasp of outrage, a ripple of violence, but he took no notice. He had bargained with the Lord of Love. He would annihilate them all, Moon-struck fools that they were. But first, it would be sweet to see their empty hopes come to nothing.

He was looking out over the heads of the people in and around the Temple. He looked up, over Haddon Derray and the young man, and raised his hands to the Fosca that were skimming through the night. 'There is your fate!' he said, joyously. 'There is your end.'

Look there. See how she betrays you. See, there is no fidelity, no true lasting love in the world. See how you have been betrayed.

The voice of brilliant white light cut through Lukas's thoughts. He looked at Eleanor, close to Blythe's side, so close and a terrible lifetime away.

Take her back. The voice in his mind was relentless. *Fight him, if necessary. You can do this, if you set your heart on it, if you act with courage in My name. Take her back, with violence.*

'But she must be free,' Lukas said slowly. 'It is up to her, whom she loves. I have no desire to imprison her.'

'Release me!' It was no longer a supplication. Terror had found its outlet in something else, and the creature in the centre of the Temple was beginning to erupt, breaking like a wave over the stone and flowing towards the two figures hesitating at the Temple gates.

In its efforts to escape, it was flinging itself wide. Limbs like branches grew long and thin, stretched beyond bearing. Scraping, clawing, dragging themselves over the arena, seeking an escape, anything to get away. But the Shadows were proliferating at the same rate, spreading everywhere and no part of it was free, no stem or shoot or bud without its weight of guilt. Like the visible contamination of plague, their dark claws plucked even at the robes of those who watched.

At once the young man with Haddon Derray moved forward as if to stem the burgeoning growth. There was the faintest suggestion of bells as he crossed the threshold.

They crossed into the Temple of the Lady. Its broken pillars ran in a full semi-circle, in honour of Astret, the Lady who decrees that Death shall follow Life and in Her own being as Moon, moves from light to dark.

Coron stood there, his hands outstretched to the Shadows, and they moved not at all. There were bells ringing, breaking across the words the young man struggled to say.

Haddon Derray took hold of the outstretched hands, held them fast. And the sound of the bells changed, deepened. The uneven clamour reverberated, growing and swelling through a tritone, destabilising structure and thought. Haddon Derray bent his head, his eyes closing. There were bells swinging through every acoustic now, filling the night, and the air vibrated. The sound became enormous, blocking every thought, blocking the movement of time. The black wave of agony yearning towards them was held still, cresting eternally, while noise burst through consciousness. Stones were falling from the ruined pillars. The flesh of Haddon's hands began to shiver.

Coron was unstable as dreaming.

And as they watched, there was a collapse. A dismantling of flesh, an undoing of the bonds of energy and blood. The body of Haddon Derray scattered to the ground in blackened bones and greying ashes.

The Moon shone coldly as Coron began to weep.

Tears ran down his face, and the bell-sound became muffled by cloud. There were clouds gathering all around the Temple. Defined by the shape of wide wings, they were covering the face of the Moon, swooping downwards.

An Arrarat hawk, augury of a greater Hawk yet, released into the night.

Coron wept and the wings of gold fell towards him. Salt tears ran through his being, washed over his heart.

Wings enfolded his tears, enclosed his grief.

Poor child. Poor innocent, lost one.

Come to me.

In a rush of air and light, the hawk took the weeping figure of Coron and the remains of the man returned to death. It leapt into the sky, climbing far beyond the clouds, far beyond the wailing Fosca and silent Moon. Beyond the atmosphere and stratosphere, and further yet until the pull of the earth was discarded, and the chains of mere life forgotten.

The constellations of the sky became distantly aware and they rested there, caught amidst the vast joys of the far galaxies.

Shining there beyond Sun and Moon, they were released from pain. Released from power and responsibility. They were brighter than jewels. And those watching, wherever they were, whoever they were, whenever they were, wept at such beauty.

Abandoned. Without hope, the thing that had been Lefevre spread itself wide. Creepers ran from it like entrails, fastening it to stone. Nailed beneath the weight of Shadows, it called again. And its servants, its only enduring creation, answered.

The Fosca began to gather.

Phinian Blythe drew his sword.

Eleanor caught his arm. 'Phin, no, they'll never let you near it—' She meant the Shadows, he knew.

He knew better than anyone there what it was like to bear Shadows. And he would not abandon anyone, not even Lefevre, to them.

And then the Fosca closed in. Flaming arrows littered the ground. Fires sparked and flared. There was no wood, nothing obvious to catch, but everyone there was vulnerable. They had no shield, no defence. . .the people from Sarant began to scatter, to run away from the Temple. Like a sunburst of flesh, they ran down the hill on all sides, away from the place where silver stone was stained by Shadows and fire.

Blythe saw a flurry of arrows fall through the air, around the three Mages. He saw one of them pin the cloak of a preoccupied Mage.

Before anyone could move, anyone react, Aylmer Alard was engulfed in fire. His colleague Thibaud turned towards him and as he did so, the triangle of power which had contained Lefevre failed.

Flame sped around the framework of light. Shocked, too slow to avoid the leaping electric charge, Thibaud Lye was held rigid at the point of the triangle.

His hands blackened and flame sprang from his eyes.

Matthias had already stepped back, informed by intuitions that did not depend on sight. His hands were hanging free from the framework of light. He smelled the burning flesh, felt two consciousnesses ripped from his mind.

Death, the death of magic, coming close now. My friends, Matthias thought, have you left me already? Am I finally alone?

And although he was appalled, and unseeing, he knew that he could not yet afford to mourn. Every sense was finely wrought with horrors, attuned to violence. He heard the air above him part, heard a rush of leathery wings; drew back as the stink of decomposition hit him. Only a few yards away, the Fosca baron settled on the Temple floor.

Before he could react, Matthias was pushed roughly aside. He heard his brother warn him, between gasps, to keep out of the way. He heard the clash of a sword on bone, the clawing bone of a whipping tentacle, and hoped that that would be the end of it.

He knew that on the other boundary to the Temple a Sun priest waited for him. He turned towards Dion Gillet.

Not the end, yet. Lukas Marling was no longer passive. Sword drawn, he was running with wild fury at the Fosca baron. He drove at it with massive force and then threw himself to one side, not counting the cost of injury. He had no fear that mattered.

The baron lashed out, catching his cloak. It was torn from his shoulders, ripping, and Lukas heard his name half-breathed, half-screamed. *Eleanor*. He did not dare look round, not while Fosca were dropping to earth all around them, not while the tendrils of flesh, nailed with thorns were still writhing their way across the cold stone towards him.

On the edges of his peripheral vision, he saw Blythe move into the arena. And Matthias. There were Fosca all around them, skimming through the air just above their heads. He knew that soon they would settle, and then there would be no chance, not against so many. Lukas saw the Sun priest leave his position at the eastern edge.

He saw Matthias move, like Blythe, towards the centre.

The sky was black with Fosca. There were hundreds of them circling overhead, and every atom of air was soured by the stench.

He saw Eleanor hesitate, and then try to follow Blythe into the centre.

'No! Out of here!' Lukas was shouting, running fast across the Temple floor to Blythe and Matthias. To Eleanor. . .

The cloud of Fosca was settling all around them. Black, ungainly shapes squatted on the cold stone. He grabbed Eleanor's wrist, Matthias's shoulder, pushing them roughly towards the Temple boundary. He felt a claw rip into the cloth of his shirt, saw that Eleanor's arm had been raked by thorns.

There were ashes everywhere, ashes from the dead, clinging to their limbs and feet. Blythe had turned aside, was hanging back. Matthias too was resisting, turning round, back to the arena.

Lukas knew he had to get Eleanor out, no matter what it cost. But before he could even look at her again, the Fosca baron was suddenly there between them, its face turned towards him. Marking him.

Lefevre was aware of the presence of Mages. Claw-hands raked the air between three men, and acknowledged old rivals.

Matthias, Mage of the Lady. Dion Gillet, Priest of the Sun. And Phinian Blythe, who had promised to give Lefevre death.

Each movement was curiously crippled by the Shadows, dead weights which clung to its elongated limbs. The three men circled a creature of blossoming thorn.

For a moment the Fosca held off and watched.

Gillet spoke to Phinian Blythe, 'This is the will of God. You interfere at your peril.' His eyes were glinting with triumph. 'This is the just punishment of the Lord, and will run its course.'

Phinian Blythe hardly heard him. He was watching the way the Shadows drifted across the face of his old enemy. He saw the scaled skin crack and twist as it uselessly winced away from the Shadow touch. He remembered what it was like struggling for breath against their weight. He saw the shadows waver, presenting face after face, memory after memory. Horror upon horror, sins without number, vivid and potent and present.

He thought, so this is vengeance. And where is its satisfaction, where is its sweetness? He tightened his grip on the sword.

Matthias said to him, 'Can you do this without guilt? Remember the cost, for the Shadows will take you again if you act from flawed motives. . .'

Blythe looked at Lefevre and for a moment the Shadows gave him glimpses of the past, stories from long ago. Symbols of love, of fear and guilt.

He saw his wife Karis, murdered by Lefevre.

He saw Idas, sacrificed into evil by Lefevre.

He saw Marial, gentle musician caught and destroyed in a war he did not understand, because of Lefevre.

And then he saw the child Coron: lost to them all because Coron, the healer, had attempted to reverse death. He had denied the Lady within Her own Temple, just as Lefevre had always denied Her. He had entered Her realm in order to heal Lefevre.

Blythe saw the knowledge of all these acts, and so many others, which chained Lefevre to the earth. And he felt only pity. That such overwhelming ambition, such great love for God, should be brought to this.

He stepped forwards and raised his sword, double-handed. He looked into the barred eyes, the tortured mouth. No words this time, no fluent requiem. With all his strength, he brought the sword down on the Rose-head.

Once was enough. Petals scattered like blood. A toppled figure falling to earth. It lay on cold stone, unmoving, but still there was movement. A stirring, a shift of lightening relief as the Shadows lifted.

Flowers bloomed where a brain had lodged. Petals spilt out of the skull-case, scarlet and white. Small, perfect, and sweetly scented, blossoms flowed over the Temple floor.

Phinian Blythe saw the Shadows drift away from the Temple, drift away from the people left there. There was no burden of guilt for them to express now. No suffering soul in need of the purgatory they offered.

The only blood on Blythe's hands came from the thorns of a rose as he picked it up.

He looked at the fragile scarlet petals for a moment. Turning, he saw Eleanor watching him, such complexities in her eyes. He gave the flower to her.

The Fosca baron turned from Lukas Marling to Phinian Blythe. For once, an expression was revealed on that blank, rotting canvas. It snarled at him, drawing back thin lips from jagged teeth.

Blythe raised his sword. It was still running with sap. He was deathly tired, as if what he had just done had drained every ounce of energy. With effort, he moved to one side, knowing there was no real defence to be made against such a creature. Its swinging claw caught against his side. He hardly felt it in the shock of what happened next. He knew at any moment he would die, that the next blow would kill him, but it never came. He saw Lukas very close, sword raised high in attack, but there was no need.

The Fosca baron was assaulted by light. A deadly beam transfixed it, froze it, the snarl of fury welded on its face.

A blind Mage held it there: Matthias, acting without staff or sight, from intuition only.

He said one word and the Fosca baron shattered, span apart into the void of light surrounding it. Shards of brittle, desiccated flesh fell like dust, and the Fosca circling in the night sky screamed suddenly, a sound that lifted to the stars in disappearing discords. . .

They fled that place, spinning like drunken mosquitoes, shooting out into the clouds, driven from the explosion of power. Wide and disparate, they were thrown over the island and far beyond.

Eventually, they lost volition and fell like dead leaves: some into the sea where they were lost in its deep secret. Others fell on earth, and rotted quickly, quietly into the soil, the sand, the green fields and damp marshes. . .

None survived. There was no King to direct the Fosca now, no creator to order their existence. Their god had found judgment, as do all gods, in the end. It had died.

And so did they.

Chapter Twenty-nine
Freedom

A field of flowers, a field of ashes.

Eleanor looked at Lukas helplessly. Her fingers still held the flower Phin had given her. Phin, who was standing only a little way from her, watching doubtfully. He was very white, but so was Lukas.

'Why are you here?' She spoke clearly, her voice remarkably steady. 'I came home.'

'Felicia? The baby? What about Shelt?'

He looked at her and didn't move. 'They don't need me, Eleanor. I'm free now. There are no other claims.'

His eyes were bright as diamonds, but his voice was relaxed and light. There was no pressure there. Freedom, such as the Gods never gave.

She swallowed. How to say this? She had no doubts, no regrets.

There was an Arrarat, a dark grey creature coming for him. She saw Astrella alight in the middle of the Temple, saw Lukas move towards his great hawk. He stood there for a while, his hand on Astrella's shoulder. He looked only at Eleanor.

'Go free, my dear,' he said softly. 'If that's what you want. Fly free as a bird, free from chains and promises and the difficult restraints of the past. I will never hold you back. But if you still want me, or need me—' He paused. 'It still holds good. I love you as much now as I ever did.'

He felt the pressure of cold light to his left, the obsessive jealousy of the Moon.

What of fidelity, of the past you have shared, of the trust you possessed, the promises you made? Take her, fight for her, win her and destroy the other.

And be Mine for ever.

The burning heat of the Sun flared on the right. *What of passion, what of the desire of the flesh, the heat in the blood. . .? You have the right to this, take it. This is your nature, you are a man.*

He tried to articulate it. 'We can do better than that,' he said slowly. 'And whatever has happened must be allowed to pass away.'

He looked at Eleanor, her eyes so large, the flower falling from her hands, and from her to Phin. He saw compassion and wide understanding, and knew that Phin recognised what these words cost. She would be happy with Phinian Blythe. She could have children with him, and live in content and peace.

The dark crystal, hard and undeniable. His life had been forfeit long ago. There was nothing for him now.

He had turned towards Astrella, thinking to leave, to get away, anywhere, anyhow.

There was a hand on his shoulder. A delicate touch, hesitant, gentle. He took a deep, shuddering breath, his eyes closing momentarily.

'Lukas. . .?' she said, quiet, steady. So sure.

He knew that this couldn't be happening, that there are no second chances.

He could smell the scent of her, the warm sea-smell of woman. He raised his head, looking at her hand resting on his shoulder, and saw the slight shiver of tension in it.

If he turned now, it would be for ever.

Her voice again, sweeter than music to him. 'There have been separations, there have been lies. But through it all, there was only ever you. Only you, in this world, or any other.

He turned around and saw miracles in her eyes. He lifted his hands and slowly their fingertips touched. A bridge across unmeasured distances, unmeasured time.

His fingers curled around hers, drawing her closer.

He had waited so long.

His hands moved, brushing the golden hair from her face, finding and tracing the moon-scar at her temple. He touched the softness of her cheek, touched the fine line of her mouth.

He saw that she was hardly breathing. Her lips were parted, and then he could wait no longer and took her into his arms, holding her tight, locking his mouth on hers. The intensity of it drove the past from them, kept the future at bay.

Such wanting, such loving. They were clasped together in starlight.

Phinian Blythe looked beyond the two lovers, out into the wide night. Beyond the Temple he saw an Arrarat hawk lift into the air. Astrella, he thought. She was gaining height swiftly, reaching away from the Temple. Endlessly fascinating, the careless curve of grace, the wide sweep of strength. . . .

In the pulse of her wings, in the power of her flight, another resonance took life.

Brighter than flame and darker than death, the Benu grew from the world around them, its wings lifting free from the hills, its body the great plain beneath them.

Its wings flexed, spreading vast and curved. In exaltation it cried out, soaring beyond the stars, and echoed with its flight the augured path of the Arrarat hawk. It looked clearly through all worlds, all dimensions, no longer blind.

The Benu took from this world its Gods. In its left eye the cold light of the Moon shone. In its right, the blazing glare of the Sun. The Hawk swept with it all magic, all illusion.

The Gods would no longer walk. The ancient rivalries would be reflected only through the lives of ordinary people. No distortions, dreams or manipulations. Created in the imagination of men and women to explain and justify their worst actions, the Gods were no longer needed.

We can do better than that.
Humanity set free, responsible only to itself.
No magic or revenge. No chains, no saviours.
No excuses.

Chapter Thirty
The Death of Magic

Dion Gillet saw the Benu fly, saw his God transmuted into something he did not understand.

Something he did not want to understand. He saw the Shadows, the Children of the Night, nestling beneath the wide-flung wings and knew that there was no escape.

He saw his followers in disarray, running crazily across the plain, terrified and defeated by the advent of the Great Hawk. He saw two lovers, and knew that the separation he envisaged would never now take place.

He remembered, with deepening despair, the existence of Katriana. Where was she now? Now that the Lord Lycias had been subsumed into something else?

Across the arena, he saw Matthias turn towards him. And this was something else he could not face. Without planning, without even considering at all deeply, he manufactured a cloud of obfuscation, a sharp and nippy exeat from a situation fraught with untold difficulties.

Dion Gillet was still powerful. He felt that power flicker at his fingertips, he felt reality bend before his will. He moved himself away from the Temple of Astret, away from the carnage and the two lovers locked in each other's arms. And from that dangerous blind Caver Mage. He made a loop in distance, and removed himself to a seashore not far away.

But far enough. No one would find him quickly. He looked at the boat his followers had pulled up beyond the tide those few days ago, and sighed. It was a long row, back to Peraldon.

It would be better to fly. He wondered whether to spend time searching for a Fosca mount. It would be of use, these shifts in time and matter were so exhausting, and rowing even worse. . .But the

Fosca were gone, and although he was arrogant he knew better than to attempt an Arrarat summoning. Especially now.

In desperation, he sent his mind into a waking dream. Find a way out, he told himself. Range through the pathways, physical and metaphysical, and find a way to get out of this place.

'Dion.' A voice spoke to him from within the trance. He recognised it immediately. Katriana, flesh of his creating. The female side of himself, someone he had used to distract the God. He took a deep breath and braced himself. His thoughts had given her a pathway back to the world of humanity.

The light fractured around him and he blinked, trying to clear his vision. And when he looked again, she was there, his beautiful ward, standing naked in the waves before him. Her eyes were shadowed by her blowing hair.

'You want a way out of here?'

Something in her voice.

He knew there was no point in regrets. He shrugged. 'Well, little one, so the great gamble has failed. The Lord of Love has left us both. He has left all humanity. We're alone now. There's no way anyone is ever going to forget what happened tonight.'

'No. The world will never forget.'

He thought that she ought to be cold, standing there in the waves with no clothes, but she was not shivering. Her skin was smooth and touched with blush like a young peach.

'I will give you your way out.' She walked towards him and water fell from her limbs, sparkling in the early morning light.

He saw, then, that there was nothing in her eyes.

'An angel of death, are you?' He smiled, still not understanding. 'You should not dare approach me, Katriana. I am puissant yet.'

'And I am not. But still, I am more than you.' She was standing before him, and suddenly he was struck by a double realisation. He had to get away from her, for the nothingness in her eyes was indescribably dangerous. But at the same time he found that he could no longer move.

'Be nothing, with me.' She leant towards him, and he felt her breath chill the air. Her hands reached out to his face and there was nothing he could do to stop her.

Too quickly for thought, the sharp nails of her two index fingers ploughed furrows through his eyes.

The soundless scream split his mind apart.

He was on his knees in the waves, toppling forward. He fell face down into the surf, and there was not enough strength in all the world to lift him up again. White foam filled his nose and mouth, filled his brain and soul. Brain-bubbles of aerated water. His life drained away with the ebbing tide.

She watched the waves take his body, watched it roll back and forth in the shallows, watched the crabs investigate, the sand worms and small scavengers start their busy work.

And when Cassun and the rest of Gillet's followers stumbled down the cliff path, some days later, there was not enough left of the corpse to identify their erstwhile leader.

They knew who it was, nonetheless. The Sun-medallion still hung round the ragged bones of the neck. Exclaiming, they did not at first see the woman standing beneath the shadow of the cliff. Only when they began to dig the grave did they realise that they were being watched.

Cassun recognised her, even though her eyes were so empty.

'Well, Katriana. Do you want passage with us?' He was wary, holding out his cloak to conceal the fragile perfections of her beautiful body from the other men.

'I want only one thing from you.' She ignored the cloak, walking towards him. He felt suddenly cold, and glanced to his companions for support.

They were loading the boat, and seemed not to notice that she was there. None of them looked at him, or her. . .

'*What*? What is it you want?' Instinctively he had stepped back.

'This,' she said, raising her hands.

Angel of death.

The Emperor, recovering slowly, mourned his Mages. There were none left anywhere. He called for advisors, and three people who knew nothing of magic answered his call.

The High Priest of the Sun, newly elected to a position which was to be redefined.

The High Priestess of the Moon, similarly bewildered.

The Warden, secular power in the city of Peraldon.

They discussed the way forward, they discussed terms and treaties, and approaches to the Northern Continent.

And in the end, they wondered if there really was no magic left in their world.

Xanthon said, 'The College burned to the ground. There is no one, now, who can interpret the few remaining texts. And even if we find someone to research and revive the forms of magic, what use will it be? There is no context for magic now, not in that formal, powerful, world-changing distortion. Or are we wrong about this?' He raised one saturnine eyebrow at his advisors. 'Does magic still exist, can men travel between worlds and hold back time, and alter the shape of reality?'

Only the Priestess answered him, her palms held upwards to the ceiling. 'There is only this reality, and what we make of it,' she said, knowing that the others would believe her.

But still, she wondered where Matthias was.

Chapter Thirty-one
Massiq

His hands trace her eyebrows, her cheekbones, the line of her neck, the fullness of her breasts. His blue gaze, clear as the sky, runs through her like water and she feels as if she might melt, right then and there.

He is with her every night, every day. She feels long fingers stroking her hair, touching, so lightly, every part of her. At night, sometimes caught in dream and not realising, she moves uneasily, disturbed by memory. His hand is warm, unmistakably living, true and real as it clasps hers. At once she wakes, staring in the faint light from the dying fire. She sees him then, still unbelieving, and the remnants of sleep fall away.

Her breathing is unreliable. And there are no words left in the world, not one thing she need say.

'No, don't try,' he says, his finger on her lips. His voice is light and easy as ever.

As if in a trance, she sees him, his arms widening, held out to her. She sees the glint in his eyes, the half-smile on the long, expressive mouth. She moves, but she has no idea how. Their fingertips touch, delicate as moths.

'It's all right,' he says softly, words forever true. 'Eleanor, it's all right, I'm here now, now and for ever. . .'

She rolls against the soft sheets, letting them slide across her bare skin, towards him. His hands tighten, drawing her close. His mouth is against her hair, his fingers strong on the curves of her body.

'Ah. . .and now?'

His lips brush hers and this is like fire, like electricity, but now she is equal to it. Not swamped, not overwhelmed. She feels vividly alive, suddenly reborn. She knows every nerve is aware, every sense alert and tingling with anticipation.

It is another chance at happiness, a gift of grace. More than she ever hoped for, more than she ever deserved.

His hands move down the side of her face, circling her neck, spreading wide over her shoulders and breasts. He is gentle, gentle all the way, and still she knows that it is urgent that they join together immediately, without further delay. There was no need to hold back, nothing to stop them, alone on this quiet island for the length of the winter.

Sometimes they hold each other close all day, breathing the same air, their bodies moving together, twining together, entangled in desire. And when they are apart, they move as if they are following the patterns of a dance, slowly, sensuously, like the stars in the sky, the fish in the sea, like birds flying in formation.

This movement between them, this constant proximity, informs every day and every night, wherever they are, whatever they do.

She knows it will not last, not like this. In time, they will become accustomed to each other and this proximity will feel ordinary and unremarkable. She looks forward to this, recognising that there is no higher fortune.

She hopes that Phin is content now, back in Peraldon, hopes he has conferred with the Emperor, returned to his family. She looks forward to meeting him again. She half expects him to walk down the herringbone paths to the home he has lent them. They often talk of him, and wish him well.

No other thoughts intrude. They keep each other warm, lighting log fires in the old hearths, the shutters closed tight against the cutting sea-breezes. On fine days, they walk the length of the cold island, their breath clouding in the damp air. They watch ducks and geese hiding in the grey-green reeds, and the water is silver grey. The mist hangs there white and loose, all colour soft and muted, quiet and subtle. But his eyes blaze with blue and his voice is light and easy, and warm as summer. And his touch makes demands that drive her beyond this ordinary world of water and earth, air and fire.

She wonders sometimes if this is too perfect, as if they are living in dream of paradise and will one day awake to find life tedious again.

'But we have the Arrarat,' he says. 'How can things ever be ordinary?'

And she smiles at him and thinks, yes, we have the great hawks to carry us beyond this quiet world, to open our thoughts to perspectives wider than our imagination allows. This is true, but whether there are great hawks in the world or not, our lives are still touched by a different magic.

For we are travellers in each other's lives, carried down the paths of time, touching here and there in strange moments of intimacy. And the intersections, where the paths meet, give meaning to it all, mark the paths with light and shade.

Losing one world and finding another.

Envoi

He holds Matthias's hand until it is quite cold. Gently, he lays it back on the frail body, and covers the empty face with the blanket.

Phinian Blythe knows that, soon, others will come looking for Chorolon's last Mage. That the Emperor will eventually be impelled to seek him out, and that all the Cavers on Sarant will want to know what happened. Matthias's strange death, this quiet drifting away, will be a mystery to them.

He will not be there to explain that this death was a gift. Something long-desired, a peaceful conclusion to a life that had held too many terrors. He knows that Lukas and Eleanor, at least, will understand.

Standing at the mouth of the sea-cave he sees Amery, Matthias's golden hawk, waiting for him.

For a moment they stare into each other's eyes. He feels the warm delight, the knowledge of companionship. He is too close to Matthias's death to smile, but he moves calmly and picks up the diary from the rocky ledge above Matthias's head.

In the bay, still within the shelter of the cliff, he holds in his hands shapes made of coloured glass. He has built a fire, and the wind from the turbulent tide has fanned it to a roaring blaze.

To his side, the diary lies face down on cold rock. Its pages are covered with cramped, blotted, untidy writing.

He has wondered whether to take it with him. As insurance, in case he ever needs another way out. In case it proves impossible, again. He has decided to leave it behind, to leave it here below the high-tide mark, where the waves will soon swamp the dark ink and wash the pages clear once more.

Phinian Blythe is no Mage, and has no desire to follow such paths.

He has decided to take a chance with this Arrarat hawk. Amery, a chance to escape. And then he will be free, free of the past, free from this world where the Gods walk no more and there is nothing but loneliness.

He throws the glass shapes.

There is a flight over fire.